PRAISE FOR A NOBLE CALLING

A rookie FBI agent battles through adversity and danger to rediscover his true identity in this story of intrigue and suspense.

"The characters are entrancing, and Weaver describes scenery like a poet, slipping the reader into the comfort of a Yellowstone cabin where one can almost feel the heat from the nearby hot springs or hear the pound of bison footfalls."

—*Arkansas Democrat Gazette*

"Loved it! Awesome book that flat-out rocks! It really honors park rangers, FBI agents . . . [shows them as] real people with real strengths and weaknesses. Great descriptions of the scenery and pure adventure! Can't wait to see what happens next!"

—Central District Ranger Kevin Moses, Shenandoah National Park

"Read the book in two days! Absolutely loved it, especially how it depicted the problems (and successes) between agencies and different groups within the FBI. Can't wait for the next one!"

—Diane O., FBI, retired

"*A Noble Calling*: Mysteries, mayhem, and the maturation of an FBI agent. Win [Tyler] remains determined to honor his sacred oath as an FBI agent, even at the cost of his own physical and emotional well-being."

—*Philological Review*

ALSO BY RHONA WEAVER

A Noble Calling: An FBI Yellowstone Adventure

2021 Bill Fisher Award for Best First Book in Fiction
(Independent Book Publishers Association)

2021 Best Action/Adventure Novel (Next
Generation Indie Book Awards)

2021 Best Christian Fiction (Next
Generation Indie Book Awards)

2021 Finalist for Best Thriller (Next
Generation Indie Book Awards)

2021 Finalist for the Eric Hoffer Award for
Commercial Fiction (Eric Hoffer Foundation)

2021 Finalist for the Christy Award for First Novel
(Evangelical Christian Publishers Association)

2021 Bronze Medalist in Regional Fiction
(Independent Publisher Book Awards)

A SACRED DUTY

A SACRED DUTY

✦ AN FBI YELLOWSTONE ADVENTURE ✦

RHONA WEAVER

Two Oaks Press

Published by Two Oaks Press, Little Rock, Arkansas
www.rhonaweaver.com

Edited and designed by Girl Friday Productions
www.girlfridayproductions.com

Design: Paul Barrett
Project management: Sara Spees Addicott
Editorial production: Jaye Whitney Debber
Cover photos by Bill Temple

ISBN (hardcover): 978-1-7347500-3-4
ISBN (paperback): 978-1-7347500-4-1
ISBN (ebook): 978-1-7347500-5-8

Library of Congress Control Number: 2022906752

To Bill, the love of my life and my true FBI hero

CHAPTER ONE

The bones were stark white. . . . *Maybe they aren't real.* The long, slender finger bones were still attached to the delicate metacarpal and carpal bones. They extended only a few inches above the wrist to a jagged break. He remembered just a few of the bones' names from his single biology class at the University of Arkansas—anatomy hadn't been one of his big interests. Sweat stung his eyes as he shifted his boots on the hot wooden planks and cocked his head to squint through the drifting steam. The hand looked so much like it belonged on one of those fake plastic skeletons that were ever present in science classes. *Maybe it isn't real,* he told himself again.

He and the two park rangers had already taken dozens of photos and measurements of the site. As far as he knew, no one had disturbed the bones since they'd been belched up from Yellowstone's volcanic depths. Lord only knows how long they'd laid there. He eased his six-foot-three frame into a low crouch, balanced on the balls of his feet, and worked his damp hands into the thick black polypropylene gloves. He resisted the urge to hold his breath as foul-smelling vapor whirled around the eight-foot-wide caldron of muddy goo that lay just beyond him. Blinking the sweat away, he eased the bones back from the edge of the hissing steam vent that was draining into a bubbling pool. He flinched when the vent burped up a glob of thick, whitish mud—it seemed to be protesting the removal of its prize.

No one spoke.

Geez . . . how did this get here? He gently lifted the featherlight bones away from the hot crust, afraid they might disintegrate under his touch, but they didn't. They were solid and smooth, and frighteningly real. He examined them, turning the remains in his hands, brushing away the pasty muck that was clinging to their underside. The sun made a sudden appearance from behind a cloud bank—something between the skeletal fingers gleamed and sparkled in the bright light.

"It's a ring. . . . Win, there's a ring on the third finger. See that?" The ranger poised next to him spoke in a reverent tone.

"Uh-huh." He slowly turned the hand to reveal a blood-red stone encircled by pale-green gems, glistening against the background of bleached bone and tarnished gold. A woman's ring on a woman's hand. *Whose ring? Whose hand?*

Special Agent Winston Tyler was squatting on wooden boards above chalky-white ground just to the right of a five-foot-tall steam vent and only a few feet from a large sinkhole that was breathing noxious vapor. A fumarole was spitting streams of water ten feet into the air on the other side of the steaming white plain, which measured less than five acres. Vapor rose from fissures and jumbled piles of stone. Dead trees, stripped of their bark, were scattered about the scorched ground at odd angles—frozen in shades of gray and white—monuments to the heat that had killed them. The superheated ground crested on a slight rise where a gaping hole roared every few minutes as it breathed more steam and fumes. He'd heard the rangers call it the Devil's Breath Spring. An apt name, since the seething thermal landscape had a hellish feel. Tall lodgepole pines stood at the periphery of the chalky ground—silent spectators watching the scene unfold; dark mountains rose on three sides, close and claustrophobic. The turquoise lake a few hundred yards beyond the thermal area was a redeeming quality, Win supposed, but this morning it too was shrouded in swirling steam.

Win cradled the ghost-white bones in his hand as if he were holding an injured bird, aware now that the amateur geologist's report of human remains at the remote geyser field was sadly accurate. *These reports usually turn out to be animal bones or even pranks,* the rangers had said. They're often just false alarms—nothing to find, nothing to investigate. Win blew out a deep breath as jagged emotions fought an internal battle to push away his professional detachment. No hoax today. A woman had died here.

Park Ranger Trey Hechtner was wobbling on another of the thin boards they'd brought along on the helicopter to support their weight on the unstable crust of the thermal site. Both young men were athletic and fit, but the balancing act in the intense heat was no easy feat. The ranger pulled off his dark-green Park Service ball cap and wiped a gray sleeve across his face. Sweat was coursing through his short blond hair, staining his shirt. The 170-degree heat from the ground was permeating both men's clothes. Win could feel it beginning to seep through the soles of his leather hiking boots. He slowly stood and stepped backward on the boards as he continued to study the lost hand.

In his three years in the Bureau, Win had concentrated on white-collar crime and public corruption. Until very recently he'd never seen a dead person, and he'd never assisted in the retrieval of remains, as the process was formally called. Most anywhere else in the country, he'd be standing on the sidelines while an FBI Evidence Response Team went about this unsavory business. But his field office was in Denver, over seven hundred miles away, and his supervisor hadn't opted to call out the ERT for an excursion to the middle of nowhere, especially when there was no evidence of a crime. Win found himself in the role of an ERT member, since time was of the essence—there was the very real possibility that the skeletal remains might sink back into the superheated goo.

Win took several steps back toward more stable ground and delicately placed the bones into the plastic evidence bag that Ranger Jimmy Martinez handed him. Everyone flinched when a geyser erupted thirty yards away, spewing water high into the air. Win's eyes left the bones to watch the sunlight form prisms of red, yellow, blue, and violet within the scalding spray. *Beautiful.* A fitting farewell from this otherworldly place for the precious package he held.

* * *

The Park Service's canary-yellow medevac helicopter had its main rotor slowly turning as Win climbed into the rear passenger compartment ten minutes later and buckled himself in. Trey gingerly handed him the evidence bag that contained the bones, grabbing his cap with his other hand to keep the rotor updraft from pulling it away. Win nodded to the ranger and raised his voice over the whine of the copter's revving engine. "Make another sweep for anything we mighta missed and get with me when you get back to Mammoth. I'll call this in and hit the missing persons database." Trey gave him a wave and ducked away from the chopper.

Settling his ball cap and pulling the headset on, Win closed his eyes against the dust and sand kicking up from the rotors' increasing spin and pulled the side door closed with his free hand. He fought down a brief wave of nausea as the craft pitched sharply upward while his stomach tried to stay at the lower altitude. He hated helicopters.

This wasn't at all what he'd expected on his first day back at work. The doctor had told him to take it slow and easy for several more days. He doubted a crack-of-dawn chopper ride to a remote geyser field in a far corner of Yellowstone, three hours of tromping around the bubbling, hissing, spewing thermal features in intense heat, and a second bumpy helicopter ride back to the office had been what the neurologist had in mind. He cradled the bag in his lap, leaned against the web seat, and let his mind float back to the previous days—days that had changed his life and his soul, forever. He hadn't come to grips with all of it yet, nowhere near. Instead he'd focused his energy on physically healing. He figured that needed to come first. The weightier things of the soul could wait just a bit until he pulled the rest of himself back together.

The firefight that had nearly claimed his life had been fourteen days ago. *Touch and go*—he'd heard that over and over after he awoke from a three-day induced coma. It had been touch and go. By the grace of God, for him it had been a *go*. Not so for several others.

They'd kept him in the Med Center in Idaho Falls for over a week; he'd been back in his rented house in Mammoth Hot Springs since last Tuesday night. His mother had insisted on staying with him after his father flew home to Arkansas. He might be nearly thirty, but he knew better than to argue when the head of the Tyler clan announced she'd stay until he got back on his feet. And during those first few days of fighting the headaches, nausea, and pain, he'd been content to let her care for him.

He'd spent parts of those days sitting on the stone house's front porch, watching the tourists traipse up and down the boardwalks of Mammoth Hot Springs' Lower Terraces, which lay just beyond his yard. By the third day home, he'd begun walking at daybreak; just a hundred yards at first, now he was up to a mile. He'd consumed enough of his mother's Southern cooking to regain most of the weight he'd lost during the ordeal. He'd gone through countless phone messages, notes, and cards from friends and well-wishers . . . nice to know so many people cared that he'd nearly died.

The gun battle and its aftermath had made the national news several nights in a row, and he'd been hailed as a hero. *A hero.* He didn't feel like a hero; he didn't know how he felt. During those infrequent times when he'd allowed his emotions to seep to the top, he'd felt an odd mixture of gratitude, sadness, elation, and anger. He'd thought he would come through the ordeal closer to God—deeper in his faith. But he hadn't. Not yet, anyway. He wasn't wise enough at twenty-eight to understand why.

He'd come back to Yellowstone to a crisis that hadn't ended. Four of the domestic terrorists, as they were being called, had slipped away and disappeared into the park's vast wilderness. The mastermind of the debacle, Prophet Daniel Shepherd, had escaped with roughly two million dollars' worth of diamonds; there wasn't even a lead on his whereabouts. Win's life had been in the balance more than once in his dealing with Shepherd—no one could assure him that the danger had passed.

No, it wasn't over yet. But it hadn't been his concern for the last two weeks. Others were handling the False Prophet case, as they called it. Colleagues from the Denver Field Office were collecting evidence, executing search warrants, interviewing witnesses, and testifying before grand juries. The process of investigating and preparing for prosecution ground on—he hadn't been asked to assist.

He was also on the outside looking in while the Bureau rotated units of its elite Hostage Rescue Team and countless SWAT teams into the deep forests of Yellowstone in pursuit of the four fugitives. A restricted zone had been established over a vast area west of Mammoth, including the northwest quarter of the park and parts of two national forests. Checkpoints were manned, trails and roads were closed, law enforcement activity was intense. And it was all happening without him. He wasn't accustomed to being sidelined—it wasn't in his nature to sit on the bench.

Wes Givens, one of the Denver Field Office's Assistant Special Agents in Charge, or ASACs, had given Win his marching orders over the phone before he'd left the hospital. "Ease back into work, Win; no need to jump into the thick of things. Deb Miller is handling the False Prophet case, and it's only a matter of time until we bring in those four remaining fugitives. There's no intel that Daniel Shepherd is still an active threat to you, but don't completely let your guard down. Take some time off, Win. Let yourself heal."

But the ASAC knew the workload in Yellowstone, apart from the terrorism case, was nearly nonexistent. He'd offered Win some hope. "We're trying to get you transferred to Denver. In the meantime, Ken Murray said you could handle some background work on several old missing persons files—interviews with witnesses, rangers, and local law enforcement folks who originally worked those incidents. It's a good time to clear that backlog." Mr. Givens had wrapped up the call on an upbeat note: "You're in line for a commendation from the Director, Win. You've made the office proud, so ease back in."

Win's mind snapped back to the present as the helicopter banked and dropped for its approach into the park's headquarters at Mammoth Hot Springs. His stomach fought to stay at the higher altitude; he clenched his jaw and stared out the window to stymie the queasiness. His motion sickness was temporarily forgotten as the chopper flew over the tall steel bridge above the Gardner River and made its final approach. Seeing Mammoth from the air was mesmerizing. There was such a sharp contrast between the vintage vibe of the Historic District, with its sandstone-and-frame structures surrounded by bands of shady trees, and the modern crush of hundreds of cars, RVs, and buses clogging the highways and parking areas. In a sense, Mammoth felt just as otherworldly as the geyser field he'd just left.

Mammoth sat on a plateau in the northernmost part of a park nearly the size of Rhode Island and Delaware combined. The location had been the park's headquarters since the horse-soldier days of the 1880s, when the U.S. Cavalry wrestled the world's first national park away from the profiteers who were rapidly destroying its features. While the structures within the Fort Yellowstone National Historic District maintained their original look, the landscape had changed since the early 1900s. The cavalrymen's wives hadn't approved of the fort's sterile terrain of sagebrush and stunted pines. They'd planted dozens of hardwoods and evergreens on the mostly barren plateau and piped in water to nurture the trees and to green their yards. The result was an oasis-like setting for Yellowstone's old buildings.

When Win had arrived here in early April, it was still winter by park standards—the community was barely shaking off its long hibernation. The town ballooned in size from fewer than three hundred permanent residents to several thousand with the influx of seasonal park workers and tourists during the brief summer season from late May until mid-September. The bustling activity below him was evidence that peak tourist season was fast approaching.

The pilot made a sweeping turn that provided a view of the area's namesake white terraces and hot springs. The steaming water cascaded down a mountainside in alternating pools and terraces for hundreds of feet before nosing up to the parking lots and the Grand Loop Road just southwest of Win's stone house. The terraces were gleaming white, orange, and gold, and although earthquakes had sharply diminished the thermal activity of the hot springs over the years, they were still an amazing attraction.

The helicopter rocked back on its skids and settled onto the temporary landing pad that the FBI had installed weeks ago. Win waved to the pilots and walked several yards to a large stone building that once served as a cavalry barracks and was now used by the Park Service as their fire and rescue center. For the last two weeks it had become the tactical operations center, or TOC, for the continued search for the four fugitives—it was bustling with activity at all hours of the day and night.

The FBI Hostage Rescue Team operator guarding the entrance was outfitted in full tactical garb; his black MP5/10 was swung in a ready harness across his armored chest. Win flashed his credentials as he spoke a greeting. He got barely a nod in response. Win felt the tension when he entered the large staging room. Three analysts from the Bureau's Critical Incident Response Group were poring over live drone footage being fed to them from above. The two twenty-seven-foot Predator drones, on loan from the military, were being flown from a small airport outside of Livingston, Montana, sixty miles away. Someone on the far side of the room was calling out for a tech guy, loudly griping that he was losing his drone feed. Logistics and communications at the remote park were difficult, and the droves of tourists made efforts at subject containment almost impossible. It wasn't an ideal situation.

Shelia, one of HRT's liaison agents, waved him over from across the cavernous room. She brushed her long blond hair back behind her shoulder and peered up at him from her cluttered desk. "Win, so great to see you again! Lookin' good! Hey, you've even got the hair growing back." He self-consciously ran a hand to the back of his head, where, thankfully, his dark-brown hair was beginning to cover the scars. The agent didn't seem to notice his unease. "Have you heard? We may shift Gold Unit to some even more goshforsaken spot, a wilderness area across the park boundary in Montana—another anonymous tip that the subjects have been spotted. My plants are all gonna be dead at my apartment if this crap doesn't wrap up soon." She glanced back at her screen, then shifted gears. "Oh, I saw the Park Service bulletin on possible human remains at a geyser field . . . anything to it?" She adjusted her dark-rimmed glasses and leaned back in the chair.

Win held up the bundle containing the skeletal hand. "Yeah, unfortunately."

"Related to the mission?"

"No. Probably a missing tourist, probably an accident. But I'll be working it. The brass pulled me from the fugitive hunt for the time being—"

"Pity. We could use you." She shrugged and abruptly turned back to her screen, since he had nothing to contribute to the mission. *Her* mission. That was her focus and he knew it. She couldn't be bothered or distracted by the mere death of another unfortunate human being.

He knew he shouldn't be so critical; everyone was stressed, tired, frustrated. The FBI had the best surveillance and detection resources in the world, yet after two weeks they still hadn't been able to locate four guys in the woods. Not to mention the lack of progress in finding Shepherd, the ringleader. The press, sitting in their satellite vans just up the street, were clamoring to know why. The lack of success or even a hint of positive news was wearing on everyone.

Win made the required brief verbal report to HRT's on-site commander that the remains from the geyser field appeared to have nothing to do with the fugitive hunt, then he headed out the way he had come. No one had time for chitchat, barely time for a greeting or a smile—the fatigue from the relentless search gave the TOC an oppressive feel.

He took his time walking the two hundred yards to the divided street that ran in front of the Justice Center. He passed the rear of the Park Service's huge stone Administration Building, paused beside the large white retro post office, and glanced at the activity across the street at the Justice Center. The park's Justice Center was one of the few modern buildings in Mammoth; it had been constructed in 2005 to more or less blend in with the Historic District. It housed the Federal Magistrate's office, a courtroom, and offices for the Assistant U.S. Attorney, the U.S. Marshals Service, and, for the time being, a large contingent of FBI personnel.

It was a bit early for the Bureau's daily press briefing, but it looked as if they were setting it up. The FBI press agent might have been announcing the new lead just to make it appear that headway was being made. Real news had been nearly nonexistent; the press had reverted to reporting public interest stories to justify their continued presence in the park. Win had even been interviewed in the hospital three or four times before his discharge last week. Reporters had been scrambling for stories and had even quizzed him on Yellowstone's missing persons files.

He decided to skip the press conference as he walked to the FBI satellite office that occupied a stout, two-story stone building just up the street. It was rare that his curiosity didn't prevail, but the headache that had remained at bay all morning had returned, and his doctor's warning about dehydration was moving him toward the office and coffee and the quiet of his desk.

* * *

"Didn't think you'd make it back in this soon." Denver's Violent Crime Squad Supervisor, Ken Murray, was speaking into the video camera and shuffling papers. "Good to see you're still in one piece. . . . But, Win, are you sure you're not coming back a little early?"

The FBI satellite office's 32-inch communications screen showed the older agent crisp and clear. The senior agent's short brown hair was slightly disheveled, his eyes were red and puffy, and worry lines creased his brow. Win knew the Violent Crime Squad was deep into an investigation of a brutal gang in Denver, three armed bank robberies in the metropolitan area last Friday were a problem, and half of their personnel was serving on the SWAT team stationed in Yellowstone. Everyone on that squad had several balls in the air. It was only 11:45 and Murray already looked like he'd had a long day. Win leaned forward toward the screen and did his best to smile and look competent. Truth was, he wasn't feeling great; the headache hadn't lessened. A bottle of water and two cups of strong coffee hadn't done a thing to ease it.

"Yeah, good to be back . . . was gettin' real tired of sitting around the house. May not get in the field to run down the fugitives, but I can make sure the paperwork isn't piling up on the False Prophet case."

Win watched Murray dip his head. "Even with Deb spearheading the indictments, you'll have plenty on your plate there—I wouldn't push it tromping through the woods after those yahoos. HRT and our SWAT boys are more than capable of handling that part of the gig. You can't screw around with a head wound. Take time to heal."

Win felt self-conscious talking about his injuries. He switched back to the main reason for his call. "You've seen my preliminary report on the bones we found this morning? I'll get the 302 to you later today, but I wanted to give you a heads-up on it."

Murray, as everyone called him, shrugged with his thick, bushy eyebrows and nodded. It was clear from his countenance that he thought the young agent should still be recuperating at home, but he didn't push the point. Murray knew he would have done the same thing—over a week in a hospital, a good bit of it in intensive care, and five more days at home staring at the walls, he'd be back on the job too. FBI special agents typically weren't the sit-around-and-hope-to-feel-better types; most were type A personalities all the way. There was work to be done.

"Those remains could clear a file . . . hope so. I'll have one of our forensic techs call you and go over the procedures to get them processed. In the meantime, you know I read through those missing persons files while we were screwing around waiting for something to happen in Mammoth in early May. I've done a little research, and in most of the four hundred or so national parks or national monuments the Park Service and the local police would do the heavy lifting on any missing persons calls. Yellowstone is different. The park was established well before any of the three states that surround it were formed, so the Federal Government has exclusive investigative jurisdiction. No locals involved unless we want to invite them in. And the Park Service appears to be totally understaffed, especially in law enforcement. We've had several missing persons reports up there that haven't even had cursory investigations."

Murray paused. "I'm not blaming the Park Service folks—it's *our* jurisdiction." He held up several of the files. "Your bones could be tied to any one of these—it will take some legwork. There's next to nothing in some of these folders, and even less on our digital file system." His expression didn't change on the screen, but the disgust in his voice over the substandard investigative work was clear.

"Johnson's been here five years. . . ." Win let that trail off. He wasn't going to cast blame on the office's only other agent, even if he knew that was where much of the blame lay.

"Yeah, well, Johnson turned everything over to Park Service special agents and never really followed up. Half the time, those agents were off in Alaska or Florida, at some other park. They obviously didn't have the time or the resources to run down even half of the leads. I'm holding eight reports—all in control files, none of them raised to official case status. These are missing adults, going back several years. And that doesn't even count several others that are almost certainly accidents, with no bodies recovered."

"I know, I looked 'em over too," Win said. "Some of those folks may have resurfaced long ago. Sometimes people just want to disappear for a few days . . . or years. Start a new life." The FBI Academy taught agents that in any given year, of the 650,000 or so persons reported missing in the U.S., most all are found, and most are found alive. The vast majority of adults who are reported missing contact relatives or friends within days of their disappearance.

"Some of these could be suicides, but the rangers tell me that suicides are pretty rare in Yellowstone. It's a long drive from large population centers; folks who want to kill themselves would have to work at it just to get here." Win sighed as those morbid thoughts crossed his mind. "We could probably close out several of the open files with just a few phone calls to the next of kin listed in the paperwork or to their local police. Some of these folks may have turned up."

"I was thinking the same thing. You need to get on that, but while you were in the hospital, after one of your press interviews, we got a call from a lady in Philadelphia. Her daughter . . . look at 70A-DN-615412."

Win shifted in his chair and keyed in the numbers on the computer beside the larger video screen. In seconds the Bureau's Sentinel Case Management System flashed the control file up in front of him.

Murray kept talking as Win scanned the smaller screen. "It's one of the more recent incidents. Look it over. My FD-302 interview on the call with this woman's mother is the last entry, just a few days ago."

Win's eyes quickly locked on the pertinent information: Janet Goff, thirty-two years old, from Philadelphia, Pennsylvania, reported missing in Yellowstone National Park just over two years ago. She was with something called the Yellowstone Geothermal Expedition. She'd just finished her doctorate from Carnegie Mellon University. Two color photos of a serious-looking young woman stared back at him. Mousy-brown hair, heavy black glasses, pale skin, impatient, stern eyes. The scene was somewhere outdoors; it appeared she was annoyed with the photographer. Another candid photo from a restaurant. Dressier clothes, some modest jewelry, but her sour expression was the same in both pictures. *She doesn't look like a happy camper.*

Murray was still talking while Win continued to scan the digital file. "Ms. Goff was out in Yellowstone with one of the research groups that work on earthquakes or geysers, something along those lines. Her mother told me that no one with the Bureau had even called her back after the search for her daughter shifted outside the park. No wrap-up, no official handoff of the file to the Montana Highway Patrol." He paused. "And based on what I *don't* see in the file, she may be right. Follow it up—" Murray glanced away from the screen as someone spoke to him. He quickly turned back to Win. "Gotta go. Got a lead on our bank robbery suspect." The supervisor raised his chin and smiled. "Real good to see you back."

The big screen went dark, and Win's eyes went back to the young woman's face on the computer monitor. Janet Goff scowled at him from two photographs. For just a moment he allowed himself to wonder what she was thinking, what she was feeling, when the pictures were taken. He hoped she'd had better days.

CHAPTER TWO

He caught his mother's smile through the back door's screen as he moved up the steps.

"I was getting a little worried," she said as she watched him unlace his hiking boots in the mudroom. "You know Dr. Shari wanted you to start back slowly, Win."

He grinned at her as he pulled off the second boot. "Duty calls, Mom, pretty easy morning."

She wasn't buying it. She'd raised three boys, she knew when he was fudging. He hated the worry he'd caused her, hated what she'd endured during days and nights which must have been nightmarish at the hospital. That's one reason he hadn't protested when she'd declared her intent to accompany him back to Mammoth, to stay with him until she was sure he'd recovered. He couldn't fault her for wanting that, for needing time to reassure herself that her eldest son was healing, that her boy would be okay.

"Well, come along. Jason's here. We'll show you our latest project after you've had dinner. You'll have to rest for at least an hour—if not, well, I may have to delay that flight tomorrow. . . . What's that smell?"

"Ahhh, been in one of the geyser fields, around those mudpots, like we saw near Old Faithful yesterday. Uh, maybe I need a quick shower." He sniffed the air and came up empty. His sense of smell had been slow in returning since the head injury.

Jason Price raised a slender hand in greeting as Win padded across the tile floor of the mudroom, eased past his mother in the dining room, and moved toward the back hall. The kid was sitting at the antique oak dining table, intent on his phone. The seventeen-year-old never raised his eyes as he tossed out a comment, "News says the FBI's Hostage Rescue Team is pulling out of Yellowstone." He scrolled down with his thumb. "Hmmm, they got a lead that the militiamen were spotted somewhere, hmmm, somewhere in southwestern Montana . . . Sage Peak. Where the heck is that? . . . Says they're converging on that mountain. Did you know that, Win?"

Win's trek to the shower interrupted, he turned and cocked his head. "Can't comment on an open case, Jason, but if the internet says it, you *know* it's true."

The boy rolled his eyes and shrugged in disappointment. No way Win was giving him insider information on the biggest manhunt in recent history. Win changed the subject.

"You're not working today?" Win took in Jason's Montana State hoodie and jeans—no Park Service uniform.

The kid gave him a *duh* look. "It's Memorial Day, Win. *Most* people do get some time off."

Win stopped in his tracks and considered that. He knew it was a holiday, at least he'd known it yesterday. But when the call had come in at five this morning that suspected human remains had been found at a remote geyser field, he hadn't hesitated. The park's dispatcher told him that Agent Johnson was in the field with the SWAT team, the local coroner was out of town at a conference, and if there was any chance this could relate to the fugitives, it had to be nailed down ASAP. She said she could send rangers to secure a perimeter, could wait until the FBI had more folks available, but he'd said no—he'd said he'd go. It was time to saddle up, to get back in the game.

Jason had already polished off one bowl of his mother's homemade beef stew when Win came back ten minutes later, looking considerably more presentable. His mother offered grace and he dove into the stew and cornbread. They rehashed yesterday's sightseeing trip through the park and looked back over Jason's phone photos of Old Faithful and the Canyon waterfalls. Win had been embarrassed to admit that he'd been stationed in Yellowstone since April 8th but hadn't seen any of the major attractions. Bad weather, snow-covered roads, a fanatical prophet, and a band of murderous militiamen had put a crimp on his sightseeing. His mother had suggested the day trip, her way of assessing his continuing recovery, he suspected. Jason had volunteered to serve as their driver and tour guide, and the seven hours on the Grand Loop Road that made a figure-eight through the park had been relaxing and fun. *I need more days like that,* Win told himself as he finished his lunch.

Twenty minutes later, Win sat on his front porch and watched Jason drive away. The kid's father was the park's facilities manager, and Jason served as his assistant. Jason had overseen the renovation of Win's rental house and the FBI satellite office—the kid had talent galore. Since Win came home from the hospital, the boy had hung around, especially this weekend, as his parents were out of town. Win's mom was used to feeding hungry boys, and the kid knew a sweet deal when he saw one.

Win's mother handed him a glass of ice tea as she sat down in the empty Adirondack chair beside him. She followed his gaze. "Jason's dad told him they were still doing tests today; she's been moved to a regular room. He thinks they'll be in Billings at least until midweek." She sighed. "Good that he's grown—or nearly so. It reminds me of those months you had to stay with Granny. . . . You were so little, you didn't understand."

"Do we ever understand?"

She drew a deep breath and turned her eyes to the cascading hot springs that rose less than seventy feet from the driveway. "Trials. There will always be trials and hardships we don't understand." Then she tried to lighten the mood. "It's good that Jason has the part-time Park Service job. He loves the work, and it's wonderful that you've taken some time with him. He's really been working on those SAT practice tests you bought him. With his mother's illness interrupting his homeschooling these last few months, I'm not sure he would apply to college without your prodding."

Win turned his head and smiled at her. "You taught me how to be a big brother, Mom. I've had some practice."

They watched from the shade of the wide porch as troops of tourists trekked up and down the boardwalks merely yards away. Sounds of laughter and loud voices blended with the noise of road traffic into a blur of background sounds he'd learned to tune out as he watched the spectacle. The white calcite that formed the terraces was almost blindingly bright in the midday sun. Streaks of orange bacteria meandered through the cascading pools, adding to the splendor of the scene. A large pillar of travertine called the Liberty Cap rose thirty-seven feet into the air. It stood a hundred yards from his porch—he'd measured the distance. The Yellowstone guidebook said it likely hadn't sprayed scalding water in hundreds of years. It simply stood tall and white—a silent sentry guarding the mountain of steaming hot springs. Win's stone house had some fascinating neighbors, that was for sure.

"You're going to do the mental health work they've recommended?" His mother threw the question out casually.

"Think I need a shrink, Mom?" he asked in a teasing voice.

She looked into his deep-blue eyes. "You've seen some things . . . had to do some things . . . that no one needs to face alone." She knew he wasn't one to share his emotions. She touched his arm. "I've always taught you that we're never alone—that God is with us. He places family, friends . . . *and* counselors in our lives to help us cope. You need to accept that physical healing is just part of it. Not even the biggest part. Yes, I want you to get some help. This isn't the time to be stoic, to pull back, to buck up. I want you to take advantage of what the FBI offers you."

He looked away and took a sip of his sweet tea. He didn't look back at her, so she waited him out.

"You've teamed up on me. Dad said the same thing on the phone last night." He sighed. "Okay, I'll call them . . . I'll do it." He looked back into her strained face. "I don't want y'all to worry."

She stood and smiled down at him. "Good. That's settled then. Rest awhile before you go back to the office. I've got two pies to make, chickens to cut up, packing to do. I'm glad you're letting Jason take me to the airport. You don't need the stress of driving to Bozeman and back."

Geez, glad I didn't tell her what I've been doing all morning.

She opened the door and looked back at him. "I'm glad you let me stay."

"Gruff will miss you."

She bent down to shoo the big orange cat back inside the door. "Is he the only one?"

He smiled. "Thank you, Mom."

* * *

Win cradled the landline receiver on his shoulder as he sipped coffee and rummaged through his desk for the candy bar he was sure he'd seen there weeks ago. It was closing in on five, hours since his lunch of beef stew. The Denver Field Office's Evidence Response Team leader had transferred his call to a forensic analyst at the FBI Laboratory in Quantico. He was getting nowhere fast, and the fact that he was expecting answers on a holiday was compounding matters. He tapped his pen on the desk. He hadn't expected the lack of enthusiasm he'd received thus far in his quest to find a home for the evidence bag of bones that sat on his desk.

Finally, the woman's unconcerned voice came back on the line. "So, you've got no missing persons investigations connected to a criminal case in . . . where did you say this park is?"

Lordy! Who hasn't heard of Yellowstone?

"It's Yellowstone National Park. The Denver Field Office has jurisdiction." He was trying hard not to let his tone convey his annoyance.

"You don't have an urgent situation . . . not even a criminal case opened." She seemed to be looking at her computer screen. "You could ship the remains here, but I'm looking over our backlog—all the active cases that would be ahead of you. You're looking at two months or more to get anything useful back. And that's before we could do DNA sampling and carbon dating for age."

Win drew in a deep breath and tried an appeal to the woman's humanity. "There's no way to move it along? This is someone's daughter, someone's mother, someone's friend. A person died here."

"I'm sorry, but you know our protocols, Agent Tyler. If you could tie the bones to a criminal case, we could move on them ASAP, but we can't test every random bone that comes in. Do you have any idea how many bones we get that turn out to be early Native Americans or settlers from the 1800s?"

Win changed tactics. "Okay, I understand. So what do you suggest?"

"See if you can get your local coroner involved. Maybe a state lab or even a private lab. Can't hurt to try. Just be sure to document every movement of the bones on the off chance you do find some evidence of a crime. The chain of custody has to be uninterrupted for the remains to be admissible at trial."

Win got off the frustrating call and leaned back in his chair to stare out the 115-year-old windowpane toward the front of the park's Albright Visitor Center and the open area that had been a parade ground back in the day of horse patrols. The three-story limestone Visitor Center had housed cavalry officers back in 1909. It sat directly across the street from the compact gray stone building with the green-tile roof where Win's office was located.

His second-story window view was front and center for the comings and goings at this hub in the northern part of the vast park. The current attraction across the street was an elk cow and calf that were bedding down in the shade of a towering cottonwood tree. A dozen tourists jockeyed for position to snap a photo. Two tour buses pulled past, probably headed for the Mammoth Hot Springs Hotel, a hundred yards to the west. Even with much of the northwestern part of Yellowstone within a restricted area, there was no shortage of visitors hitting the park.

He redirected his focus to the bag that held the skeletal hand. There was no evidence locker here—not in a two-man office. His home office in Denver was hundreds of miles and a full day's travel away. *Not an option.* But it didn't feel right leaving the bones on his desk in a plastic bag, like some discarded trinket. He gently picked up the package and moved it downstairs to a low compartment in the newly installed gun safe. Not an ideal spot for part of a once living, breathing human, but better than the superheated muddy goo he'd retrieved it from hours ago. He addressed the remains as he laid them inside the vault. "I'll do my best to get you home. Back to someone who cares." As he closed the heavy metal door, he self-consciously glanced around to make sure no one had overheard.

*   *   *

Trey Hechtner, the Mammoth District Ranger, was waiting in Win's office when Win climbed back up the oak staircase to the old building's second floor.

Trey glanced up from his phone and grinned at the agent. "Your mom's planting flowers at your house—elk or deer will eat them tonight. I'm guessin' you're hiding out in the office to avoid being an accessory to horticultural murder."

Win blew out a long breath as he slid into his desk chair across from the ranger. "She means well. . . . It's like she wants to make everything homey. Wants to baby me."

Trey shrugged. "She watched you darn near die in intensive care. Can't blame her for wanting to hold on tight."

"I know. I know. Her flight home is tomorrow morning. Jason Price is taking the SAT in Bozeman, so he's taking her to the airport. . . . Planting flowers—for real?"

"Elk will eat them." The ranger was staring back at his phone.
Geez.

"I'll bring some chicken wire over this evening and cover them. Give 'em a fighting chance. I'm guessing your mom will want progress reports and pictures of them every week."

Win rolled his eyes at that thought.

"Back to business," he began. "The FBI Laboratory is not gonna move fast on the bones. They recommended the local coroner or a private lab to give us an initial read. There's a woman who was associated with one of the geyser research groups who went missing two years ago." He slid the file with Janet Goff's photos across the antique oak desk.

The ranger studied the photos and the brief profile. "Ah . . . I vaguely remember. I was in Grand Teton National Park, coordinating the rescue of several climbers up on Teewinot Mountain. Took us days to get that mess under wraps—two climbers fell, and three more were trapped after a rock fall. It was a rough deal, and I stayed down there for another several days, clearing up the paperwork." He flipped through the sparse file. "But I don't recall any big push to search for this woman. Says here they found her car at the Norris Geyser Basin lot."

"Yeah. The file said rangers began a search of Norris Basin, then got a tip she'd been seen in Livingston. They had pings off her cell phone in Livingston and a day later in Missoula. File got turned over to the Montana Highway Patrol. I've got a call in to them, but it could be that's as far as it went."

They both sat and stared at the photos of the apparently unhappy young woman staring back at them.

"Okay then," Win finally said, "get me the Park Service file on Ms. Goff and I'll follow up with the highway patrol. Not lookin' like I'm gonna hear anything back today."

"It's Memorial Day, Win. Some folks do take off—"

"Yeah, yeah, I got that. I guess I can wait till tomorrow for the photos and measurements you took at the site. The remains we found today were over thirty miles from where Janet Goff's car was found—that's as the crow flies. The bones might match up better with a different file. I'll hit the missing persons databases tomorrow. You wanta check in with the local coroner's office and see if they have any interest in looking over the bones?"

"Well, their office is just two folks—I know they were out of pocket this morning—but I'll call them tomorrow. I'm sure they'll give it a look. Anything else you need me to do on this?"

"Just round up any other open files y'all have on missing persons in the park in the last few years. Let's see if we can make some sense of this in the morning."

Trey rose from the wooden chair. "Cindy and I'll see you tonight at supper; we've found a babysitter for McKenna. Real nice of your mother to cook for us again. Kinda hate to see her leave, she's been feeding us real well for the last few days."

"The cooking has taken her mind off me. You won't believe all the stuff she's cooked or baked and left in that freezer in the basement. I'll be eatin' good for a while."

The ranger smiled and picked up his flat hat as he stood. "Don't suppose you called your bear girl to come to your mom's going-away dinner tonight?"

"Uh, no. Thought about it, but no."

Trey's smile widened. "You better not think on it too long, or someone else will have the good sense to sweep into that girl's life and you'll be left standing in the dust. She's beautiful, kind, and thoughtful. You said that yourself."

"She's also camped out with her research team out of cell phone range somewhere south of Tower Fall in the Antelope Bear Management Area. She won't be back to Roosevelt till middle of the week."

"Sooo . . . you *have* been keeping up with her." He patted the top of the chair on his way out and glanced back, raising his eyebrows in a mocking salute. "Good man."

* * *

Trey hadn't been gone five minutes when heavy boots tromped up the stairs. Win thought the ranger might be returning, but instead the office's only other resident FBI agent appeared. Special Agent Spence Johnson's hefty frame took up most of Win's doorway as he leaned in from the hall. The deep voice wasn't particularly friendly. "Whata ya doing here?"

"Couldn't take sitting around the house any longer. Mr. Givens cleared me to come back. Rough day?" Win replied as he took in the older agent's dirty camouflage fatigues, scuffed combat boots, and heavy ceramic-plated body armor. It was obvious that Johnson was still in the thick of the hunt for the fugitives. Win motioned him toward a chair.

Instead of sitting, the man leaned against the doorframe, fatigue weighing on his wide shoulders. He squinted down at Win. "I'm too damn old for this crap. . . . I've been in the field with our SWAT team for three days now, and I'm gettin' the rest of the day off, and maybe a couple more if I can swing it. Shoulda retired months ago." Johnson ran a filthy hand along his chin—three days of graying stubble. At fifty-five, Johnson was nearing the Bureau's mandatory retirement age of fifty-seven, and he was way past the allowable retirement age of fifty. He didn't have to be trooping through the mountains for days on end.

Johnson had been transferred to the FBI's Yellowstone Satellite Office over five years ago. Win was sure whoever had sent him there had hopes of him quitting the Bureau. No agent worth his salt stayed in a backwater posting like Yellowstone—it was the equivalent of exile to Siberia. A transfer here was a career killer. Win Tyler knew that only too well. He may have redeemed himself with his handling of the False Prophet case, but the LOE, or Loss of Effectiveness transfer, that landed him in this remote office in early April still clawed at his gut.

His focus turned back to the big man in his doorway. "Anything new on the militiamen?" Even as he asked the question, he knew the answer. The Bureau spewed out regular email updates. The manhunt was one of the biggest things the FBI had going in the country right now, and the national news networks hadn't tired of the drama. Yet there hadn't been a confirmed sighting of the fugitives in five days, and that report had been sketchy. A backcountry hiker had reported armed men in an area three miles west of Mammoth. That tip was a "maybe" at best, since the hiker had been caught in the restricted area, had reeked of weed, and had refused to take a polygraph test. Still, it was one of the best leads they'd had.

Johnson growled back at him, "You know as much as I do. Nobody has a clue where those guys are. Well, except maybe Bordeaux. He was a honcho in that militia. Have you talked to him since you got back?"

Win shook his head. "Gonna try to get out there this week. Heard he made it home from the hospital."

Johnson switched hands with his gear bag and sighed. He was clearly running on fumes.

Win tried to be conciliatory. "Hope you can get a few days off. . . . Did you hear about the human remains we found at that little geyser field called Maxwell Springs?"

Johnson nodded back in the affirmative, disinterest obvious on his ruddy face. "Probably one of those damn fools wantin' to hot tub in the wilderness. Let the rangers handle it. You're gonna be up to your butt in paperwork on False Prophet for weeks, even if we never catch those boys in the mountains."

Okay, lots of sympathy there.

"Anything I need to deal with since I've been out?" Win asked.

"The Park Service managed to get two of their special agents down here, and I moved all of our active cases over to them so we could concentrate on False Prophet. Guess you saw that everything's being coordinated out of the Justice Center or HRT's operations center down the street. The surveillance folks are still downstairs off and on, but that may not last long. At least a third of the contingent shifted today to follow up on that lead near Sage Peak." He drew a deep breath. "Is Deb the case agent on False Prophet now, or are you picking it back up?"

"Don't know. Waiting for the brass to make that call." Win could tell the guy was fading and starting to move away. "Nothing else?"

"Since you've been out"—Johnson stretched his six-foot-five frame, stared up at the ceiling, and thought about it—"we've got several minor drug cases, a couple of domestic battery cases, one pretty bad assault, and a bunch of smaller stuff. The park's folks are handling all that." He started moving away again, then turned. "You did get a boatload of personal mail the last several days that I haven't had time to get over to your house. It's stacked up in the conference room." The man's mouth moved into an almost smile. "It's probably fan letters from dozens of lonely women who've seen your face plastered all over the TV news." He raised his voice several octaves to mimic a reporter. "Handsome, dashing FBI agent saves Yellowstone!" He chuckled and shook his head. "How many marriage proposals have you gotten so far?" His eyes squinted even tighter, and he smirked. "Better yet, how many hot propositions have you gotten? If you're not interested, throw a few my way." He ambled off down the hall without waiting for a response.

Win felt his face flush. He'd received dozens of notes and letters from citizens who professed their appreciation for his reported heroics . . . and, yes, a few of those writers had been downright graphic about their idea of sharing their gratitude.

* * *

He was at the office the next morning before seven. His mother and Jason had left for Bozeman at dawn, and without his mother to monitor him, he'd kicked his exercise routine up a notch and run two miles before breakfast. While he jogged, three Humvees filled with SWAT agents slowly passed him on the highway; the weariness in their faces told him they'd served as the night shift guarding possible escape routes out of the mountains. As he stood at the crosswalk and watched their convoy disappear down the road, a longing to be part of the team filled him. He knew it was time to get back into the thick of things.

By midday he'd handed off the evidence bag with the bones to Trey for their trip to the Park County Medical Examiner & Coroner's Office in Livingston, and he'd spent hours phoning colleagues and reviewing files to get himself up to speed on the False Prophet case and the fugitive hunt. He decided to tackle the postal bins of mail sitting on the downstairs conference-room desk as his next task. As Johnson had suspected, the imposing bundles of letters contained fan mail, typically notes of appreciation, some a little kooky, a few erotic, most quite sincere. There were dozens written in crayon from kindergarten and elementary school classes. Several were from folks he knew in Arkansas; he set those aside for more personal responses. For most, he wrote brief comments of thanks on Bureau stationary. Win knew he could get a clerk in Denver to send boilerplate replies, but he figured if folks had taken the time to write to him, they deserved his personal attention. He moved through the stacks of letters quickly. He wasn't comfortable with the role of a hero.

Three hours later, he was getting near the bottom of the pile when an international airmail envelope caught his attention. No return address, but the stamp had Turkey's red flag with white crescent and star displayed. *An admirer from afar!* He slit the nondescript white envelope with his pocketknife and a second, smaller envelope fell from the first. *Odd.* The smaller envelope contained two newspaper clippings and a folded letter. Both clippings were written in a Cyrillic print. *Turkish? Some Slavic language?* A grainy photo of Janet Goff stared back at him from a short, yellowed column. The second article was longer; it contained no photo, but handwriting ringed the text. *Weird.* The letter was dated May 18. *While I was in the hospital.* It was written in stilted English.

Win scanned through the formalities and read the body of the letter:

I SAW YOUR TELEVISION INTERVIEW ON THE INTERNET.
YOUR COMMENT TOUCHED MY HEART. AS YOU SAID, THE
MISSING ARE NEVER LOST TO THOSE WHO LOVE THEM. AND
SO WE MUST DO ALL IN OUR POWER TO FIND THEM. I WAS
WITH A RESEARCH EXPEDITION IN YOUR YELLOWSTONE
NATIONAL PARK WHEN NATASHA PAVLOVNA YAHONTOVA
GOES MISSING. SHE WAS DEAR FRIEND AND AS YEARS
PASS, I HAVE REGRETTED NOT BEING MORE HONEST
ABOUT SOME INCIDENTS WHICH SHED LIGHT ON HER DIS-
APPEARANCE. I HAVE HELD THIS CLIPPING FOR THE MANY
YEARS SINCE SHE WAS LOST AND THEN I READ OF JANET
GOFF, ALSO MISSING IN YOUR PARK. I HAVE ASKED A
FRIEND WHO IS AN AIRLINE HOSTESS TO POST MY LETTER
TO YOU. SHE WILL DO THAT WHEN SHE IS NEXT OUT OF OUR
COUNTRY. I AM NOT FREE TO TALK WITH YOU BY TELE-
PHONE OR EVEN EMAIL, AS I FEAR MY COMMUNICATIONS
ARE MONITORED CLOSELY BY MY GOVERNMENT. MY
HEALTH PREVENTS ME FROM TRAVELING. IF YOU COME
TO MY RESIDENCE, I WILL GRANT YOU AN INTERVIEW

WITH HOPE THAT IT TAKES YOU CLOSER TO DISCOVERING
THE TRUTH FOR NATASHA PAVLOVNA AND MS. GOFF.

It was signed VLADIMIR ORSKY, SVETLYI, RUSSIA.
Russia? For real?

The articles were probably written in Russian. Win stared down at them in frustration. If he scanned and sent them to Denver, he'd get an official translation within one or two weeks. It wasn't like he had a hot case here. In fact, as of yet, he didn't even have a case. He could type them into a language app and get some semblance of a translation. *That will have to do.*

He'd been so engrossed in the foreign letter that the beeping of the secure locks on the front door hadn't registered. He flinched in surprise as Trey moved into the room. Win relaxed back in his chair and smiled. He needed a break, and the calm, easygoing ranger was fast becoming a close friend.

Trey laid his flat hat and a stack of file folders down on top of the conference table, then dropped a sack of sandwiches nearby. "Had a great time at your house last night. Your mom makes the world's best fried chicken." He spotted the piles of mail. "Whoa, boy . . . these are all from admirers?"

"Yeah, Americans are grateful to their men in law enforcement!" Win shot back the smart retort.

"Yup, they're grateful, all right, but I was in the same firefight and I haven't had an influx of fan mail. Suppose it helps if you're the tall, dark, and handsome type who looks good giving interviews on television—even from a hospital bed."

Win fished a sandwich out of the sack. "Hey thanks. How'd you know I hadn't eaten?"

"Does it matter? You're always hungry—Wow! Women are sending you *these* kinds of photos?" Trey was thumbing through the small stack of erotica that lay to the side on the table.

Win hitched his eyebrows a couple of times and gave a sideways grin. "Some days it's a tough job."

Trey was staring at the foreign letter. "Turkey? You got mail from Turkey?"

Win switched into a more serious mode. "It might relate to our missing persons files"—he pointed to the note and clippings—"but I'll be darned if I know. The articles and letter are actually from Russia. Can't read Russian."

"You can't read Russian! I'm shocked!" Trey grinned at him, then looked more closely at the articles. "Well, I know someone who can. Can I send him a screenshot of the longer article? It's not case related?"

"Nope, have at it. We don't have any official case files open on this. Might actually lead to a tip."

Trey pulled out his phone and took photos of the lengthier column, then typed a quick text. Win was more interested in satisfying his hunger than finding out where the text was going. They were only halfway through the meal when Trey's phone chirped to signal a message. The ranger glanced at the text, dropped his chin, and frowned. He held up the phone for Win to read: **It is directions to the entrance to Hell.**

CHAPTER THREE

The message was not, to say the least, what Win or Trey was expecting. *Directions to the entrance to Hell? Seriously?*

"Luke Bordeaux reads Russian?" The surprise in Win's voice was clear.

"Yup, speaks it pretty good too. Russian, French, Spanish, Arabic, and one or two of those other Middle Eastern languages, not to mention his Cajun talk, as he calls it. Luke has a gift for language. When he was a Green Beret, the Army sent him to language schools." Trey glanced back at the phone. "He just texted that he's tied up at the hospital in Bozeman for the rest of the day. Seein' a new doctor." He looked back at Win. "I guess we'll have to solve our Russian mystery later. You haven't been to visit him since—"

"No. He's been home, what? Two, three days from the Med Center?"

Trey nodded.

"I'll call him and drop by his place tomorrow. I should have gone sooner."

"You've been healing yourself. Give yourself a break." The ranger gathered up the sandwich wrappers and bag. "Wait. I nearly forgot." He pulled a small FedEx package out of a hefty file folder. "Headed off the FedEx delivery guy at the door when I came in. I signed for it."

Trey held the package out to Win. It was lightweight, with insurance endorsements and security wrapping on it—must have cost a fortune to overnight it to Mammoth. Win took it, and for just a moment it didn't click that the return address on the label was New Orleans. Then he saw the handwriting through the label's plastic sleeve. His breath caught and he fought to keep his emotions off his face. He bit down on his lip and nodded. He had to look away.

Trey could see his distress. "Ah, well, I've got a planning meeting with our folks. I'll catch you tomorrow." He quickly turned away and moved out the door.

Win just stood there. He held the package and stared at the handwriting. He knew what he was holding. The parcel was light—the packaging made up the bulk of it. *Open it. Don't be a coward. Open it,* his mind counseled. But he didn't. He couldn't. He carried it upstairs to his office and put it in his lower desk drawer, the one he could lock. And he locked it.

* * *

It was well after five now, and Win was getting next to nowhere on his efforts to insert himself back into the False Prophet case. He had called his supervisor early this morning; the man's voicemail said he was unavailable. Win figured that counted as touching base with the boss, and he proceeded to call several of the agents who were doing the heavy lifting on the indictments. He'd worked as an Assistant U.S. Attorney for a year after law school. He knew he could contribute to their efforts, but he got a firm brush-off. He also reached out to the agents who were still chasing down leads in the field. Everyone politely told him they were good, the case was moving along—and oh, by the way, shouldn't you be resting, taking care of yourself, healing? Was there a memo he'd missed, *Don't let Tyler back in*?

He gave up on the *ease back in* approach and called again for his direct supervisor, Jim West, at the Jackson Hole Resident Agency. During the summer, that Bureau office was a three-plus-hour drive through Yellowstone and Grand Teton National Parks. The 150-mile trip from Mammoth to Jackson, Wyoming, was clogged with bear and bison jams and further slowed by the parks' forty-five-mile-per-hour speed limit. Win had been stationed at the FBI Yellowstone

Satellite Office for six weeks now, and he'd never even been to the Jackson Hole RA.

Jim finally came on the landline and was apologetic. "It's my fault, Win. I should have gotten back with you sooner. I honestly didn't think you'd be medically cleared for duty this quickly." He paused. "Ah, that's good, really good." Win heard the stress in the man's voice. "The Bureau's shutting down the Jackson RA—been in the works for a couple of years, but suddenly, outa the blue, I've got to close down the office next month. Consolidating with the Lander, Wyoming, RA. That's another 160 miles down the road. I have to sell my house, buy a house. . . ." He sighed. "And with the fugitive hunt in our territory, I've been up to my eyeballs in issues."

"I didn't know—"

"We have to get your shooting inquiries out of the way before you go off desk duty. You can handle the missing persons files and some of the other lightweight stuff while the inquiries go forward. But until the Inspection Division's results come back clearing you on the shootings, you have to tread lightly. Can't let you back in on False Prophet for the time being."

"I didn't know I'd be sidelined like this."

"Hey, it's just policy. It's sure not a reflection on your work. Wes told you that you're in for a commendation from the Director. That's a big, big deal. And they're working on your transfer to Denver. You need to be thinking about what you want to work, because I heard Mr. Strickland is going to try to let you pick your squad. I know you did white-collar and public corruption for your first three years in Charlotte, but think about the terrorism squads, or violent crime. . . . You could apply for SWAT. You've got great skills."

Win could tell the conversation was turning into a pep talk. Maybe that was what he needed. He asked a final question. "Our SWAT team and HRT are still rotating up here on the manhunt. Am I allowed to tag along, get to know some of the other agents, get myself back in shape?"

"Sure, sure. If the team leader is good with it. But keep a low pro-file, okay? Most agents don't get in shootouts *in their entire careers.*

You've been in three years and you've got several shooting inquiries going—*right now.*"

* * *

After the call wrapped up, Win sat at his desk and considered his options. He could knock off, go home, and chill. His doctor and his mother would approve of that move. He could change into his workout clothes and hit the little gym that was located behind the hotel and open to park employees, or he could satisfy his curiosity about the Russians and do an internet search. He chose the latter option, and two hours later he was still at his desk.

Win's internet search produced next to nothing on Natasha Yahontova, but Dr. Vladimir Orsky was the real deal as far as geyser and volcano experts went. There was nothing on the guy within the Bureau's system except for notations of his State Department requests for visas and customs information—no red flags there. But Win had no trouble finding numerous internet hits on him from previous years. There were professional papers he'd presented at conferences, expeditions to several South American volcanoes—the hits went on and on. Curiously, there was nothing on the web for the last four years. Orsky dropped from sight, at least on the internet, just as abruptly as the missing persons on Win's list had vanished.

Natasha's Park Service hard file contained brief reports from the State Department of two contacts with a grandmother in Russia who was listed as next of kin, but there didn't appear to be any follow-ups after the year she disappeared. The file held eight slips of paper with sparse details describing witness interviews by a Park Service special agent. The first interview Win pulled was with Dr. Orsky. He was the colleague who'd reported her missing to park rangers on August 26th of that year. They were both working with a group called Yellowstone Geothermal Expedition; Dr. Preston Ratliff was listed as the lead researcher. *Same group that Janet Goff was involved with . . . hmmm.* Ratliff's interview was even more concise than Orsky's. The interviews didn't give him much. Natasha was working alone, measuring temperature fluctuations in the Mud Volcano area of the park. She couldn't be found when two of her coworkers stopped to pick her up for lunch. Her work van was in the Mud Volcano parking lot, and her rental car was at the cabin where she'd been staying in Canyon. She was neither seen nor heard from again.

The file included a black-and-white photocopy of her Russian passport photo; its quality was so poor that Win could barely make out her features. It listed her age as thirty-six—brown hair, five foot six. Her place of residence was shown as Novokuznetsk, Russia; there were no other contacts except the grandmother. She was in America doing thermal energy research, and the paperwork said she was affiliated with Russia's International Geothermal Institute. Their website looked legit. Win thumbed through the file again; something was missing. There were no FBI 302 forms. *Was the Bureau not contacted?* She'd been reported missing nearly two months after Johnson arrived in Yellowstone. *Where are the other law enforcement contacts? Did the Bureau drop the ball?* Win's internal dialogue continued. *Geez, this is shoddy work.*

He leaned back in his chair and thought about it: two missing women—both connected to the same research group. *Coincidence?* The Bureau didn't believe in coincidences. *Neither do I.*

* * *

He'd forgotten that he'd silenced his personal phone during the call with his supervisor earlier that evening. When he turned it back on, he was met with a chorus of message alerts. A local number got his attention, and the soft voice on his voicemail caused his pulse to jump. He replayed the message twice, and his smile grew wider each time.

"Hi, Win . . . it's Tory. Hope you're feeling much better. . . . We're back in Roosevelt tonight. You said to call when I got here. Cell service is sketchy, at best; I'm using the landline at the gas station. I've got the day off tomorrow, so if you'd like to come down . . . I know it's last-minute, but I'll be around and they're opening the Roosevelt Lodge dining room tomorrow—maybe we could have lunch or dinner? If it's not a good time, no worries. Hope to see you soon."

He really didn't know her well—they hadn't even had a real date. But as he'd come out of the drug-induced stupor in the hospital, he'd made a mental list of things he wanted to do with the gift he'd been given: a second chance at life. Getting to know Victoria Madison had been on the short list. And yeah, he wondered if he was jumping the gun, moving too soon. It had only been four months since the breakup with Shelby. And yeah, Shelby had been there for him; she'd taken an emergency leave from her residency at Tulane to fly to Idaho Falls for four days while he was in the hospital. They had talked. . . . He let his thoughts wander back there for a second too long and the tightness returned to his chest, the hollow feeling settled in his heart. *Too soon?* Maybe so, but there was only one way to find out. He stretched as he rose from the chair. Time to get home. Tomorrow he had some visiting to do.

*   *   *

Luke and Ellie Bordeaux had moved to Montana from Louisiana a little over five years ago. They lived with their two young children on a forty-acre inholding within the national park. Their place was east of Highway 89, about halfway between Mammoth and Gardiner. The frame house was two miles off the highway at the end of a rough gravel road. No neighbors for miles. It was an isolated location, but on this clear, crisp morning it was also beautiful. The sky was azure, with white fluffy clouds that seemed to dance in the breeze. The views of the Absaroka Range to the east and northeast were breathtaking; every peak retained its cap of snow. A reminder that May 28th was still spring along the Wyoming-Montana border.

Win had had no luck reaching Luke by phone last night or this morning, so he'd finally called Ellie. She'd seemed rushed, said she had the kids and was fixing to walk into the drugstore in Gardiner. She said Luke was doing better, that he was down the back trail behind their house—said he'd been going down there in the mornings ever since he'd come home from the hospital, said it would be good for him to have a visit. He noticed that her usually friendly voice was strained; she'd hurried off the call. He didn't read too much into it—everyone in Gardiner was on edge over the hunt for the militiamen.

The trail behind Luke's house to the Yellowstone River meandered for a quarter of a mile, gently sloping downward from the plateau, where the ranch-style house sat among towering spruce, to the yellow bluffs flanking the river. The path cut through a large open field covered with fragrant sagebrush that had taken on late spring's mint-green color. Win entered a stand of lodgepole pine at the edge of the clearing and could hear the water flowing just ahead. Luke was sitting on a low boulder with his back against the trunk of a large spruce. His thick black hair was shorter since the hospital stay, and his black beard and mustache were trimmed close. He was wearing faded blue jeans, a red flannel shirt, and moccasins, not his usual hunting boots. His face was turned toward the river that flowed at the bottom of the yellow limestone cliff; Win could glimpse the water through the trees. The gentle drift of the green-hued river was nothing like the brown raging torrent it had been the last time Win had stood above it nearly three weeks ago.

Bordeaux never turned to acknowledge Win's approach. Win stopped about twenty feet away. He could see the sling cradling Luke's left arm, noticed his face had lost some of its tan, thought he looked a bit thin. He listened to the gentle rush of the river. A bird was calling in the trees nearby. Luke Bordeaux never made a sound.

"Been on the phone with Ellie. She said your shoulder was comin' along pretty good." Win said that as a greeting. For a good minute there was no answer, then Luke shifted on the rock and looked at him.

"Uh-huh." The dark eyes slowly took him in, from his hiking boots to his brown Indiana Jones–style felt hat. "And you're lookin' a sight better than the last time I saw ya."

"I've been tryin' to get ahold of you—you haven't been answering your phone."

"No, reckon I haven't. I emailed Trey the translation of that Russian clipping and handwriting he sent me. He said it was for you." Luke's eyes looked almost black. "We're done."

Win closed the gap between them and stood near the man. "You got a problem with me?"

"Should I?"

"What is it? Your foolish pride? It's the informant payment, isn't it?"

"I never asked for money from you . . . from the Feds. It's blood money. That's how I'm seein' it. You think you own me now."

Win dropped his gaze to the dust on his boots. He heard the bird call from the trees again. "I knew you might not take it well, but I was trying to make good on my promise to you—to take care of your family if something happened to you in that church militia mess." He looked up and met Luke's eyes. "And something did happen. Just by the grace of God, we both lived."

Luke's dark eyes bore into his. "How 'bout you hike back outa here the way you hiked in. I've got nothin' to say to you."

Win blinked a couple of times at the unexpected hostility. He raised his chin and met the man's angry eyes again.

"I've got a feeling I'm missing somethin', Luke. I came to check on you, to thank you—"

Bordeaux didn't let him finish. He slid off the rock and stood in one quick, fluid motion. The injury hadn't diminished his presence; he was as tall as Win and maybe more physically imposing. His voice was as hostile as his stance. "I've already had three visits from the Feds wantin' me to *help* find Eriksson and the other three boys who bugged out of the firefight." His eyes narrowed even further. "Those visits at the hospital weren't real friendly." He raised his chin. "Like I said, you think you own me now. Well, you kin have your money back—I never asked for it and I ain't selling out the militiamen. You hear me, boy!"

Whoa! Might shoulda got here sooner.

Didn't look like being shot had done anything to ease Luke's Cajun temper. Win held his hands out to his sides, palms up. That was his subtle sign of surrender, an attempt to calm the man down. "It's a far sight harder to give money back to the government once you get it," he said. "Maybe you just need some time to cool off and think this through a bit more." He tried to change the topic. "Y'all had any threats or blowback from the Prophet's people?"

Luke shook his head *no* and answered softly. "Everyone 'round here knows we all got took by Daniel Shepherd. No one we know woulda stuck with the Prophet iffen they'd known what was goin' down. And that includes Eriksson and those boys. None of us are outlaws."

"I get that, but there's still consequences for breaking the law . . . and a whole lot of law got broken. People died." Now Win was getting a little hot. "So, everyone just wants to claim they were misled? To claim it wasn't their fault? Our rule of law counts for nothing if everyone just declares a do-over and pretends nothin' happened." His voice was harsh. "People died," he repeated before he turned and walked back up the trail.

Win's hike back to his Bureau-issued Expedition wasn't nearly as pleasant as his hike in had been, but Bordeaux needed to get his head on straight, and continuing to debate the rights and the wrongs of things wasn't likely to win any points. Win also needed to find out who in the Bureau was putting pressure on Luke regarding the fugitives. Luke Bordeaux didn't respond well to strong-arm tactics; Win had seen that firsthand.

* * *

Tory was wearing a tan safari jacket over a light-blue denim shirt. She was leaning back against one of those rustic rail fences, with one leg raised and her hiking boot resting against the graying rail. The ranger had his summer flat hat in his hand, and he was leaning in toward her, using his other hand to emphasize some aspect of the story he was telling. Win zeroed in on her pretty face. She seemed totally absorbed by what the man was saying; she covered her mouth with a hand and laughed at something he said. Win watched her brush back a strand of dark hair that had escaped her barrette. She looked, well, she looked captivated by this guy.

Win swung his attention to the ranger. Not in law enforcement, or
if he was, he wasn't wearing a gun belt today. He was maybe six or six
one, about Trey's height. He had light-brownish-blond hair that was
slightly longish, and a scruffy, short beard. He wore his uniform well—
pretty athletic looking. The guy reached over and hugged Tory; she
pushed him back in a playful way and then they both laughed. *Damn.*
Win felt his chest tighten. This could complicate things. For some reason it hadn't occurred to him that he could have competition for Tory's
attention on her day off.

He'd cleaned up a little at the office after the trek to Luke's place,
and he'd driven the nineteen miles from Mammoth to try to catch
her before lunch. He'd just pulled into a parking spot in front of the
Roosevelt Lodge. He was admiring the hickory rocking chairs that lined
the front porch of the sprawling 1920 log building that housed the dining room, lounge, and gift shop. He read the sign saying the lodge had
been built on the site where President Teddy Roosevelt camped during
his horseback tour of Yellowstone back in 1903. That's when Win spotted the couple at the rail fence near the entrance to the rustic cabins.
He sat there with his hands gripping the steering wheel and considered
his options. *Walk up to them and introduce yourself to this guy? Stage
a strategic retreat and come back later? Sit here and stew about it like
a wimp?* His lack of confidence with women was rearing its ugly head.
Just when *strategic retreat* was winning his internal debate, the ranger
gave Tory a wave and moved off toward the Roosevelt General Store.
Problem solved.

Her smile was just as beautiful as he'd remembered. Her brown
eyes were just as soft. Those eyes sparkled and gleamed when she told
adventures of the last few days along Antelope Creek. Her enthusiasm
for the Interagency Grizzly Bear Research Project was contagious. He
found himself smiling more and more as she recounted the last week's
achievements. Her group had caught and tagged three more bears, her
research paper for Vanderbilt was coming along nicely, and for the first
time in days she had more than a nylon tent over her head. All good.

They ordered the opening-day barbecue special at the dining room
and debated whether Tennessee or Arkansas barbecue was better. They

went for a walk through the trees around the historic log lodge and watched the wranglers corral the horses that would soon be fitted out for summer trail rides. He discovered that she'd grown up riding too, that she loved throwback tunes from old bands like the Eagles, that she seemed respectful of all living things. They hiked away from the buildings and up a wooded rise to get a better view of the open, rolling hills to the east. Win managed to deflect most questions about his injuries; he couldn't tell her much about the harrowing events that had nearly ended his life—anything on the case that wasn't public knowledge was totally off-limits.

"You're back at work full-time then?" she asked.

"Sorta easing back in, on everything. I've worked up to a couple of miles on my morning run. I'm mostly going though paperwork at the office." He paused. "Making progress, I think."

"But you haven't begun to deal with the weight on your soul."

He blinked. *How does she read me that easily?*

She drew a breath and nodded. "You're thinking the physical part is best handled first—I get that. I'm sure you're praying about it, waiting for God to lead."

Well, actually I'm not. And I don't know why. Someone down below on the highway shouted and interrupted his thoughts. He pulled his eyes away from her and spotted the kids near the road.

"Bears! There's bears!" The teens obviously hadn't gotten the word that you were supposed to be quiet around the wildlife. One of Tory's hands went to the bear spray hanging from her belt; Win followed her lead as she moved out of the cover of the trees. The crowd of onlookers near the road was growing, and someone had convinced the kids to quit the yelling.

They were about a hundred yards from a large black bear and its tiny cub. The bear was grazing on the new grass and slowly progressing up the ridge away from them. Its ebony coat glistened in the sunlight. The cub couldn't have weighed more than ten pounds; it was tiny. Moments later a second cub appeared. Then a third. The cubs ran, rolled, and tackled each other, following in the general direction of mama bear. They were just like kittens or puppies, or any baby thing,

Win supposed. The mother bear turned her head and murmured to her brood; they rose on two feet as one, then tumbled quickly after her.

Tory was transfixed. "Isn't she amazing?" she whispered.

"Yes, she is." Win Tyler wasn't looking at the bear.

CHAPTER FOUR

Maybe I shoulda listened. Taken the boss's advice. Sat this one out. Win slumped down on a gray boulder just off the main trail. The last HRT guy in the line of operators glanced toward him as he moved past. The guy gave a quick questioning motion with his head toward the trail, and Win shook his head. "I'll wait on the rangers," he whispered in response. The operator paused long enough to mouth the words *Careful going down.* There wasn't any condemnation in the other man's eyes. Win didn't need to prove his toughness to him or to anyone else, yet he still felt a wave of embarrassment as he sat to the side while they quietly climbed the steep, rocky path.

He'd hiked with the nine-man HRT unit up and down game trails on the precipitous slopes of Clagett Butte and Terrace Mountain all morning. They'd just ascended a steep section of Sportsman Lake Trail and Win had nearly collapsed. It had been four hours with hardly any stops since they'd left the vehicles at the turnout at Glen Creek Trailhead. These guys were locked in and super fit. It wasn't an outing for anyone not one hundred and ten percent in shape. Win had known that, but his pride had gotten him miles into the mountains, where he finally hit a wall. He'd stumbled badly twice in the last twenty yards; he couldn't safely go on. And there was no need to. He'd volunteered for this gig to try to prove to himself that he was ready to get back in the action. *I'm not ready and I should have known that!* The Scripture *'Pride cometh before the fall'* floated through his mind. Now he'd have to sit and wait on the six Special Response Team park rangers who were coming up behind HRT.

He'd spent much of the last three days suffering through shooting-inquiry interviews and staring at his office walls. The Bureau's Inspection Division folks had descended on Mammoth with the suddenness of a storm. Recounting the horrific experiences of the firefight to the FBI's inspectors had brought the nightmares back to life. His efforts to tamp down his emotions for the last two weeks were now for naught—everything felt raw again; the headaches and flashbacks returned with a vengeance.

He wasn't sure how to handle the inspectors, but he'd taken Jim West's advice and clung close to the office, projecting what he hoped was a model for the consummate competent, responsible FBI special agent. Jim West told him the inspectors needed to see that, needed to see him going about the business of the Bureau in a low-key manner. Jim told him there might be a time and a place for his gung ho, damn-the-torpedoes attitude, but this sure wasn't it. Win had felt like an actor in a deadly serious play, but between interviews, inquiry paperwork, and mandatory video sessions with a psychologist, he'd managed to make progress on the missing persons files. He was sure he didn't hide his relief when the inspectors pulled out late on Saturday afternoon, just as abruptly as they'd come. Their decisions would be reported later—that was out of his hands—but at least this phase in the awful process was complete.

The three-day grind held one positive: he'd managed to get his exercise routine back in full swing, so on Sunday morning when the call came through that the fugitives may have been sighted by a drone three miles west of Mammoth, he thought he was ready to hit the field with the A-team. He was very wrong.

He breathed in a deep sigh, shifted on the boulder, and took in his surroundings. He'd been resting for ten minutes or so, and nature's sounds had returned to the woods. A woodpecker was tapping out a steady drumbeat somewhere deep in the forest. He wondered which woodpeckers made these mountain forests their home. Did they have the big, prehistoric-looking pileated woodpeckers, the redheads, or the flickers he'd grown up with? He made a mental note to research that. Two mule deer timidly crossed the trail less than forty feet away. They paused to look at him with wide eyes, their large gray ears moving back and forth. They found him to be of little interest and disappeared into the thick forest below the trail.

The calmness of his surroundings was helping—the headache and crushing fatigue that had sidelined him began to retreat. He'd hoped Trey and the rangers would be coming around the lower switchback at any minute. But the HRT guys had set a brutal pace; he wasn't sure how far behind the rangers were. He'd head down and meet them, borrow one of their guys, and make the trek on down to the trailhead. He was thinking they'd been held up. He was also thinking it wasn't too smart to be sitting out here alone.

He was less than a quarter mile down the trail when he saw it. Just a flash of light from the forest below. *A reflection off metal or glass?* It flickered again in the deep woods—slightly closer now, he thought. He stopped and drew in a breath of relief. *That would be Trey's guys.* The trail had dropped down to a bench on the mountainside, and he was now standing within a short stretch of gently sloping open ground straddling thick stands of Douglas fir. This band of old-growth forest hosted evergreens more than eighty feet tall; moss-covered boulders were scattered among them, and smaller evergreens competed with the giant trees for sunlight. Win remembered that the trail was near vertical for a ways just beyond this little clearing. His legs were still a bit shaky from the exhausting hike, and he didn't relish the more difficult parts of the climb down. He'd wait for the rangers here.

Thick bunches of yellow daisies got his attention; they seemed to grow wherever the sun hit a patch of exposed dirt. He remembered someone calling them arrowleaf balsamroot, and he supposed the last few days of above-average temperatures had brought the blossoms on. There were flowers everywhere he looked. He wished they'd been blooming before his mother left last week—she'd have loved this sight. He'd been so intent on keeping up with the HRT boys on the way up the trail that he hadn't noticed the flowers before. He absently wondered how many touches of beauty he missed every day because his mind was too focused on one objective. It was a failing of his, he reckoned.

He'd pulled out his personal phone and bent to take a photo of one really impressive yellow bouquet, when he felt it. The hair on the back of his neck tingled. The woods had gone quiet. Win knew enough about his instincts not to ignore the internal warning. Something was wrong. He did some quick calculations: He was still at least three miles from the trailhead and the vehicles. He was maybe half a mile from where this path intersected with Snow Pass Trail, which led directly east toward Mammoth. There were still four desperate militiamen somewhere—and he was way too exposed. *It's probably the rangers . . . but what if it isn't?*

He unclipped the MP5 from its ready harness and scanned the trees from a crouch. Even before his eyes cleared the forest, he heard the sound of metal on metal on the trail far below. He paused to make sure. The doctor had said his hearing should return completely in his left ear, but he still found himself turning his head to better pick up faint sounds. He heard it again, this time a bit closer. He moved out of the clearing to the uphill side of the trail and eased down on one knee beside a huge tree. *Be cautious, be smart,* he told himself. He had a reasonable view down the slope toward the trail, but the woods to either side of him were dense. He scanned the forest for movement. When he turned his eyes to the left, he was staring directly into a familiar face.

"What . . . what are you doing—"

"Keep it down, dammit, we ain't the only ones up here." Luke Bordeaux was standing beside a moss-covered boulder, less than ten feet away.

"You're in a restricted area. You can't be here!" Win hissed.

"That so. . . . Well, just out gettin' some exercise, musta took a wrong turn."

"Sure you did!" Win moved into a crouch. "This isn't a joke, Luke. You know HRT doesn't have a sense of humor!" Win took in Luke's twill hunting clothes: the heavy boots with gaiters, the brown canvas pants, jacket, and day pack. A camo field cap was turned with its bill to the back. Bordeaux was dressed to bushwhack through the wilderness, not casually hike a well-used trail.

"Seriously, it'd be a felony if you're apprehended in this area," Win whispered.

"Well then, I reckon I'd best not get apprehended," Luke softly replied. His dark eyes moved back to the path. "Somebody's comin' up the trail."

"That'll be the rangers. Trey and some of his folks—"

"No, it ain't. Trey's got a man down from a fall. They're more'n a mile down the trail. I skirted 'em and was movin' on up, then I seen you lollygagging around by yourself, takin' in the flowers. Couldn't hang with the big dogs?"

Win glared at the man.

"Whoever it is, they came from the east. . . . They're armed," Luke said softly. "I've seen glimpses. Looks like several."

"The fugitives?"

Win watched Luke study the slope below them, watched his face for a tell. He saw nothing.

"Ain't likely," came the quiet reply.

Luke knows exactly where Eriksson and those boys are. Win shifted to try to see through the trees better. Luke's eyes stayed on the slope, but he raised his hand slowly. A huge pistol had appeared in that hand; it was pointed toward the trail.

"Who y'all got out here?" Luke asked without turning his head.

"HRT above and Trey's rangers below. That's it." Win flexed his fingers on the cool metal of the rifle. He caught a glimpse of movement below them. "Can you see anyone?" he whispered.

A bullet slammed into the tree just above Win's head before Luke could answer. Win dove behind the solid trunk as two more rounds thudded into the wood. As he flicked off the safety, he heard garbled shouting from below—someone calling out that he had two on the screen.

"He's got thermal imaging!" Win nearly shouted it to Luke. Luke was leaning against the boulder with his gun braced against it. Win saw the recoil from the large handgun. Heard the loud report.

Luke ducked behind his cover and looked Win's way. "They *had* thermal imaging. Don't have it now. That's how they spotted us. How they got so close."

"FBI! FBI! Cease fire! Put down your guns!" Win yelled down the hill. A barrage of rifle fire was the immediate response. *Sheeees! Who are those guys?* Win sank lower behind the tree as another burst of fire raked the boulder where Luke had stood seconds ago. He fumbled with the key on his shoulder radio "FBIY-2 under fire . . . a half mile above Snow Pass Trail . . . need assistance! Under fire! Copy?"

"HR-6, roger that . . . hold your position . . . on our way," came the HRT team leader's tense response.

Where has Luke gone? Win hazarded a peek around the base of the tree and saw nothing. He could hear branches cracking and breaking down below. Then more garbled voices. The report of Luke's big handgun cut the air again, this time from somewhere to Win's left and farther down the slope. Luke wasn't just holding his position; he was going after them. Whoever *them* were.

"Throw down your guns! You're under arrest! Citizen's arrest!" Someone far to Win's right called up.

Citizen's arrest? Are you kidding me!

"*You* throw down *your* guns, and I don't mean maybe!" Win shouted in response. "FBI here! Identify yourselves now!" Luke's pistol fired again, and someone yelled that they were being surrounded. Win heard something crashing through the woods below him.

"You said the Feds were on Quadrant Mountain. . . . Damn, you better have that right!" an angry voice said.

Win could hear the man clearly; he was less than forty yards below, in the rocks. Win swung the MP5 and sighted toward the voice. He saw movement—a shoulder, an arm in green camo. He hesitated with his finger firm on the trigger. *Dang, I don't want to shoot anyone.* He whispered a prayer and yelled down to the man in camo. "FBI! You better be talking to me now!" He glanced left and right to make sure he wasn't being flanked, but he couldn't see twenty feet into the dense trees beside him; he knew he needed to change his location. He heard other voices, heated but lower this time.

"You come out where I can see you! Enforcement agents! Show yourself!" someone yelled from below.

Enforcement agents? Bounty hunters? Geez! Before Win could respond, he heard a familiar shout from below: "Police! Hands up now!" Trey and the cavalry had arrived. He saw the man below him slowly stand with his hands up. Win lunged from behind his tree and dodged from tree to boulder to tree, rifle at the ready, as he moved down the slope. "FBI here!" he called so as not to become a target. He pulled up behind a stout trunk, sweat burning his eyes and relief flooding over him. He could clearly see the rangers' black Kevlar helmets bobbing among the trees below him. Trey was standing in the trail, shouting orders. Three men in green camo were on their knees in front of him, hands raised.

Suddenly there was a blur in the woods moving away from the rangers. A guy in camo was coming straight toward Win, running for all he was worth. Win stepped from behind the tree and the guy dodged, quick as a deer. Win yelled "Halt" and lunged for him. The man stumbled, dropped his rifle, and let loose with swearing. He swung hard for Win's head and luckily missed; panic mixed with rage was etched on his broad face. Before Win could get in a lick, one of the rangers plowed into the guy, knocking him square on his backside. That ranger's rifle now held the man at bay.

Win reached for the handcuff pouch on the back of his belt. He slapped the short ranger on the shoulder and moved to secure the thug. "I've got him, buddy."

"Like hell you do," came the terse reply. "This is my catch, back off." He blinked as he saw the face under the black helmet. *A girl?*

She was sorta out of breath but all business as she went about the chore of making the man lie spread eagle, frisking, and cuffing him. All in short order, completely professional.

A girl on the Park Service's Special Response Team, who knew?

The captive was sitting with his hands cuffed behind his back; she checked his pockets for more weapons and Win kept him covered. It occurred to Win that the guys they were holding looked rougher and meaner than the fugitives they were hunting. The bounty hunter's thick arms and neck were covered in garish tattoos, he wore a tight black tee under his camo body armor. A scruffy beard, long unkempt hair, jagged teeth, and a nose ring completed his badass look. Being tackled by a woman wasn't setting well with the guy either. He let loose another string of profanities directed at her.

"Shut up or I'll kick your ugly teeth in!" the female ranger snapped back. Win was afraid she might do just that—he lugged the guy up by his arm and pushed him toward the trail.

Trey had climbed the slope to them just as HRT swooped in and completely took control. "It's four bounty hunters outa Cheyenne," Trey was telling the team leader. "They claim they spent the night in Gardiner and came up the Terrace Mountain Trail before dawn. They're probably the ones the drone spotted. I don't know how they got around our trailhead checkpoints outside of Mammoth."

Win knew how they'd gotten around them. Many of the local deputies and rangers who'd been assigned to highway and trail checkpoint duty weren't taking it very seriously. The fugitives hadn't been spotted in well over a week, and it was tiresome, boring duty. Everyone had become too complacent.

The HRT team leader was livid. His mission was to find four domestic terrorists, not break up a firefight between the Bureau, the Park Service, and a bunch of trigger-happy bounty hunters. And the man who seemed to be in charge of the motley group was winning no points with the Feds. He might have been handcuffed and on his knees in front of the rangers' guns, but he hadn't yet conceded defeat.

"You can't arrest us! We're sworn enforcement agents. . . . This is Wyoming. There's no legal restriction on hunting indicted criminals in Wyoming! Why'd you dangle that $500,000 reward out there if you didn't want us here?"

Real good question, Win was thinking.

"Not one more word!" the team leader barked at the man. The other three guys looked a little more contrite, with HRT's intimidating firepower now on display. The HRT guys had formed their defensive perimeter and were taking control of the captives, checking the cuffs, looking for weapons.

"They had a handheld thermal device," one of the operators reported to his boss. "Tyler's shot must have gotten it. It's in about a hundred pieces."

"That'll cost you! That's $7,600 for the Flir K65 mobile. We'll sue!" one of the men yelled.

Win stood back to let the HRT guys and the rangers hash out the *who does what now* with their prisoners. The team leader was still fuming that his mission was fouled up. Win's headache had made a reappearance, and he was weighing the pros and cons of mentioning Bordeaux.

The team leader swung his head toward Win. "How many rounds did you fire?"

Win dropped his eyes and studied the MP5 in his hands. "Uh . . . none, sir. I . . . didn't fire."

The guy's eyes shot back to Win's face. He stepped closer. "I heard someone fire. Not a long gun, a big sidearm. Three shots. None of these yahoos are carrying handguns bigger than a 9mm—and the rangers say they never opened fire. You wanna explain that, Agent Tyler?"

Before Win could formulate an answer, Trey stepped beside him. "Sir, as the senior paramedic here, I'm ordering Agent Tyler out of the incident zone. You've got things under control. He doesn't need to give his statement now. He's just come off medical leave and he's done too much too fast. Not good with a head injury." Trey stepped between Win and the operator as he dug through his medical bag. "I need to check his blood pressure."

The HRT guy seemed shocked that the ranger was trying to call the shots, but before he could object, one of the bounty hunters started thrashing around and cussing his captors again. The team leader glanced back at Win, his eyes narrow under the olive-green helmet's brow. "All right, all right. Go on down. I'll get with you later."

Trey spoke to Win softly as the other man turned away. "You look like crap. This mess will take forever to sort out, and that's even if HRT doesn't call in your evidence response folks." Trey was attaching a blood pressure cuff to Win's arm and looking straight into Win's eyes. He lowered his voice even more. "I heard that big pistol. . . . *We*

know someone who owns a 10mm gun like that—" One of the operators moved a little too close, so Trey didn't finish his sentence. He
addressed Win a little louder, "Think you can make it down with some
help?"

Win nodded as Trey made a show of taking his blood pressure and
heart rate, gave him a *We'll talk later* look, then called one of his rangers over. "Jazz, this is Agent Tyler. He's going down for medical reasons. Had a head injury three weeks ago. Hike him out slowly and then
check on Gentry. We'll be there as soon as we finish up here . . . not
likely anyone's going any further after the fugitives today."

Win looked into the woman's face and tried to smile, but she was
scowling up at him, so he gave up the attempt. "Appreciate your help,"
he mumbled as he moved around the commotion and on down the
trail. He figured she'd follow; he never turned to look.

*   *   *

It seemed as if half the law enforcement complement still in Mammoth
was rushing up the trail toward the incident. Win and Ranger Jazmine
kept moving to the side of the path; they silently watched the parade
move up the steep slopes past them. It was a complete callout. *And
why not,* Win thought. Beautiful Sunday afternoon, first of June, and
everyone on duty was bored spitless with nothing to do except stand
around and wish something would happen. Well, *something* had
happened, but it would only make for more confusion, more hassle,
and probably lower their chances of achieving their real objective:
finding the four rogue militiamen.

Most of the higher-ups at the U.S. Marshals Service and the Park
Service no longer believed the four fugitives were anywhere near
Mammoth. They'd had no reliable sightings since that first week of the
incident, around the middle of May. The thinking was that someone
had ushered them out of the area, but the recent tip at Sage Peak had
turned out to be a bust, as had several others. Truth was, nobody had
a clue where they were, but the FBI brass wasn't about to pull the plug
on the manhunt yet. Not even close. Win's bosses had long memories.

They remembered the fugitive case of Eric Rudolph, the Olympic Park bomber, who in 1998 escaped to a North Carolina national park and evaded HRT and the Bureau for five years. He'd been right under their noses the entire time, in a wilderness area much, much smaller than Yellowstone. Rudolph was captured when he finally came out of the woods to scrounge for food from a grocery store dumpster. The search in Yellowstone might get scaled back, but Win knew there was no quit in the Bureau.

The restricted zone was an area roughly the size of a small state. That wilderness was pocketed with cliff overhangs, caves, and other perfectly good hiding places. If those four men had stayed holed up in one spot, even the dogs wouldn't have found a scent, and the infrared, thermal, and high-resolution cameras on the drones and surveillance planes couldn't see through solid rock. The militiamen could be right on their doorstep. Win had been out of the loop for so long that he wasn't sure exactly which way the intel on the fugitives pointed, but one thing he did know for sure: Based on what he'd seen today, it should be pointing right square at Luke Bordeaux.

CHAPTER FIVE

He felt her gently brush against his face, his chest felt heavy, and again she softly touched his nose, a calm *purrrrrrrr* . . . he reached for her hand and forced his eyes open. Mere inches from his face, slitted green eyes stared back at him. Fourteen pounds of cat sat on his chest, purring a contented cat song, willing him to awaken.

"Geez, Gruff . . . c'mon, buddy, get off me." He breathed a deep sigh and rubbed the big orange cat's ears. "Man, I need to get a life." They both stretched and Win reached for his Bureau phone. When he'd gotten home from the fiasco with the bounty hunters, he'd taken a shower, turned off his phones, and laid down for a nap. He never took naps, much less turned off the Bureau phone—he was technically on duty 24/7. He'd signed up for the fifty-hour work week, which often extended well beyond seventy hours, and the "always on duty" requirement when he'd joined the FBI. He was always on call. He sat there and weighed his options. For a moment he was tempted to leave the phones dark and take one of the heavy-duty pain pills the doctors had prescribed. He thought about it. But it wasn't physical pain he was feeling. It was loneliness and loss . . . and something else he couldn't quite put his finger on. He sighed again. Those pills wouldn't do a darn thing to dull those feelings—not in the long run anyway.

As he suspected, the work phone told him he'd missed a call from the HRT team leader, who was kind enough to leave a message saying that he hoped Win was feeling better and he'd get with him at the office tomorrow for his 302 interview. Trey had also called to check on him; the ranger's message reported that he'd probably be in the middle of their little crisis with the bounty hunters until late tonight.

Win's phone said it was only three. He thought about calling Tory and seeing if she'd like to get dinner tonight. But he'd seen her on Wednesday afternoon and they hadn't talked since. Win's insecurity surfaced—he figured Tory was likely spending the day with that good-looking ranger he'd seen her with last week. *How will I know if I don't call? Call her!* He remembered that Shelby hated to be called at the last minute. Said it made her feel like an afterthought. Was Tory an afterthought? *No.* Was he an insecure coward? *Maybe . . . possibly . . . probably.* He'd been with Shelby for five years—*five years*—and he'd forgotten how dating was done, not that there'd been many girlfriends before Shelby. He could feel it coming on: the pain, the hollowness in his chest, the regret. He blew out a deep breath, stretched again, and forced the rising emotions down. He shifted to other tasks.

Win made calls to his parents, brothers, and grandparents back home—that was part of his Sunday routine. Nothing really to report . . . taking it easy . . . just had a nap. No mention of the grueling mountain hike, the debilitating headache and fatigue, or being shot at by a bunch of loons. Just a typical Sunday afternoon.

Next on his list was Bordeaux. He had to talk with the guy before he gave his statement tomorrow. No way he was fudging in a Bureau interview to keep Luke in the clear. He downed a coke and a ham sandwich and geared up to go find the man. Luke wasn't answering his phone. Not that Win was expecting him to, but it still annoyed him. He'd thought they'd bonded during the firefight weeks ago, but maybe that was just his perception in the heat of battle, maybe that was just how he'd wanted it to be. He was getting ready to walk out the back door when a text came in on his personal phone: **front of ur house in five. L**

That's more like it.

Win walked around to the front porch, pausing for a few seconds to make sure the chicken wire was still keeping the elk out of his mother's freshly planted shrubs and flower bed. He sat on the front steps between the two tall evergreens that gave his house some privacy from the parking lot and highway just beyond the small yard. The lot and road were bustling with activity. It looked like every tourist in the country was in Yellowstone on this spectacular Sunday afternoon.

The dark-green Ford-150 SuperCab pulled up in front of the house, and Win walked to the open window. Bordeaux barely glanced at him.

"Get in," he commanded.

Win glanced in the rear window to make sure Luke was alone. He slowly opened the pickup's door.

"You just gonna stand there? Iffen you stand there, I might change my mind on talkin' to you. I'm waffling back and forth on it."

Win got in. Luke was moving the truck down the road before Win got the passenger door shut.

"What are we gonna be talkin' about?" Win pulled on his seat belt and took in Luke's jeans and chambray shirt; he'd lost the bushwhacker look. He was reminded again how much Luke had a rakish, Caribbean pirate appearance. Win watched him navigate the slow traffic with his right hand on the wheel; he could tell there was padding under the left side of Luke's long-sleeve shirt, but he wasn't wearing a sling. He saw a knife on Luke's belt, but no sign of a firearm. He'd never known the guy to be unarmed.

Luke turned down the Grand Loop Road that led toward Roosevelt; he fell in behind a massive RV with Florida plates. They passed the stately two-story historic houses on Officer's Row and the gray stone Yellowstone Chapel in silence. They drove off the mostly barren plateau surrounding Mammoth, crossed the high metal bridge over the Gardner River, and meandered through the steep, forested terrain to the south. They drove for a while. Luke finally spoke without glancing his way. "You looked like hell up on that mountain. You ain't ready fer that kind of action yet."

"I appreciate you pointing that out to me," Win replied sarcastically. "I probably hit the field a little too soon."

"You think?"

"At least I was *supposed* to be within the restricted zone. What were you doing there?"

"Buildin' up some strength and gettin' my wind back." Luke breathed a deep sigh. "It's slow, slow goin'. Ellie is pushing me on it . . . guess I've been a little underfoot. Like I told ya, just gettin' a little exercise."

"I'm an FBI agent, Luke. Do I really look that stupid?"

Win saw the man's lips nearly turn to a smile, watched him force back a smart-aleck response. Luke shrugged with his good shoulder and turned the truck into a small parking area just off the highway. The brown wooden sign said *Phantom Lake*.

"Let's stretch our legs a minute. This is a nice spot. Not many folks here," Luke said.

Win figured he didn't need to push it. Bordeaux had texted him for a reason. He needed to let it play out. Luke tapped the steering wheel a few times with a finger; he seemed to be considering something.

Before opening the driver's door, Luke started talking. "Hypothetical question. If those militia boys wanted to turn themselves in . . . how would they go about it without gettin' shot?"

Win studied the man. *He knows where they are—he's been in touch with them.* "Hypothetical answer. Would probably work out best if someone could get word to them to meet at an agreed-upon place. Without their weapons. Away from the public. We could have an arrest team there and an ambulance if Cabe McDonald still needs medical assistance. Does he?"

Luke eased back in the seat and turned toward Win. "How would I know that? Hypothetical question, I said." Luke pushed the door open, stepped out, and walked to a smooth boulder at the edge of the small lake. He stretched his left shoulder and grimaced.

Win followed him to the large rock. "I'm not on the case now. They've got me working through some old missing persons files, but Eriksson and those men need to turn themselves in and do it soon. The longer this goes on, the worse it will be for them. If an agent gets hurt, even accidentally, while they're on this manhunt, the charges will keep ratcheting up."

Luke was staring across the shallow lake. He waited to answer until a car full of picnickers finished loading up and pulled out.

"They don't feel like they've done nothin' wrong. They helped get those folks free," Luke said.

"Yeah, and that will count for something, but you know as well as I do there's consequences for actions." Win was still treading lightly.

Luke seemed to be thinking on it. Win pressed him. "Luke, I'm mighty beholden to you for more than I can even express, but I can't protect you if you're helping those guys. If you know where they are, that's aiding and abetting. That's a crime and you know it. And as long as they're out there, they're in danger; the public could get caught in the middle and *they're* in danger; and every law enforcement type who's after them is in danger. It needs to stop."

Luke sat down on the boulder and looked off across the lake again. "They call it Phantom Lake 'cause it only holds water in the wet season. Dries up and completely disappears in late summer and fall. Ain't much of a lake. Not like you're used to—those big blue lakes in the Ozarks. When I was little, we used to drive to north Arkansas in the summer to camp and fish . . . real nice country."

He's stalling. This is like pulling teeth. "I know this isn't easy for you," Win said.

"The Feds—some FBI boss from Salt Lake—come down pretty hard on me when I was in the hospital. Called the militiamen terrorists. Started spoutin' violations and federal prison sentences— threatened to go after their families and *my* family on anything they could find." Luke was still looking across the flat water. "Happened more'n one time. Scared Ellie."

"I'm sorry. I didn't know about that until you told me. It shouldn't have happened that way, but those folks are above my pay grade. You've been in the Army; you know the grunts aren't the ones calling the shots."

Luke nodded. "I do know that. And I do know that the militiamen can't run forever. It ain't doing nobody any good."

"Maybe we can work—"

Luke cut him off. The dark eyes had swung back across the little lake. "Somethin' ain't right."

"What?" Win's eyes followed Luke's to black specks above the far ridge. Luke stood up and walked two cars down to a group of young men who were pulling their packs and hiking poles from a small SUV. Win was surprised to hear Bordeaux sound just like a park ranger.

"Sorry guys, this trail is closed this afternoon. Looks like we've got a winter kill or carcass on the ridge. . . ." Luke was pointing them back to the highway, telling them about the Hellroaring Creek Trail just a couple more miles down the road. "Much nicer views, super wildlife watching, suspension bridge crosses the Yellowstone River. Have a great afternoon, and carry that bear spray!"

The hikers loaded back up and Luke returned to the truck. He slid into the driver's side and pulled the huge pistol Win had seen earlier that morning out of the center console. Win's right hand instinctively went to his Glock. Luke looked up with a frown. "Easy, boy."

Win watched Bordeaux unbuckle his belt and attach the holster. "What kinda cannon you carrying?"

"Wilson Combat Hunter, 10mm—a bear gun. Popular with guides in Canada and Alaska. Can stop a grizzly. Few handguns can do that."

"You'd shoot a bear?" Win was shocked.

"No, but it makes me feel good that I *could* shoot a bear iffen it come down to me or him."

"What were you shooting at this morning? You got off three rounds."

"One fer the thermal monitor . . . one to get those fools' attention, and another one to *really* get their attention." Luke switched gears and nodded toward the ridge with his chin. "There's a problem across the lake, and I didn't wanna let those kids walk into a bear or lion kill. Let's go make sure before we call the rangers to shut this area down." He pulled on a light jacket to conceal the weapon, handed Win a canister of bear spray, and started off for the trail on the south side of the lake.

"Why don't we just call and have the rangers come check it out," Win offered.

"Big bunch of ravens, flying in low. Wouldn't wanna waste their time iffen it's nothing."

"You've been a commercial hunting guide out here for years. I figure you'd know if it was nothing."

Luke just kept walking. "Pay attention and talk loud. It ain't real smart to surprise a grizzly. Some of the big snowbanks are still melting. Could be a bison or elk got stuck and didn't make it through the winter."

They trooped along the edge of the shallow lake and up the side of a modest ridge into thick lodgepole pines. The trail wasn't steep or rocky, it was a gentle upward trek; Win was grateful for that after his misadventure in the mountains this morning. He watched Luke from his spot ten feet behind him. The man might still be recovering from a serious wound, but he moved up the trail with ease: no wasted motion, no obvious focus on the path itself. The guy's special ops training was evident. Luke held up a hand and stopped as they crested the low ridge.

"Kin you smell it?" he asked.

Win shook his head. "Just now getting my sense of smell back—comes and goes." He scanned the pine forest and saw movement to his right. Shafts of late-afternoon sunlight cut through the trees. A large silver-gray canine darted into view. Then a darker one joined the first, their yellow eyes fixed on him from less than twenty yards away.

"Coyotes! Uh . . . wolves!" Win called out.

"I see 'em."

Win was spellbound. "I've never seen a wolf . . . they're huge." The piercing stare from the wolves' buttery eyes was chilling on a primal level. Win felt a wave of fear collide with the sense of wonder. They looked much bigger than he'd expected wolves to be—he was guessing 120 pounds—the Discovery Channel didn't do them justice. The two wolves turned and trotted down the ridge, quiet as shadows. Win hazarded a glance toward Bordeaux. "That means no bears?"

"Not necessarily. Stay put and keep your head up." Luke had the big pistol out now. He moved off the downhill side of the ridge, away from Phantom Lake. Win pulled out his phone and was relieved to see service bars; he tucked it away and wondered if it was real smart to be this trusting of Luke Bordeaux. Just when he was about to conclude that it wasn't, Bordeaux materialized from the woods with a hard look on his face.

"Got a body—a man, from the look of it. Big snowdrift is melting 'bout fifty feet off the trail down yonder." He motioned with the gun. "Wolves were digging to get to it . . . ravens and some critters already had." Win started to move in that direction. Bordeaux grabbed his arm. "You don't need to see that." He shook his head. "Call 911, the rangers will handle it."

"I'm an FBI agent, Luke."

"You keep telling me that." Luke held up his phone with a photo of the gore. Win took a sharp breath and quickly looked away. Luke kept talking. "I'll keep the varmits off, you go down, meet the rangers at the trailhead, and send 'em up here." Win clenched his jaw and nodded. He suddenly had no desire to see the carnage.

*　*　*

A Park Service Tahoe finally pulled into the small Phantom Lake parking lot with its lights flashing and stopped in front of him. Jazmine Jackson, the female ranger who'd escorted him down the mountain six hours ago, was riding shotgun in the big white-and-green SUV. She swung out and looked him over as her partner called in their location.

"You again?" She shook her head as she pulled a ball cap on over her tight braids. "Does trouble just follow you or is it the other way around?"

Win ignored the remark and gave them an overview of the situation. The guy in the SUV was checking the sky above the ridge with binoculars. "Yeah, I see the ravens. You think we've got a crime scene?"

"We need to treat it as such. There was a man reported missing in this area in April."

The gray-haired ranger nodded. "Yeah, I remember, we found a car abandoned in this lot. Never found a trace of the driver."

"Well, we may have now. Luke Bordeaux is guarding the site; wolves were trying to get at the body."

Ranger Jazmine moved to the back of the SUV and began removing equipment. Win turned back to the older guy. "I've called this in to our folks. They've given me an ETA of about seven, ten more minutes. They want y'all to wait for them before you approach the site."

Jazmine gave Win a sharp look. "You want us to wait on *your* people? We're in charge in this park."

"No, Ms. Jackson, you are not. The FBI has jurisdiction." He left it at that and walked away. He wasn't in the mood to argue technicalities. She huffed off carrying a *Trail Closed* sign, and the other guy walked over to tell some curious tourists that the parking lot was closing. The *big dogs*, as Luke had called them, would be here any minute—they would want answers. Win stood beside the Ford F-150 and tried to formulate a reasonable, logical explanation for what he was doing—without authorization—way out here at Phantom Lake with Luke Bordeaux.

He couldn't come up with a thing.

* * *

Monday was another in the string of perfect-looking days in the park. For much of Win's time in Yellowstone, during April and May, it had alternated between icy, rainy, and snowy; the spring weather had been downright awful. But everyone said it would suddenly transition to deep-blue skies, warm days, and cool nights. Everyone had been right.

Win had wrapped up his morning routine of exercise, Scripture reading, prayer, and coffee; he stepped out his back door at 6:15 into bright sunshine. As he started for the Bureau SUV, a sharp snort from the side of his house got his attention. He tentatively moved toward the sound. He'd learned that caution was *always* the best policy in Yellowstone; many of the animals here had the potential to gore, trample, or eat the unaware. Win caught sight of several early risers standing on the boardwalks, taking pictures back toward his house at whatever it was, so he warily peered around the corner of the dwelling. Four large rust-colored heads swung toward him in unison, and four mouths stopped mid-chew.

"Dang it!" He lunged toward the elk cows, who were having his mother's flowers for breakfast. Win had grown up on a farm in Heber Springs, in the Arkansas mountains. He knew what to do when the gate was left open, when the cows got out, when livestock got in the hay-field. *Run 'em out!* The four Yellowstone elk might have been very dis-tant relatives to the cattle Win had grown up with, but that was about as far as it went. As he charged toward them, they lowered their heads and charged right back—they were each over five hundred pounds, and the distance was closing fast. He threw up his hands and yelled. They stopped, he retreated. They confidently resumed their feast while he stood at the corner of the house, fuming.

Seconds later, Trey pulled his Tahoe into the driveway that ran beside the house. The proximity of the ranger's big SUV caused the elk to trot up the trail behind the dwelling. They smugly passed Win without a glance.

Trey was grinning when he got out of the truck. "Wish I had a video of that. It would go viral!" Then he got serious. "Next time you get a ticket—stay twenty-five yards from the elk. You do know that wasn't real smart—"

"Yeah. Yeah, I seem to be making a habit of *not real smart* lately."

Trey was inspecting the damage to the plants. "I'll fix this back . . . maybe add extra wire to keep them out. They didn't eat everything." He looked back over at Win. "Dropped in to tell you I'm on my way to Livingston to pick up the bones. We've got preliminary results from the Coroner. Want to meet on it today?"

Win nodded. "I'm pretty free. Gotta do an interview with HRT on the bounty hunter deal . . . and I'm gonna talk with that Sims lady. Her daughter, Missy Sims, went missing several years ago. The Park County Sheriff's Office handled most of that case since her car was found outside the park's boundaries, but she was never seen again after she left work here in Mammoth." Win shook his head at the thought of the incomplete files. "We shoulda had jurisdiction. Mrs. Sims lives in those hills north of Gardiner. Got to wait for her to call and give me a time." He sighed. "We did clear one file up late yesterday."

"I heard about it from my folks. Is it the informant who went missing a few weeks back?"

"Yeah, they found a billfold with a driver's license. Body is in bad shape, but it looked like a blow to the head got the guy—a sharp edge, maybe a hatchet or a shovel." Win drew a breath as yesterday's images floated through his mind. *Well, at least I didn't throw up.* He focused back on Trey. "The Coroner finally got there, body's been sent to the Wyoming State Crime Lab in Cheyenne."

"You had to work it?"

"No, I lucked out. The Bureau rotated in a new on-site commander yesterday, some ASAC out of Chicago. She didn't know anything about Bordeaux's involvement with the militia, nothing about my history with Luke—she called in the Coroner, the ERT, and had her SWAT team secure the site. Luke hid his gun, we both gave quickie statements, then we slipped outa there like tourists. Got home before dark." Win turned to look for the elk. "Uh, you know I asked you about a ranger down at Roosevelt—"

"The guy who was makin' a move on Tory?"

Win glanced away, then glared back at the grinning ranger. "Yeah, that one."

"Well, it isn't great news. Based on your description, and my snooping around with the staff down there, I'll bet the guy was Chris Warren."

"You know him?"

"Know about him. One of my rangers—real nice girl—had a short fling with him last year." Trey paused and seemed to be recalling something unpleasant. "He's a playboy, a heartbreaker. Real son of a—" Trey stopped and swallowed the expletive. "Well, you get the picture. Chris is a seasonal ranger out of California; he's been coming to Yellowstone for the last several summers, just here for three to four months each year. Technically he's a volunteer, but he works as an interpretative ranger giving educational programs. I've heard he's a highly educated, wealthy trust-fund guy who does the Park Service job for kicks. We have a few of those. He's a doctor of something or other in geysers or thermal energy." He paused. "Nobody I talked to knew if they were dating for sure."

Win drew a breath and dropped his eyes. "Thanks for checking . . . it's not a big deal." *Yes it is.* He glanced back at Trey and forced a smile.

Trey could tell Win wasn't wanting to go there. He leaned back against his SUV and changed the subject. "You and Luke hash anything out?"

Win shook his head. "Luke was real quiet on the way back yesterday. I'm wondering how much he knows about the body, uh, the guy we found. Luke said he'd met him at Prophet Shepherd's church. He said that in his statement. I'm wondering if there's more." He paused. "I need to get myself inserted back into the False Prophet case, get a lot more cooperation from Luke, and bring those four militiamen in."

"You know it's never as simple as that." Trey's radio was crackling to life in his rig. He waved as he opened the truck's door and reached for the mic.

"See you directly," Win called. He opened the door to his own vehicle and slid into the seat. *No, it's never as simple as that.*

CHAPTER SIX

The big red one is a ruby." Win gently turned the bones so that the ring sparkled under his desk lamp.

"How do you know that?" Trey asked. "Wouldn't pick you for a jewelry expert."

"It was Shelby's birthstone. She was born in July, same as me. She had all sorts of ruby stuff: necklaces, rings, bracelets, you name it." Win didn't have to explain who Shelby was; Trey had sat with her in the intensive care waiting room for more hours than Win wanted to think about.

"Huh . . . so those smaller ones are, what? Emeralds?" Trey was hunched over the desk above the light, giving the ring a closer inspection.

"Well, they're green . . . sorta pea green . . . emeralds. Maybe." Win turned the bones gently in his gloved hand again. "We need to see if there's any inscription on the ring, need to have an expert look at it. I hate to take the ring off the bone . . . it's sorta stuck there by the way the fingers lay. Finger bones were kinda fused by the heat, I'd guess. No cartilage remaining." He grimaced. "Gotta do it." Win kept staring down at the delicate finger bones that laid claim to the ring. He handed his Bureau phone to Trey. "Tape this."

"There's a guy up in Paradise Valley who's some sorta gemstone guru," Trey said as he took the phone. "He has a cool crystal and rock shop that we took McKenna to last fall. Real nice, talkative guy, moved here from Oregon—he said he was in the jewelry business out there. Want me to check him out? See if he'd look it over?"

Win nodded his response, then reported the date, time, location, and all the other pertinent information for the evidentiary video as he slowly eased the ring off the finger bone. Trey ended the recording as Win held the ring under the light.

"Wow, lots of bling," Trey said. "Any inscription?"

Win turned it again. "Looks like . . . maybe some scratches, but I'm not seeing much. My evidence response folks don't seem to have any interest in this since it's not tied to a criminal case. Yeah, make the call. I'll take it up to your guy or drive it on to Livingston or Bozeman to a jewelry store. I've got some time later today." *It's not like I have much else to do.* Win sighed and dropped the ring into a small evidence bag. "Also, let's keep the ring's history to ourselves. It may be the only clue we've got to her identity."

Trey sat back and flipped open his notepad. "The Park County Coroner guesstimates the woman's age at over twenty-five and under forty. He said the bones were strong, well formed, from a healthy female."

Win raised both eyebrows skeptically. "Well, healthy up to the point she died in that hellish bubbling caldron." They both grimaced at the thought.

"Let's hope she was already dead when she went in there," Trey added.

"Has your expert come up with any answers on how the bones and ring could have survived that superheated bath? How long could they have been in there?"

Trey leaned back and avoided Win's eyes. The ranger suddenly took an interest in the room's artwork. "Win, you're not gonna be thrilled with our choice of thermal expert for this case."

Win laid the bones down in the slender padded box that the Coroner had provided and focused on Trey. "You're not telling me it's—"

"Yup." The ranger's eyes were still adverted.

"C'mon, Trey. Tell me you're not serious."

"Wish I could—it's not my call. Dr. Christopher Warren should be reaching out to you real soon to set up a meeting. Chief Randall went over our file with him early this morning."

Win pulled off the purple nitrile gloves. He was trying to be cool about this, but he wasn't fooling Trey.

"You think they're seeing each other?" the ranger asked.

Win tried to be nonchalant. He shrugged it off. "Don't know. I haven't exactly been around a lot." He shrugged again, his indifference not as convincing this time. "Don't know where I stand with her."

"Why don't you ask her to the Gardiner barbecue and rodeo. It kicks off Thursday night around six. My sister is picking up McKenna, and Cindy and I are going. We could meet you there, like a double date. Take some of the pressure off you." Trey picked up his hat and smiled as he stood. He seemed pleased with his role as a potential matchmaker.

"That might work." Win was considering it.

As Trey started out the door, he made a teasing appeal to Win's competitive nature. "Or you could just assume Chris Warren has beat you out with Tory and cast your eyes elsewhere. I heard Jazmine telling one of my guys that she thinks you're a stud."

* * *

She never woulda just left . . . walked away . . . run off. The telephone contacts all had a slightly different variation of the same message. Their voices were all different, yet each was filled with the same mixture of disbelief, desperation, and grief. There had been no closure, no final resting place, in most cases not even a spot to visit where their loved one had last been seen. Win had methodically moved through each file during the last several days. He'd spent hours reviewing reports from NCIC, the National Crime Information Center, and going through NamUs, the National Missing and Unidentified Persons System. He was trying to categorize the files: those who disappeared on purpose, the probable accidents, and then the really difficult ones, the possible crimes. It was a gut-wrenching task that he found he handled better in short stretches.

After Trey had left the office, Win sat staring at the stack of remaining files. Thin files filled with more questions than answers. He'd already narrowed it down. One elderly man who'd been reported missing last year near Old Faithful had turned up days later in Whitefish, Montana, and no one had bothered to update the paperwork. A female hotel employee had skipped town with a coworker to Spokane three years ago; she hadn't bothered to call her family for more than two years. One of the missing had been discovered to be a suicide; they'd found his farewell notes months later when a relative managed to hack into his laptop. He'd apparently taken a dive off one of the Canyon waterfalls at night. No body had been found. Suicide was rare in Yellowstone, but it did occasionally happen. Win had written up reports and officially closed those files.

Then there was the missing informant they'd found yesterday, a man named Wayman Duncan. An investigative case had been opened in the Denver office; they hadn't yet named the lead agent. Johnson was the logical choice, but his long history of poor work—or, to be more blunt, no work—would likely rule him out. Win was still sidelined because of the shooting inquiries. No chance of getting case-agent status on that one.

Win now had four open files going back six years. His extensive review of missing persons reports in Yellowstone led him to conclude that several much older incidents were very likely accidents where the bodies had never been recovered; the scant evidence they had pointed to mishaps rather than crimes. The park's cold, rushing rivers and deep mountain lakes were no more forgiving than cliffs that dropped off hundreds of feet. And then there were the thermal features—those acid-filled, scalding pools of water and mud claimed lives most every year. Not to mention the wildlife: bear, bison, moose attacks. There were lots of ways to die in Yellowstone. Somebody had even written a book about it. He figured he'd read it if he stayed here much longer.

* * *

"I keep it . . . ah . . . I keep her room the same." She swung the door open and stepped to the side as he moved into the small bedroom. His height and broad shoulders made the room seem even smaller. He noticed his sense of smell was improving as he took in the musty scent of the unused space. The light cut through slatted blinds in thin lines and threw a jagged pattern over the blue chenille bedspread; it looked like one his grandmother would have used. A string of dusty ribbons from horse show wins sagged above the headboard and draped behind the lonely lamp. He doubted it had been used in a good long while. The once-blue walls had faded to a sad shade of blueish gray. Framed pictures sat on the single chest of drawers. One photo showed a younger version of a beaming Missy Sims sitting on a gray horse. She was wearing blue leather chaps and holding a first-place ribbon. Blue must have been her color. A picture of her laughing with her mother, another of her and her brothers. Just like the bedroom, their smiles frozen in time.

She had come in behind him, and he watched her smooth the bedspread. "I used to come in here every day just to sit . . . just to wait. Just to hope."

"Ma'am," he said softly, "you can wait for me downstairs. You don't have to stay. I'll be down shortly."

Her hand went back to touch a stuffed brown bear beside the pillow. "No, no, it's just that . . . just that I haven't been in here in a few weeks."

He guessed it'd been months, maybe years.

"It's not that I've given up. It's not that, but after Ben left me . . . after the boys graduated and moved out, and . . . and so much time's passed. . . ." She didn't finish.

He watched as the light caught dust particles floating in the air, caught a tear sliding down her cheek. He clenched his jaw and fought the tightness in his chest. He cleared his throat and managed to get a grip on his emotions.

"Mrs. Sims, I can't even imagine what you've gone through . . . what you're going through. Do you mind if I sit?" She nodded, and he sat on the edge of the straight-backed chair. He could picture Missy slinging her jacket over it and piling her schoolbooks on the seat. It wasn't much of a sittin' chair.

He needed to hint at his main clue. "Did she have any favorite jewelry? Anything that she wore often?"

"Yes." The woman smiled. "She always wore a small gold cross. I gave it to her for her sixteenth birthday. She wouldn't wear rings because she was afraid they might snag in the saddle or on a rope. Always the horse thing." She smiled again.

"Take a minute, tell me what her interests were that summer. Tell me anything that you remember that might seem a bit unusual. Was there anything that's jumped out at you as time has passed?"

Her eyes were wet, and she blinked several times before looking away, into the past, back into her nightmare. She sat down on the bed, and her voice sounded distant when she finally spoke. "I told the rangers and the deputy sheriff about her job that summer. I told them about how excited she was. . . . It was between her freshman and sophomore years in college. It was a horse job, and she loves anything to do with horses."

She was a wrangler, Win thought, and the story began. He knew he'd sit there way more than a minute. He would hear Missy Sims's story. And that was how it needed to be.

When he walked to his truck forty-five minutes later, he finally let himself breathe deeply. He felt drained and numb from forcing the woman's anguish down deep inside, away from his reason, his logic, his focus. He fought to compartmentalize his emotions. Same as he'd done yesterday, when against Luke's advice, he'd viewed the informant's body. This was part of his job, he told himself. He'd spent the first three years of his FBI career in Charlotte working bank and securities fraud—white-collar crime and public corruption. Before the April 8th transfer to Yellowstone, he'd never pulled his weapon, seen a body, or walked a person through depths of grief he couldn't fathom. He told himself again, *This is part of my job.* He whispered a prayer for Mrs. Sims as he started the SUV. He hoped he was doing this right.

* * *

He'd just finished inputting his interview notes into the computer at the office when the landline rang. It was Mrs. Sims's voice, with just a hint of hope floating in it. "After you left, well, I . . . I sat in her room for a long time and thought back. Like you told me, was there anything I might have called the Sheriff about and never heard back." She cleared her throat. "And . . . and one thing did come to mind. I told that deputy, I know I did, but he never said anything else about it." She cleared her throat again and paused.

"What is it, ma'am, what came to your mind?" Win asked gently.

"Missy had been really upbeat about her last trip into the back-country. She'd taken a group of scientists to a geyser field."

Win felt his pulse do an uptick; he gripped the phone tighter.

"Do you recall where?" he asked. "What group of scientists?"

"No. No, nothing except she'd been wrangling for that group on at least two other trips that summer already. She always seemed keyed up, more excited when she was getting ready to take that group out. She'd just gotten back from two weeks in the backcountry with the geyser people right before . . . before she disappeared. She was only home for three days, but she wasn't feeling well, she seemed moody. That wasn't like her, but I remember we talked while she was getting ready to go to the Gardiner rodeo. She was happy that afternoon, and I remember saying it sounded to me more like she'd met her a man out in the wilderness rather than gotten all worked up over some new geysers."

Win heard her take a ragged breath.

"Me saying that, it seemed to embarrass her . . . she got real quiet. And I remember thinking that she'd gotten involved with someone I might not approve of—that was just the feeling I got from how she responded. We never talked about it again." She paused a long time, and he could hear her breathing through the phone.

"How long before—"

"It was the Saturday rodeo. She went missing two days later. Never came home from work that Monday. . . . It's been nearly six years. Six years, August 19th. How could it be *six* years?" Her voice was fading. He could tell she was trying to regroup.

"Yes, ma'am, I know." *How can I know?* He forced his emotions down again.

"She was going to meet three high school girlfriends at the rodeo. They hadn't seen each other in weeks, since they'd been scattered, working all summer. She was closest to Sharon Schmidt back then. Sharon also went to Montana State, and they rode back and forth to college some. If she had a new boyfriend, she would likely have told Sharon. She still lives in the area, I used to hear from her from time to time. It's been a couple of years now, but she married a cattle rancher— Jim Benz is his name. They live north of Cedar Creek, off Highway 89." She gave Win a phone number.

"It might mean nothing, I'm sure the Sheriff or the rangers followed up with her backcountry clients . . . I'm probably bothering you for nothing." He could tell she was about to cry. She was hurrying off the phone.

"No bother. This could be helpful. I've got the girls' names she saw that night. No one mentioned anyone new she was seeing when they were interviewed back then, but I'll reach out to Sharon, Mrs. Sims, see if this jogs any memories. If anything else comes to mind, you don't hesitate to call me. Anything." He hung up and wiped beads of sweat off his forehead. He drew a deep breath, leaned back in his chair, and covered his eyes with his hands.

* * *

There was nothing in the file referencing a new boyfriend, no mention of geyser scientists, and next to nothing on Missy's backcountry clients. There were several very brief interviews by a local deputy, a park ranger, and an FBI agent, of clients who'd hired Missy for backcountry horseback trips. Those included scout troop leaders, a couple of fly-fishing clients, and a few that didn't specify the group. He flipped over to the final page of the FBI interview with one of Missy's clients. It read "She was good with the horses, a competent wrangler, but I didn't know her. No idea where she'd go." Win squinted to read the faded name of the interviewee: Christopher S. Warren.

The ranger who might be seeing Tory. . . . Huh. Win sat back in his chair and thought about it. Trey had said Dr. Warren had a reputation as a womanizer. He picked up the phone number Mrs. Sims had given him a few minutes ago.

Sharon Benz was still local. He did a quick trace for her driver's license and turned up an address. Same phone number. A soft-spoken man answered on the fourth ring.

"I'm Win Tyler with the FBI, and I'm calling for Sharon Benz, please."

The man sounded surprised. "Is something wrong? The FBI?"

"It's a routine call. I'm following up on an old case, Missy Sims's disappearance." He waited to hear the man's response.

"Oh . . . Missy. Oh, yeah . . . well, Sharon talked to the police years ago. Has, uh, something been found?"

Win assured him it was a routine follow-up. The man introduced himself as Sharon's husband, and he said that Sharon was in Gardiner, picking up a load of feed. "She's got a few errands to run, you could try her on her cell if you need to reach her today."

He gave Win the number, and Win made the call. He could have done the interview over the phone, but he'd learned that face-to-face meetings were generally more productive. He wanted to see the other person's reactions, gauge their truthfulness, judge their character. He'd see if she'd meet him in town.

"I'm waiting for them to load bagged feed at the co-op—I'll be here at least another twenty minutes," she said. "It's been so long, I can't imagine anything I'd say that could help you now."

Win wasn't so sure that was true.

* * *

It took every bit of twenty minutes to drive the five miles from his office to Gardiner and the park's north entrance. The tourist traffic was as slow as cold molasses. Win pulled into the feed store's gravel lot and found Sharon Benz leaning against her white one-and-a-half-ton pickup, talking on the phone. She looked like she worked on the ranch: faded jeans, plaid shirt, scuffed boots, and a misshapen straw cowboy hat. She had a horsewoman's slender build and a pleasant face. A face that paled slightly as she glanced up and saw him step out of the Bureau SUV.

She was nervous, and that, in and of itself, wasn't a bit unusual for any citizen when they got a call from the FBI. But he thought she looked too stressed, way too nervous. She was biting her lip, the fingers of one hand absently playing with her long hair. *Way too stressed,* he thought to himself. It didn't take long to find out why.

Win took off his sunglasses, showed her his credentials and shook her hand. The woman's palm was damp. He played his hunch immediately. "Mrs. Benz, so kind of you to meet with me on such short notice. I'm following a lead that Missy Sims might have given you some . . . well, some delicate information the last time you spoke with her. Is that true?"

The young woman swallowed hard and dropped her eyes. She bit down on her lip again and blinked. "It would just kill her mother to find out . . . they were real church folks, you know."

Win knew what she was saying.

He moved a step closer and spoke quietly. "She was pregnant?"

The young woman nodded.

"Who was the father? What did Missy tell you?"

She rubbed her hand across her face and the story, pent up far, far too long, spilled out. "For the longest time I thought she'd just decided to run off with him, you know. I thought once the baby was born, she'd get back in touch with her folks, come home. But time went on . . . and I wasn't so sure. I could never imagine her leaving—for good." She took a deep breath and finally looked into Win's eyes. "I never knew who the father was. She never said. She said he was older, said she'd met him that summer on her job, said he was real smart." The woman dropped her eyes again. "She said he had money. Uh, Missy and I weren't super close, but I remember wondering why that mattered so much, that he had money." She sighed. "Missy was really excited. But at the same time I know she was scared to death to tell her mother."

"When did she find out she was expecting?"

"It was the day before I saw her at the rodeo. She said she'd gone to a drugstore in Livingston and bought a test. She couldn't go to a store here because everybody knows her. Small town."

He knew what she meant.

They talked awhile longer, but Win didn't learn much more. She was relieved that she'd finally told the story. Before he left her, he asked another question. "Why didn't you tell this to the investigator who interviewed you?"

"Like I said, I thought she'd left town with the guy. I didn't know who he was. I didn't think she was really, you know . . . *missing*." She bit her lip again and blinked back tears. "I told her I'd keep her secret. And . . . and as the years went by, I kept calling her mom, but after a while it was just too hard to talk to her. I kept picturing Missy and her baby living with an older rich guy someplace nice." She sniffled back tears.

"But you knew better?"

She looked back at him. "Yeah, after a year had passed, I knew better. Missy would never have left her horse. Something happened to her . . . do you know what happened to her?"

"No, but I'm going to try my best to find out."

* * *

Rock Man's Rock Shop was just off Highway 89, twenty-two miles north of Gardiner in a scenic area called Paradise Valley. The towering mountains of the Absaroka Range rose on the east, the Gallatin Range on the west, and the rushing Yellowstone River paralleled the highway down the middle of the valley. Cattle grazed in lush pastures or lounged under cottonwoods as they watched the traffic pass. The idyllic setting and the beautiful views were almost enough to take Win's mind off his somber task. Almost, but not quite. He still had work to do, and as he pulled into the nearly empty dirt parking lot, he was glad he'd thought to grab the evidence bag with the ring before making the trip to Gardiner to talk with Sharon Benz. Now he was dropping by to see if the rock guy was in—kill two birds with one stone, so to speak.

No one was in the shabby structure that passed for the guy's show-room, but two carloads of tourists were perusing the plywood plat-forms that held all sorts of colorful rocks in front of the building. Inside, vibrant sketches of gemstones adorned the walls, and an amaz-ing display of fossils, jasper, topaz, agates, and crystal clusters lined every sagging shelf. Win could see why Trey's four-year-old daughter loved this place. It had a bohemian feel, but the owner's résumé was impressive—he held all the national gemologist titles. This shop was his escape from the big city into a relaxed retirement, Win supposed.

Win rang the silver bell on the counter and a jovial man appeared from behind a screen of colorful beads.

"Hey, hey there! And what can I help you find?"

"I'm Win Tyler, FBI." He pulled out his credentials and they shook hands. "Ranger Trey Hechtner said you'd be expecting—"

"Ah, the ring. He said you had a ring for me to look over. Wait . . . lemme guess . . . Mississippi? No? Ah, not northern Alabama . . . no, not quite right. . . ."

"Arkansas."

"Well, of course! Delightful Southern accent! My ex-wife is from Hot Springs—best quartz crystal veins in the Western Hemisphere are near Hot Springs, Arkansas!"

It was a good thing Win wasn't particularly busy, because Rock Man was a trip. The guy had '60s hippie written all over him: tie-dyed T-shirt, baggy cargo pants with Birkenstock sandals, a blue bandanna holding back his long white hair, and a gray beard that reached nearly to his waist. He could have stepped out of a ZZ Top poster. They visited for ten minutes about the metaphysical characteristics and healing powers of Arkansas's quartz crystals, of which he had an impressive selection. Win said he loved the beauty of the stones but wasn't a believer in their magical qualities. Rock Man seemed disappointed, but he wasn't deterred; he kept showing Win samples, hoping for a conver-sion, while ignoring the rest of his potential customers. The man also exhibited his array of vivid art—just a hobby, he declared; the stones and gems were his true passion.

"Uh, the ring?" Win finally said, pulling the small evidence packet from his shirt pocket.

"Ah, yes." Rock Man moved behind the makeshift wooden counter, put on the nitrile gloves Win offered, slid the ring out of the plastic bag, placed it on a black velvet cloth, and studied it. "My, my, my . . ." Win thought he looked perplexed, or maybe surprised—hard to tell with all the facial hair. The man produced a magnifying device and a small bright light. He turned the ring, held it up with long tweezers, turned it again, and studied it a while longer.

After about two minutes, he looked up at Win and smiled. "Thank you."

Win was puzzled. "Why?"

"This is the most exquisite piece of nineteenth-century jewelry I've ever touched. It's flawless, museum quality . . . priceless." His tone was reverent.

"What?" Win leaned forward on the counter.

"Well," he corrected himself, "technically not priceless, everything has a price. But a two-and-a-half-carat ruby of this quality and age, and the four one-carat demantoid garnets—so rare—the setting . . . just magnificent."

Win was shocked. "Does it have an inscription?"

"It has a great deal of wear, and it needs a deep cleaning, but yes, there is a faint inscription." He looked into Win's eyes. "There's the stamp of the designer and what I'm sure is a profession of love." He smiled a dreamy smile. The guy was really into this.

"Can I see it? Can I read it?" Win asked.

"Of course." Rock Man held the magnifying device up to the ring and turned it into the white light for Win to see. "Not a problem, as long as you can read Russian."

CHAPTER SEVEN

He placed the evidence bag with the ring, now in a lovely red velvet ring box, in the Expedition's center console. Carrying around a ring worth hundreds of thousands of dollars in his shirt pocket didn't seem wise. He checked a voicemail from Trey before he even started the truck: *Chris Warren wants to meet with us on the bones and the thermal feature issue at three in our conference room, if you can make it. Just text me when you get this; I'm working a vehicle accident now, but I should be able to get there. Oh, and the Mammoth Hotel Map Room is hosting a program at six . . . some prominent geyser expert, ah, Dr. Ratliff. I've met with him a few times on research permits. He's a real elitist—you'll love him. I checked, and he's been out here several years in a row. Gotta go.*

Win texted back an answer, pulled onto the highway, and headed back toward Yellowstone. He felt a rising excitement that told him he was on the hunt, beginning to slide pieces of the puzzle together, answering the critical questions. It was a big part of what had drawn him to the Bureau as a career: finding the missing pieces, making things right, restoring order. And there was a lot of order that needed to be restored in the thin files that held the brief stories of the lost. There were other loved ones, just like Mrs. Sims and Sharon Benz, waiting for answers—waiting for closure. And there were way too many coincidences to ignore. Three missing women in the last six years, all related in some form or fashion to geyser research groups operating in the park. And the Russian connection? *How does that tie in?* In Win's mind those files were looking less and less like a series of random accidents, and more and more like an interconnected crime.

Win put in a call to his supervisor as he drove. He needed to bring Jim West up to speed. But Jim was in no mood to talk about missing persons. Jim was more than a little hot.

"What in the world were you doing with Luke Bordeaux, not once, but twice yesterday? You were told to stay out of the False Prophet case . . . you can't be involved in *any* aspect of that case as long as your shooting inquiries are ongoing. Bordeaux is a central figure in that case! What part of that did you not understand?"

Whoa. This ain't good . . . maybe I'll pass on my plan to stop at Luke's on my way back to Mammoth.

Jim kept talking. "I've fielded calls today from that ASAC from Chicago who just came on, from HRT's on-site commander, and from two of the lead agents investigating the militiamen. I'm sure Wes Givens will be calling me next." Jim took a deep breath. "Win, nobody is happy that you're trying to insert yourself back into the case."

Win made an attempt at defense. "I'm trying to get Bordeaux to finger the fugitives—"

"Are you certain he knows where they are?" Jim still sounded angry. "You . . . still can't . . ." The supervisor's voice began breaking up as Win's Expedition entered a series of narrow, winding curves. Win passed the sign for Yankee Jim Canyon just as the phone call dropped. For once, Win was glad to have such poor cell reception.

*   *   *

He was gripping his leather-bound notebook just a little too tight as he moved through the open doorway of the Park Service's large conference room. Chief Randall and Trey were across the room by the coffee pot with their backs turned to him. The ranger Win had seen talking to Tory was seated at the end of the long table, focused on his notes. His straw flat hat was resting alongside a stack of papers and brochures. Win's eyes went to the scruffy beard, the sun-bleached hair, the broad shoulders filling out the short-sleeve gray uniform shirt. Those muscular arms had held Tory. Win felt his chest tighten.

The man raised his head and appraised him. Win knew that look: It was the look of the opposing quarterback—the look of a winner. This guy wasn't intimidated by Special Agent Winston R. Tyler, FBI—nope, not one little bit. This guy was a player.

He stood and held out his hand. "Dr. Chris Warren, and you must be Win Tyler. I understand we have a mutual friend." The pale-blue eyes twinkled, and the corner of his mouth rose in a smug smile.

Win accepted the handshake and gave a curt nod. "Is that so, Dr. Warren?"

Chris Warren dropped the quick handshake and took a step too close to his competition. Win's hands went to his hips, pushing back his jacket. He had the height advantage, and he used it as he glared down at the man. Win's aggressive stance was usually reserved for the bad guys—his black .40 caliber handgun was visible, his physical size was imposing, and his eyes had narrowed and darkened to cobalt blue. But the other man didn't blink, he just stood there invading Win's space, waiting for him to back down.

Trey swung around the conference table with a cup of coffee in hand. "Hey, hey . . . did that old thermostat get stuck again? It's gotten real chilly in here all the sudden." His attempt to lighten the mood went nowhere. Chief Ranger Richard Randall gave the standoff a curious glance and moved to shake hands with Win. Chris Warren stepped away and sat back down.

"Great to see you, Win." The tall, gray-haired ranger seemed genuinely pleased. "Gus wanted me to tell you he's hoping your recovery is going well, that he's thinking of you." The Chief was referring to Gus Jordon, the Deputy Chief Ranger, who was on a temporary duty assignment in Glacier National Park.

Win nodded at the greeting, and they visited for a few moments about the apparent FBI pullout while Win poured a cup of coffee. With Warren in the room, nothing confidential could be discussed, so Win couldn't have provided any details even if he'd had them—which he did not. He'd learned of the sudden activity within HRT and several of the SWAT teams just minutes before he walked through the door. He could hear the rumble of heavy trucks and Humvees on the street below. Something big was going down.

Trey started the meeting with an overview of the discovery of the hand bones at the relatively new thermal field called Maxwell Springs, in the remote northeast corner of the park. Then Chris Warren launched into his lecture like a public speaking pro. Warren's audience might have been small, but Chief Randall, his big boss, was there, and he was playing it for all it was worth. He handed out flyers and graphs detailing various parts of his talk. He lowered the room's big projection screen, dimmed the lights, and presented a *National Geographic*–worthy PowerPoint that he'd prepared on the park's newer thermal fields and activity. Win had to concede: This guy was good.

"The earthquakes are nothing unusual; the park has an average of one thousand quakes under 2.5 on the Richter scale every year—swarms can push that number over three thousand. It's uncommon to feel those small quakes. Generally activity must be over a 3.0 on the scale to be noticeable to the public. We registered a 4.3 magnitude quake on May 15th, centered near Maxwell Springs; it altered geysers and features all the way southwest to the Mud Volcano area, within the caldera. We assume there were major impacts at Maxwell Springs. I'll be a part of a research team that will begin documenting those changes later this month."

Win knew the caldera was the thirty-mile-by-forty-five-mile crater rim of the Yellowstone supervolcano—it was squarely in the middle of the park. He remembered reading that the caldera was created by an eruption 640,000 years ago, and that it was long overdue for a violent eruption that would obliterate parts of several states. He shut that unsettling thought out of his mind and focused back on what Warren was saying.

"The magma core is most shallow at the Norris Geyser Basin, where we estimate it at only three miles below the surface. The magma is much, much deeper at Maxwell Springs, but the volcanic core is slowly moving to the northeast . . . any shift in the magma can contribute to localized earthquake activity. For that reason, there are event cycles that occur within that thermal field frequently—where localized tremors cause moderate eruptions of vents and geysers. In this case, it's most likely that the human remains were regurgitated from either the nearby caldron or a widening steam vent during the more pronounced May 15th event."

"You mean, the bones just got belched up from the depths of the volcano?" Trey asked in an incredulous voice. "What kept them from being eaten by the heat or the acid?"

Dr. Warren paused, glanced at Trey, and tried to sound less than demeaning. He didn't pull it off. "Ranger Hechtner, the Maxwell Springs thermal field is in flux; the heat and the acidity from feature to feature can change overnight. If a person slipped and fell into one of those hot springs' pools, or even got into a pool intentionally to soak, there are any number of ways to die. Just the toxic bacteria in the water could generate enough poison to render a person unconscious within minutes, even if the acidity was low and the heat was within reasonable levels. But not all the pools are dangerously bacterial, acidic, or super-heated; a hot spring's pool could be perfectly safe one day and abruptly change in a matter of hours, maybe minutes. *Abruptly change.*"

Dr. Warren still sounded condescending. "You should know that's why we monitor the water so closely in areas such as the Boiling and Firehole Rivers, where we allow swimmers each summer. If the water feeding into the streams from the thermal features were to suddenly change in bacterial content, temperature, or acidity, we could warn swimmers not to enter. We've had to do that several times during the last few years because of heat fluctuations, as you'll recall."

Trey raised his eyebrows and leaned back. Win doubted that Trey, having been properly chastised, would ask another question. So he threw one out. "The bones were firm, not degraded or brittle. How could they sit in hot water, even if it wasn't scalding hot, for any length of time without disintegrating?"

The expert turned his cool eyes on Win. "The hot springs and cal-drons at Maxwell Springs haven't been completely cataloged yet, but some of those features are forty to fifty feet deep, a few much deeper. The hot springs' pools are often interconnected with the nearby geysers and heat vents. The body could have been sucked to the bottom when the pool drained after a seismic event. The skeletal remains may have rested far below the surface for years—high and dry, until the earthquake on May 15th forced water back into the cavity and shot the bones to the surface. Several of Yellowstone's springs have had explosive eruptions in the last few years. Ear Spring blew artifacts from the 1930s thirty feet into the air—dozens of items that tourists had thrown into the pool were regurgitated. That event was fairly recent. It's certainly not out of the realm of possibility that the bones you found could have been underground for years."

Win was intent on Chris Warren's features as the man wrapped up his presentation by casually describing the horrific deaths of animals and humans who'd fallen into the thermal pools. There was a cavalier tone to his voice, no hitch in his breath. His eyes didn't waver, his brow didn't crease. Win detected no change in his demeanor. Was it just professional detachment? *Maybe.* Or was it the sign of a psychopath—a person who was totally unfeeling and uncaring? *Could be.* Whatever it was, it sure didn't do anything to improve Win's opinion of Dr. Christopher Warren.

After Warren wrapped it up and moved toward the front of the room to brownnose with the Chief, Win sat fingering the brochure that some backcountry outfitter had put together on Yellowstone's wilderness hikes. *Maxwell Springs: Fascinating Thermal Features and a Magical Lake.* He wondered if the woman whose bones he'd held had been thinking along those lines before she ended up in the bottomless depths of that superheated pool. He grimaced as those thoughts wound through his consciousness. His mind's eye saw the faded face of Natasha Yahontova staring up from her passport. Something in his gut told him this wasn't an accident. Something in his gut told him this was murder.

* * *

Ten minutes later, Win stepped out of the wide doors of the park's Administration Building, rounded the corner, and watched as a convoy of Bureau SUVs lined up in the big parking lot. He waved at the driver of the nearest vehicle and walked over to the open window. It was one of the Denver SWAT Team members he'd visited with a few times. Win noticed that the guy didn't have on his tactical gear.

"What gives? Not a callout?"

The agent shook his head. "No, a repositioning. Just be glad you're still on desk duty. We're headed to a wilderness area in the Gallatin National Forest. As the crow flies it isn't too far—thirty miles, just across the park boundary—but it's a five-to-six-hour trip to the staging area. It's the same area HRT scoped out last week—uh, Sage Peak."

"Thought that was a dry hole."

"It was, and this probably will be too. A series of tips came in this morning." The agent put up his fingers to mimic quotation marks. "Anonymous tips," he said as he shook his head again.

"That New America militia has a lot of sympathizers over that way—could be that bunch trying to throw us offtrack."

"You know that, and I know that, but our new boss lady does not know that." The guy sighed. "She is *not* into sitting around and waiting for something to happen." The man sounded tired and frustrated. "Back to tent camping—I haven't camped out this many days since Boy Scouts." He sighed again. "It's gettin' old."

"Who's goin'?" Win asked.

"HRT's whole contingent, and we're also shifting the drones and most of the surveillance planes to that sector. San Francisco's enhanced team, us, and the Salt Lake team are rolling." The agent glanced in his rearview mirror. "That just leaves the Omaha team, the Park Service SWAT guys, or whatever they're called, and a few of our folks working the investigation on False Prophet." He shifted the Suburban into gear and grinned. "You're gonna be downright lonely."

Win patted the side of the door and stepped back. "Y'all be careful out there."

* * *

Win dodged between groups of tourists who were watching the Bureau folks pull out; the normally concealed blue lights on every vehicle were now flashing. A flurry of activity surrounding the Justice Center told him that the press vans and satellite trucks would also be on the move. He stood and watched for a moment. He didn't like this feeling of being left behind. He drew a breath and reminded himself that his work with the missing had significance as well—it was desperately important to many.

He knocked on Johnson's doorframe when he got to the building's second floor. The heavyset guy was leaning back in his chair; Win could tell he'd been dozing. "Sorry to interrupt."

"Whata ya want?" Johnson yawned and squinted his eyes tight against the light. He rolled his head and stretched his shoulders before he focused back on Win.

"I may request that some of these missing persons files be taken to the investigative case level. Just wanted to touch base again before I send them in. See if you've had any more thoughts on—"

"No. I told you I'd handed off all those files to the Park Service's investigative branch. I did the initial 302s. That's it."

"There's no FD-302 in Natasha Yahontova's file," Win countered. "Nothing from the Bureau."

Johnson yawned again. "Oh, yeah, that one. Yeah, well, that was right around the time I got here . . . I passed it back off to Denver, but I told you I'd nose around a little."

Very little, I'll bet, Win thought to himself, but to his surprise, Johnson opened a drawer and slid several pieces of paper across the desk. "I got this back from Denver this morning. Apparently, they did send some agent"—he glanced at the papers—"Julie Cordsmier, up here for the interviews. It's been in this Natasha lady's file in Denver the whole time, but no one bothered to upload it into Sentinel or to shoot us a copy. Sloppy excuse for work."

You would know sloppy work. Win motioned toward the papers on the desk. "Anything significant in there?"

"How would I know? It's your deal. I've been too busy to read it."

Too busy. Uh-huh. There was nothing resembling work on the agent's desk, unless the David Baldacci novel counted. Win scooped up the loose papers and turned toward the door. Johnson's words followed him.

"Since our SWAT team is on the road, I'm gonna take a few days off. Take some leave."

Win stopped at the door and turned back. He couldn't believe anyone would be granted annual leave in the middle of the biggest manhunt the Bureau had going.

Johnson shrugged; he knew what Win was thinking. "Not likely to be much happening here. My knee is bothering me again—got a medical waiver from a doc-in-the-box in Livingston. That'll keep me out till I can see the office's doctor in Denver." He shrugged again and almost smiled. "Who knows when they'll work me in."

* * *

Win walked down the hall to his office and closed the door, then sat down at the antique oak desk and drained the entire water bottle he'd picked up from the break room earlier. He tried to get his disgust with Johnson's total lack of motivation off his mind. *I don't need that distraction.* He leaned back and thought about the files. *Do I really have enough on the missing women to point toward a crime? Am I just trying to see what I want to see? Creating a case?*

He stacked the three missing women's files together: Missy Sims, six years ago; Natasha Yahontova, five years ago; and Janet Goff, two years ago. All three women were tied in some way to thermal research groups in Yellowstone. *Could these disappearances be linked? A serial killer?* He paused and shook his head. *Or have I watched too many cop shows since I've been stuck at home?* He sighed. *Maybe.*

And what about Conner Chen? The young man, an employee of a park concessioner, had been reported missing within three days of Natasha's disappearance in the same general area of the park. Could that be an outlier or a coincidence? The missing women were all related to the geyser researchers, but Conner apparently was not. Win had been taught that serial killers generally had a specific type of victim, and if the attacks were sexual, that type was usually young women. Often the victims were similar in appearance or had jobs or professions that were akin. Conner and Missy were both park contractors, but they weren't employed by the same park concessioner, so there didn't seem to be a connection there. He tapped his pen on his notepad. Conner wasn't tracking with the others . . . still, his instincts told him the young man's disappearance was somehow related to theirs.

What Win needed was some actual evidence of wrongdoing, not simply a gut feeling. He had to put together a detailed timeline and reach out to anyone else even remotely connected to these four cases. But first he wanted to bounce it off someone with more experience, someone who could read through any attempts he could be making to create *real* work for himself. Johnson obviously wasn't an option, and Win had been told his supervisor was out for a few hours, seeing a Realtor. Probably a good thing, since Jim West might not be finished chewing him out over his contacts with Bordeaux. He'd just reached for the landline to call Murray, on the Violent Crime Squad, when there was a knock at his door.

She moved through the door without waiting for a response, and Win immediately stood. The unexpected visitor had chin-length blond hair, in a straight cut. She was tall and slender and dressed in a crisp navy blazer. The sharp creases in her khaki slacks matched the sharp angle of her nose and cheekbones, giving her a fierce, predatory look. She swept into Win's office, a large guy in full tactical uniform following in her wake.

"Angela Holmes, ASAC Chicago." She was still moving forward as she held out her hand. Win had enough presence of mind to move around his desk and meet her piercing eyes as they shook hands. The guy behind her wasn't introduced.

"Winston Tyler, I'm sorry, I wasn't ex—"

She dropped the handshake and smiled. "Yes, I know, Agent Tyler. I just wanted to meet you and tell you how pleased I am that you're back on the job so soon. I've heard so many good things about your work here."

Uh-oh, I'm fixin' to get hammered.

She turned and took in his office. Her minion just stood in the doorway.

"Please have a seat—can I get y'all some coffee?"

The minion shook his head and the honcho eased into the chair.

"Some other time, perhaps. We're on our way out, have a helicopter waiting. I'm sure you know about the redeployment. We'll just take a moment of your time. Please, be seated." She shifted in the chair to admire the large 1904 oil painting that adorned one wall: a grizzly bear standing over a fallen elk. "Tom Strickland told me that you renovated these offices single-handedly in just weeks. We glanced in the rooms downstairs. All the original antique furnishings, blended so well with the modern conveniences and technology. And the artwork . . . just stunning."

"Thank you. I actually had a lot of help from some very talented folks. Since the building is on the National Register of Historic Places, we were able to use paintings that the Park Service has collected for years—most have hung in one of the park's lodges at one time or another . . . many are over a hundred years old." She smiled and nodded. He knew she wasn't here to peruse the art.

"Tom is really high on you—as is Wes Givens. Wes and I were classmates at Yale." *That explains the upper-class aura,* Win thought. The Denver ASAC had Ivy League written all over him. "Wes tells me you'll be transferring to Denver as soon as the paperwork clears," Ms. Holmes was saying. "I don't want anything to trip you up, so let's clear up a few issues."

Here it comes . . .

"I know you must be anxious to get back in the action, but as you're aware, I am now the on-site commander, and everything related to the search for the four fugitives goes through me. *Everything.*" She looked down her sharp nose at him.

"Yes, ma'am."

"I do not want you contacting Mr. Bordeaux or in any way interjecting yourself into the False Prophet case or the fugitive hunt. Is that clear?"

Win nodded. "Yes, ma'am. My supervisor got with me on that today."

"Good." She leaned back in the chair. "As I understand it, you are basically on desk duty until such time as your shooting inquiries are concluded. Is that correct?"

"Yes, ma'am. I'm working missing persons files."

She lost a bit of the harsh tone. "Win, I can appreciate that tracking down domestic terrorists in the wilderness and some of our other more high-profile activities are appealing. Especially since you were directly in the middle of it for weeks. I would remind you, however, that *all* of the Bureau's work is vital." She gestured toward the files on his desk. "I worked a few kidnapping and missing persons cases early in my career. Believe me when I say that the subject of each of those files is the most important thing in the world to someone. You may not be able to bring those people back, but you may be able to bring some peace into broken lives. A worthy goal while you're on desk duty, wouldn't you say?"

Win took a breath and nodded. "Yes, ma'am, of course."

She smiled as she stood. "And while you're working those files, you can stay off my radar. Wouldn't that be for the best?"

"Yes, ma'am. I understand."

"Such a pleasure to meet you. You'll have to show me all the building's art one day." And with that she was out the door.

The minion glanced back at Win as he started away. He spoke softly. "You *do not* want back on her radar, bud."

"Got it."

CHAPTER EIGHT

Win hoped his face wasn't showing his deep disappointment. He hoped his averted eyes weren't giving him away. He hoped his shrug showed indifference, not the hollow grip of despondency that swept through him. "No problem, Boss," he replied.

But Jim West didn't make supervisor by being a poor judge of human nature. Even on a video screen, he saw right through Win's efforts at nonchalance. "It's just one of those bureaucratic snafus, Win. Headquarters won't approve your transfer to Denver until six months after your official posting to Yellowstone." When Win didn't respond, Jim continued, "Hey, you've earned your ticket out of Yellowstone. More than earned it. Wes is leaning on them for a waiver. Tom is leaning on them for an exception. You'll be in Denver before the summer's out if our bosses have their way."

Win cleared his throat. Twice. He forced down the obvious feelings of letdown and moved on to other aspects of the call. But the vacant, hollow feeling didn't go away.

After the screen went black, Win sat in the empty communications room and thought about it. He'd called Jim West's cell to report the visit from Ms. Holmes as soon as she'd left the building. Win had been surprised to find Jim at the office; he'd been even more surprised when Jim asked him to get on a video call. The guy was a good supervisor, that was for sure. It's never good to deliver bad news over the phone, downright rude to do it by text or email, and while having a face-to-face on a video call wasn't ideal, it was the best of all evils given the distance between their offices.

Win was thinking his gut reaction to the unwelcome news was a little more extreme than warranted. He wasn't normally that emotional. Not normally. *The lingering effects of the trauma I've suffered? Maybe I do need to be talking to that shrink more often.* He blew out a deep breath and stared at the wall. He knew what he'd done wrong. He'd screwed up after the hospital stay and let his mind take him to the Bureau's expansive green glass office building in Denver—which he'd never even seen in person. He'd pictured himself working big-time terrorism cases with a squad, going on training exercises with the SWAT Team . . . being invited to join. He'd seen himself enjoying the camaraderie of other agents, learning the ropes from the older guys. He'd pictured himself moving up in the ranks, back to where he'd been just over four months ago: quickly moving up the ladder in the Bureau.

Just three years out of Quantico, in his first office posting at Charlotte, he'd been working with the heavy hitters on a case of national significance. They were closing in on a U.S. Congressman, days away from an indictment for public corruption. Then on January 25th, his world came crashing down—he learned the hard lesson that the good guys don't always win, not in this world anyway. He'd been told again and again that he was lucky to still have his job. They'd exiled him to Yellowstone National Park—an isolated posting for the FBI's banished. *And it looks like I'll be here a while longer, dammit.* He pushed off from the communications room desk and headed back to his office. He was gonna be late for that geyser guy's lecture, he hadn't had dinner or supper, and his natural good-natured optimism had flown the coop. *Lordy, it's turnin' into a crappy day.*

*   *   *

They slipped into the back of the large, bright Map Room just as the question-and-answer session was wrapping up. The distinguished man behind the lectern was in the process of thanking those in attendance, but his eyes found Win and Trey when they entered the room. Win removed his hat, leaned against the wall, and waited for the audience of about forty to begin clearing out. He took in the expansive wooden map of the United States that gave the room its name; its 1937 workmanship was impressive even at a distance. They finally moved toward the volcanologist at the front of the room. The man turned from thanking several admirers as Trey and Win approached. Trey did the introductions.

"Dr. Preston Ratliff, this is Special Agent Win Tyler with the local FBI office."

Ratliff's handshake was strong—maybe a little too strong, as if he were playing a dominance game. Win noticed that the man's rough hand didn't fit with his perfectly coiffured short gray hair and beard. But it was his gray eyes that upped the contradiction; they were flat and cold even though his words were warm and friendly.

"So good to meet you, Agent Tyler, I got your message this afternoon, just before the lecture. Great to see you again, Ranger Hechtner."

"I'd like to visit with you for a few minutes when you've finished here," Win began.

"Of course, of course, glad to help in any way." Ratliff turned to speak to a small man who was handing out copies of the lecture. "Simon, will you make sure everyone gets the materials."

He turned away from Simon and smiled back at Win. "Just be a few moments more." He stepped to the side and smiled down at an effusive woman who had approached with an open book for the professor to sign.

"If you could make it 'To Madeline. . . . Oh, Dr. Ratliff, it's such an honor to finally meet you," the woman gushed.

It went on like that for several more minutes with the doctor's devoted fans, mostly women, asking for a photo, a book signing, the lecture material autographed, or all the above. Win couldn't see what the attraction was. The man had to be closing in on sixty, maybe more, but he did look fit and the air of confidence and authority he conveyed was evident. Still, a *volcanologist*? Everyone was treating him like a rock star. Finally, the doctor ushered Win and Trey out of the Map

Room to the hallway where the Mammoth Hot Springs Hotel's administrative offices were located.

"I'm using one of these offices while we're in Mammoth," he was saying. "Do have a seat."

The guy was clearly taking charge of the meeting, and Win was letting him run with it. Let the good doctor think he was calling the shots.

"I wanted to ask about a couple of women who worked with your research team here in Yellowstone several years ago," Win said. "Let's start with Janet Goff. She was with your group two summers ago . . . she disappeared on July—"

Dr. Ratliff cut him off. "Ah, I was in contact with the authorities back then. . . ." He stared toward the ceiling and seemed to be thinking. "I'm sure I told them everything I knew." He sighed. "Janet was a disturbed woman. I . . . I don't want to speak out of turn, but I believe I heard that her car was found—that the police suspected suicide."

"Where'd you hear that?" Win asked.

"Oh, perhaps the park rangers, or it may have been in the newspapers . . . ah, Simon, thank you." The little guy had slipped in as silently as a shadow and deposited a steaming mug of something in front of him.

Win shifted in his chair, and Trey glared at the intrusion. The professor didn't seem to notice.

"Let me introduce my assistant, Dr. Simon Dravec." The smaller man turned indifferent eyes on them. He was terribly thin; Win's granny would have called him wormy. Win had guessed his age at early forties when he'd first noticed him in the Map Room, but that was an incorrect guess. On closer inspection, Dravec was much older than he first appeared, maybe even in his mid-fifties. He was nearly bald; wispy white hairs covered his scalp. His pale skin matched his eyes; they moved back and forth between Win and Trey as if he were trying to decide on a menu item for dinner. Win felt an unnerving twinge just watching the guy.

"These men were asking about Janet," Dr. Ratliff said, turning his gaze to Dravec. "You do remember Janet Goff?"

"Ah, she did her doctoral work at Carnegie Mellon. It was two years ago, nearly three. Didn't they decide she'd killed herself somewhere in Montana?" There was no emotion in the soft voice.

"Yes, that's what I'd heard too."

"What about Natasha Yahontova?" Win threw out the name to get a reaction. The scientists just stared back at him blankly. *Geez, these guys are cold.*

The volcanologist finally leaned back in the chair and rubbed his beard. "Ah, I haven't heard that name in so long. Dr. Natasha Yahontova ... such a talented researcher. Really gifted. That was what? Five years ago? Natasha just dropped off the face of the earth."

"In my line of work, Dr. Ratliff, people don't often drop off the face of the earth without someone pushing them," Win said.

Ratliff's assistant gazed at Win, unblinking. "Oh my, my. You're not implying foul play in their disappearances?"

"I'm not implying anything, Dr. Dravec," Win replied. "I'm just following up on some matters, trying to close out some old files. Give some families closure." Appealing any more deeply to these men's humanity didn't appear worth trying—he hadn't spotted any humanity in either man yet.

Trey asked the next question. "We're also wondering if you remember a young woman named Missy Sims. We think she was a horse wrangler on some of your backcountry trips." Win and Trey were taking a leap on that one; accurate records of Missy's clients hadn't been found. If the men recognized the name, they didn't show it.

Ratliff glanced back up at his assistant. "We haven't done horse trips in ... what? Five summers?"

Trey leaned forward. "Missy Sims was reported missing nearly six years ago—"

"Such a long time ... how sad," Ratliff said.

"How sad," the skinny little guy echoed.

Win took a breath. This was going nowhere. "I'd like to take formal follow-up statements from each of you—separate statements."

The doctor rocked back in his chair and Dravec shifted his stance.

Win jumped in before they could protest. "It's standard practice in cold cases. Just tying up loose ends, you understand."

The smaller man drew himself up and glared at Win. "We've got a very tight schedule. Dr. Ratliff is to be back in the field day after tomorrow. We have lectures in Bozeman tomorrow afternoon." Win thought it was a bit off that the underling seemed to be running the show, but he waited out the doctor's response.

"Well, well, Simon. We want to cooperate in any way that we can. Natasha was a brilliant mind, her research could have been noteworthy. Could have been widely published. But Janet . . ." He shook his head. "She was just a troubled soul. And this Missy person . . . well, you can't expect me to remember the help." Win was liking Ratliff less and less.

Win studied Ratliff before he spoke. "These women haven't been declared dead, yet you're speaking of them in the past tense."

"Am I? Yes, I suppose I am." Ratliff shrugged with disinterest. "It's just that I've assumed Janet ended her life—very little talent there. And Natasha, well . . . she could simply have misstepped in one of the thermal areas. Yellowstone's thermal features are no safer than other geothermal sites in the world, even if some of them are surrounded by hordes of tourists. It's dangerous work." With that he seemed to tire of the meeting. He gave Win a patronizing look. "I doubt you could appreciate the hardships required to advance in this profession."

Win shifted forward in his chair, then stood. "I need separate statements from each of you. Tonight would be fine, or I can ask Judge Walters to instruct you to stay here tomorrow and I'll work you into *my* schedule." It was time to lean on them with a bit of the Bureau's weight.

Win got the interviews that night, not that they yielded any more information than he originally had. He and Trey sat in the FBI conference room and mulled it over after escorting the scientists from the FBI building. It was nearly nine. Win's headache had returned, and he was hungry and tired.

"Whata ya think?" Win rubbed his eyes and looked at the ranger.

"That you look spent . . . that you need to be getting more rest, eating better. That you should pace yourself a bit more."

"I mean about our volcanologists."

Trey frowned. "I know what you meant. We learned nothing more than what's in the files—and those guys have put these women behind them. They don't care. I really doubt that either of them has given Janet and Natasha a thought since they disappeared. And Missy was a long shot . . . she may not have even been with them." Trey sighed. "They are totally, and I mean totally, wrapped up in their research."

"Yeah, Dravec said twice that being interrupted to answer questions during the original investigation of Natasha's disappearance, such as it was, put them six and a half hours behind schedule on their fieldwork. He could remember the exact hours of research time they lost—five years ago—but nothing else about the particulars of the day she vanished. Completely focused on their all-important geyser statistics."

Trey stretched his arms behind his head. "Yeah . . . neither one is gonna win any points for concern or caring, and Dravec is creepy as hell. But are they suspects?"

Win stood up and shrugged. "Don't know. We've gotta look a lot closer at Chris Warren too. Some of this research seems to overlap among these groups. He could be our best suspect. If there's a reason to have a suspect."

"Well, let's knock off for tonight. Get fresh eyes on this tomorrow." Trey waved as he moved for the outer door.

Win walked up the stairs to his office and noticed that the two downstairs offices were dark. The FBI surveillance teams who'd been rotating in since back in mid-April had either pulled out with the repositioning or moved to the more modern facility down the street. Either way, with Johnson out on his questionable medical leave, it was looking like Win might indeed get lonely, as the SWAT guy had told him this afternoon.

He sighed as he sat down at his desk. Spending hours dealing with folks who were so blatant in their lack of regard for other human beings was wearing on him. Being stuck in Yellowstone National Park for who knows how long, with little real work to do, was wearing on him. Being politely reamed out by the new boss in town was wearing on him. *Yep, it's been a crappy day.* His tired eyes went to the red velvet box containing what he suspected was Natasha Yahontova's elegant ring. The ring was just as lost as the woman who'd worn it. His mind went back to this afternoon, to the Chicago ASAC's words: *"You may not be able to bring those people back, but you may be able to bring some peace into broken lives. A worthy goal. . . ."* Win stared at the velvet box for a moment longer, his thoughts still on the lost. It was more than a goal, he thought. *It's my duty to do my best to bring them peace, to bring them justice. A sacred duty.*

He sighed again and stood. It was nearly ten; he needed to get home, feed the cat, and scrounge up something to eat. He picked up the clear evidence bag containing the red ring box. He'd put it in the gun safe with the woman's bones. It didn't need to be lying here on his desk. Then he paused and sat back down. *Well, hell. I might as well get this over with . . . couldn't make this day any worse.* Of course, he was wrong about that.

He used the tiny antique key to unlock his lower desk drawer, then pulled out the small FedEx parcel and used his pocketknife to carefully open it. He looked inside.

The dark-blue velvet box was the same one he'd picked out at the jeweler's in Heber Springs nearly three years ago. As he opened the ring box, the memories spilled out. The man and woman behind the glass counter had been lavish in their praise that crisp fall day. He remembered that. He and Mr. Thurman, the only jeweler in the small town, had sat at a table at the front of the store and talked through the Arkansas-Auburn game as they waited for the woman to finish cleaning the ring.

"Our boys sure coulda used you, Win. You wouldn't have dropped that ball in the end zone! No sirree! How many touchdowns did you catch your senior year? Wasn't it some SEC record?" Win tried to be modest and deflect the praise. He was nervous. The jeweler switched gears as the clerk finished her tasks, laid the velvet box on the table, and moved on to other chores. "She's one lucky girl, that's all I can say. To have Miss Dovie's ring . . . one lucky girl. Yes sirree!"

He remembered reverently opening the box and looking down at the newly sized ring, which had been handed down through his family. It was a one-carat blue diamond set in white gold. His great-grandfather found the diamond at the Crater of Diamonds State Park, in southwest Arkansas, back in the '30s, before the mine was even a park. It was the only place you could find diamonds in North America, and even now it was still finders keepers at the state park. Win's great-grandad was twelve when he found the gem, and it became a treasured part of the Tyler family history. Win's grandfather had the diamond made into the engagement ring that he'd given the prettiest girl in Velvet Ridge. Win remembered Papa telling that story over and over and smiling every time he told it. Win had seen his grandmother wear the ring to church and on special occasions those many years ago. They were farm people; you didn't wear your finer things for day-to-day living. When his grandmother passed, Papa had given the ring to his oldest grandson and asked him to keep the tradition alive.

Shelby had said all the right things when he gave it to her. He didn't remember exactly *what* she said, but he did remember the pride he felt when she saw the ring—when he slipped it on her finger. They were up on Hawksbill Crag, a magnificent, remote overlook in the Arkansas Ozarks. It was one of those crystal-clear fall days when the sky was so blue it didn't look real, when you could nearly reach out and touch the cottony white clouds. Every leaf had been painted and the mountains were blazing in red, yellow, and orange. A stream was tumbling in the valley far below, a melodious backdrop for the breathtaking setting. They'd been in Heber Springs for a friend's wedding and had driven over early that Sunday morning. Shelby thought they were just going for a hike on a beautiful day. He'd planned it well, and she'd been surprised. And it had been perfect. *Just perfect.*

Win touched the ring that he knew she'd been the last to hold. He found himself blinking back tears, his throat so tight he couldn't swallow. The memories continued to drift through his mind. Some hikers had come up the trail just as he was down on one knee, proposing.

They'd politely stopped at a distance and then applauded when it was obvious she'd said *yes*. The hikers had made a big fuss over the engagement; they'd taken photos—good photos. He still had the pictures on his computer and his phone; he hadn't been able to force himself to delete them. Couldn't do it.

Still can't.

CHAPTER NINE

It was one of those happenstances, as his mother would call it. The next morning he'd only been at his desk for five minutes, drinking coffee and rereading Luke Bordeaux's translation of what Luke had called *directions to the entrance to Hell*, when the landline rang. Win glanced away from the Russian news clipping, with its handwritten subtext, and answered the phone.

"FBI. Win Tyler here," he answered absently, still holding the old newspaper article, examining the Cyrillic letters.

"This is CIA, Langley, calling for Special Agent Winston Tyler. Please hold for Deputy Chief Casson, Directorate of Operations."

Win nearly dropped the phone. *CIA? Deputy Chief? Seriously?* He laid down the clipping, tried to calm his pulse rate, and focused on the caller. There was a long pause—apparently the CIA didn't use elevator music to fill the void—then a man's deep voice. "You're Winston Tyler?"

"Yes, sir."

"John Casson at the Agency. I'm going to conference in Clark Timms, Deputy Assistant Director for the FBI's Office of International Operations, and Barbara Winter, the Agency's Mission Chief over Eastern Russia. Can you hold for just a minute, while we pull them into the call?" Win was stunned. *Can you hold? While three of the top spooks in the U.S. Government get on the line? Naw, I'm thinkin' about goin' out for breakfast.* Win's inner dialogue kept it up while he waited. Maybe they did need elevator music; he was getting more anxious by the second. He knew higher-ups at the CIA and the Bureau didn't routinely call rookie FBI agents. Probably *never* called rookie FBI agents. *What is this about?*

Nearly thirty seconds dragged by, then two more acknowledgments that the secure conference call was being filled, then a friendly voice on the phone. "Agent Tyler, this is Clark Timms at Headquarters. I have a copy of your Country Clearance Request to visit Dr. Vladimir Orsky in Svetlyi, Russia, for an investigative interview. Something about a missing woman . . . Natasha P. Yahontova, last seen in Yellowstone National Park five years ago."

"Yes, sir. I sent in that request on May 27th, the day I opened the letter from Dr. Orsky indicating he might have information regarding the woman's disappearance."

One of the other higher-ups spoke. "Why? Just a missing person. Why aren't the locals handling this?"

"The Bureau has sole investigative authority in Yellowstone—no locals involved unless we want to bring them in. I'm trying to close out several missing persons files."

"Win," Mr. Timms interjected, "give us an overview of the investigation thus far. Tell us what you have, what precipitated Dr. Orsky's letter to you."

Win sucked in a breath and delivered what he thought was a succinct accounting of the information he had so far. He covered the discovery of the bones with the valuable ring; the unsolicited letter from Dr. Orsky, with the Russian newspaper clippings; the scant information he had on the missing Russian woman; and his concerns that two other missing women were also related to thermal researchers within the park. He ended his short summary with a question. "Is there a problem?"

There was silence for several seconds.

Finally, Ms. Winter, the CIA lady for Eastern Russia, answered, "Well, I don't know that it's a problem, but it is *highly* unusual for the Russian Ministry of Internal Affairs, which controls all Russian police departments, to approve your request for an interview within two days of receiving it. In fact, the Russians don't usually approve our requests

for in-country interviews. Period. We're not"—she cleared her throat—
"shall we say, on the best of terms with them right now."

The Bureau guy, Timms, spoke up. "We don't typically ask to go
over there. And even if we did, the Russians don't do anything quickly.
They are cautious, methodical, calculating. It's been one week to the
day since you sent in your request. One week. That's unheard of."

Win was stunned again. He hadn't realized that a Country
Clearance Request was such a big deal. He'd seen it as another step
toward solving a mystery—Natasha's disappearance. But he'd also
thought it was a shot in the dark; he had no reason to think the request
would be granted without significantly more documentation. He'd simply found the correct form on the Bureau's digital system, typed it up,
and sent it to his bosses. He had no idea it would sail through Denver,
get shipped to Headquarters, then the U.S. Embassy in Moscow, then
who knows where, and then be authorized—by Russia. *And someone
had to approve it at each juncture—how did that happen?* But Win
wasn't the one asking the questions in this conversation.

The CIA folks launched into dozens of rapid-fire questions, which
Win answered to the best of his ability. Mr. Casson closed out with
a blunt assessment of Win's request. "Let me make sure I've got this
straight. You're a three-year man with no experience in counterintelligence or advanced training in any of the intelligence sectors, either
before or after you joined the Bureau. You don't know any Russian
nationals or speak Russian. You have never been out of the country.
You're in a two-man office in Yellowstone National Park. You don't
have conclusive evidence that the bones are Ms. Yahontova's. No DNA.
No carbon dating. And you have no idea why the Russian police would
invite you to one of their most sensitive, closely guarded regions for a
missing persons interview."

Dang, it doesn't sound too good when you put it that way. "All of
your statements are correct, sir." Win thought about adding that maybe
the Russians were just trying to be nice, or cooperative, or maybe they
wanted closure for this woman's family, same as he did. But he thought
better of it.

Mr. Timms wrapped up the call. "Thanks for your time, Win. Let us chew on this a bit more. Someone from the Denver office will be in touch with you soon. Don't reach out to anyone on this until you get clearance from Headquarters or Denver. Have a great day."

Win hung up the phone and sat staring at it. *What just happened?*

*   *   *

Win had just finished writing up an internal memo related to the phone call with the three honchos from Washington when the landline rang. It was the secretary for the Violent Crime Squad at the Denver Field Office. She was pleasant and more than a little puzzled.

"Washington has approved your interview with Dr. Vladimir Orsky on that missing geologist," she said. "You must be quite the darling of the brass at Headquarters. Those TV interviews you gave after the incident with the militiamen, I suppose." She paused and seemed to be shuffling papers. "It's unheard of for a three-year agent to be sent overseas, even for a routine case interview—much less sent to Russia." Her incredulous tone was followed by a sigh. "Well, maybe they know your request for a ticket out of Yellowstone got squashed by the Transfer Unit. The trip . . . well, I'm thinking they're throwing you a bone."

Win wasn't loving her choice of words or her lack of interest in the missing persons cases. But the news on the interview request—*So cool. I'm going to Russia!* She told him to be prepared to leave whenever word came down. She said Country Clearance Requests generally took weeks to firm up, but someone or something seemed to be moving this one along at warp speed.

"Sit tight," she said, "the Bureau's Legal Attaché in Moscow will be doing the legwork, handling all the paperwork with the local authorities. Someone will eventually be in touch."

Win began to feel a hint of excitement. After several dreary days of shooting inquiries and plowing through all the heartbreak and tragedy within the cases of the lost, maybe a little adventure was down the road.

The supervisor of the Foreign Counterintelligence Squad in Denver called right before noon and gave him some reassurance that he wouldn't be on his own in Russia. "We have standard protocols with any country that allows us in—I haven't personally seen a case where we went to Russia, but I'm sure it's done, and this is probably routine for our Moscow Legal Attaché. We call them Legats, by the way . . . you'll meet with one of our Legats when your plane lands. He or she will be with you every step of the way—no worries about the language or procedures, the Legat will handle all of it. You just need to get your interview questions together. Be ready to take notes, I doubt you'll be permitted to tape or photograph anything. Don't expect a call from our office in Moscow anytime soon. Win, I wouldn't hold my breath on this—it's not like it's an urgent deal."

* * *

She was sorta plain—a short, chunky woman with dull brown hair wrapped in a tight braid, tied off with a gray bow, and draped over her shoulder. Her sun-weathered face didn't announce her age—she could have been forty, but he was guessing she was younger. Her long gray cotton dress and hand-knit blue shawl made her look as if she'd just stepped off the set of *Little House on the Prairie*. Oddly, she wasn't as out of place as you'd think, since there was a back-to-nature, semi-hippie fringe that populated this part of the country. She'd been sitting on the store's side porch, watching him, for the last fifteen minutes as he finished his sandwich at the picnic table near the Mammoth General Store.

The woman wasn't hiding her interest in him. She was watching him as if she knew him. If he was honest with himself, he'd admit that he caught women watching him everywhere he went. His first year in college, he'd dated a girl who was the jealous type and hated that his good looks drew other girls' attention. But Shelby seemed to love it. She always said it just proved that she had what it took to snag the hottest guy on campus—should have occurred to him then that in Shelby's mind, everything revolved around her.

He finished the turkey sandwich and dabbled at the handful of chips that still lay on the napkin in front of him. A thieving magpie dropped out of the nearby tree and lunged past his boot to nab a chip that had gotten away. He admired the bird's ebony head and beak. The iridescent teal feathers on its side and wings looked like racing stripes, and its long blackish-green tail was impressive—it was a fancy bird by his standards. As the magpie hopped away with the stray chip to eat it, Win turned his attention back to the watchful woman on the porch.

He'd started back in on the chips when he saw the woman move down the steps and walk his way. His right hand drifted away from the Fritos and down to his sidearm. He'd been trying to remain hypervigilant, given the events of the last few weeks. The undercurrent of fear that had been a frequent companion moved into his consciousness as she stopped across the table from him.

"You're Win Tyler." It wasn't a question. Her voice was soft and subdued. He noticed then how tired she looked.

He was straddling the picnic table bench, but he rose a little and touched his hat brim with his left hand. His right hand stayed under his jacket, on the Glock. He scanned the surroundings to see if anyone was with her. Nothing set off alarm bells, nothing felt threatening.

"Yes, ma'am, can I help you?"

She tried for a smile, but it came across as sadness. The light breeze was playing with the fringe on her shawl. "I'm Rose Shepherd Bufford . . . I've come here from Rapid City to see you."

His hand involuntarily tightened around the handgun's grip, and he blinked at her in surprise.

"Do you mind if I have a seat? Won't be taking up much of your time." The sad look hadn't left her lined face, and he realized it was her normal look. She'd seen lots of heartbreak in her time.

"Sure . . . sure. You mind keeping your hands where I can see them, Mrs. Bufford? You here by yourself?" His eyes kept scanning the steady stream of tourists and park employees who were going in and out of the store at lunchtime. His back was to the highway and the open parade ground; he didn't like being this exposed.

She settled herself on the bench across from him and nodded. She kept her hands on top of an older leather handbag that she'd laid on the table.

"You here by yourself?" he asked again.

Her tired eyes continued to look at his face, not so much making eye contact, just mapping out his features. "Ah, ah . . . my husband, Roy, and our two kids . . . they're over in the pickup, sleeping." She nodded toward an older GMC twin cab parked beside the nearby gas station. "We drove all night to get here, it's nearly an eight-hour drive. I . . . I just wanted to get here and get this over and done with. . . . We were gonna find your office after lunch. Roy's got to be back at work on Thursday."

Get what over and done with? With her father, Daniel Shepherd, on the FBI's Ten Most Wanted list, he knew she should be under FBI surveillance. But if she was under surveillance, they wouldn't have let her approach him. *Where are her FBI watchers?* Daniel Shepherd had tried to kill him—and had darn near succeeded. *What is she doing here?* His mind was going in too many directions at once. He didn't respond, and she continued to talk.

"The FBI agents who've come to see us these last few weeks . . . they said I could lose the kids, they said we could go to jail, both me and Roy, if Daddy showed up and we didn't tell them. I hadn't seen him in years, not since right after Mama died. Like I told those agents, I never heard from him in all this time 'cept for things he'd mail to the kids at Christmas or their birthdays. We haven't been close since I was a little girl. He was in the service—gone most of the time, to the wars . . . then there was the prison time."

She dropped her gaze from his face, as if repeating those words shamed her. She drew a deep breath and continued. "When he got outa prison, he started up his church. We didn't see eye to eye on the church, so we completely lost touch. He didn't approve of me marrying Roy . . . Roy's a Methodist, you see."

As if that explained it.

"But Daddy showed up yesterday morning . . ." She raised her gray eyes and looked into his for just a second. Win saw a flicker of a smile there, as if she were remembering someone or something good and joyful far in the past, buried deep in her heart. "Roy and I live on the old homeplace, and I plant my garden just like folks did when I was little—Mama used to make a big garden each year at the same spot down near the creek." She glanced up again. "It's best to get your canta-loupe and pumpkins in about the same time as your herbs . . . May 21st is ideal if you plant by the moon, but we had a real late spring."

He nodded that he understood. "Yes, ma'am, planting by the *Farmer's Almanac.*"

"Yes, well, yesterday . . . I was putting in the cantaloupe and he just showed up down at the garden and asked me to come see you. Said that you were the one who had to have this. Not them other agents back home."

She started to reach into the big purse, and he stopped her with a firm hand over hers. "I'm sorry, but how 'bout you let me look in there. You don't have a weapon in there, do you?" He kept his voice calm and steady.

She didn't try to pull her small hand away, but she shook her head *no.* For the first time he sensed that she was fearful. "You kin look. It's the envelope and the little doeskin pouch. He gave me those things. The letter is for you . . . the other, well, he said to keep 'em, but they don't belong to me."

*   *   *

She hesitated at the conference-room door and waited for her husband and the others to file out. The kids were thrilled with the prospect of a real park ranger guide, and they'd already run ahead to catch up with the two rangers who were leading the tour.

"You do look like him. Not so much straight on, but when you turn, when you smile . . . I kin see how Daddy would take you for Dennie." She pulled the shawl higher on her shoulders and nodded to herself; that look was in her eyes—that look of seeing something good far in the past. "He wasn't always a bad person, he just got away from God. There were some good times . . . Dennie was a precious little brother. He loved horses; he loved the rodeo. He got in with the wrong crowd at school—I don't know how it come to this . . . this nightmare. I'm sorry for what they did with their lives, for what Daddy put you through."

He thought she might cry, but she pulled herself up straighter and her misty eyes met his. Her fingers were fiddling with the fringe on her shawl. "You've been kinder to us than I had any right to expect."

"We can't live anyone else's life for them, Mrs. Bufford. Your father and your brother chose their own paths. The Bureau appreciates what you've done here. I appreciate what you've done." They walked out of the building, and she waved to her youngsters, who were drinking cokes on the Visitor Center's wide porch, under the watchful eye of a female ranger.

"Y'all enjoy the park and have a safe trip home." Win watched until she and her husband crossed the street before he returned to his office.

* * *

He'd waited until he got approval from his supervisor before he opened the white envelope with his name printed on the front. He already knew what was in the small leather pouch Mrs. Bufford had given him: four perfect one-and-a-half-carat diamonds—part of Shepherd's loot. Probably worth more than $25,000, maybe even $50,000; he didn't really know. He hoped she'd receive a reward for turning those in; he wasn't sure how that worked.

What he did know was that someone with the Bureau's Special Surveillance Group was in deep trouble. The Buffords were supposed to be under twenty-four-hour watch on the off chance that Daniel Shepherd turned up at the home of his only known family in the States. Somebody was gonna catch hell over that lapse, not to mention the fact that the blunder could have put Win's life in danger. Maybe someone at the Bureau had assumed that since Shepherd was on the run, he was no longer a threat to Win. Win knew that wasn't a safe bet, and this surveillance snafu did nothing to ease his concerns.

He propped his cell phone up on the desk, set it to record his actions, and recited the necessary preamble of evidentiary facts. He paused with his pocketknife over the envelope—it still had garden dirt on its exterior—then carefully slit it open and removed the one sheet of paper with his gloved hand. It was handwritten, short and to the point.

To Agent Winston Tyler:

Three times I tried to follow what I saw as God's leading regarding you. Three times I failed. Since you claim to be a Christian, you know that three is a number of completion set out in Scripture. I will not dishonor God. Since His mighty hand of protection is on you, I swear that I will not raise my hand against you again as long as I live.

Daniel Shepherd, Prophet of the Lord

Win sat back in his chair and turned off the phone video. As he read the note again, he felt a flood of relief—no more scanning every crowd for Shepherd's face, no more looking over his shoulder, no more fear. He leaned his head back and closed his eyes. *Thank you, God.*

* * *

It wasn't quite eight that night when Trey knocked on Win's back door.

"It's open," Win called from the kitchen. The ranger sat the grocery sack on the washer and took off his boots in the mudroom.

Trey smiled at him as he deposited a six-pack of beer and two bags of chips on the granite countertop. "Remind me again why we're watching *baseball*?"

Win opened a beer and saluted Trey with it. "'Cause football season hasn't started, and college basketball is over." Trey nodded and seemed to agree that the reasoning made perfect sense. "Plus," Win added, "it's the Razorbacks in the late game tonight in the regionals for the College World Series. We've got a shot at a sweep."

Gruff made an appearance as Trey was trying out the cheese dip that Win had lifted from the microwave. The big orange cat ambled into the kitchen, did a head bump against Win's shin, and wrapped himself around Trey's leg. The ranger was fanning the dip with his hand. "What's with your cat? Didn't he used to hate you?"

"Not a clue," Win said with a shrug. "Those days after the hospital, when Mom was here—well, Gruff was crazy about Mom. Maybe he figured if she liked me, then I was alright. Whatever it is, we're buddies now." The cat knew he was being discussed; he gave them a flick of his tail and a superior look before walking away. "Jason's comin' over too. Kid's mother is still in the hospital in Billings. He's havin' a rough go of it."

Trey seemed to approve of the dip, downing two more cheese-laden chips as Win kept talking. "Thanks for arranging for the Buffords to have a tour of the park today. I sorta felt sorry for them—they wouldn't even take any gas money from me. Seemed like good folks caught up in a bad deal."

The ranger nodded. "Yup, been a lot of that going around lately." He wiped his hands on a paper towel and glanced over at Win. "I got the word to Luke that you'd been ordered to stay clear of him, no communications for the time being—that your bosses had come down on you."

"Thanks." Win paused, then brought up something that had been on his mind. "I, uh, got the impression Luke doesn't remember much of the firefight."

"Did he say that?"

"Not in so many words." Win shrugged.

"He lost a lot of blood . . . he nearly bought it that day, same as you." Trey leaned back against the counter and dropped his eyes. "People process trauma differently, plus he's seen more heavy action in his lifetime than either of us can imagine. He was special ops in the Middle East for years. His mind may have just let the images go. He may have no idea what he said to you or what he did that day. It wouldn't be unusual."

"You learn that in your EMT training?" Win knew Trey had an Advanced Emergency Medical Technician certification; he'd seen the guy use that expertise. Trey was a pro. "Is it like the fog-of-war thing you hear about?"

Trey gave a sad shrug. "Something like that, I suppose. Happens often to trauma victims . . . sometimes the memories return weeks or even years later. Sometimes never." He drew a wistful breath. "I wish I could forget that day. Are you still having nightmares?"

Win thought about his answer before he nodded. "How'd you know?"

Trey took a drink of his beer and glanced away. "You aren't the only one . . . and I didn't even shoot anyone. It's gettin' a little better, but some nights I still relive it when I close my eyes and it's been, what? Three full weeks. You and Luke had the heavy-duty drugs too. It's gonna take a while, Win. They got you seeing a shrink?"

"Yeah, I've done a few sessions with a guy out of Headquarters on the video. Had a session late this afternoon, and he recommended I do more regular stuff, get away from work more . . . have a little fun."

Trey dug into the cheese dip again, then looked up and smiled. "So, ball game watching with the guys is a homework assignment. Let me guess, you were also told to make that date with Tory."

Win felt his ears go red. "Wasn't told to but did it anyway. She's gonna stay with a friend who's at the Mammoth Hotel Thursday night. We're going to the rodeo."

Jason came through the back door without knocking, pulled off his tennis shoes, and headed for the kitchen. "Thanks for the invite, Win." His eyes lit up when he saw the big container of cheese dip. "Oooh, nice! Who're your Hogs playing?"

Win handed Jason a coke just as his Bureau phone buzzed. He waved them toward the den, where the game was starting, and answered the phone.

The man's voice on the call sounded far away. It was. "Hi, Win, this is John Bennett, Legat in Moscow. You're booked on flights from Bozeman to Petropavlovsk-Kamchatskiy on Friday. If you've got a minute, let's go over a few things. . . ."

CHAPTER TEN

"Hey, hey! Got your text—are you kidding me? Russia? You're flying to Russia today?" The enthusiastic voice on the call brought a broad smile to Win's face.

"Yeah. Petropavlovsk-Kamchatskiy. Just got off the plane in Anchorage. Leavin' here in just over an hour."

"Can't believe you can pronounce that, much less know where it is . . . uh, where exactly is it?"

"Far Eastern Russia, the Kamchatka Peninsula. They call it the land of ten thousand grizzlies."

"No kidding? Kamchatka? That's where the Baileys took their top execs fishing last summer. Caught twenty-pound trout, dozens of 'em. Saw big bears everywhere, some of the best hunting and fishing in the world. You gonna get to stay a while?" The tone was almost reverent. Win could tell Tucker Moses was impressed.

"Naw, just a quick-turnaround trip to interview a potential witness. No time to hunt or fish, but I oughta see some volcanoes. The place is eat up with 'em. What've you been up to?"

Tucker ran through the highlights of a jury trial he was preparing for in Vicksburg and lamented his continued slump in the girl department, as he put it.

"You seen Tory?" Tucker asked.

"A couple of times, yeah. Took her to a rodeo last night. Had a real good time."

"And?"

"And what? It was just our first real date . . . and I may have some competition."

"Like a little competition's gonna bother you? Win Tyler: Sigma Chi class president, All-SEC receiver—two years in a row, smokin' Assistant U.S. Attorney, FBI hero who saved Yellowstone . . . let's see, what am I leavin' out?"

"Second-team All-SEC," Win corrected.

"Whatever. You got this, Win. I'll bet that girl hasn't stopped thinkin' 'bout you since you took her home." Win grinned at the comment and hoped Tucker was right.

Tucker Moses had been his best friend since law school, when they'd shared an apartment at the University of Arkansas for three years. Tucker grew up on the Moriah Plantation in Louisiana and was doing real well for himself in his law practice in Oxford, Mississippi. He came from new money stacked on old money, but there wasn't a snobby, arrogant bone in his body.

Win ended the call with a promise to fill Tucker in on Russia as long as nothing got elevated to official case status. He found a Homeland Security officer and was ushered into a TSA office on the concourse. The young man sitting at the desk was impressed with Win's destination.

"We get law enforcement locking up their sidearms on stopovers to Canada all the time, even Japan or South Korea, but Russia? Man, that's cool." The uniformed TSA guy kept talking as he checked to make sure Win's Glock was unloaded before attaching an ownership tag. Win powered down his personal phone and handed it and the gun's extra magazine to the young man, then waited as the officer filled in the lengthy forms.

"I had no idea any of our folks even worked over there. You been there before?"

Win tried hard not to show the mix of excitement and tension building inside him. He shrugged. "No, never been to Russia, but the Bureau works with foreign police agencies all over the world. It's really not that big a deal."

The guy glanced up from the paperwork and raised his eyebrows. "Uh-huh . . . well, you couldn't pay me enough to go there, official business or not. It's *Russia*, they aren't like us. Everything's run by the mafia and the KGB. People just disappear over there."

Win shrugged again. "That's probably ancient history. I'm on a planeload of American tourists going to see volcanoes, geysers, and bears. Russia's trying to attract visitors; they're not looking for trouble." The TSA officer locked Win's personal phone, the Glock, and the extra magazine in his safe and swung his eyes up. He wasn't convinced. Win heard the boarding announcement for Yakutia Airlines through the open door. He scribbled his name and date on a final form and nodded back to the officer.

"Keep them safe for me, I'll be back real soon." He carried his leather satchel briefcase and his carry-on toward the boarding area. Sure, Russia was safe—he'd meet the Bureau's Legat, get the interview, and be back on American soil in less than thirty-six hours. Still, he felt naked without his gun.

* * *

He stowed his jacket, bag, and the leather briefcase in the overhead bin and tried to match the seasoned travelers' looks of bored indifference. But he couldn't pull it off. His excitement for the trip transitioned to a wide smile when the gray-haired woman sitting next to him asked if he'd like the window seat. She patted his arm as they rearranged the seating, and he introduced himself to her and her husband.

"I saw your ticket when you came down the aisle," she said. "Bozeman to Seattle, on to Anchorage, then to Petropavlovsk-Kamchatskiy. Have you been there before?"

He shook his head and she kept talking. "Well, everyone calls it Petropavlovsk, not that ridiculously long version of the name." She was a talker. "We took one of the first flights from Anchorage to the Kamchatka Peninsula back in 2006. That was the year before the horrible landslide hit Kamchatka's Valley of the Geysers and buried so many of the spectacular features. It's still a wonderful destination, but sadly not nearly as magnificent as before." She poked her husband for affirmation.

"We were thrilled when Yakutia Airlines began their seasonal flights from Alaska again last year. They're upgrading, you know. A modern passenger terminal is set to open soon in Petropavlovsk—and aren't their new jets nice?" She brushed her hand across the smooth leather on the armrest. "The Russians are certainly putting their best foot forward." She beamed at him in anticipation. "We'll be there before you know it! It's less than a five-hour flight." Win nodded and placed his paperback novel into the back pouch of the seat in front of him. He had a feeling he was going to get real well acquainted with his seatmate during the next few hours.

"Oh, and you'll never forget the view from the plane of the volcanoes that flank the city of Petropavlovsk," she was saying. She sighed at the memory. "It is breathtaking, truly breathtaking. You must see the volcanoes from the air." She cut a glance at her husband. "Remember how thrilling air travel was for us once, Herbert?" Her eyes teased Win for a moment more. "It's so good to see someone young excited about a new adventure."

*　*　*

Thirty minutes later, Miss Emma Jean finally turned her attention to the drink service, which Win politely declined. He used the interruption to put in his earbuds, lean back the seat, and pretend to take a nap. There was no longer anything to see out the window except the navy-blue Bering Sea far below. And it wasn't that he wasn't friendly—he was generally friendly with everyone—but he was finding it harder and harder to conceal his anxiety from the gabby lady.

He'd never been comfortable flying. But he knew that wasn't the main issue. His mind kept going back to his work. He needed this trip to produce some results, to fill in some blanks. He felt as if he was getting nowhere in the search for the lost. He had three missing women—all tied in some way to geological research expeditions. He had a missing young man who didn't seem to be connected to any of the others, but the timing of his disappearance was suspect—within days of when Natasha Yahontova was last seen. As frustrating as this was for Win, he couldn't imagine how heartbreaking it must be for the families. He'd gotten no response on his inquiry with the State Department regarding Natasha's next of kin, but he'd spent much of the last two days on the phone with family members and others involved in the initial investigations. He sighed. *I need a break on these cases.*

The jet hit a patch of light turbulence and his anxiety went up a notch. To calm his nerves, he replayed last night for at least the tenth time. He'd pulled his ten-year-old Explorer into a gravel parking space behind the Mammoth Hot Springs Hotel, next to the row of rustic cottages, and turned off the engine. He was early—and nervous. His granny had an expression for it: as nervous as a long-tailed cat in a room full of rocking chairs. That fit. He sat in the truck and drew in a deep breath as he pocketed his keys with a sweaty palm. *Get a grip, Win! It's a date with a girl . . . this isn't your first date. Get a grip!* His internal lecture did nothing to ease his stress as he glanced at his reflection in the rearview mirror. That didn't help—he thought he looked as anxious as he felt. He needed to chill for a few minutes before he worked up the nerve to walk to her cabin.

Tory had sounded excited when he invited her to the rodeo. The connection on their brief phone conversation had been terrible, and they'd only talked for a couple of minutes, but she'd sounded upbeat and pleased that he'd called. So maybe she wasn't seeing Chris Warren after all. She said she had a college friend, an artist, who was staying in Mammoth for a few nights, and she'd planned to visit her for a couple of days. He figured she'd probably gotten into Mammoth earlier this afternoon from the bear-research base camp somewhere in the wilds southeast of Roosevelt.

He drew a deep breath, finally screwed up his courage, and walked under the late-afternoon shade of the towering cottonwoods to the cream-colored cabin. She was sitting on the small front porch, working on her laptop. She turned her head when she saw him and smiled that beautiful smile. He felt his knees go a little weak as he nodded to her. "Hey, good seein' you."

"You too, Win. You just missed Lauren, she left with some folks to get supper. I was hoping you could meet her." She began talking about her afternoon of visiting with her college friend, and he found himself watching her more than listening. Her jeans fit her well, and she was wearing a light-green blouse. She had on the black cowboy boots he'd seen before. He reckoned everyone had to wear cowboy boots to the first rodeo of the year in Gardiner. Her long brunette hair was tied back with a ribbon that matched the shirt. She had on gold drop earrings—first time he'd ever seen her wear jewelry. She looked totally amazing. And he realized she was waiting for him to answer some question she'd asked that he hadn't heard 'cause he'd been so caught up in looking at her. He dropped his head and gave her a sheepish grin. "You wanna repeat that?" He figured she got that a lot.

She laughed. "I asked if you were ready to go? I just need to put this up and grab my jacket. I haven't been to a rodeo in ages—this is so exciting!"

Yes it is.

They met Trey and his wife, Cindy, at the barbecue that volunteers for the local library held as a fundraiser before the rodeo. Cindy and Trey were the perfect example of the adage that opposites attract. Where Trey was cool, calm, and deliberate, Cindy was exuberant, vocal, and dramatic. She was barely five feet tall and built like a fireplug, with short blond hair that seemed to have a mind of its own. They'd met fighting a wildfire in Nevada, not long after Trey joined the Park Service. Cindy had been a medic with the smoke jumpers, while Trey was just a novice working the fire line. Trey had been enthralled by the cheerful, spunky woman—and it was clear that after several years of marriage, he was still impressed.

There was a country band playing, and it looked like most of Gardiner's nine hundred residents had turned out for the opening night of events. "Got some real cowboys riding here tonight," Trey commented. Win figured Trey should know; he'd grown up on a large cattle and sheep ranch in central Idaho. Trey Hechtner was a top-notch park ranger, but he could easily transition into cowboy. And he wore that outfit of straw hat, snap-button shirt, and boot-cut jeans with a silver belt buckle just as well as he did the green and gray of his ranger uniform. They all had another round of cokes, then listened to the band and tried to guess the names of the throwback country tunes in the group's repertoire. Everyone was competing to make up the silliest song titles. Being with Trey and his bubbly wife was just plain fun.

The weather was perfect, with the deep-blue sky fading to lilac as the sun began its descent after nine. Days were long this far north; it wouldn't be full dark till nearly 10:30. Win pulled Tory's jacket around her shoulders as the chill air moved in; the temperature dropped twenty degrees as the sun began to set. He was sitting close to her in the bleachers, pointing out things that she probably already knew; she'd been around horses, same as he had. But she let him take the lead on things and he liked that. He didn't tell her about his short-lived bull-riding career as a senior in high school. *Young and foolish* came to mind. That story probably wouldn't score any points with the smart woman sitting beside him.

The serious events, like team roping, steer wrestling, and barrel racing, were interspersed with fun events for the kids. The children's goat roping—which didn't include any actual roping—turned into a circus, with indignant rams chasing every child who dared dismount to remove the ribbons from their horns. At the end of the event, it was Rams 5, Little Cowpokes 0. Everyone in the stands cheered the kids on and laughed with the children at the outcome. Tory's laugh was light, sincere, and free. Win liked her laugh, and he noticed how good it felt to laugh with her. As they were walking back to the truck after night fell, he realized how long it had been since he'd laughed with a woman he was interested in—since he'd laughed with anyone except Shelby. *Five years. Woulda been five years last month.* He'd been thinking of taking Tory's hand, but he didn't. *Maybe I'm pushing it. Maybe it's too soon.* Those thoughts kept floating through his mind.

When they got back to the Mammoth Hot Springs Hotel, he found himself thinking of kissing her good night, and that got him nervous again. He parked in a dark area beside the hotel and went around to open her door. She slid out and sidestepped him when he moved in a little closer. He couldn't see her face real well, but she placed a hand on his arm and spoke softly. "I . . . I had a great time, Win."

Uh-oh.

"I really did. But I need you to know that I'm coming out of a long-term relationship . . . I . . . I'm trying to ease back into dating."

He could sense her wanting to move away. *Say something!* his mind screamed. "That's okay, it's okay." He managed to get out.

She squeezed his arm lightly. "It's just that . . . just that I'm starting to like you, and I have some issues with trust right now. I got blindsided on some things in that last relationship and . . ." She drew a breath and gripped his arm even tighter.

He pulled her in to him and held her there, just for a few seconds. "You can trust me, Tory Madison. I promise you that—you can trust me. And just for the record, I'm also comin' off a long-term relationship *and* I'm starting to like you too. So how 'bout we take this real slow, see where the Lord leads us. How about that?"

He saw her white teeth flash a smile in the near darkness. "I'd like that a lot, Win Tyler."

* * *

A short, pale girl in a light-blue uniform held up a sign reading *American Tours of Kamchatka*. Her uniform reminded him of pictures of 1960s airline stewardesses—right down to the pillbox hat. Maybe ninety percent of the passengers from the Alaska flight were retrieving their bags and following her through the drab concrete terminal toward the customs booths. Other passengers were ganged around a thin flight crewman who was offloading gun cases and fishing equipment from a battered luggage cart. Three big men who looked to be the outdoorsmen's guides were standing near the small group, calling out names and instructions in broken English. The American sportsmen could have been models for North Face and Arc'teryx ads—high-dollar duds. Hunting brown bears and fishing for lunker trout in a wilderness encompassing millions of acres apparently wasn't for the middle class.

The Legat, Special Agent John Bennett, was to meet him here at the luggage drop-off. *Where is he?*

The vintage luggage carousel was squeaking and grinding as it slowly spit out their flight's last few bags. The far wall was covered with a large red sign warning in several languages, thankfully, one of which was English: *No telephone use before Point of Entry.*

Point of Entry? Customs, Win guessed. The walls and concrete floors were painted an institutional gray that seemed to match the low clouds and drizzle falling outside the windows. The dim flickering of fluorescent lights overhead added to the gloomy feel. It was cold in the corridor—the temperature couldn't have been over fifty—and the smell was a mixture of cigarette smoke, mildew, and disinfectant. Two armed guards or policemen, Win wasn't sure which, leaned against the wall near a bathroom. They carried identical black submachine guns and wore identical scowls. Kamchatka was not a welcoming place. If the Russians were trying to lure tourists to this remote spot, the airport needed a very different marketing director and a major facelift.

Win sighed and once more scanned the dwindling crowd waiting for their bags. Someone nearby was softly humming an old church tune he remembered from his childhood. He tried to place its source, gave up, and slowly followed the herd for the short walk down the corridor toward the front of the building.

Passengers were now flowing out of a second plane into the far side of the terminal. Win watched through a dirty window as more sportsman types and tourists climbed the stairs from the tarmac. A wave of Russian soldiers moved past him toward the front doors, their boots clicking loudly on the scuffed floor. The Russians weren't into casual fatigue dress while traveling; each of the young men in the group of thirty or so wore spotless dress uniforms, right down to the medals on their green chests. At least half of them were already lighting cigarettes as they joined the throng moving down the dingy corridor. An announcement was blaring through the small terminal in Russian as the last passenger exited the second jet. Still no sign of Bennett, and Win's seatmates, Herbert and Emma Jean, had disappeared as well. Win drew in a deep breath and moved toward the customs booths near the entrance. Maybe the Legat was waiting outside.

Win followed the last of the tour group's clients into line and pulled out his passport, credentials, and visa. He continued to scan the entrance for the Legat. He'd been sent two photographs of the guy— he'd recognize his face. Bennett was supposed to have arrived early this morning after a nine-hour overnight flight from Moscow. Win wasn't ignorant of geography by any means, but it was hard for him to wrap his head around the distances in this vast country. Moscow was 4,204 miles to the west—a direct flight from Petropavlovsk to Seattle— had there been one—would be nearly 1,000 miles shorter. He sighed and scanned the faces around him again. *I'm a long, long way from anywhere.*

Bennett had said there could be issues with customs given the current U.S.-Russia relationship. But the Legat spoke Russian and knew the system; he'd told Win he'd be here to run interference. *Where is he?* Win felt a tightness in his chest and realized he was now more anxious than annoyed.

The line shuffled forward a few feet just as the sandy-haired guy behind Win shifted his bag and dropped his passport nearly on top of Win's carry-on.

"Dang it. Ah, sorry about that. Got too darn many things in my pockets. . . ." The voice was pure Texas.

Win reached down for the open U.S. passport and discreetly matched the photo and name with the man behind him. *Jacob T. Stedman,* he silently read. He calculated the man's age from the birthday shown as thirty-six. He was tall, maybe an inch shorter than Win, and broad-shouldered, with a square jaw anchoring a good-natured face. He wore his brown bomber jacket loose, but Win could still tell the man was into lifting weights. He looked solid.

"No problem," Win replied as he handed over the passport.

"Hey, thanks . . ." The guy grinned. "You don't sound like you're from around here either. I'm guessin' East Texas? Maybe Mississippi?"

"Pretty close. Arkansas." He glanced back at the delay in the customs line. An older woman was fumbling for more travel documents. She was holding up the show.

The man kept talking, forcing Win to refocus on him. Win lectured himself internally: *There's no reason to be impolite just because my ride hasn't shown up.*

"You don't look like a volcano watcher. You here with oil and gas?" the man was asking.

"No, I'm not in the energy business . . ." Win didn't really answer the question, but he kept the conversation going. "What brings you to the far side of the world?"

The guy held up a worn black leather briefcase with *Southwest Energy & Natural Gas* stamped in silver above a company logo. "The Russians are trying to ramp up production in this region. We're in natural gas exploration. I've been here a few times trying to scope things out—before our company makes a proposal." He nodded to Win that the line was finally beginning to move, and they stepped forward a few spaces.

Win scanned the entrances again for Bennett—still no luck. He'd call him as soon as he got through customs; maybe Bennett's concern about his entering the country was overblown. There were only two more tourists in front of him; he'd soon find out. Win's palms were getting a little moist, but the fellow behind him was still chatty.

"You staying in Petropavlovsk? It's eighteen miles southeast of the airport and 1,300 rubles for the ride into town . . . that's nearly twenty bucks. Wanna share a cab?" the stranger asked.

"Thanks, but I'll pass. Supposed to be meeting someone here at the airport. He may be running late." He looked into the friendly green eyes and smiled. "I'm Win Tyler. I'm sorry I'm a little preoccupied. It's my first trip to Russia." Win extended his hand.

The handshake was very firm; his first impression of the man's strength was correct. "Don't worry about it. Jake Stedman. Grew up in Houston. Don't sweat the customs deal here—they just make it look intimidating." He laughed softly. "I think we've all seen way too many spy movies."

Win grinned back at him and nodded his goodbye as the stern customs guard motioned him forward.

CHAPTER ELEVEN

He'd had harder times getting a beer at a bar back in college than he did getting through customs at the airport in Russia. The jaded customs agent's flat eyes had given Win's documents a cursory glance as he stamped the passport and visa. He'd mumbled, "Enjoy time in Kamchatka," as he handed the paperwork back. Win stood on the crowded sidewalk and scanned the rush of taxis, vans, and cars. Every driver seemed to be honking their horn, every officer seemed to be shouting. He continued to watch for his contact as the crush of travelers began to thin. He found himself subconsciously humming the old hymn he'd heard inside. *Prone to Wander, Lord, I feel it; Prone to Leave the God I love . . .* He couldn't remember the song's name. A cabbie called in broken English for him to come aboard a van filled with middle-aged ladies. Win waved him away with a strained smile.

A graying older woman hobbled toward him with two rolling suitcases. She could obviously see the concern in his face. "Oh . . . my, my, lad," she began in a pronounced Scottish accent. "They don't have an endless supply of cabs here. . . . Come along with us. We'll all get into town. You don't want to be stuck at the airport for hours in this weather."

She was right. It was beginning to spit rain and the sidewalks were starting to look deserted. Her portly husband was frantically waving them toward a small black van. "Got to reserve a cab here ahead of time, laddie! You're not back in the States!" He gave Win a toothy grin.

To heck with it, Bennett can find me at the hotel. Win grabbed his bag and thanked the good folks, and they arrived at the three-story wood-frame hotel less than thirty minutes later. The weather was making no effort to improve—the town's famous volcanoes were still completely hidden by low cloud cover and fog. The cab ride from the airport through shabby industrial areas, decaying commercial dis-tricts, and sprawling blocks of fifty-year-old apartment buildings was anything but scenic, and the gray weather didn't help, but Win kept his eyes out the window, eagerly watching the unfamiliar landscape. He concluded that the city of Petropavlovsk was squashed between the steep foothills of the volcanoes and the large bay. There was so much he wanted to see.

His Scottish cab-mates were exhausted from their cross-continent series of flights from Edinburgh, so conversation was sparse. Win tried Agent Bennett's cell number twice—the rings went straight to voicemail. At least they had cell service in this far corner of the globe. The Legat hadn't checked into the hotel or left a message at the desk, and Win was beginning to get worried. His phone buzzed just as he walked into his second-floor room. The connection wasn't great, but Win could hear him.

"Win, hey man, I'm so sorry. My flight was diverted to Vladivostok—mechanical problems, they said. I've been trying to get rebooked all day. I'll be on a plane out of here in three hours. Ahhh . . . it's a three-hour flight. So, I'll be there before midnight. Was customs okay? You okay?"

"Yeah, everything's cool. I slept some on the planes, so I may get in a run, maybe get a bite to eat first. Call me when you get to the hotel. We can go over the plan then . . ."

The connection was breaking up. "Sure, sounds good." Static for a couple of seconds, then it cleared. He heard: ". . . careful there. Lots of strong-arm robberies—they prey on tourists and foreign businessmen. Don't let your guard down."

"Got it. See you later tonight. Whenever you get in, call. I'll get up."

The connection dropped. He wasn't sure Bennett had gotten the last of the call. He glanced at his watch and calculated the time; it was nearly five in the afternoon. He had at least seven hours to kill before they could meet and go over the details for tomorrow's witness interview. He wanted to eat something light and get in a workout.

But first he checked out his small room. It was adequate—nothing fancy for sure, but the bed was fairly firm, the shower had hot water, and everything looked clean. Tourism brochures were neatly arranged on a wooden desk next to a 24-inch TV that had probably been manufactured before he was born. He tried not to be too critical, his trip had been last-minute. He figured the better accommodations in town were already booked, and if they weren't, his FBI per diem probably wouldn't cover a room at a nicer hotel even if one existed. He looked out of the room's only window to a cozy inner courtyard that was ablaze with red and yellow flowers. The modest attempt at beauty pleased him; someone was trying to brighten their corner of Russia.

He shaved, then stood under the shower until its one minute of hot water ran cold. He felt the need to wash away the weariness of hours crammed on airplanes. He pulled on a warmer wool shirt with his khakis and light jacket. He followed the worn wooden stairs downward toward the smell of food.

The other travelers all had the same idea, and the harried little hostess at the tiny restaurant told him in halting English that he was welcome to wait in the bar until a table opened up or he could order a sandwich in there. A glance out the window at the pounding rain ruled out his finding another café in town. He nodded to the Scottish couple, who were having soup in the dining room, as he made his way back to a much larger room that housed the bar. He'd never been much of a bar kind of guy, but hunger was driving him on, and he maneuvered through the dimly lit room past a group of well-heeled sportsmen to a small table near the corner. A wispy layer of cigarette smoke drifted above everyone's heads, and American music from the '90s played a little too loudly in the background. The waitress handed him a lacquered menu with photographs of six items. He picked the one that looked the most like a hamburger with fries and tried to ask for water. He wasn't sure what she would bring. A glass of water appeared in front of him, and a few minutes later he was scarfing down a reasonable facsimile of an American hamburger as he scrolled though his missed calls and texts from back home. He'd have to call his brothers soon—they wouldn't believe he was eating french fries on the other side of the world.

"You look like you need some company." The accent was probably Russian, and the voice was soft and smooth. He was surprised that he heard her so clearly above the thumping of the music. She didn't wait for a response as she slid into the empty chair beside him.

Uh-oh.

"Where do you live? America? Yes?" The smooth voice asked as she leaned in closer. She was tall and slender. Her age was impossible to read, but her skirt was too short, and her blouse was too low, and he had enough sense to know he was fixing to get into trouble if he sat there much longer.

"Uh . . . yeah. I live in Wyoming." *Get out of here, Win . . . this ain't good.* Warning bells were going off in his head.

"Wyoming," she purred. "Ah . . . yes, American West. You are a cowboy? Yes?" Her brown eyes flickered beneath layers of black mascara. Silky strands of dark hair framed her flawless face. Win pulled back a little and quickly scanned the room for his waitress; she was taking an order from the sportsmen across the crowded room.

How he could smell the delicate scent of roses in the smoke-filled room was beyond him . . . but he could. She moved even closer, and her red lips parted to show perfect teeth. She cocked her head and smiled in delight. "A cowboy! You want to buy me drink? Yes?"

"Actually, no . . . I'm not a cowboy, and no, I'm sorry I can't buy you a drink. I'm waiting for my bill and then I'm leaving." He raised a hand to get the waitress's attention and the young woman suddenly leaned hard into him. He reached upward to steady her as she tried to stand. *Is she okay? Is she drunk?* Someone else was suddenly on the other side of her. Win stared up at the newcomer in surprise—it was the man he'd met in line at the airport.

"Hello, darlin'," the tall Texan drawled. His left hand clamped down on the girl's thin wrist. "Why don't you give the man's wallet back."

She struggled to twist free, but the man had a firm hold. "What you talk about! Let go! Let go!" she hissed at him.

"You want to cause a scene? You want the police here?" He pulled her closer to him and she stilled. "Naw . . . I didn't think so, sweetheart." He glared down into her eyes, his face hard as stone.

She tossed Win's leather wallet down on the table and tried to pull her arm loose. "Not so fast," the man said. He glanced at Win. "She get anything else? Check."

Win was stunned. He quickly reached into his jacket pocket for the thin pouch that held his travel documents and creds. His phone was still on the table. He nodded to the man, who released his grip. The woman stumbled away into the dense bar crowd and snarled back something in Russian that Win was glad he didn't understand.

Win was standing now. "Whoa . . . thank you. I . . . I had no idea," he stammered.

The Texan shrugged. "I've stayed at this hotel several times. I've seen her in the bar before . . . seen her kind. They're Gypsies, you know. They train their children to steal from birth, and they're very, very good at it." He shook his head. "Sad way to live."

"Can I buy you a drink?" Win offered. "I sure owe you one."

"Yeah, maybe one beer. I'm thinking of taking a run when the rain lets up. It stays light till after eleven here in early June."

"I'm a runner—was gonna run later too. Your name's Jake, right?"

"Jake Stedman, and you are . . . ah . . . Win?"

"Win Tyler." They shook hands again and reclaimed the seats. Thirty minutes later they were sipping their beers and eating salted vobla fish—Russia's version of bar snacks. They'd discussed last year's football and basketball seasons and the price swings in the energy industry, and highlighted their respective colleges. Jake had his degrees from the University of Texas, and he had a Texan's characteristic superiority complex on anything related to Texas. He was wearing a wedding ring, but they hadn't gotten into discussions about family and Win had been able to deflect the conversation away from his work. Given the current political climate, he didn't want to discuss the FBI, proud as he was of it, in a crowded bar in Eastern Russia.

"You here on some top-secret mission? Folks don't just happen into Kamchatka; takes a helluva lot of effort just to get here," Jake finally remarked as he downed another small dried fish. He was apparently a little tired of Win's lack of candor on the job issue.

Win wiped his hands on a napkin and started to rise. "Tell you what, let's get out of here and talk about it on that run. You're welcome to go with me. I need to work the kinks out."

"Okay, good. I'll meet you in the lobby in fifteen minutes. Sound like a plan?" The Texan slid some tip money under his empty glass. He smiled. "Probably be safer to run in pairs. You've already seen that you have to keep your guard up out here."

Yep, heard that twice now . . . won't have to be told that again.

*   *   *

The rain stopped just before they set out on their four-mile run, but a cold fog was forming in its place. Win had explained that he'd been slowly working his way back up to his more typical five-mile outing because of a recent head injury, so they both loped along at a moderate seven-minute-mile pace. Win could see that the Texan could have pushed it much harder. The man was barely out of breath when they finally stopped to stretch at the boardwalk along the downtown's waterfront.

They'd run past a small lake that adjoined an even smaller park populated by trees that reminded Win of river birch. There was a gigantic bronze statue of Lenin, and directly across the square stood a more modest statue of Saints Peter and Paul holding a cross. *A bit of a paradox,* Win thought. The downtown area had a couple of large brick theaters and some modern office buildings; nothing was more than a few stories tall. The predominant structures were drab, Soviet-era five- to seven-story apartment buildings, where Win guessed the town's 180,000 residents lived. To most anyone else on the planet, this dreary city center, on this cold, gloomy evening, would feel outdated and depressed, but to Win it felt exciting, exotic, fascinating. Friends had teased him about his boyish enthusiasm and boundless curiosity his entire life, and he was having trouble concealing his excitement from Jake as he took in the simple wonders of this foreign place.

A mist was forming over the whitecapped bay, and the clouds lay thick against dark hills that ringed the opposite shoreline. Two massive naval vessels were moving up the foggy waterway toward the bright lights of the big naval base that sat farther up the churning channel.

"Wow . . . are those destroyers or cruisers?" Win's knowledge of naval weaponry was down in the little-to-none range.

The other man leaned forward on the metal top rail, his hands balancing his considerable frame as he stretched his calves during the cooldown. "Ahhh, no idea. Not really into military stuff . . . but they're big rascals, that's for damn sure." He glanced away from the ships and looked toward Win. "You know the Russkies have one of their largest naval bases just up this bay? The whole Kamchatka Peninsula was completely off-limits to civilians until 1992—much of it is still reserved for either the army or navy."

"Well, yeah, read a little about it. That's the naval base that caused the South Korean airliner to be shot down by the Russians back in the 1980s. Hundreds of innocent lives lost, all because of stupid Soviet paranoia."

Stedman didn't respond right away; he was watching the two huge steel-gray ships steam past. The noise from the massive engines was drowning out any hope for conversation; even the sound of the waves striking the rocks twenty feet below them was overpowered. Win could catch glimpses of sailors on the ships' decks through the wispy vapors; colorful flags snapped in the wind near the bridge and the bow—announcements of their arrival in port, he guessed.

He wanted to take a picture of the ships before the fog enveloped them and text it home to Will. His fifteen-year-old brother would think this was awesome. He was about to pull out his personal phone when he remembered it was locked in a safe in Anchorage. Using his Bureau phone was out of the question. Win thought back over the warnings during the call from the Bureau's Legat several nights ago: *"Don't do anything to give them a chance to hassle you . . . no questions, no interactions with military personnel or police, and, for sure, no drawings or photos. Your room could be bugged. . . . Always remember: the Russians are not our friends."* Win sighed and decided to buy a few postcards at the hotel; at least he'd have some mementos of the trip. He leaned into the fence to continue his stretching.

"Hey, you never did tell me what you're doing here. But if it's some big secret—well, hell, I get that, I guess."

Jake sounded a little hurt by Win's stonewalling on the job thing. The guy had saved his wallet and his dignity by nabbing the pick-pocket. *What the heck.* Win did a quick glance around to make sure no one could overhear. There wasn't anyone within twenty yards—the only other people nearby on the bay's boardwalk were an older couple watching the ships. They looked vaguely familiar—maybe the Scottish couple from the cab ride—he wasn't sure. *I reckon a little rain shouldn't stop the sightseeing.* Win turned back to Stedman.

"I work for the FBI, Jake. I'm here on an assignment, so I can't really discuss it. I don't want you to think I'm hidin' something. I'm on a flight back tomorrow night. Short trip."

Stedman straightened and his expression showed surprise, then a look Win was accustomed to seeing when he announced his employer: a mixture of wariness and awe. "No kidding? . . . The FBI? Wait till I tell the guys back in Houston I've met an FBI agent on assignment! Man, that's gotta be exciting!"

Win leaned into the fence to finish his stretch. "It can be, but not this trip. Just routine stuff, no excitement. But I'd like to keep it quiet, you know—who I work for while I'm out here."

"Sure . . . sure. I won't say a word." Jake nodded his head and grinned a conspiratorial grin. "Not a word."

"You ready to walk on back? It's lookin' like it might start raining again."

They headed away from the waterfront, crossed the street, and walked down a winding gravel path that cut through the waterfront park. It was only a little past 7:30 in the evening, but the nasty weather seemed to be keeping most everyone inside. Two bundled-up dog walkers and a small group of European-looking tourists were walking along the boardwalk that overlooked the bay, but the damp park looked deserted. They lapsed back into talk of football to pass the time for the hike back to the hotel.

"You remember that Cotton Bowl game a few years ago? Texas lost it on the final play?" Win asked.

"Naw . . . that's my team, but there were a few years when I wasn't really into the Longhorns. Family issues and such."

"That was a big, big game . . ." *Me catching that pass knocked Texas out of the championship race. No Texas fan coulda forgotten that.* Win couldn't conceive of anything that could totally override college football in any guy's mind. *Hmmm, that's kinda odd.* He went a different direction.

"Where'd you grow up in Houston? My dad had a good friend who was at MD Anderson for cancer treatments. Dad drove down there to visit him a couple of times. The cancer center is north of downtown in that rough area—The Woodlands, right?"

"Uh-huh, yeah . . . The Woodlands is a tough neighborhood," Jake replied. Then he said something about the weather. Win wasn't listening.

Uh, no it isn't. The Woodlands is the high-rent district and it's nowhere near the cancer center. Something ain't right.

Just as those unsettling thoughts were coming to roost, Win caught sight of a tall, slender female jogger moving through the park far to their left. Her face was hidden behind a fleece neck scarf, and her dark hair was pulled back in a ponytail. She was wearing black running tights and a black jacket. *Why is a woman running out here alone? Doesn't she know the dangers of this place?* There was a familiarity about her movement when she dodged a puddle in the trail. *The thief in the bar?* Win was suddenly on high alert. Stedman's own words, *Don't let your guard down,* flashed through his mind. He tried to tamp down his suspicions. *Geez, Win! You're gettin' as paranoid as the Russians. Lighten up!*

Jake was still rambling on about something related to energy production and the Siberian winter, but Win wasn't tuned in to him. His focus was on their surroundings as he tried to formulate a plan to separate himself from the guy and get back to the hotel alone. He might be overreacting, but he figured he'd play it safe. They were just entering the concrete pedestrian tunnel that ran under one of the town's main highways. Win hated dark, damp places to begin with—too many spots for spiders to hide—but his sense of unease climbed a few notches as he and Jake passed the rusted iron security gate and walked into the musty, dripping tunnel.

He'd hardly noticed the hundred-foot-long concrete cylinder when they'd run through it a few minutes earlier, but now the creepy factor was ramping up real high. Wild graffiti in red, black, and purple covered every inch of the walls. Dim yellow bulbs were struggling to light the gloomy interior. At least he could see the gray evening light at the other end. No one was lurking there. He took a deep breath and told himself again to settle down. He'd make some excuse and split from Jake when they cleared the tunnel.

Win had been so focused on what was in front of him that he flinched when Stedman quickly turned. Just then a raspy voice called out from behind them. "Stop there! Hands up! Get hands up!" The commands were in rapid succession from the heavier of three scroungy young men who stepped around the iron security gate. One of the men was holding an amber beer bottle, the second held an unlit cigarette, and the third was gripping a silver revolver that was pointed right at Stedman. Win and Jake obediently raised their hands as the men trooped under the dripping lip of the tunnel and into the faint light just ten feet away. The thugs were dressed in mismatched pants and jackets. All three were bareheaded, with stringy hair, unkempt beards, and darting eyes. The man holding the gun had colorful tattoos on his neck and on the exposed part of his wrist. He was moving the handgun in a circular motion and saying something to one of the others in rapid Russian. Even in the dull light, Win could tell that the revolver was rusted and pitted—these bad guys were classic street thugs.

Win might have suspected that Jake wasn't being straight with him, but now he had much bigger problems standing right in front of him. One of the lowlifes moved toward him, holding the beer bottle up like a club while stretching out his other hand in the universally understood gesture: *Give me your money!* Win was carrying all of his documents and his wallet—he hadn't felt safe leaving them at the hotel. That was not looking like a good decision; he was fixing to lose his wallet for the second time this evening. The gunman said something else in Russian and the third thug took several steps outside the tunnel to act as their watchman. They'd obviously played this game before.

Win and Jake were standing nearly shoulder to shoulder as the bottle-wielding thief approached. Win hazarded a quick glance at Stedman and saw him lean forward a tad and gesture with a slight nod toward the advancing bad guy. Stedman wasn't going down without a fight. That didn't seem real bright since they were unarmed, but Jake had apparently made a unilateral decision not to lose his money to this gang of miscreants. *So here we go . . .*

When the bottle swinger got within arm's reach of Win, Jake sprang toward the tunnel wall and shouted something in Russian. Win grabbed the thug's outstretched hand and twisted it backward as he pulled the guy into him as a shield. The bottle shattered on the concrete floor, and the man shrieked in pain as his wrist snapped. Win pushed off and the thug stumbled backward into the gunman. That guy got off a wild shot that ricocheted off the concrete wall before Stedman was on him. Jake delivered a punishing blow to the gunman's jaw, dropping him like a sack of flour. The cheap pistol hit the concrete path beside him. Win's opponent was still screaming in pain when Win drove two punches into his face that dropped him unconscious on top of his companion.

For a moment it seemed to be over, then the sharp crack of a handgun erupted nearby. The third thug had a gun, and he was shooting. Stedman was nearly in front of Win when Win saw him reach under his heavy sweatshirt and pull a small, black semiautomatic from a pancake holster on the small of his back. *Whoa! The Texan has a gun!* The guy was also amazingly quick and accurate with it. Stedman went down on one knee and fired twice toward the tunnel's entrance. Win heard the dull thud of bullets hitting their mark. He caught another glimpse of the slender female jogger. This time he saw her face—it was the woman from the bar, and she had a pistol in her hand. She was moving quickly through the trees toward the third thug's position.

Now Win *knew* he had another problem. Stedman turned his head just enough to meet Win's eyes as he started to rise. Those green eyes were cold and flinty. This man was *not* an oil company rep. Win had a split second to decide.

He lunged at Stedman before he could stand, grabbing for the pistol. After weeks of convalescence from last month's injuries, he knew he wasn't at full strength, but he was fighting for his life, and he fought hard. He knocked Stedman's gun hand into the hard wall of the tunnel and the small pistol fell and skidded away on the concrete. Stedman swung downward with his free hand—Win blocked the attack with his shoulder. The Texan kicked back, landing a blow to Win's midsection with his knee, but he was still slightly off balance and didn't connect with power. As Win fell backward, he kicked out and connected right behind Stedman's knee. Stedman groaned and went down hard against the wall. Win landed near the pile of unconscious thugs. His right hand scooped up the ancient revolver and brought it to bear on Stedman in one smooth move.

"Stop!" Win quickly rose to a low crouch, the rusted pistol now cradled in a two-handed grip.

Stedman froze, slumped against the side of the tunnel, his palms out in front of him as if to ward off the bullets. For a moment Win was aware of the flickering yellow light, of the damp, musty smell, of the low rumble of traffic on the road above their heads. Both of them were gasping for air and looking for a way out.

"Win . . . I . . ."

"Save it! You're with that girl . . . you're thieves too. You were setting me up, but these lowlifes beat you to it."

"No . . . no, man, you got that wrong."

"You were speaking Russian!"

"I told you I'd been over here some. I've picked up a few cuss words. C'mon, man, put the gun away." The Texas drawl was casual. Stedman started to stand.

Win cocked the hammer; the gun was steady. Stedman froze again.

Win dropped one hand from the grip and pulled out his Bureau phone. He remembered the emergency number that the Legat had given him. "I'm calling the police." He fumbled one-handed with the phone and prayed that he'd get a signal in the dingy tunnel. He didn't.

Stedman blew out a breath. Then, "Win, I am the police."

"What?" *Are you kidding me!* The guy looked serious.

"We were keeping an eye on you . . ."

"Show me some creds . . . your badge." Stedman didn't make a move. "Do it now!" Win glanced toward the tunnel's security gate and the pile of unconscious thieves. *Where has the girl gone?* "Slowly, just use two fingers . . . I want to see a badge!"

Stedman gingerly reached into the side pocket of his heavy gray sweatpants. He pulled out a small black case and held it up.

"Pitch it over here." Stedman threw it with two fingers. The credentials landed at Win's feet. He knelt lower and unfolded the case with his free hand, holding it up toward the light. A small photograph fell from the case and fluttered to the ground.

The credentials weren't so different from the ones Win carried. But there was no law enforcement badge. *Maybe they don't carry real badges in Russia,* he thought. He turned the credentials slightly in the dim light to try to make out something of the Cyrillic alphabet, and when he did, his breath caught in his throat. *CBP PФ* in large red letters. English translation: SVR RF, or Sluzhba Vneshney Razvedki Rossiyskoy Federatsii. Russia's intelligence agency, the modern-day successor to the KGB. This guy wasn't a policeman; this guy was a spook. A very dangerous spook. Win stared at him over the top of the credentials. Stedman sensed the shift in Win's eyes.

"You shoot me . . . you . . . you won't get away." He didn't sound as casual now.

Win stuffed the man's credentials in his pocket, put a knee down, and picked up the little photo. His mind was going in lots of directions. He was looking for options. The color photo looked like an elementary school portrait: a handsome little blond boy in a blue military jacket. "Who is he?"

"It doesn't matter." The Russian's voice was as hard as his face. He'd lost the Texas accent.

Win glanced again at the photo. The boy looked like a miniature version of the man he was facing down with the gun. "I would think it would matter more than anything right now," Win replied softly. "How old is he?"

The SVR officer swallowed hard and blinked a few times. "Is five. His name is Victor. Is his first school picture." The words were broken English with a Russian accent. Thoughts of his child had shaken the man.

Win was still hesitating. A large truck lumbered on the road overhead and the tunnel seemed to shudder. He was still processing his limited options. He wasn't sure where the small semiautomatic had fallen, but if he made a run for the end of the tunnel, there was a real good chance that Stedman, or whatever his name was, would shoot him in the back before he cleared the entrance. He'd seen how quickly the guy could move. But he couldn't pull the trigger on an unarmed man. He knew that wasn't one of his options, but Stedman didn't have to know that. Win realized that his window for escape was closing fast. He caught sight of movement in the dark trees beyond the security gate.

"Get up! Hands behind your head. You're going out of here with me—now!"

The Russian stood up and locked his fingers behind his head. Win crammed the photo in his pocket and pushed Stedman down the tunnel ahead of him.

Win stayed tight behind him, with one hand on his collar and the gun pressed into his back. Not the ideal way to move a prisoner, but he wanted to use the man as a shield in case they had company on the far side of the tunnel. And they did. He saw two armed men dart across the trail just before they cleared the entrance. He pulled Stedman to a stop and eased him back into the gloom. He heard movement back toward the security gate. Another large truck passed overhead; a trickle of gravel rolled down from the roadway. The steady drip of water from the tunnel ceiling added to the cadence of sounds. Things seemed to be moving in slow motion for Win. He felt his heart pounding in his ears. His breathing was heavy and his grip on the handgun was damp with sweat. Sticking the gun solidly into the guy's ribs, Win dropped a hand to check his phone again. Still no signal. No way to even call back home and report that he was in trouble. As he regained his grip on the collar, he realized he'd just run out of options.

"Take it easy," Win heard the Russian say. The Texas accent was back. "If you step out of the tunnel with a gun on me, they'll cut you down. No need to play that *Butch Cassidy and the Sundance Kid* scene . . . no need to die here."

Win didn't say a word. He silently prayed for God's protection—there was nothing else to do. He could see at least three people moving from tree to tree just beyond the tunnel's entrance. He glanced back down the length of the tube and saw a shape duck back behind the iron security gate. Someone from beyond the entrance yelled something in Russian, and Stedman called back a short answer. Win did nothing to stop him. He drew in a long breath and let go of the man's collar. The gun was still in his back.

"What did y'all say?" Win poked him a little with the revolver. Stedman kept his hands locked behind his head, but he turned slightly to look into Win's eyes.

"He asked me if I wanted them to kill you. I told him not yet." The green eyes didn't waver.

Win didn't know how to respond.

"Give me the gun, Win." The man was speaking just loud enough to be heard over the roadway's traffic. "You didn't kill me when you could have . . . that counts for something, believe me. You've just got to trust me on this. The gun?"

Win drew in a deep breath and nodded. He took his finger off the trigger, eased the hammer forward, and moved the weapon to the side. He closed his eyes for just a second to keep the man from seeing the fear that had risen in his chest. The last few minutes of his life had been relatively awful, but things really went to hell after that.

CHAPTER TWELVE

Win had used the "sweat 'em out" method in interrogations before: leave the subject handcuffed to a stationary metal table for an hour or so in an empty room to contemplate his or her fate. The Russians took that method to a whole new level. More than two hours after Stedman pushed him face-first into the damp concrete wall of the tunnel and then cuffed and blindfolded him, Win found himself zip-tied to a stout wooden chair with a cloth sack over his head, tissue in his ears, and a dirty gag in his mouth. They'd done a thorough search, stripped him of his jacket and running shoes, and left the blindfold on under the dirty sack. No one had spoken during the entire ordeal—not that he could have understood them if they had. Now he was sitting in an icy room, reliving the traumatic experiences over and over in his mind.

He'd been dragged out of the park and shoved into the back seat of a car with men on either side of him. Panic had nearly overwhelmed him when they'd gagged him, stuffed wadding in his ears, and dropped the dark sack over his head. He struggled to breathe through the gag and dense cloth. He pleaded with himself to remain calm, to take shallow breaths through his nose, to pray. But the sensation of suffocation was incredibly powerful—several times he thought he'd black out. And it wasn't a convenient time for his sense of smell to return. The cloth hood smelled of sour vomit. They'd used it before. He gagged down his own sickness; he knew he could drown in it if he started throwing up.

Sheer panic wasn't an emotion he'd experienced often in his life. There had been moments of it during the horrible episodes with Prophet Shepherd only a few weeks earlier, but nothing like this. . . . The Russians intended their cruelty, they meant to terrify him, to break him. And he had no earthly idea why.

He knew they'd driven for at least fifteen minutes; his usual excellent sense of direction had escaped him—he didn't know which way they'd traveled. When the car stopped, they'd yanked him out and roughly steered him up several steps into what he supposed was the first floor of a house or building. When they first entered the building and tied him down, he heard muffled noise through the wadding in his ears, but he couldn't distinguish the sounds. He was guessing at the time, but he figured that for over two hours he'd heard nothing, seen only blackness, smelled only the putrid cloth that covered his head. Despite his pleas to God for help, fear was sitting like a heavy weight on his chest.

Finally, he felt rather than heard someone come near him. Slight vibrations as people walked across the cold wooden floor. The sack was yanked from his head; the earplugs and the gag were removed by rough hands. The blindfold came off last. He squinted to adapt to the sudden brightness. As his vision cleared, he found himself staring directly into the deep-green eyes of Jake Stedman. The man was sitting less than four feet in front of him, still wearing his running clothes. He was leaning forward in a wooden chair with his elbows resting on his thighs, his hands clasped in front of him. His gaze reminded Win of a cat patiently waiting for the mouse to move—in no hurry to finish off its prey. Win tried to swallow, but he couldn't.

"Well, Cowboy . . . looks like the game's changed." Stedman's Texas drawl continued, "Why don't we make this as painless and brief as possible. Why don't you tell me who you're really working for and why you're here in my lovely country?"

Win blinked in confusion. As he tried to formulate a coherent response, his eyes raced around the drab room . . . a bedroom maybe? There was faded wallpaper; heavy curtains were pulled tight. Other than the chair Stedman occupied, he could see no other furniture.

Some sort of high-beam light clicked on. It was strung directly above his head; he could feel its radiating heat on his damp hair. He became aware of others in the room who'd been standing behind him. Two men in dark jackets and black balaclavas moved to Stedman's side and stared down at Win through the masks' openings. He felt the presence of others outside his line of sight. Win's breathing was rapid as his lungs tried to compensate for the hours with so little oxygen. His mouth was so dry that he had a hard time forming words, but he finally managed to answer.

"I . . . I don't know what you're talking about. You have my credentials . . . you know . . . you know who I work for . . . the United States Federal Bureau of Investigation. I'm here . . . here for a witness interview . . . it's been cleared with the local police."

Stedman didn't move at all; he didn't acknowledge the men who'd stepped beside him. He kept his focus totally on Win. He simply shrugged with his eyebrows and narrowed his eyes a tad. "My superiors seem to think that's just a convenient cover. They seem to think you've been sent here to harm a Russian citizen—your so-called witness perhaps? . . . Or are you a CIA operative up to some other mischief? Which is it, Cowboy?"

This has to be a nightmare. This can't be happening.

"*Как вас зовут? Что вы здесь делаете?*" Stedman softly asked him.

Win pulled back a little in the chair, confusion and frustration apparent in his face. *The guy is talking to me in Russian?*

"What's your name? What are you doing here?" Stedman shook his head. "Rather short-sighted of your people to send an operative here who doesn't speak the language." He sighed. "Either that or you're a great actor." He leaned back in the chair and drew a breath, "We'll know soon enough, I suppose."

Win flinched when someone behind him touched his head. He felt long fingers, gentle fingers, run through his dense hair; he smelled the faint scent of roses. "A pity that he wasn't friendlier to me earlier . . . sad that it had to go this way." It was the voice of the woman in the bar, yet it was different. There was a subtle Russian inflection to the educated

English accent. She was moving to his side as she kept talking in that alluring voice. "Such a handsome American . . . we would have had such a nice time." She ran the tips of her fingers across the T-shirt that was tight against Win's chest. "Da, a pity. We could have avoided all of this unpleasantness."

Win didn't look up at her, but the big Russian did. He smiled a thin, humorless smile. "You have great confidence in your powers of persuasion. As you say, it's pity we'll have to use mine."

Thirty minutes later, Win was still holding it together mentally; he'd suffered through a seemingly endless barrage of questions, accusations, and threats hurled at him by Stedman's two goons. It hadn't gotten physical, not yet, but Stedman allowed his two buddies free rein to threaten Win with every form of torture known to man. Win tried to reason with them at first, to point out that his documents contained agreements signed by Russian law enforcement, to tell them about his scheduled meeting with the FBI's Russian-speaking Legal Attaché, to give them any publicly known information. But he wouldn't talk about the deeper investigation or how he'd come to have information that a Russian citizen was needed as a material witness in a missing persons case. He wouldn't tell them about the ring. He wouldn't violate his oath not to speak to outsiders about pending case-related matters. And based on their questions, Win didn't think any of that was of great interest to them anyway. They were convinced there was a much more sinister motive for his arrival, and as time dragged on under the intense questioning, he began to realize that these men were determined to force some hidden truth from him.

Win's pulse accelerated as his interrogators moved away from him to confer with Stedman on the other side of the room. He could read it in their body language—things were fixing to ratchet up a notch. Win tried to regroup as he watched them. Even with the masks, he'd been able to recognize two of his tormentors as the Scottish tourist, who'd somehow lost his heavyset look, and the guard who'd manned the customs booth at the airport. *Does everyone in this town work for Russian intelligence?*

He'd long since exhausted everything he learned in his two-hour session at Quantico entitled "Proper Response If Held Against Your Will." The objective of the FBI's training was to humanize yourself, find something in common with your captors, appeal to their humanity and compassion. It hadn't taken Win thirty seconds to recognize that those elementary tactics weren't going to work with these folks. It was obvious these men had no qualms about using the enhanced interrogation techniques that the Bureau and American law enforcement forbid.

But even after the threats and strong-arm tactics, Win kept trying to assure himself that his captors wouldn't really harm him. *I'm in Russia on official business, for Pete's sake!* He kept telling himself that this was some sort of misunderstanding, some mistake that needed to be corrected, some heavy-handed misstep that would quickly end. *Be cool, be calm . . . it will soon be over,* he counseled himself.

The four Russians were huddled like a football team near the closed door on the other side of the room. The girl walked away from the group, produced a bottle of water from somewhere, and offered Win a drink. Fear of being poisoned was moving up his list of concerns as she held the bottle in front of him, but his parched throat cried out for the liquid. He nodded when she moved it closer; he took two long swallows. As the woman pulled the water away, he saw no malice in her eyes. But he saw no compassion either. His focus was on the girl, and when the smaller of the two goons backhanded him with a gloved fist, it caught him off guard. His head snapped back and he groaned, trying to shake the stars from his vision, just as another strike to his chin rocked him. Win tasted blood as his head slumped forward. Stedman said something in Russian and the thug stepped away.

The goon with the Scottish accent moved behind Win and yanked his head up by his hair. The room slowly came back into focus. Stedman was now in front of him, leaning onto the back of the other chair, his eyes intent on Win's. "My friends are becoming impatient, Cowboy. It's way past their suppertime . . . they are irritable. What can I say?" He shrugged. "It should be apparent that this line of questioning could go on for some time. As of now, well, they've just gotten your attention, just a tap to wake you up. It can get much, much more uncomfortable if you don't tell us what we need to know. You haven't been very forthcoming about this missing Russian woman . . . ah . . . what was her name?"

The Russians had upped the ante, but Win was far from folding. He was angry. "You know damn well what her name is! Natasha Yahontova! She's a geological researcher and a Russian citizen. She was reported missing in Yellowstone five years ago." He spit blood out to the side and glared at Stedman. "We've gone over this again and again! I'm here to try to find her, or at least give her family closure. Are you people so damn cold and cruel that you don't care about her, about her family? Is this your typical way of cooperating with foreign law enforcement? You're nothing but a bunch of godless barbarians!"

Stedman's face took on a harder look, and his eyes flicked up at the man still gripping Win's hair. Something unspoken passed between them and the cloth sack suddenly came down. Win's world returned to darkness and stench.

*　*　*

He wasn't sure how much time had passed. At least there was no gag or blindfold. At least he could still hear. He closed his eyes, reminded himself to breathe shallow breaths, and tried to still his frantic thoughts. Win knew any prospect of rescue was out of his hands. He had no leverage, no control whatsoever. He hoped against hope that the Legat's plane had landed, that Bennett was somewhere nearby, trying to straighten out this mess. He worked to calm his thoughts, ease his anxiety, lose the fear that kept gnawing at him. The Russians were trying to terrify him—he had to admit they were succeeding.

He asked God for the hundredth time for protection and realized that his prayers needed to get a bit more specific. He thanked God that he was still alive, that he'd had a second chance at life these last few weeks, and he asked Him for a bit more time in this world. Win told God he was sorry for pulling away since the shootings . . . for not feeling worthy to even approach Him. He confessed that he didn't understand it. He asked God for wisdom and courage to face whatever these goons would throw at him—to keep him from bringing any disgrace to his family, the Bureau, or his country. The fear and anxiety began to subside with the prayers; he began to silently repeat the Twenty-Third Psalm over and over as a mantra. There was nothing else he could do.

It had only been a few minutes—less than ten, he figured—when the heat from the intense light above his head began to permeate the rancid hood. Sweat was streaming down his face and breathing was becoming nearly impossible. The sensation of being smothered in the hot, putrid air was nearly overwhelming. He flexed every muscle against the restraints holding him fast to the heavy chair—they didn't budge. The feelings of panic began to resurface as he gasped for air. *Have they left me here to die?* He fought the pressing desire to call out for help—to plead with them for mercy. *Hell no! I won't give them that satisfaction!* He bit his bloody lip to keep from crying out; he tried to go back to reciting the Scripture, but he wasn't getting it right. He didn't know how long he could hold on.

The hood came off as abruptly as it had gone on. Suddenly he had air, suddenly he could breathe. The smaller goon was down on one knee in front of him. The guy clipped off a leg restraint, stripped off Win's sock, and held his bare foot up in a grip as tight as a vise. "Happens all the time," he was saying, "tourists get heroin . . . get in drugs. . . . So easy to overdose. Is easy. Find them in ditches, by the waterfront, behind bars. Overdose . . . happens all the time." He never looked at Win as he spoke. Win was trying to blink the sweat from his eyes, get oxygen to his lungs, get his mind back in gear. At first the words didn't compute. The Scottish-sounding guy moved around behind the kneeling goon. He pulled down his mask a bit and turned to face Win. He was checking the dosage in a syringe with a needle that looked at least two inches long.

"Too bad, laddie," he said. "He told me to give you one more chance—no more waste of time—one more chance to tell us how Dr. Orsky contacted you . . . why you think those bones are Russian . . . if anything else was found. Why you are here." His eyes were flat and indifferent. Win knew that look; he'd seen the eyes of an assassin before. The man held the syringe up to the light and tapped it.

They're going to kill me, Win realized, in shock. Time seemed to stop. The fear slipped away. He knew God was with him—knew he had seconds to do *something.* He knew he should forgive them. Knew it was the right thing to do, for his soul if not for theirs. He closed his eyes tight, then opened them to stare down his killers. *I should try to forgive.*

"One more chance, laddie," the man said again. "Tell me what we need to know . . ." He bent forward and moved the syringe toward Win's foot.

"Go to Hell" was Win's reply.

* * *

He tried to blink his heavy eyes open . . . but there was darkness— the blindfold was back in place. He smelled a sour mixture of strong coffee and his own sweat. A scratchy wool blanket was draped over him, and he was surprised to be able to move his left arm and tug it away from his neck. His right hand grasped metal chain links . . . he was handcuffed by one wrist to an iron bed frame.

One of Stedman's goons shook his shoulder and pulled the warm blanket away. "Sit up! Up with you now!" It was the man who'd been impersonating the vacationing Scotsman, the man Win thought was going to kill him . . . *How long ago?*

Win struggled to sit. He swung his legs off the small bed and his feet hit the cold wooden floor. Then the blindfold came off and he was staring up into Jake Stedman's friendly face. The man was standing over him, two steaming ceramic mugs in his hands. He sat one of the mugs on a side table and straightened.

"Ah, good morning, Cowboy! You look like you had a rough night!" He took a sip of whatever he was drinking and smiled down at Win over the mug. The tall Russian was dressed in the same brown bomber jacket and khaki pants that he'd worn in the airport, but those were the only similarities. The once sandy-blond hair was now wavy and dark. The once clean-shaven face now sported a mustache and dense beard, both nearly black. His green eyes were now brown, and his brows matched the beard. The same Texas drawl, the same man—yet unrecognizable. Win wondered for a moment if he was still caught up in a horrifying dream.

Stedman glanced at his wristwatch, "My, well after midmorning. You've had five hours of sleep . . . not bad."

Win blinked again. He drew a breath and tried to clear the cobwebs from his mind.

Stedman continued to talk. "The mock execution sometimes works. Sometimes doesn't." He shrugged. "Figured it was worth a shot, was gonna have to give you the SP-117 anyway." He cocked his head and studied Win. "Headache? Sick stomach? Disoriented? Complete loss of memory? Uh-huh . . . nasty stuff, that drug. We're really well acquainted now, Win. You just don't know how well acquainted, do you? You don't remember anything after the needle went in."

Actually, Win did remember the intense, burning pain from the injection between his toes. He remembered the horrible sensation of live fire flowing through every tiny vein in his body. He remembered his last defiant words to the Russian before his mind dropped into a bottomless black pit. Then nothing. He dropped his eyes and fought down the wave of panic sweeping over him. Several hours of his life were just gone. Gone. *Dear God, what did I tell them? What do they know?*

Stedman was still talking in a conversational tone. "Got you the closest thing I could find to American coffee and some bread with cheese and meat . . . need to eat a little to settle your stomach." Win raised his eyes. The man picked up the second mug from the table and held it out to Win. Steam was rising off the top of the black coffee.

He took the offered drink with his left hand and saw that the ceramic mug was shaking as he held it. *Get a grip, Win,* he warned himself. He steadied it against his running pants, lifted it again, and tried to take a sip. His mouth felt like it was stuffed with cotton.

Stedman stretched back and smiled. "Yeah, boy, we've got an exciting day comin' up. Beautiful out there this morning! The big mountains are shining, bright blue sky. . . . Hey, hey, don't look so glum. My superiors have taken a modest interest in your mission to find our countrywoman . . . ah, what is her name? Natasha? Ah, yes, Natasha Pavlovna Yahontova."

Win managed to swallow some of the hot liquid. He hoped he could hold it down. He took another sip. Then he asked, "Is . . . is that why I'm still alive?"

The Russian dropped the charm offensive. He pulled the wooden chair to within three feet of Win, sat down, and glared at him. Win saw the flinty glint in piercing eyes that were now brown. "If it had been my intent to kill you, Agent Tyler, you would be dead. After our little discussion last night, I concluded that you came here to find answers to this woman's disappearance. I happen to believe that is your only mission here. My superiors may have overreacted a bit initially, but they've had time to come to that conclusion as well. So now we must move that investigation along and get you back to America."

Win drew a deep breath. "I want to talk to the American consulate."

The other man leaned back and crossed one ankle over a knee. He looked at Win over his coffee mug and smiled. "Good luck with that. You're working with me today, buddy. We've got an investigative interview to conduct."

"I'm doing nothing with you! I demand to talk to the FBI Legal Attaché!" Anger was rising in him; he couldn't let these thugs break his spirit.

Stedman set his coffee mug on the floor and drew a credentials case from his jacket pocket. He flipped them open in front of Win and smiled again. "Well, you *are* in luck there, Cowboy. Special Agent Jacob Stedman, FBI Legal Attaché to the Russian Federation, at your service. You can call me Jake."

Win stared at the very real-looking FBI credentials in disbelief. The Russian waved one of the goons over with his free hand.

"Let my colleague hear my conversation with Special Agent Bennett at 4:00 a.m. this morning. Sorry you weren't available for that call, Win."

The masked man hit the PLAY button on a handheld recorder. Win heard static for a few seconds, then Stedman's voice in broken English.

"Hello? Special Agent Bennett, FBI? Yes . . . yes. Colonel Nikolay Kuznetsov, District Police Directorate for Petropavlovsk-Kamchatskiy. Is sorry for early hour." Win caught just enough of the response to recognize Bennett's voice in response. "The American FBI agent . . . Winston Tyler? Yes . . . yes, is in our custody since late last evening." There was a pause, and Win couldn't make out Bennett's reply. Stedman's voice again: "Yes . . . Agent Tyler is in good health . . . ah, perhaps feeling not so well . . . too much drink . . . too much . . . ah, how to say it . . . party? Is told he met women at hotel bar early evening . . . he goes to other bars. . . . was unruliness, fighting . . . heavy drinking." A garbled response from Bennett. Then Stedman again. "Young men can be unwise away from home, yes? Your Agent Tyler has no money left, perhaps no dignity left . . . but he is unharmed." Bennett's response was still not clear, but Win could tell it was the Legat on the call.

"He says he was to meet you . . . an interview with a citizen . . . I have papers here." Another response that Win couldn't understand, then, "Unfortunate your flights have delays; air travel in this region is sometimes problem." Bennett's indistinct answer, then, "No, no, you may not speak to him. I call you as a courtesy . . . Special Agent Bennett. I will be firm. Moscow wants this to stay at my level so as not to escalate. Young men can do childish things if they think no one is watching, but we are unhappy a U.S. federal agent has played the fool on Russian soil. We could file charges against him . . . jail him indefinitely. A great embarrassment for your government." Another pause for Bennett's response. "Yes, we will escort him to the interview and then to airport for his flight to . . . ah . . . Anchorage in Alaska. . . ."

Stedman waved the rest of the conversation away, and the man clicked off the recorder. Stedman stood up and looked down at Win. His tone was a soft Texas drawl, but its undercurrent was deadly serious. "This is how it's gonna go down, Agent Tyler. My friends are going to make sure you drink that coffee and eat this food, then you're going to shower and get dressed. Your things are here from the hotel. In forty-five minutes, *we* are going to drive to Svetlyi and *we* are going to interview a Russian citizen who may have some information to share about a missing woman. You will handle that interview, since you've prepared for it. If you cooperate, you will be on your flight back to America this evening, right on schedule."

Win's voice now had an edge. "And if I don't cooperate?"

Stedman squared his shoulders; he towered over Win. "Perhaps there's a time for foolish pride . . . this isn't one of them."

CHAPTER THIRTEEN

There was no conversation on the initial part of the drive from wherever they'd been to wherever they were going. Win was sitting in the back seat of a medium-sized, olive-green Russian SUV with a light bar on top and police insignia on the side panel. The driver and the man riding shotgun wore sidearms. They were dressed in the dark-blue uniforms of police officers, but Win figured they were part of the SVR team; their deference to the man he knew only as Jake Stedman was obvious. Stedman sat beside him, staring out the side window. He seemed lost in thought.

The modern two-lane highway snaked up the wooded slope of what could only be described as the most perfect-looking volcano Win could conceive. If you looked up *volcano* on the web, that sucker's photo would have been there. The perfect cone, far above them, was snow covered, and the scale of the mountain was immense. The sparse traffic seemed to consist mostly of military vehicles, minibuses, and an occasional small car. Some sort of aspen-looking tree species and brushy cedars made up the bulk of the vegetation. Houses and buildings became few and far between and the trees snuggled closer on either side of them as they continued climbing higher up the winding mountain road.

Win concluded that they'd been holding him somewhere in the outskirts of Petropavlovsk. He hadn't spotted any of the vintage Soviet apartment buildings that had been evident near his hotel, but he did glimpse the gleaming blue roof and gold onion domes of Trinity Cathedral, which stood on a hill overlooking the city. He'd seen it during his research on the internet, and he knew it was a couple of miles from downtown. They'd been driving for over an hour now, and most of the homes in this outlying area appeared to be wood frame with a shed or two and a garden area. Everything carried a layer of mud. Given that he could see his breath when they exited the house earlier, it was clear that early spring was still holding on in Kamchatka.

Stedman finally said something in Russian to the guy in the front seat with the broad yellow stripe on his blue lapels. That man nodded and spoke to the driver. Less than a minute later, the SUV slowed and pulled off the road into a scenic overlook. Stedman turned to face Win. "You've noticed that Dr. Orsky lives quite a distance from the city. In a rural district, as we say. We'll be at his house in a few minutes. You're concerned about his safety, about his facing some punitive action from us because of his contact with your authorities."

Win gave him a questioning look.

"I gathered those bits of information from you last night," the Russian explained.

And I'm sure that isn't all you got.

"You don't need to concern yourself with those matters, Agent Tyler. If Dr. Orsky can provide useful information about this missing woman, there won't be repercussions for him. Like you, we simply want the truth."

Sure you do.

"I'll let you conduct the interview. The sergeant"—he nodded toward the man riding shotgun—"will attend. That was arranged by your Legal Attaché and is the normal procedure during these types of interviews. I will be there as your translator, to assist you. Dr. Orsky is expecting us, I called him last night," he paused and smiled, "when I arrived here from the U.S. Embassy in Moscow. *I am* your FBI Legal Attaché in Moscow. Remember that." Stedman tilted his head toward the fake sergeant. "Dr. Orsky was also contacted by the local police this morning to confirm the appointment."

Win nodded that he understood—no *real* police were involved. Win looked away and stared out the window at the sweeping view of the city and the dark-blue bay far below them; he was in no mood to talk to the man.

But Stedman wasn't finished with his little briefing. His tone became sharp. "We are professionals. You are a professional. I expect you to act like it. . . . I expect you to do your job today."

Win swung angry eyes back to Stedman, who cut him off before he could speak. "Your ordeal last night was unfortunate, but it's behind you. Get over it. You'll be back in America in a few hours. Remember why you are here. Some good may come from your efforts." With that lecture hanging in the air, Stedman left the vehicle and headed for the public toilets on the far side of the parking lot. The driver signaled Win out, and they all hit the facilities.

A few minutes later, Win walked to the edge of the overlook while the two fake cops stood by the police SUV, smoking cigarettes. Win wasn't taking in the view. He was trying to compartmentalize his jumbled emotions, trying to cut through feelings of being violated, of being controlled. He couldn't seem to get a handle on the awful sensation of having lost several hours of his life once those drugs hit—he had no memory at all. Stedman's lecture had actually helped. *I am a professional—act like it. Just keep it together . . . get the job done.*

"You come from a beautiful part of the world, but you haven't seen anything compared to this," Stedman said as he came up behind Win. "The big lake in your hometown, Greers Ferry Lake . . . it is lovely."

"So we discussed my hometown during that drug-induced interrogation?" Win asked bitterly.

"No, no. I looked you up on Google: Win Tyler, football star from small-town Arkansas." Win turned his head toward the man in surprise. The Russian smiled. "Even godless barbarians have the internet, Agent Tyler."

The Russian stepped to Win's side. "The Kamchatka Peninsula is about two-thirds the size of your California, yet it has the largest concentration of volcanoes on earth, hundreds of them. Twenty-nine are active now. We are on the lower side slope of Avachinsky. It stands

2,741 meters above Petropavlovsk. Its last eruptions were in 1991 and 2008, not so long ago. Later in the summer the trails are open all the way to the top. . . . Actually, volcano trekking is a bit of a thing here." His hand swept over the unimpressive skyline of the city's Soviet-era apartment buildings, toward the waterfront. "The Avacha Bay is one of the world's best natural harbors, and twenty kilometers across the bay . . . see the town there? That is Vilyuchinsk, a restricted city, open only to the military. It is home to our largest nuclear submarine base.

"The other two volcanoes that encircle the city are Kozelsky and Koryaksky. Neither of them are highly volatile at the moment." He shook his head. "But at any second they could erupt—rather like your Yellowstone, just a different type of volcano. It's a risk to live atop a monster, I suppose." He scanned the horizon again. "Ah, but such beautiful monsters on a day like today!"

"You sound like a tour guide, Stedman. . . . What's your real name?"

"Ah, let's not worry about real names—that doesn't matter. And this place? I was stationed here for short periods off and on early in my military career. There are some good memories here." He smiled at those memories, then lifted his chin toward the SUV. "Let's go solve a mystery, shall we?"

* * *

They pulled off the highway onto a muddy two-track with grass growing in the middle. They weaved through a thicket of wispy trees to a clearing boasting a low frame house with a rusty minivan sitting in front. It wasn't an upscale place by any stretch: the walls hadn't seen paint in years, weeds had overtaken a flower garden, and a rickety wheelchair ramp extended from the small porch to a gravel landing. A very large woman in a yellow cotton dress and lace apron stood on the porch and ushered three of them in. The driver stayed put and pulled out his cigarettes.

All three of the visitors shed their shoes after they walked in the door. Win was glad he'd worn a good pair of socks. The Russians had rituals that had to be followed before a meeting began, just like down

South. Win was accustomed to sitting with coffee or a coke for a few minutes—talking about the weather, hunting, fishing, or the latest sports event—getting to know the folks. Where he'd grown up it was rude to just jump into business. The Russians seemed to have that same civilized tradition.

The woman, who'd been introduced as Dr. Orsky's sister, seemed to be his caregiver as well. Win watched her adjust the oxygen canister that sat beside his wheelchair. The geologist was thin and frail, nothing like the photographs of the vigorous middle-aged outdoorsman Win had seen on the internet. A folded blanket covered his legs, but his handshake was firm, and his eyes were clear when he turned to Win during the introductions.

The woman set a tray of porcelain teacups and a steaming kettle down on a low table in the center of the room. There were already small plates with some type of pastries there. It was just after three o'clock, and Win figured this must be the Russian version of high tea, like the British observed. He wasn't hungry, but he didn't want to offend anyone, so he followed Stedman's lead, picked up a plate, and ate a doughnut-like thing. He smiled and nodded when the woman poured more tea into his delicate cup. Stedman carried on a cordial conversation with them in Russian—so that the lady could be included, Win guessed. The fake police sergeant was pleasant; he threw in a few comments. After the formalities, the woman added a couple of logs to the black iron stove in the corner and left the room. Dr. Orsky set his teacup on a side table and switched the conversation to perfect English.

He thanked Win for coming, for making such an effort to find the missing. He glanced at the fake policeman and sighed. He said he hadn't done international communications in years, said he'd feared someone in his country suspected him in Dr. Yahontova's disappearance and was watching him. Admitted that he'd been paranoid for far too long. He apologized for not being more forthcoming when he was interviewed by the authorities in Yellowstone five years ago. He said it had nagged at him. He told them that he'd been injured during an eruption of Shiveluch volcano on the upper end of the peninsula over four years ago. Too close to the summit when it blew, he shook his head sadly. Just one more sample, he remembered saying, just one more risk, tempting fate one more time. He shook his head again. Others had died that day. He'd lost the use of his legs and the heat had damaged his lungs. He'd never been a religious man before that, said he wasn't sure if he was now. But after his accident, some force prodded him to come forward about Natasha Pavlovna Yahontova. Still, for years, he'd done nothing.

Then two summers back he'd seen an article in a scientific journal about the disappearance of Janet Goff in Yellowstone. He'd known then that he must reach out. But he didn't. Not until he saw Win's interview replayed on the internet a few weeks ago. Not until he heard Win say that the lost are never lost to those who love them. At that point, he admitted to himself that he had indeed loved Natasha Pavlovna. He'd betrayed that love by being a coward, by not telling the entire truth so long ago.

The man had told his story, but Win knew it was nowhere near complete. He began the process of digging deeper to find the hidden truths. He used questions and statements to fill in the blanks, to coax out more of the details. Witness interviews was one area of Bureau work where Win didn't lack confidence. He'd honed those skills in long, difficult interrogations during his work on one of the largest public corruption cases on the East Coast. He knew he was good at it. He used a low, calm tone of voice to draw out Dr. Orsky's memories of the geological expedition to Yellowstone, of his unrequited love, of his impressions on the day Natasha disappeared. There was a rhythm to it, the questions and answers, the past laid out in front of them. After nearly an hour, Win began to hone in on the most critical issues.

"I don't want to be indelicate, Dr. Orsky . . . but you think she and Dr. Ratliff were lovers. That it had been going on before you joined the expedition that summer. That their relationship had become volatile in some way?"

"Yes . . . it was as you say." The man stared at his hands. "Natasha Pavlovna is a fiery woman, a person of great passion—for her work and, yes . . . yes, for that man." There was sorrow in his voice.

"Did you ever see or even sense that there was violence in their relationship?"

"No . . . but angry speech sometimes, angry looks. Shortly before she was gone—perhaps less than a week—I felt a change in her. She had been studying the open steam vents and springs, trying to understand their internal structure. The one in the Mud Volcano area was of great interest to her, it is called Dragon's Mouth Spring, if I remember correctly. There is another one, an even more intriguing one, at Maxwell Springs . . . it is called Devil's Breath." He studied his hands for a moment before deciding to go on.

"Dr. Ratliff was not happy with her study of those features, and they argued often. It seemed to have come to a head that week. She wouldn't talk about it to me. I assumed it was the danger in studying the vents . . . I assumed she was . . . perhaps . . . perhaps taking unusual risks that Dr. Ratliff didn't feel were warranted. She wanted to map the interior of those features. It had never been done."

"Why not?" Win asked.

Dr. Orsky seemed taken aback by Win's question. "Why, the danger, the extreme danger. Those features are live steam vents, wildly fluctuating heat from 170 to 320 degrees Fahrenheit. They sometimes contain hot springs—often toxic—which rise and fall in depth. Very unpredictable. They can also form an antre, ah . . . in layman's terms, they can be cave-like, with rooms beyond the entrance, tunnels, and passageways."

The entrance to Hell. Win remembered Luke's translation of the handwriting.

"Is that why you sent me the clipping with the handwriting added to the magazine article? Where did you get that?"

The geologist seemed embarrassed by his answer. "It was something of hers . . . a small thing she had, the clipping—from a scientific journal, I suppose. The article was about the cavernous nature of some unique steam vents. I had joined the expedition only three weeks before, and I . . . well, I was hopeful for a relationship with her. We were drinking vodka . . . it was June 12th. We were the only Russians on the team, so she had gone out with me that night."

"June 12th has some significance?" Win asked.

The fake sergeant shifted in his chair and scoffed. Stedman answered the question. "It's Russia's Independence Day."

"Yes," Dr. Orsky continued, "it was Russia Day—so she, ah . . . she stayed with me and the more we drank, the more she talked of how one could enter the steam vent, walk in the spring, go down into the volcano . . . go to the center of the earth. We were laughing about it, but I think now that she was serious; she thought it was possible to touch the inside of the volcano and return whole. She wrote notes on the article." His face reddened a bit. "I . . . I kept it as a remembrance of that night. As my health declines, I need to let go of some things." He paused. "So, I sent it to you, Agent Tyler. But I don't think you can take what she wrote literally . . . surely she never tried to enter an active steam vent." His voice didn't sound as certain as his words.

"Why not map the vents with thermal imagining, sonar, or satellite imagery?" Win asked. He knew the geological expeditions used high-tech instrumentation.

The man smiled. "Ah yes, that is how we know of the antre, of the open spaces. But seeing those things with your eyes, touching the inside of a volcano with your hand, even with the danger—perhaps in spite of the danger—that is exhilarating. That awareness cannot be compared with just knowing something exists."

"The day she disappeared at Mud Volcano . . . could she have tried to enter the mouth of the spring, uh, the steam vent?"

"No. No, too many tourists were there, too much equipment would be required, and an assistant would be necessary. We dropped her off at the Mud Volcano parking lot at 5:30 a.m. She didn't have any equipment . . . no protective suit, nothing except measuring devices . . . said she was going to do some heat readings in the upper area. There were tourists in the parking lot at that hour, I remember several bison were standing there and everyone was trying to get photographs. As she was getting her pack out of the van, I told her we'd pick her up for lunch—that was our normal routine. I noticed that she seemed excited, maybe anxious. I remember wondering why."

"Anything else you can add? Your original statement contained few details." Win noticed Stedman was leaning forward a bit, really focused on this line of questioning. They were getting to the crux of the matter, both Win and Stedman knew it.

The geologist paused for a long moment and stared into the past. "There was an untruth. . . . I told your authorities that Dr. Ratliff was at my research site that day. It was planned for him to be with me later that morning on the southeast side of the Sour Creek Dome, about four miles from Mud Volcano. Dr. Ratliff never came. He did not come to help us search for Natasha Pavlovna that afternoon. I didn't talk to him or see him until late the next morning. He was with Simon . . . ah, Dr. Simon Dravec. Simon told me Dr. Ratliff had been working a new site near the Norris Geyser Basin with Dr. Christopher Warren. It was odd, we hadn't worked with Dr. Warren's group often, but Natasha did occasionally meet that man for dinner—we all thought it was to make Dr. Ratliff jealous . . . more attentive to her. She trifled with Dr. Warren a bit." He looked uneasy saying things that were unflattering about the woman he loved.

He sighed and turned back to the memory. "That next afternoon, I hadn't yet given a full statement to the park rangers . . . we were still searching for Natasha Pavlovna the day after she disappeared. Simon took me aside and asked me to give very few details to the police . . . said Dr. Ratliff would appreciate my brevity. He implied that my career could be harmed if I had too much to say." The man drew a deep breath, or tried to; he fiddled with his oxygen monitor for a moment, then added, "I traded my suspicions, I traded the truth, for advancement in my field." He didn't meet the other men's eyes. "I have felt shame for those lies every day since."

"You suspect she was meeting Ratliff that morning?" Win asked.

"Yes, but I have no proof."

"Could it have been Dr. Warren instead?"

The man gave a dismissive shake of his hand. "No, no, I wouldn't think so. Christopher Warren is an amateur. A gifted amateur, perhaps, but not a committed researcher. He wouldn't be of any real interest to someone with Natasha Pavlovna's professional promise."

Win wasn't so sure about that.

"What about Simon Dravec? Where was he in this?"

Dr. Orsky seemed puzzled. "Simon? Dr. Dravec? Yes, Simon was always in the background. He planned the expeditions, the logistics, the lectures. He'd been working with Dr. Ratliff for years before we met. He is a very skilled geologist, by the way . . . but he always seemed content in his role. The perfect assistant."

Win switched back to the day of the disappearance. "You said she seemed excited when you and your colleague dropped her off. Do you remember anything else that you didn't report earlier? Anything that could help us, Dr. Orsky?"

The man struggled to draw a deep breath. Win could tell his strength was beginning to fade. "She . . . she had them on that morning."

"What?"

"She had her ring and necklace on." He met Win's eyes and smiled at the memory. "She had a beautiful ring and necklace that she'd wear on occasion . . . when we'd go out as a group to a restaurant, or even around the campfire some nights. She said the jewelry had been passed down in her family and it dishonored her ancestors' memory to keep it locked away, not to wear it. So she'd wear the jewelry sometimes, but I had never seen her wear the ring or necklace at work. The chemicals in the field are often corrosive, and that is especially true at the Mud Volcano area—one of the water-filled sinkholes there has the acidity of battery acid. Why risk damaging the jewelry? I remember wondering if someone was meeting her. I almost asked her that before we drove away . . ." He let that trail off and a penetrating sadness settled in the room. Win knew they wouldn't be getting much more.

*　*　*

The driver pulled up to the curb and let the police vehicle idle there. The fake police sergeant left the vehicle, then reappeared a few minutes later with a cardboard tray of drinks. "Coffee and tea, sir. There's a bit of a delay for the plane," he reported as he handed out the refreshments.

Stedman added a packet of sugar or something to his drink, had a taste, then settled himself back in the seat to wait.

Win took the offered paper cup and killed the time by watching a group of loud American sportsmen congregate nearby. They were gesturing excitedly, several days' stubble and sunburn on each face, eyes gleaming with satisfaction. The indistinct voices with northeastern accents invaded the closed vehicle. They were probably retelling adventures of pulling in twenty-pound salmon or trout, of encounters with the exotic wildlife in the wilderness of Eastern Russia, Win supposed. He longed to call out to his countrymen, to warn them of the dangerous men sitting mere feet away. To tell them that Kamchatka contained more terrifying creatures than its infamous brown bears. He fought the desire to flee after them; he forced down his feelings of helplessness. The Americans moved away and blended into the throng of travelers entering the terminal building. Win turned his attention back to his captors. Everyone had been silent on the nearly two-hour drive to the airport. He wondered again how this was going to play out. *Will they really let me go?*

Stedman had donned a police officer's jacket and cap before they'd driven to the airport. Now he adjusted the cap's visor to shield his face. A real policeman in a crisp blue uniform walked toward the car, annoyed that a colleague would park directly in front of the terminal. Stedman pulled his credential case from a pocket and held it up to the closed window. The officer glanced at it, saw the red SVR designation, and visibly stiffened. He saluted awkwardly and quickly moved away from the vehicle.

Stedman pocketed the credentials and shifted toward Win. "You've got a couple of choices, Agent Tyler."

"Is that how you see it?" Win took a long sip of his coffee and watched the Russian's eyes.

"Your agency thinks you've botched this assignment . . . played the fool . . . managed to get in your witness interview and safely leave our country only through the good graces of the Russian government. To say it politely, they think you're a screwup. It wouldn't be the first time your bosses have come to that conclusion, would it?"

No, it wouldn't be. . . . Lord only knows what he drug out of me last night. Win didn't respond, but his expression probably gave his morbid thoughts away. He took another swallow of the coffee and tried to figure out where this was going.

"They'll do lab work, but the drug we used last night leaves no trace after twelve hours," Stedman said. "There's no one here to corroborate your story of being detained and interrogated by our intelligence service."

"You're suggesting?"

Stedman cocked his head and shrugged. "Much better for you if your superiors think this was just a police matter, the simple arrest of a drunken young fool. . . . If they even *suspect* you were drugged or in our custody for a number of hours, your chances of advancement in the FBI are completely blown. You're compromised . . . your government would never be able to trust you with its secrets. You'd immediately lose your top-secret clearances. Much better to be viewed as a bumbling screwup than a national security threat, wouldn't you say? You're a smart man . . . you've already thought that through."

Actually, Win hadn't thought that through. It had never occurred to him to fabricate his report to keep his career. And thinking wasn't happening real well all of a sudden. Stedman's face was fading in and out as Win tried to focus; dull pain was suddenly pounding at his temples.

Win didn't have a chance to answer. Two men in blue police uniforms abruptly pulled him and his belongings from the vehicle. Tourists and soldiers scattered out of their path as they marched him, arm in arm, through the airport, down the jetway, and to the plane's door. A stewardess stood at the entrance and glared at him. No one else was boarding; the plane appeared to be waiting for them. The headache and the blurred vision were suddenly worse; Win swayed as his guards handed his bag and briefcase to the stewardess. His gait was unsteady as he tried to step toward her into the fuselage.

The guy who'd originally been a Scottish tourist had Win's left arm in an iron grip. He steadied Win in the doorway and whispered in his ear. "Do not be alarmed by this sickness, lad. You had a bit too much vodka last night—a severe hangover is expected. You will sleep most of the flight, then you will be fine."

"In . . . in the . . . the coffee?" Win asked with slurred speech. The fake policeman raised his eyebrows with a slight nod of affirmative. Win didn't remember much of the flight. He never did see Petropavlovsk's famous volcanoes from the air.

CHAPTER FOURTEEN

There were three of them—stony faced, dark suits and ties—you don't see that often these days. They couldn't have been more obvious if they'd worn signs around their necks proclaiming *FBI*. Win still wasn't feeling real great as he walked out of the jetway and directly into them. The thin, late-forties-something guy in the lead stepped forward and introduced himself as the Anchorage SAC. There were no other introductions, and no one made a move to shake hands.

It was nearly eleven Anchorage time, and except for the departing passengers from Kamchatka, the international gate concourse was deserted. The agents took Win's briefcase, phone, and carry-on and herded him down the concourse, bypassing the customs booths, to a sterile security room where a burly man in a white coat sat him down in a metal chair, removed his jacket, rolled up his sleeve, stuck in a needle, and took three long vials of blood. The med tech dabbed some sort of ointment on the small cuts under Win's chin, on his knuckles, and near his jaw. He began checking his vital signs. One of the agents was methodically searching Win's carry-on, as the Alaska FBI boss glowered down at him. Foul smells were filtering through the small room from Win's open luggage. The agent pulled out Win's crumpled wool shirt and khakis—they reeked of blood and liquor. The Anchorage Field Office boss obviously didn't like being ordered to the airport in the middle of a Saturday night to deal with an errant agent. He began hammering Win even before the med tech finished his tasks.

"You've embarrassed the Bureau and your country! I can't image how many strings had to be pulled to get your ass out of there! A bar fight! Call girls! A simple interview trip—you turn it into an international incident and land in jail!" The red-faced man's anger was barely controlled; he wasn't shouting, but it was close.

Win started to give a reply, but the SAC held up his hand to silence him. He stared back down at Win. "We'll make sure nothing's planted in your bags or on your phone . . . we'll get the lab results down to Seattle, and Reed here will be shadowing you till you meet our guys in the lower forty-eight. You listen to me, Agent Tyler"—he nodded toward the short redheaded guy rifling through Win's briefcase—"Reed doesn't leave your side until he hands you off to our counterintelligence folks when you get off the red-eye in Seattle. You don't go to the head without him. You don't talk to him. In fact, you don't talk to anybody after you take a call from Brent Sutton, Counterintelligence Supervisor in Seattle. You got that!" It wasn't a question. He turned on his heel and stormed out of the room.

The red-haired agent placed a call and handed Win the phone as the med tech pitched his latex gloves in the trash, gathered his samples and notes, and followed the SAC out the door.

The Seattle Counterintelligence Supervisor was direct. "What happened?"

Win closed his bloodshot eyes and cleared his throat. "It wasn't the way the Russians are telling it, sir. It wasn't that way at all. They nabbed me. They were SVR. A man they called Jake Stedman was running it. . . ." There was silence on the other end of the line. Win started talking faster. "Big guy, blond hair. He approached me at the airport, right after I got off the plane, said he was from Houston. He sounded like a Texan—"

The supervisor cut him off in midsentence. His voice was so loud that Win knew the other two agents in the room could hear every word. "I don't want to hear this crap! The Russian police sent us surveillance video and still shots from the bars. No spies involved in this, just you being incredibly reckless and stupid! SVR? Not a chance! You're trying to cover your butt!" He paused for a second to let that sink into Win's shell-shocked brain.

"I don't want a word about your little misadventure communicated to anyone until you get to the Seattle office for a formal debrief. Not a word spoken, written, texted, nothing done before that debrief. Then . . . then you get your story straight. You understand me!" That wasn't a question either. Win was at a total loss. He couldn't even respond.

The supervisor's harsh tone softened just a bit. "I'm disregarding what you've told me on this call . . . this isn't going on the record. You're under a lot of stress, I get that. But you better have your report in order when you hit this office!"

Thankfully, the Seattle flight was boarding when Win finally left the security room with Reed and another agent in tow. It was feeling way too much like a fugitive escort. He'd managed to get his small Bible from his bag and stick it in his pocket, figuring he needed all the Divine help he could get, but his Glock was in his carry-on, not on his person, and he wasn't liking that a bit. Agent Reed didn't have ten words to say to him as they filled out their handgun transport papers at the gate. Win signed the paperwork, then did a double take at the date—it was still Saturday, the 7th of June. They'd crossed the international date line on the flight back to America. He was doomed to continue living what had already felt like the longest day of his life. The drug-induced headache and queasy stomach had completely subsided by the time they went wheels up for the long flight, but bewilderment, frustration, and despair were now his traveling companions.

* * *

Win's greeting party in Seattle was no more welcoming than the agents in Anchorage. After the initial introductions at the gate, his two-agent escort didn't say a word. They drove him from the airport into the secure underground parking area at the Seattle Field Office on Third Avenue, up the elevator to the fourteenth floor of the massive office building and deposited him in Brent Sutton's empty office. A kind clerk gave him a weak smile, pointed out the facilities, and brought him a lukewarm cup of coffee. She left him there to cool his heels for another twenty minutes.

Win knew Seattle was one of the Bureau's larger field offices, with several hundred agents. He knew that was where part of the Bureau's East Asia counterintelligence efforts were based. He remembered a lecture at Quantico where they pitched that line of Bureau work. The "other side of the house," he'd heard it called. Not the criminal or public corruption cases that so many associated with the FBI, but the equally critical work of tracking down spies, disrupting foreign intrusions, and nailing any Americans suspected of selling out the country's secrets.

That Bureau career path didn't appeal to Win. He thought of himself as more of a "get 'er done" kinda guy—he liked the relatively rapid resolution of cases, the wide variety of casework, from bank fraud to kidnappings, and the satisfaction of seeing bad guys brought to justice. He'd been told that counterintelligence work was often covert, that surveillance work on subjects might last years, not days or weeks. And espionage indictments were few and far between—often the subjects of the Bureau's considerable efforts simply slipped back to their own countries before punitive action could be taken. Nope, counterintelligence work wasn't for him.

He was reflecting on that when Brent Sutton stuck his head in the office and told Win, in a none-too-friendly voice, to leave his bags and follow him. Then he started down the hall without looking back. Win fell in behind him and the queasiness immediately returned. He tried to get his mind off his discomfort by focusing on the supervisor. Sutton wasn't tall, six feet at most, with a runner's slim build. He was probably in his mid-forties, with receding brown hair. His crumpled gray suit looked like he'd worn it for days. There was an air of tension and urgency about him that made Win wonder if something big was going down. He hoped like hell that *he* wasn't the something big.

They entered the large, wood-paneled conference room, with its sweeping panoramic view of Elliott Bay and the city's waterfront. Win's attention was immediately drawn to the jaw-dropping vista of blue water, green islands, and white-and-green ferries. He forced himself to turn his attention to the unpleasant matter at hand. He'd worked for hours to shut the horrible experiences in Russia out of his mind. Now it was time to open that door, drag the nightmare into the light, and let these experts make sense of it all. Win desperately needed allies, but a glance at the three other faces in the room told him none were in attendance. *I'm on my own here.*

Two nondescript men were seated about halfway down the long mahogany conference table. They hadn't stood when the supervisor and Win entered the room, and they didn't look happy to be there. Sutton introduced them as Barry Jones and Charles Smith, both with the State Department. Win knew enough now to realize that Smith and Jones weren't their real names, and they certainly weren't with the State Department. They'd been sent to downtown Seattle at eight on a weekend morning because an inexperienced FBI agent had screwed something up overseas. Win could tell from their condescending looks and their lukewarm handshakes that they both thought they had better things to do.

The fake Mr. Jones was thumbing through his phone messages, frowning. He ran a hand through his hair and started talking before Win even hit his seat. "Doesn't look like you had an uneventful flight on Yakutia Airlines into Alaska . . . let's see . . . you vomited in the john twice. Staggered up and down the aisle three times after that . . . passed out in your seat, then had to be awakened when the plane touched down." His eyes shot up from the screen and met Win's. "That about cover it?"

"We had someone on the plane?"

"Of course we had someone on the plane! And in the airport and outside the terminal! We don't have FBI agents land in Russian jails all that often, Agent Tyler. Like never."

The older CIA officer leaned back in his chair and folded his hands over his stomach. "In case someone hasn't already explained this to you: You are in big trouble."

Win started to speak, but the guy held up a hand to silence him. Win normally had a slow fuse, but he had reached his limit. He rose halfway out of the chair and glared at the men. "I don't get the impression that any of you gives a damn about what really happened over there!"

He felt Sutton's hand on his shoulder, pushing him back down into the chair. The supervisor's words were forceful, but not heated. "Calm down. You'll get your say. You'll write your report . . . just stay calm and keep quiet while we go through this." His hand squeezed Win's shoulder again, and he repeated himself for emphasis. "Agent Tyler, Win, it's in your best interest not to say a word during this meeting." Win swallowed down an angry retort.

Sutton spread out an array of black-and-white photos in front of him. Photos in the hotel bar with the female pickpocket talking to him, leaning into him, smiling provocatively, laughing as she hung onto him, way too much cleavage showing. Taken totally out of context, but damning. Then there was the video that Sutton pulled up on his laptop. It appeared to be some type of surveillance tape of a bar fight—the two-minute film was blurry, and Win knew it wasn't him, but the clothes matched. As he watched it through for the second time, even he couldn't be sure it wasn't him. He sat back and blinked a few times after the tape ended its second run. *Lordy, this ain't good.* The sick feeling in his stomach returned with a vengeance.

Sutton started talking as they all stared down at the evidence the Russian police had provided. "Lab tests in Anchorage still showed 0.06 alcohol in your bloodstream . . . that was nineteen hours after our Moscow Legat, John Bennett, got the call from their police that you were in custody. Your vital signs were dead on for a man your size who had really tied one on—drunker than Cooter Brown the night before, and obviously drinking again yesterday. No other drugs showed up in your system. I have no idea how you managed to conduct your witness interview in that condition. Thank goodness the Russians let you tape it." Sutton wrapped it up. "We found nothing on your phone or in your luggage that suggested they'd been compromised."

But I have. That jarring thought reverberated through his being. *I have. No one is going to believe a word that I say.* Win felt as if he were leading someone else's completely fouled-up life. His world had been turned upside down in the last forty-eight hours, and he had no idea how to right it.

The events that followed were a little foggy in Win's mind. The conference-room door opened wide, and a woman handed the Counterintelligence Supervisor a note. Sutton glanced at it and was suddenly on his feet, nearly yelling at the CIA men that the Bureau would deal with their own problems and that Win was still an FBI agent. The CIA men both stood up and shouted that Win should be prosecuted for some federal violation and that they would have him arrested if the FBI didn't move on it. The woman backed into the wall with a shocked look, the door still ajar. Win glimpsed startled faces in the hallway, people peering around cubicles to see what the ruckus was about.

Sutton shouted out the doorway to a short African American guy who appeared to have had the misfortune of just walking past the open door. "Humphrey! I want Tyler out of here! He's admitted to a drunken brawl in Russia. I want him on that plane back to nowhere today. Drive around, sightsee, I don't care! I just want him out of this office and out of my sight. Get him on that plane, then he's Denver's problem!"

* * *

"I didn't admit to anything."

The guy gave Win the same answer he'd given him three times before when Win had tried to bring it up. "Not my issue."

"Why can't I call someone?"

Humphrey patted his jacket pocket. "Because I have your phones and they stay with me until I'm told otherwise. You did call Denver and as I recall, they bumped you up to your ASAC and he shut you down right quick. Your boss mentioned a letter of censure, if I overheard that correctly."

Win closed his eyes for a moment and drew a long breath. Then the agent seemed to have a little pity. "Just chill, Tyler. It isn't the end of the world, man. I've been in the Bureau twelve years . . . I've seen stuff.

Likely you'll be censured, maybe a cut in pay, maybe a few days off on suspension. Ain't the end of the world."

He grinned a little and pulled into the heavier traffic on a busy highway that ran through the center of the city. Skyscrapers shaded the streets, crowds surged through the crosswalks, and the noise of the urban area seeped through the closed windows. Win tried to keep the conversation going. The burly agent had hardly spoken to him since he'd hustled him out of the office over four hours ago.

"You heard the CIA guys yelling about arrest . . . about prosecution," Win said haltingly.

"Oh, they were just spoutin' off. Trying to one-up Sutton. We don't have a long track record of playing nice with the Agency. The Bureau isn't gonna throw you under the bus . . . not over something like this." He grinned. "Being stupid isn't a crime yet." He tuned in to a rap station on the radio and merged onto an elevated highway.

"You don't seem to mind this little assignment," Win said.

"What's not to like about this gig? I'm outa the office on a beautiful summer day in the great Northwest; I had one of the best seafood lunches in town at Ivar's—all at government expense." He glanced toward Win. "Now true, the company was a little gloomy, but you take what you get. Got to see the skyline and magnificent Mount Rainier from Kerry Park—best view in the city! I never get tired of it! And now we're hittin' the open road." He smiled and tapped his fingers on the steering wheel to the loud music. "You likin' my tunes? . . . Hmmm, no? You more of a country-western guy?" He left the rap station blaring.

"Where are we going?" Win stared out the windshield and grew more and more annoyed. He was wondering if Agent Humphrey had been selected for this "gig" because he didn't contribute too much to the work ethic in the office. Win glanced down at the dashboard GPS. They were now headed east on Interstate 90 out of downtown Seattle. They crossed the bridge over Lake Washington, entered a tunnel, then climbed gradually toward dark-green mountains. Humphrey casually switched off the GPS map and replaced the screen with a different station—more rap. They took an exit at Issaquah, looped around a couple of blocks, cut through two residential neighborhoods, then looped back onto the interstate three miles further east.

"Tell me where we're going." Even with his normally great sense of direction, Win was getting more than a little lost.

"To the country, man. All that press you got during that shoot-'em-up in Yellowstone . . . it was clear you was a country boy. Uh-huh, gonna see a little of the country. Got several hours before your flight, and based on Mr. Sutton's mood, you won't need to go through a security line, no sir." He nodded and seemed to be talking to himself. "No sir, I'm gonna put you right on that little plane. So we got some time to kill. It's real pretty out this way . . . oughta make you feel right at home." As Humphrey sped down the mountainous interstate, rocking along with a booming song Win didn't recognize, Win sat back in the passenger seat and desperately wished he could hit the restart button on the last two days of his life.

The bright, clear weather in Seattle had given way to low clouds and mist only a few miles into the surrounding Cascade Range. Humphrey eventually eased off the interstate, meandered down a highway for a while, then pulled the sedan into an empty parking lot just past a sign saying *Snoqualmie Falls Park*. By Win's estimation they were about thirty miles east of downtown, in an area of heavy evergreen forests, rushing streams, and legions of upscale houses. They had hit the chic new subdivisions that housed many of the four million souls who called greater Seattle home.

Humphrey parked and killed the engine. He glanced at his phone, eased his stocky frame out of the car, and stretched. "I'm hittin' the john." He nodded with his chin toward a stone-and-frame structure that sat next to a closed gift shop. Two workers in yellow safety vests and hard hats were restriping part of the lot with white tape. The small lot appeared to be closed; the workers glanced their way and gave Humphrey a hard look.

Humphrey kept talking. "I've got calls to return." He held up his phone and flashed a wide grin. "Somebody mistakenly thinks I'm still workin' today. How 'bout you get your track shoes on and hit the trail here. It's real nice, paved and gravel. Runs for nearly a mile down the hill." Humphrey glared back at the workers. "Looks like those dudes may run me outa here—I'll pick you up in the parking lot at the bottom. Take your time. Big waterfall, 270 feet tall. Very cool, lots of birds and such . . . might help you clear your head." He moved to a bench under a towering evergreen and began responding to a text.

Win wasn't really in the mood for a nature walk, but then again, he'd soon be cooped up on yet another airplane, plus the two-hour drive from Bozeman into Yellowstone. He pulled his Nikes out of his bag, dropped his sports coat in the back seat, and stared down at his locked gun box. It still chafed him that he wasn't allowed to wear his sidearm. He drew a deep breath and tried to regroup. The quiet of the woods would be welcome; Humphrey's thumping rap tunes were still echoing in his head.

*   *   *

"It's a western sword fern," the old man sitting on the massive fallen log remarked, as Win continued to stare at the four-foot-tall plant standing beside the trail. It was the most prominent of its kin; dozens of the dark-green, draping ferns populated the steep slopes under the enormous trees of the rain forest.

Win glanced down the sloping trail thirty feet to where the man sat. The guy was leaning forward, stroking a hunting dog's head. It was comforting to hear a friendly voice, to see a normal scene. The brown-and-white spaniel glanced Win's way and gave him a dog smile.

"We have fiddlehead ferns down South, too, but not this big—they're huge here . . . hundreds of them. Doesn't the cold and snow kill them this far north?"

The man continued to pet the dog. "It's actually pretty mild here, we don't get much snow. Hardly ever stays below freezing for more than a few hours at a time. It's a wonderful climate if you don't mind the drizzle and rain."

Win did mind the drizzle and rain, but he didn't want to disagree with the older guy's idea of a perfect climate. He turned his face back to the depths of the woods and looked inward. His focus on the stream, the trees, and the plants was calming him. The low mist from the thundering waterfall clung to the tops of the massive evergreens and formed an insulating canopy. The sounds of vehicles on the nearby highway were muted by the forest. Other than the occasional bird call, it was quiet. He'd met only two runners on the trail for the last quarter mile. Maybe Humphrey was right—he just needed to get away from the crap. He'd deal with the issues of his nightmare in Russia, his downwardly spiraling career, and his less-than-friendly colleagues later.

The curly-haired dog suddenly nosed at Win's pants leg; the man had dropped the leash. Win bent to pick up the supple leather strap from the gravel pathway. He lowered his hand for the dog to sniff and then rubbed its chest with his free hand. It smiled that silly dog smile that spelled total delight. Melancholy feelings of failure washed over Win again. *Wish I could find joy in such a small thing.*

Then an unexpected question from the seated man: "Why don't you come over here and sit down on the bench beside me?"

After the events of the last forty-eight hours, Win had thought nothing could surprise him—he was wrong about that. He straightened and focused on the man. He realized this wasn't just an old geezer out for a dog walk. The full head of gray hair hinted at older age, but he was likely only in his late fifties. His oilskin jacket spoke of sophistication and class. He had an authoritative air, as if he wasn't accustomed to having to ask anything twice. But he repeated the request.

"Agent Tyler, bring Champ over and come have a seat."

Can this get any weirder?

As Win cautiously walked down the gravel trail with the dog, the man stood and held out his hand. "I'm Donald Langford, AD Counterintelligence from Headquarters." Win returned the firm handshake. He had no idea what to say to an FBI Assistant Director. The FBI's chief counterespionage boss sat back down on the smooth log that someone had converted into a bench. He spoke casually, as if clandestine meetings in deserted rain forests were a common event.

"Brent Sutton and the Agency both reached out to me last night after they were sure you were on that flight home. Tom Strickland tells me you're a straight arrow, he had good things to say about you.

I flew out here after Brent got your comments over the phone from Anchorage. We're not buying the line the Russians are feeding us—I want you to know that, Win."

Win sat on the log and shared his disbelief in that statement with raised eyebrows. *Everyone in the Seattle Field Office seemed to be buying it. My folks back in Denver are treating me like a pariah, and I haven't even made my report. And why are we meeting out here in the woods?*

Win didn't have to voice his concerns; it was as if the spy chief was telepathic. Langford shifted on the bench and kept talking. "The CIA had people in Petropavlovsk who tried to keep up with you, but there was serious heat on them, and the Agency had to keep them away from your hotel. They basically lost you right after you arrived there. It's almost impossible to work countersurveillance in a small city with such a high military presence. The Russians have that area blanketed with GRU, their military intelligence folks. We had assumed you'd been detained by the GRU, just to yank our chain a little. That's a bad enough situation—it would show that the Russians are getting very bold—but after you told Sutton about the Texan, our concerns really ramped up."

Ramped up enough to bring a frigging Assistant Director all the way across the country to meet a Bureau peon?

The man paused to rub Champ's ears. "Your debrief with the two CIA agents this morning was for show, as was Brent's little tirade in the office. Word will get around fast that you haven't disputed the Russian police report . . . word will get around fast that you fouled up big-time on your first overseas assignment."

Win drew in a shallow breath and stared up into the boughs of a two-hundred-foot Douglas fir that stood beside them. He fought the urge to protest but didn't know where to begin. He managed only a question. "Why are you here?"

"You denied the police arrest in your call to Brent—and you told him about the player you thought was SVR with the Texas accent. That cast a very different light on things. If there was even a chance you were detained by someone in their foreign intelligence service, I knew I needed to get together with you today. Meet with you face-to-face."

His voice hardened. "For the moment, we're officially going with Russia's version of events. We've thanked their government for their restraint and compassion for not pressing charges, for releasing you. It's been kept out of the press. Now I need your story before you're officially interviewed." His tone softened and he glanced back at the dog. He was changing course to let Win think it through.

"We're meeting out here because it's within walking distance of my sister's home. With my job, I occasionally have a tail. It's a nuisance, but it's all part of the counterintelligence game. My trip out here won't raise suspicions—they don't bother to follow me on every weekend dog walk."

Win's eyes caught movement farther down the path.

"My people form a perimeter. Everyone you've seen or met in the lot or on the trail has been part of my detail. We closed the parking lot and this part of the park to the public early this morning. We have a cell phone jammer in place and overhead surveillance, such as it is with the mist. But, bottom line, we won't have interruptions here. We just needed to get you clear of them in Seattle and set this up—that was the reason for the long sightseeing trip and the cloak-and-dagger ride to the park. You're clean. Humphrey made sure of that; he's one of our best agents on the counterintelligence side of the house. The Russians have no idea I'm meeting with you." He paused and shifted to meet Win's eyes again. "And neither does anyone in the Bureau or the CIA who isn't read in. This is strictly a *need-to-know* operation. Do you understand what I'm saying?"

"Yes, sir. But I'm not clear on the need for this level of deception."

An emotion drifted across the older man's face that Win couldn't quite decipher. Sadness? Or resignation? The spaniel nosed into the man's hand, and he gave his dog a contemplative look. "If everyone was as loyal as Champ, none of this would be necessary, Win. But that's not the world we live in. The Russians, among others, I'm afraid, have eyes and ears in our government. We must use great care, even in the Bureau. We have to protect the integrity of the Bureau, Win."

Stedman's final warning ran through Win's mind. *"Much better to be viewed as a bumbling screwup than a national security threat, wouldn't you say?" Confess to a royal foul-up or tell the truth and lose everything?* Win fought to project calm; his palms were sweating, and his pulse had kicked up several notches. Tell the truth and potentially lose it all . . . or go with the Russian police story and come through with a reprimand and his job intact.

The Assistant Director's eyes came back to Win's. "If your captors were SVR, we need to know what's going on—they're a major step up from GRU or any of our other Russian opposition. And any play on their part would indicate they may carry it back here . . . back to America, to infiltrate the Bureau." He pulled a small color photo from his jacket pocket. "Is this the man who was running their show?"

Win stared down at the surveillance photo and made the decision he knew he'd make. He nodded. He felt his stomach clench and his chest tighten as he looked into the intense green eyes of the man in the picture. "Yes, sir. It's an earlier photo, but that's him. He called himself Jacob or Jake Stedman . . . said he was an energy rep from Houston."

"His name is Sergei Sokolov. He's not just SVR, he's A-team SVR. The Russians are big on military rank, even for their intelligence officers, but this guy is the real deal. He's a major who served in their Alpha Spetsnaz, Russia's equivalent of our Delta Force. Then he moved on to the Zaslon Spetsnaz, the SVR equivalent of our HRT. He was highly decorated during his military stint, mostly for running covert operations in several of the former Soviet republics, in Afghanistan, and in Syria. He's also been an SVR clandestine operative on and off for several years now—in Ukraine, Germany, and Great Britain . . . and probably other countries."

Langford rubbed his chin with a hand and shook his head. "We've been afraid they'd move him to the U.S. when the time was right. He did thirteen months of graduate work at the University of Texas several years back, when our relationship with the Kremlin wasn't as rocky and no one had any idea he was with Russia's Foreign Intelligence Service. Quite frankly, there were years when the Bureau's attention was focused almost totally on the threat from Middle Eastern extremists. We let some wolves in the door during those years, I'm afraid."

He reached down and scratched the dog's ears again. "We understand Sokolov can pass himself off as an American with ease."

No kidding, Win was thinking. "Why me? Why would SVR come after me? It's just a missing persons case."

"Don't know yet, Win. It's very doubtful this has anything to do with your case. Far more likely they're trying to turn you, trying to get an inroad into the Bureau for this operative and his team."

The man had shifted on the bench and was now facing Win straight on. Win tried to mask his fearful thoughts with a neutral expression. He still couldn't believe this was happening to him.

"Turn me?" he asked anxiously.

"They try to sniff out unhappy agents, men or women who are bright, innovative, but who may have reasons to feel underappreciated by our government or even angry with it. You were top in your class at the Academy. In your first office posting you were clearly a rising star, working a big-league corruption case after less than three years in—then you got caught up in the blowback from the Brunson debacle. The Bureau shipped you to a dead-end office in a national park. The Russians could have you flagged as a potentially disgruntled agent, someone who might feel betrayed by the FBI. Or could be they spotted the news coverage on your heroics in Yellowstone last month and saw an opportunity to exploit an up-and-coming agent by fabricating the story of your Russian detention. Put the screws to you with the carousing with the call-girl–bar-fight allegations. Then when your career is in the toilet, they offer you money to ease your pain during your long crawl back into the Bureau's good graces . . . they know you've got talent, and they're a patient bunch."

The Assistant Director paused and looked deeper into Win's eyes. "Then again, they could have taken the more immediate tack—we know they don't share our hesitancy to use enhanced interrogation methods. It could be they drugged or tortured you night before last and got Lord knows what all from your past to blackmail you into working for them."

Win knew he had blinked. He swallowed hard.

"Want to tell me what really happened over there, Win? All of it."

CHAPTER FIFTEEN

Win switched his track shoes for loafers and slid into the passenger seat. He drew a deep breath and stared straight ahead.

"A little overwhelmed?" Humphrey asked as he pocketed his phone and started the car.

Win still didn't face the other agent. "No . . . I can handle this." He glanced toward the guy. "Mr. Langford said you'd fill me in on the next steps. . . . He also said you were one of his best agents."

"Did he now?" The man smiled and shrugged. "We gotta go get you on that little airplane." He put the car in gear and pulled out of the empty parking lot.

"You played me. . . . Uh, I'm a little embarrassed that—"

Humphrey cut off Win's efforts at an apology. "We're cool, man. We all have our prejudices—notions of how folks are by how they look, how they talk, the music they listen to . . . I count on those biases to get subjects to let their guard down, to underestimate me. Amazing how often it works! Don't worry about it."

Win still wanted to defend himself. "I'm not a racist, Humphrey."

The man touched his tight Afro and smiled again. "Not gonna use that word, but Tyler, we're all prejudiced. It's human nature. I haven't met a person yet, even my sainted mama, who didn't have preconceived ideas about folks who weren't like us. In our business we have to work hard at losing those preconceptions—they can screw up our objectivity." He glanced over at Win. "We're cool. Just learn from it."

He nodded and his smile broadened. "Uh-huh, well, I've got my issues too. I immediately had you pegged for a country boy—self-righteous, narrow-minded, all about the rules."

He may have that mostly right, Win thought. "So what changed your mind about me?"

"Haven't said I've changed my mind," the other agent quipped. He turned up the rap music as he drove up the winding mountain highway that led back toward the interstate, back to Seattle, and back into this new world Win found himself smack-dab in the middle of—a world of confusion, distrust, and doubt.

*   *   *

Five hours later he was carrying his briefcase and bag down the concourse at Bozeman's modern airport, flowing along with the crowd exiting the fifty-passenger jet. Humphrey had told him that Headquarters' Counterintelligence Division was scrambling to get bodies there to meet him. The Bureau had a recording of the clandestine meeting between Win and AD Langford, but there needed to be a much more extensive debrief on the Russia incident, held under conditions the Russians wouldn't suspect. When Win flew out of Seattle's Sea-Tac Airport two hours ago, no one had known the plan. Humphrey had assured Win he'd be met by someone at the Bozeman airport and told him to be open to any approach.

"Tyler, if the Russkies went to all this trouble to trip you up, there's always the possibility they'll have eyes on you when you get back home. No one thinks that's *highly* likely, but dude, no one predicted you'd be a target when you hit Kamchatka either. This game they're play-ing isn't running true to their usual MO." That's what Humphrey had said before they exited the car and made the slow walk to "the little airplane," as Humphrey kept calling it. At least Win had his phones back and his Glock was on his belt. Small pieces of normalcy were returning—for that he was grateful.

Win slowed to scan the small crowd on the other side of the con-course barrier. A nervous-looking cowboy held four yellow balloons and a bouquet of yellow roses. He waved the roses and called out for Sara. *Nope, not my contact.* A gray-haired woman rushed forward to engulf two embarrassed teenage girls who were clutching their back-packs and phones. *Time to visit Grandma,* Win supposed. The greet-ers began to find their targets, and excited voices of welcome filled his ears; the group began to disperse and move down the long hall. He kept walking and spotted two guys who looked like airline workers coming up the concourse. They had on yellow neon safety vests, heavy work boots, and grease-stained overalls. Both were drinking cokes and eating what appeared to be energy bars; both looked alert and capable. *This could be it.* Win veered slightly toward the men.

He was blindsided when a petite blonde rushed to his side. She pounced on him, her voice loud enough for everyone nearby to hear. "Winnie! There you are, babe! Gimme some sugar!" She pulled him into her embrace by his jacket's lapels and planted a kiss on his lips that took his breath away. He dropped his carry-on and barely held on to the briefcase. Her lips came away from his and he heard a hushed whisper: "Play along, Tyler!" He vaguely saw several folks smiling at his obvious discomfort. He managed to get his free arm around her as she eased her grip on his jacket. She was beaming up into his red face and talking just a little too loudly. "I got us a room, babe . . . Winnie, it's been, like, forever!" Win glimpsed the tarmac workers throwing lewd looks his way. He swung her around and forced a smile. She snuggled in closer and ran a hand through his hair. The teens he'd seen a minute ago were staring at Win and the clinging woman in open-mouthed delight. Grandma wasn't amused; she threw Win a scandalized glare. Win was sure she'd be using them as an example to her granddaugh-ters of how not to behave in public.

"Well then, let's get outa here." He tried for a sexy smile and couldn't pull it off.

They exited the airport arm in arm, and he walked her to her rental car in short-term parking. It was after 9:30, and the Montana sky was beginning to darken. He'd recovered enough from the shock of her sensual display to recognize that the pert woman was kinda cute, with a short, bleach-blond pageboy, and a turned-up nose. She was maybe early thirties—hard to say on the age. Her eyes were very dark brown, not the typical color for a blonde. Probably meant the hair color wasn't for real. *Wonder what else is a sham?*

She nuzzled up to him after she opened the car door. Her look was completely sultry, but her whispered words were all business. "The Holiday Inn at 2305 Catron Street. Park, get your bags, and come to room 137. I'm Paige Lange, your hookup for the night. Act like it, babe." She stretched up and planted another long kiss on his lips. This time he managed to not pull away. She ended the kiss and dropped her head down to his chest. "Relax," she cooed. "Pretend you're in a movie or a play. Someone could be watching . . . or filming. They can read lips . . . play your part. Relax." Then she pulled away and eased into the driver's seat of the small car. "See ya in a few." She started the car, dropped the window, cocked her head, and gave him a very convincing come-hither look as she drove away.

Well, there you go.

He stood in gathering darkness and watched the two red taillights of her rental car merge into one. He drew a deep breath and tried to resist the overpowering feeling of entrapment that had settled on his shoulders. The false kisses from an ally felt no different than the blows from the Russians. He was caught up in a lethal game and he couldn't seem to grasp the rules.

Is there no way out of this? His father had taught him that he always had options. Even in his recent near-death experiences—even when he'd thought death was imminent—even then, he'd been able to make a choice. He'd reached out to God. He'd trusted. *I still have that foundation,* he told himself. But everything beyond that basic condition of his soul—*everything*—seemed murky.

If he showed up at room 137 at the Holiday Inn, he'd be choosing an option over which he had no control. He'd be choosing the Bureau vs. Russia game: play the role of an FBI screwup, lose the respect of his peers, all while waiting Lord only knows how long for a deadly spy to appear and get nabbed by the Bureau. The downsides of that route were obvious, plus he could end up dead if the Russians found out he'd told the Bureau the truth. He reminded himself that it was the option he'd signed up for. He was an FBI agent. If he kept that badge—if he walked into that hotel room—he'd be choosing a life of uncertainty and fear.

But Daddy was right; he had other options. He'd mulled it over on the plane ride from Seattle. He could call the Bozeman RA tonight, meet one of their agents here, and turn in his badge, his vehicle, and his gun. He could quit the Bureau. Walk away from it all—the Russians would have no reason to pursue him. *Just walk away.* He could board a flight and be home in Arkansas by tomorrow, get his Explorer and his other stuff later. He could spend the summer getting back in shape and solicit a tryout with a pro team. The NFL had wanted him. He was seven years out of college ball, but he knew he could still compete. Or he could just stay on the farm, live on his savings for a while, help Blake and his dad with the cattle and crops until he got his head on straight. Maybe he'd approach one of the half dozen Arkansas law firms where he had connections and apply for a position. Tucker Moses had been after him to come practice law with him in Mississippi; that was a real possibility. He could do any of those things . . . he had plenty of options.

He drew another deep breath and noticed that a cold wind was starting to blow. He picked up his carry-on and began to drift toward the long-term parking where his Bureau Expedition sat waiting. He didn't have to go to that Holiday Inn and turn his life over to a bunch of strangers who likely had no regard for his future. He didn't have to follow this Russia thing through—didn't have to solve this mystery. Someone else might be better suited to bringing peace to the families of the missing. *It doesn't have to be me. I have options . . . just walk away.*

*   *   *

It was a late sunrise because of the cloud bank to the east, but it was a dandy. Violet and lilac had morphed into pink, then orange, and now the eastern sky was going for deep red. He knew the crimson sky might be beautiful to behold, but he also knew that the ancient adage was generally true: *Red sky at night, sailors' delight; red sky at morning, sailors take warning.* The magnificent sunrise he'd been watching for the last several minutes meant storms were on the way. From Win Tyler's perspective, those storms had already arrived.

He'd been driving for nearly two hours. There hadn't been much traffic on the winding interstate leading south from Bozeman, not even too much after he made a pit stop in Livingston and wound down through Paradise Valley toward Gardiner and the park. The beauty of the predawn sky hadn't been enough to take his mind off it. Not even close. He'd made his choice. He'd gone to the Holiday Inn because he wasn't one to run away. That's what he'd told himself. *I've taken an oath to support and defend the Constitution of the United States, against all enemies. . . .* The enemies of his country were at hand. *No one said it would be easy.*

And it wasn't easy. Paige had met him at the door to room 137 with a hug and a kiss, but once that door was closed, he'd walked into the real greeting party. AD Langford hadn't sent any lightweights for Win's formal debrief. Brent Sutton, the Counterintelligence Supervisor in Seattle, was there. He looked younger and more athletic in jeans and a sweatshirt than he had at the office. A woman named Gloria Gorski from the San Francisco Field Office did the bulk of the lengthy interview. Sutton introduced her as one of their top Russia experts on the West Coast. She was short and hefty, with her red hair pulled tight in a bun. She was in her mid-to-late-forties, with a distant, condescending attitude. Win figured this little trip to "nowhere," as she'd described it, had thrown a kink into her weekend plans.

Sutton explained that they'd rented the adjoining rooms as well as the two rooms above them to form a surveillance buffer. Win wondered how they'd managed to do that at the height of tourist season, but he never got a chance to ask. They had a guy from Seattle's Counterintelligence Squad videoing the interview. Win sat on one of the room's two beds and the honchos got the chairs; the whole proceeding felt way too much like a subject interrogation.

Around midnight, a man showed up, supposedly from the hotel's maintenance department, to fix the "faulty TV." He was part of a Headquarters polygraph unit; he brought in the digital lie detector and set it up. The polygrapher materialized from the adjoining room and put Win through his second polygraph test—he'd had his first when he joined the Bureau, and although he knew it was standard procedure for agents to receive the tests every few years throughout their careers, it still didn't make the thirty-minute inquisition any more pleasant.

They'd been at it for nearly four hours when they finally took a break at 2:30 a.m. While Mr. Sutton and Ms. Gorski made phone calls, Win lay down on one of the beds in the adjoining room and immediately fell into an exhausted sleep.

Brent Sutton woke him at 4:15 by turning on the nightstand light. Sutton was standing beside the bed, holding out a cup of coffee. Win's groggy mind flew back to the image of Stedman standing over him with coffee two days ago . . . or was it three days ago? Things were running together in his mind—none of it was pretty. Win sat up, accepted the coffee from the supervisor, and tried not to yawn. The guy was talking softly; Win figured others were asleep somewhere in the adjoining rooms.

"You passed the polygraph with flying colors." The man sounded encouraging. "Are you okay?"

"Yes, sir," Win quietly replied.

"We've been trying to nail Sergei Sokolov ever since we realized what a threat he could be . . . you may be our best shot for bringing him down. If, as we suspect, he's trying to turn you, he'll show up—or someone from his team will. Could be day after tomorrow, could be next year, but when they appear, you need to be ready. The Russians have been playing this spy game for nearly five hundred years—since the days of the czars. They're very, very good at it."

Win took a sip of the coffee and nodded.

"This won't be easy for you, Win. For the time being, until we figure out what Russia's game plan is, you'll have to wear the mantle of a Bureau screwup. No one in your field office will know the truth except Mr. Strickland and his National Security ASAC, Wes Givens. They'll see a copy of the taped interview with you and AD Langford, as well as our debrief, but no one on Denver's Counterintelligence Squad will get a read-in yet. Gloria and I will be running your case along with a few of our people in Washington. Paige will probably be checking in with you from time to time. I'll be your supervisor on this for the time being. Oh, and by the way, call me Brent." Win could tell Sutton was trying to be reassuring. He nodded again.

"You'll have a file in the Counterintelligence Division in Washington with the real version of events, but your active file will reflect a letter of censure for your alleged misbehavior in Russia. We'll drag all that out as long as we can, and it's going to be difficult for you. Your willingness to play the screwup is critical to this operation, but I'll be honest, it won't make you popular among our folks."

"What makes y'all think Sokolov will come to America?" Win asked. "Ms. Gorski kept saying he's one of their heavy hitters."

"Several things: He was your initial approach, and other than that fight in the tunnel, he never laid a hand on you. He brought you food, he offered you encouragement. He let his goons do his dirty work. . . . Much of this is subconscious, Win. He set himself up as your savior— you had to depend on him to get back to America, to get home. He was conditioning you to trust him, at least on some level. It is classic espionage tradecraft. He's a pro."

Sutton ran a hand across his chin. "Come on. We need to get you back to Yellowstone so the Russians don't become suspicious that you've given us the real story on what happened over there. Grab a shower and I'll wake Paige up so that she can give you a proper send-off in the hall, in case anyone is watching."

"Are they?"

The supervisor took a deep breath, and for the first time Win saw a troubled look cross his face. "Yeah. We saw one, maybe two watchers at the airport, at least one here, and we've got one hidden camera in the hallway that we've spotted."

Whoa! Seriously? "You're surprised?"

The supervisor cleared his throat, and his face went blank. "We don't *ever* want to be surprised by the opposition. But I'd say we're concerned . . . very concerned."

*   *   *

He'd just passed under the historic stone arch that guarded the gateway to Yellowstone, and the morning light was bringing the storefronts along Gardiner's Park Street to life. He was tempted to stop at the storefront café and have breakfast, but he told himself that the microwaved ham-biscuit thing he'd gotten at the Livingston gas station would have to do for today. He flashed his credentials for the ranger holding down the early shift in the booths that provided entrance into the world's first national park. Then he told the hands-free device in the SUV to call Blake.

His younger brother answered on the second ring. "'Bout time you touched base," he groused. "Mom's been worried. We thought you'd be back from Russia early yesterday."

"Got tied up with some stuff is all," Win said in a flippant tone.

Blake was two years younger and one inch taller. He and Win were tight—Blake wasn't buying it. "Uh-huh. What went wrong, Bubba?"

"I didn't say anything went wrong." Win was defensive.

"Didn't have to say it. Kin hear it in your voice. You better not call Mom till you get your story straight—she'll get it outa you."

Win sighed. Blake was right. His mother could wring information out of him with an ease that would put the damn Russians to shame. "Well then. You tell the folks I made it back fine . . . tell them I've got a bunch more meetings, got some jet lag . . . and I'll call them later."

There was a pause while Blake thought about it. "Okay . . . I'll run interference for you on this one. You alright?"

"Yeah . . . yeah." Even Win could hear the notes of despondency in his voice.

Blake made a stab at bringing his brother out of it. "How 'bout we do a FaceTime with the kids tonight, say 7:30, 7:45 your time? Dad's gonna take the boys down to the pond to fish for a while after supper, so we'll just keep Li'l Bit up later than usual. We'll call after we get 'em all hosed down."

Win smiled as he pictured his four-year-old twin nephews and his two-year-old niece getting a shower with the garden hose.

"Sure, that would be good. I'll tell them about the volcanoes I saw over there and the big warships." He drew a long breath. "Tell Mom I'll give her a call later."

"Hey," Blake said in parting, "I'll be praying for you. Whatever it is, just know that God's got your back. Remember what it says in 2 Kings 6:16: *'Do not fear, for those who are with us are more than those who are with them.'* His angels outnumber the bad guys, Win."

"How'd you get so wise?"

Win could tell Blake was smiling. "I've got an awesome older brother—learned a lot from him. Be careful out there. Love you, Bubba!"

CHAPTER SIXTEEN

T hey decided his car went over the cliff right here." Trey was down on one knee within two feet of a seven-hundred-foot drop straight down to the Yellowstone River.

Win inched a little closer to the ranger along the shoulder of the two-lane highway as an RV came lumbering around the curve and slowed to descend the steep hill. He flinched as the huge vehicle rumbled past him. The air filled with the oily, smoky smell of hot brakes. He took off his hat and wiped his damp brow.

"What about that?" he asked the ranger, eyeing the two-foot-tall stone wall that hugged the shoulder of the highway.

"Wasn't here then. This wall wasn't built until three summers ago." Trey stared down. "Accident was almost five years ago." Win held his breath as he peered over the man's head and looked down from the dizzying height. Trey glanced at him. "You look a little green, Win. Hold on to my shoulder or get down on your butt." Trey sounded more amused than concerned. He knew Win had a fear of heights.

Win got on his knees and scooted toward the lip of the cliff. They both knelt there and stared down in silence. It was beautiful. The Yellowstone River looked like a green ribbon from above; it formed a wide S below them, lodged between two near-vertical yellow stone cliffs. Win could see whitecapped rapids along several sections of the stream. The canyon walls were stratified with layer upon layer of the golden limestone that gave the nation's premier park its name. Large birds flew from ledges along the far walls. Trey had told him ospreys were nesting there.

He forced his attention back to Trey, who was paraphrasing the accident report and interviews that Win had memorized: ". . . said he was last seen at nine o'clock at the restaurant in Roosevelt—got off his shift at the gift shop and told a coworker he planned to drive to Canyon to pick up some inventory for the next day. The concessioner's supply warehouse in Canyon is nineteen miles south of Roosevelt. It was August 29th, just getting twilight, good weather, dry roads. Found the car a few days later partly submerged . . . downriver about where the river turns into that curve." He pointed toward the water far below. "We lifted the car out with a helicopter that week, but we never found any sign of the body . . . that's not unheard of out here."

"The car was nearly new—brakes, steering, tires—everything checked out as if it had been fine before the crash," Win recited from memory. "But the transmission was in neutral—not drive, like you'd expect. Coulda gotten shifted in the crash, I suppose. Still . . ." Win leaned back from the edge a little before he continued. "Conner had been working at the Lake Hotel gift shop around the time Natasha disappeared; that's only six miles from where she went missing."

"You're thinking a connection?" The ranger sat back on his haunches. "Naw, I don't know . . . that's a bit of a reach."

Win lifted the binoculars and scanned the river again. It wasn't like he was expecting to find anything. It was more about sitting in the spot where Conner Chen had disappeared, just to take it in, just to think it through. It was a continuation of what he'd been doing for the last two days since he'd driven back from Bozeman. He was doing what Brent Sutton told him to do: go about your business, work the missing persons files, live your normal life. He'd put his trust in a select group at the Bureau to monitor his phones and keep an eye out for bad guys.

Win's assignment was to play the role of a loser. It wasn't a role that came naturally to him, but he was getting plenty of practice; the fallout had already begun. Jim West had called, stupefied and wanting answers. Win had none to give. Murray had sent him a questioning email with an incredulous tone. Win had sent back a tepid response.

Two of his Bureau buddies at his first posting in Charlotte and several Denver agents he'd worked with on the False Prophet case had reached out to him. Win had let their phone calls of concern go to voicemail; he'd sent them all vague text messages in return. The FBI was like any big organization, he supposed. Bad news travels fast.

Brent Sutton's words kept reverberating in his mind: *It's not going to be easy for you.* They couldn't take away what he'd accomplished in Yellowstone so far. His Director's Award, his cash bonus—he'd still get those. They couldn't take those away. But nothing else good would be forthcoming from the Bureau, not until the Russians played their hand . . . if they played their hand. For the time being Win was officially deep in the doghouse. He'd been exiled to Yellowstone mere months ago— he already knew how awful that felt.

Win took one more slow scan of the canyon, dropped the binoculars to his chest, eased away from the cliff, and walked back up the shoulder of the highway to the Calcite Springs overlook, where Trey had parked his Tahoe. The ranger was at the edge of the parking lot, pointing out a nesting osprey with a spotting scope to a group of eager tourists. Win watched Trey explain the difference between the male and female birds, watched him nod approvingly at the group's comments and questions. For a moment he envied Trey Hechtner's job as the friendly host to curious "visitors," as Trey called the tourists. Most of the rangers' daily contacts were positive—excited, happy people on vacation, away from their everyday cares. Most of Win's daily contacts with the public couldn't be characterized that way; he dealt with people in one form of crisis or another. This week the pleas from the friends and families of the lost haunted his thoughts. He wasn't sure what, if anything, he was accomplishing to ease their pain. He drew a deep breath. It wasn't the first time he'd wondered if he was in the wrong line of work.

Trey saw Win approach and gave a few parting comments to the enthralled tourists before walking Win's way. The ranger shed another layer of green and wiped the gray sleeve of his uniform shirt across his face. "How do you like this warmer weather, Win? Gettin' more to your likin'?" He dropped his vest over a fallen tree and sat down on the stump.

Win looked down at the sweating ranger. "Well, it's still below freezing most mornings, but it's a vast improvement over what y'all kept callin' spring a few weeks back."

The ranger was fishing a water bottle out of his day pack. "It's still considered spring here until the Fourth of July—at that point we won't expect snow for a couple of months. I'll count that as summer."

Win drank from a water bottle that Trey handed him, stretched back, and stared off into the deep-blue sky. The weather had been unsettled for the last two days, with rolling clouds, high winds, and thunderstorms each afternoon. Today was shaping up to be much nicer. At late morning it was maybe seventy-five degrees with a soft breeze; there were yellow and purple wildflowers sprouting in every sunny spot. The spruces and Douglas firs that made up this swatch of forest had light-green tips where new growth was coming in. The cool front had moved on, and the air had a fresh scent. The surroundings were near perfect, but Win was feeling edgy, he was feeling down.

His melancholy mood wasn't lost on his partner. Trey capped his plastic bottle and looked up into his face. "Somethin's been eating at you since you got back from overseas. Let me see . . . you've been declared a national hero by the press for saving Yellowstone, you've physically recovered from a near-fatal wound, and you've got a gorgeous woman interested in you . . . so why the long face?"

Win broke the eye contact and focused on a limb over the ranger's head. As much as he'd like to talk this through with Trey, the main reason for his unease was off-limits. "Maybe the missing persons files are starting to get to me. Dealing with so many parents and friends who're grasping for any flicker of hope after so much time has passed. Maybe that's it . . ." He let his words trail off.

Trey's eyes narrowed just a tad. "Maybe . . . but I heard that someone with the Bureau made a passing comment to Chief Randall that you'd run into an issue in Russia. That your bosses had come down on you pretty hard over some carousing over there." He waited to see if Win would make a response. When he didn't, Trey took another crack at it. "It's not like I've known you forever, but I just can't see you suddenly hittin' the party scene. You get set up?"

So even the Park Service guys know. Win shrugged with his eyes, then glanced away again. "It's complicated," he replied softly.

"Gotcha," the ranger responded. He picked up his vest and pack and walked back toward the SUV. Win swallowed down his pain and told himself again that he was doing the right thing, that this couldn't last forever.

*   *   *

"I understand you're the best backcountry guide in Yellowstone."

"That's laying it on a little thick," Luke answered.

The man leaned in, eyeing the ribs that remained on Luke's plate as if he might attack them. "I'm lookin' for the best—I want a real personal touch here." The prosperous-looking sportsman waved the waitress in for another round of beer. "Thank ya, hon." His friendly face smiled up at her and she blushed. Luke was thinking the guy was a charmer. They were at the Bull Moose Bar and Grill, one of Gardiner's best lunch spots. Ellie had set up the spur-of-the-moment meeting during an early-morning phone call. There hadn't been anything else on Luke Bordeaux's calendar.

"You can drive right up to Yellowstone's most amazing thermal features," Luke said. "You don't have to set out on an overnight trip to see some fascinating sights."

"I know, I know, but I want a real backcountry experience for my clients."

They both set into the meal for a few moments while Luke thought it over. This Atlanta stockbroker had told Ellie he'd scheduled a guide out of Bozeman who'd had a family emergency and cancelled on them after they'd already flown in. The man said he'd gotten Luke's name through someone at the Park Service. Luke wondered if Trey had anything to do with throwing the business his way.

Ellie had sounded downright excited about the call, about the prospect of him getting out with clients. He'd been mostly moping around underfoot at the house for the two and a half weeks since they'd released him from the hospital. He'd gotten out to exercise, to get his wind and legs back and to tend to some items she didn't need to know about, but he hadn't solicited any new guide business even though the Feds had reinstated his licenses. He had no excuse for not working. Ellie probably thought it would do him good to get a paying job and get back into the woods. Ellie was usually right.

The man washed his barbecue down with half his beer and started talking again. "We don't want the comfortable, gentleman's expedition thing, the gourmet meal thing . . . we want to rough it in the true wilderness, see some bears and such. That's what I'm goin' for. We've got our own tents, camping equipment, that sort of thing, we just need the guide. And, uh, we hope to go out day after tomorrow."

Day after tomorrow? Luke grimaced. He didn't respond right away.

The potential client frowned down at his hands for a moment, then glanced back up. "I know I'm hittin' you up last minute, but I'd be glad to double your usual rate . . . I'm kinda in a bind here." The fit-looking guy pulled a foiled guidebook from the pocket of his Barbour jacket. He spread the fold-out map in front of his empty plate.

"I've been lookin' over the maps and the brochures of Yellowstone for months . . . the original guide was gonna take us into this area—see here." He pointed to the tourism map; its colorful inset showed a photo of a turquoise lake with a geyser rising in the foreground.

Luke nodded and smiled. "Nice area. It's called Maxwell Springs. Named for Clark Maxwell, a geologist who mapped it in 1908."

The man from back East seemed excited and pleased. "Exactly! See here, it says '*Maxwell Springs: Fascinating Thermal Features and a Magical Lake.*' You obviously know the place."

"Yes sir, I've hiked in there a few times—it's pretty far off the beaten path. It's a beautiful place, and it's a relatively new thermal feature. The geysers have just started coming back to life in the last ten years or so. . . . The experts say the springs and mudpots were nearly dormant for over sixty years. It's a hard hike in; generally only researchers and a few real die-hard backpackers make the trip."

"That's just the kind of place we're lookin' for. That'd be perfect."

"It's on a side trail that extends off the Slough Creek Trail. It takes four, five hours to get there from the trailhead. Your two clients, they'll have to be in shape to do this trip. It's a hard bit of mountain hiking."

The man leaned back, wiped his hands with a paper napkin, and smiled as if he knew he'd closed the deal. "No problem, no problem at all . . . we all get out to the gym."

* * *

Win made it back to the FBI office right after two. He was reaching for Conner Chen's file when his personal phone buzzed in his pocket. He fished it out and stared down at a local number he didn't recognize. He swiped it on, expecting a telemarketer. But that wasn't it.

"Well now, Cowboy. How they treatin' ya?" Win instantly knew the voice. His breath caught in his throat.

"You're calling me here?" He tried to sound frightened. It wasn't much of a stretch.

"Sure, why not? We're partners now . . . buddies, don't ya know. You were smart to go with our version of events." *Geez, how does he know that?*

"They're treating me like I've got the plague! They've filed a formal reprimand at Headquarters, dammit!" Win tried to go for indignation, made his tone whiny. *Lordy, this is harder than I'd thought it would be.* He clenched his fist and closed his eyes to focus on the Russian.

The man on the phone chuckled softly. "So you're persona non grata, not the first guy they'd call for a beer, but what the hell, you're still in the loop, you're still on the case." He paused and his tone hardened. "More importantly, they haven't yanked your clearances. And speaking of our case, did they pull all the evidence on the missing persons down to Denver, as you'd feared?"

Win added some edge to his own voice. "It isn't *our* case, Stedman, or whatever the hell your name is . . . it's *my* case, and no, they haven't pulled the evidence to Denver yet." Win drew a breath. *Okay, Sutton said to give him something.* "I'm following several leads, but my supervisor thinks it's going nowhere." He dropped into the whiny voice again.

"They don't really care . . . these files have sat around gathering dust for years. I've stuck my neck out trying to do the right thing, to complete a full investigation, to try to give families some closure." Enough with whining, he switched back to anger: "Then you people screwed me over! Now no one will take the case or me seriously! I'm swinging in the wind here!"

"You're trying to develop a pattern to the disappearances, yes? Your line of questioning with Dr. Orsky was excellent. You're good at this, very good. Solving even one of the disappearances could be your ticket out of Yellowstone. Isn't that how you see it?" The SVR man kept up the praise and encouragement and Win kept up his pretense of angry whining for the next two minutes. Win had to admit that the guy was super smooth; toward the end of the conversation, the Russian had Win seeing him as more of an ally than his own colleagues in the Bureau. Win realized at the last minute that he was making it too easy for him—the man had to buy it, had to believe Win would sell out the Bureau.

"I see what you're trying to do! Cozy up to me to weasel into the Bureau, then set me up for a real fall. I don't need you!" The stress in Win's voice was genuine.

The Texas accent was slow and measured. "Naw, naw, you don't need me, Win. But you're a helluva lot sharper than those folks you're working for . . . solving these cases would move you up a notch. Just one notch at a time and before long, you're where you want to be—a job in Washington, maybe running part of the show. Then you could really accomplish things, you could do a tremendous amount of good—show them how it should be done."

"Yeah, right. I'll probably be stuck here in this dead-end post for another year after that stunt you pulled on me in Kamchatka. I can leave the FBI and be done with all this. Be done with you! I'm a lawyer—I'd make a good deal more practicing law than dealing with this crap!"

The voice was soothing. "They've done you wrong . . . I can see that. You can see that. But you don't need to be hasty, like you said, you're trying to do the right thing. Trust the process . . . one step at a time. Maybe I can help with this, make it more worth your time."

"Sure you will." Win tried to sound sullen and distrustful. That wasn't a stretch either.

"Hang in there, Cowboy. I'll be in touch."

The call went dead. Win leaned forward on his elbows and blew out a deep breath. He wiped a sheen of sweat from his forehead with his shirt sleeve, dropped the phone to the desk, and tried to quiet his queasy stomach. Thirty seconds hadn't passed before his landline rang.

"Good job of chumming the water, Win," Sutton said. "Now we'll just have to sit back and see if the shark strikes the bait." Win wasn't loving that analogy. After all, Win Tyler was the bait.

* * *

Sutton and his crew seemed to be expecting Win to get *the call*, as they'd labeled it. Unfortunately, Sutton said, *the call* only meant that Win was still in the Russians' sights, that the opposition still had Win on the line. It wasn't lost on Win Tyler that the Bureau's Seattle Counterintelligence Supervisor kept using hunting and fishing analogies. The Russians had him in their crosshairs, they were gonna reel him in. . . . Win understood the nomenclature. He was the hunted in this deadly game. He was the prize to be caught. Win was still trying to get his head around that awful reality.

The supervisor tried to be reassuring. "Win, that call could have originated anywhere in the world. It showed up as local, but they have telecom technology as good as ours. He was probably calling you from Moscow. The Bureau, the NSA, and Homeland Security have used face-recognition technology to blanket the international gates at airports since you got back. We've seen nothing to indicate he's in the country."

But Sutton conceded that face-recognition technology wasn't foolproof and that Sergei Sokolov's call didn't tell the Bureau who, if anyone, was on the ground or when a serious approach might be made. Sutton reminded Win that the Bureau would continue watching the borders like a hawk, that both of his phones were monitored 24/7, and that the Agency was reaching out to its field assets in Russia to try to figure out what might be going on. Then he reiterated his orders. "Just keep living your life—it could literally be months, even years, before they make an approach. The Russians never advance quickly," he emphasized again. "You have to move on."

After the thirty-minute telephone briefing with Sutton wrapped up, Win sat at his desk and wondered what to do. *Get on with your life, the man said.* He pivoted his chair and looked out the window at the multitude of tourists who were milling around the Visitor's Center. His plan for the afternoon was to work the file of the missing concessioner employee, Connor Chen, and make a few more calls on Missy Sims . . . and then there was . . . Janet Goff. Win closed his eyes, trying to will himself to focus. There were still plenty of items to follow up on. But his focus wasn't there. He didn't think he could handle any more of the lost, not at the moment. Not now, when he was feeling terribly lost himself.

He rechecked his secure email for the third time that day—still no word on the shooting inquiries. *It will take time.* Jim West had said that. And the Bureau was still spitting out updates on the hunt for the fugitives in the wilds of the Gallatin National Forest near Sage Peak. The bulk of the searchers had been there for nine days with nothing to show for it. They were still getting anonymous tips of sightings in that area, but someone higher up had finally figured out that those tips were 99.9 percent bogus—false leads meant to drag out the wild-goose chase. Win could read between the lines: the manhunt was winding down.

He glanced at his watch; it was comin' up on three o'clock. For a moment he thought about the bones and the rings he'd gently placed in the gun safe several nights ago. He thought about going down and getting them out, maybe just checking on them. But instead he picked up his personal phone and called Tory's number. He was fixin' to get on with his life.

CHAPTER SEVENTEEN

He allowed himself the comfort of blinking away the sweat that was trickling down into his eyes. Just the movement of his eyes, nothing else. No change in the rhythm of his breathing or the steadiness of his gaze through the small binoculars into the clearing far below. He was lying flat on a bed of evergreen needles, beneath an ancient, twisted tree. A gnat buzzed near his ear, but he made no attempt to swat it away. His focus was below him . . . on learning everything possible about his quarry. And fifty yards below him, the American was thinking about kissing the girl. He could see it in the lad's expression. He'd been spying on the couple for the last hour from the cover of the higher slope. Agent Tyler and the girl were sitting shoulder to shoulder on a boulder at the edge of a small clearing that was bright yellow with wildflowers. The lip of a cliff lay just beyond the colorful field. The watcher could hear the rumble of the sixty-foot waterfall; the couple could likely see the cascading torrent of water from their perch. It was a beautiful spot for an early-evening picnic.

They were all upslope off the Lava Creek Trail; they'd parked at a picnic area near the trailhead that led to Undine Falls. If it hadn't been for the occasional sound of an engine straining to climb the mountain in front of them, you'd think they were in the heart of the wilderness. Yet they were only four miles southeast of Mammoth, and not that far from the main highway that looped through the big park. He was thinking they might as well have been on the far side of the moon. He'd seen only a handful of hikers on the gentle trail, and except for the couple below, no one was off-trail, overlooking the magnificent three-layered waterfall. He doubted if this was unusual in America's wild places, as it was true the world over: very few ventured off the beaten path. That was just human nature, and what a shame that was . . . off the beaten path was so often full of wonder.

And one element of that wonder was now leaning her lovely head against the young man's shoulder. Agent Tyler had chosen well. The auburn highlights in the woman's dark hair were shimmering in the late-afternoon sun. Her brown eyes were following the agent's every word. She was tall and slender, and she used her hands to express her enthusiasm as she talked. She was very pretty, but his overriding impression of her was kindness. She looked kind.

The young woman dipped her chin and laughed at something the agent told her. She was wanting the agent to kiss her . . . she tossed her hair and ran the tip of her tongue across her lips. . . . She was flirting with him. As the young man leaned in closer to the girl, the watcher pulled his eyes away from the field glasses. He had no taste for voyeurism; he'd let them have their privacy.

He studied a delicate blue butterfly flitting above a mound of yellow flowers. He allowed himself a deep breath and scanned the surrounding forest. He didn't need to be reminded to stay vigilant. So far this phase of the operation was moving smoothly, but they were only in the initial stages. One of those first steps was discovering who Agent Tyler spent time with, cared for, trusted. The information he'd gleaned from the interrogation in Kamchatka had to be validated. The Office had already transmitted one report confirming the intense stress the agent was facing from his peers. An official reprimand had been filed, and there'd been more than one tongue lashing from his senior officers . . . those hardships would be difficult for any young man to take, likely even harder given Agent Tyler's recent professional successes.

In the three days that Agent Tyler had been back from Seattle, he'd seemed scattered, indecisive, even inconsistent. In Kamchatka he'd seen the agent as having a strong moral compass, a steely sense of right and wrong, a rigid view of good and evil. He'd seen a man who was thoughtful, deliberate, and disciplined. He had to confess that he was somewhat confused. *Perhaps I'm being too impatient . . . give the lad a chance to adapt to this new reality,* he told himself. He smiled as he glanced back into the binoculars and watched the agent deflect the woman's subtle advances, watched him choose to take her hand instead of her lips. *Yes,* he thought, *Agent Tyler is applying a good deal of that discipline right now.*

That's why the tryst at the Bozeman hotel made no sense. It wasn't this lad's style. *An aberration because of the stress he'd experienced during the last several weeks?* Perhaps it could be explained that easily. People deviated from their normal patterns during extreme stress or pressure—and Agent Tyler had experienced severe stress, no doubt about that. The drugs they'd administered in Petropavlovsk had loosened the agent's tongue, and he'd shown no signs of any training that could have helped him counter their effects. The truth serums were most effective when used in combination with long-term sensory deprivation and physical force, but they hadn't had the time or the need for more extreme measures. They'd gotten what they were after, accomplished that part of the mission, more by the grace of the Almighty than any skill on their part.

He grimaced at that thought. Moscow's planning was normally meticulous, but this time they'd thrown the mission together with reckless abandon. His legend was rushed, there had been no time to prepare. Agent Tyler had made him with the questions about Houston. *Houston, Texas*—some fool analyst at the Office thought he should be from Houston. He'd never set foot in the place, never studied its demographics, never played the role of a capitalist in the energy industry. These things couldn't be rushed. Normally he had several days, sometimes weeks, to get into his legend, his role. But not this time. And this time, the American had tagged him. Inept preparation and execution that could have had tragic results. If he'd been killed by the American, the mission could have been jeopardized—and the success of the mission was all-important. *Amateurish work!*

Even after that near disaster, the mission was still moving at blinding speed. He'd thought the Office might pull back a bit, might move forward more cautiously. But no, here he was in the American West, where some sort of criminal manhunt had the place crawling with federal police, where he was still waiting for elements of his team to arrive, where hordes of tourists clogged every road. And, worst of all, he found himself unsure who was friend or foe. And he didn't like that one little bit. He'd always been given at least a working knowledge of their inside assets. But in this case, he hadn't been privy to the identity of any of their spies on the ground. It was as if Moscow was aware of the heightened risk in their rushed operation—if he got caught, God forbid, he wouldn't be able to finger anyone within the U.S. Government. A necessary precaution, he supposed, but it certainly made working this mission more difficult and dangerous.

He scanned the surroundings again with the binoculars. Several fat, woodchuck-like things were scurrying up and down the rocks near the cliff's edge. The reddish-brown creatures had big eyes and bushy tails; they were snapping off the yellow blossoms with their prominent front teeth, then standing on their hind feet and stuffing the flowers into their mouths as if someone might snatch them away. He found himself grinning at their antics, then focused back on the couple and watched the woman point to the big rodents; she seemed to be explaining something about them to the attentive young man who was still holding her hand. Sergei shifted his position slightly and let his mind wander a bit. The amusing animals brought back to mind his last assignment—he'd been in such a different place.

Ten days ago, he'd been sitting in the formal elegance of the Gundel Café in Budapest, sipping his tea and watching excited children run ahead of their parents toward the entrance to the city's delightful zoo. Victor would like that zoo—he'd been thinking that he'd like to take him there someday. The boy adored the polar bears at the Moscow Zoo; they'd sat for an hour in the near zero cold in February and watched the bears play in the snow. Sitting there in the café, he'd wondered if the Budapest Zoo had a polar bear. The Budapest assignment had been almost relaxed. He'd recruited an asset from the Hungarian government, a man who possessed many secrets the Motherland could use. . . . They'd met at different spots in the city several times over the last year. That day in the Gundel Café they'd accomplished an attaché case switch-off while feigning confusion over a mix-up of tables. It had been seamless—the Hungarian's briefcase full of secrets sat at his feet while he finished his tea. A very profitable encounter, and he'd expected the assignment to be ongoing for several more months.

But three hours after walking out of the café, he was on a private jet to Moscow, whisked to high-level meetings in Yasenevo, the Office's expansive headquarters in the southern suburbs, and then in less than forty-eight hours he was on a flight to Petropavlovsk. There'd only been one night at home, only a few hours to spend with Krestya and Victor. It had been hard to explain to his child that he had to leave again so soon. "Your father is a soldier," Krestya had reminded Victor, "and soldiers have a duty that must take them away for a time . . ." Sergei hadn't experienced that type of rapid redeployment since he began working clandestine operations; it was unsettling.

Ah . . . no one said it would be easy. He allowed himself a soft sigh as he swung his gaze back to the woodchucks for a moment. Victor would love to see them playing in the flowers.

* * *

She'd suggested this spot overlooking the big waterfall, with its small field of flowers and the comical family of varmints. Win wondered if Chris Warren had clued Tory into its wonders, but negative thinking wasn't going to win him any points with her—he tried harder to force his insecurities away. They'd finished the sandwiches he'd bought at the Roosevelt General Store, and they'd spent the better part of an hour taking in the beauty of the place. Now she was telling him about yellow-bellied marmots, the groundhog-like rodents that were putting on a show just yards away. They're closely related to squirrels and prairie dogs, she'd told him; they can get up to eleven pounds, she'd said; they hibernate for up to eight months out of the year. . . . She quit talking and waited for him to make some response.

She wrinkled up her nose and scowled. "Win Tyler, you're not hearing a word I'm saying!"

He ran his thumb slowly up the back of her hand and leaned back against the big rock to study her. "Why, yes, ma'am, I am listening. I'm gettin' real well educated on the local groundhogs—"

"Marmots," she corrected, that cute little scowl still on her face.

"Marmots," he repeated and ran his thumb down the back of her hand. "But I'm a poor student at the moment—you'll have to forgive me—seems I'm a bit distracted by the amazing woman beside me." He was giving her his best slow smile and it seemed to be working.

The cute scowl disappeared as she blushed and shyly flicked her eyes away from his. She'd been flirting with him since they'd finished their meal, but now he'd turned the tables. Now he'd turned up the heat.

He reached behind her long silky hair to the nape of her neck; he lowered his head, and . . .

"We're being watched!" she said in a hushed whisper.

He froze for a split second while the alarm registered. His hand came down from her neck and found the small semiautomatic he'd slipped into an ankle hostler. He drew the weapon even as his rational mind screamed that first he had to assess the threat. But he drew the weapon anyway as his eyes swept the trees for the enemy, *his enemy*: the Russians.

Staring back at him from the tree line, less than forty feet away, were two big brown eyes connected to one of the largest racks of antlers he'd ever seen. At Win's sudden movements, the huge bull elk lowered its head and shook its formidable crown in warning. It wasn't at all intimidated by Win's weaponry. There were no Russians watching his clumsy attempt at a first kiss with Tory. Nope, just one massive beast that obviously planned to claim this clearing as its own.

Whoa! Geez! Maybe I overreacted a bit.

"Win! You can't shoot it!" Tory was no longer looking at the elk. Tory was looking at the gun with a horrified expression on her face.

"I'm . . . I'm not gonna shoot it." Win sucked in a deep breath as his mind frantically searched for anything to say, for any way to move time back a few beats to his fingers on her neck, not on the trigger guard.

"Hey, y'all!" A slight young woman yelled and waved from the opposite side of the clearing. An older lady appeared next to her and leaned on her hiking poles. "Hey, Tory! Figured you might come here . . . beautiful evening! We thought we'd join you!" The first woman was walking toward them. "Hey, you must be Win!" She stopped. "Is that . . . is that a real gun?"

Oh, for Pete's sake!

Win caught a glimpse of the bull elk retreating into the forest. A sinking feeling settled onto Win's chest, and he desperately wished he could join him.

* * *

The Yellowstone Chapel was more than three-fourths full—far more people than he'd expected for the Sunday service at ten o'clock. But then there wasn't any other church in the park; the nearest congregation was in Gardiner. It was Win's first visit to the handsome stone church during worship services, but it had already held an important place in his life during his brief time in the park.

Win turned and shook hands with the law enforcement ranger who was herding her two small children into the pew behind him. The ranger welcomed him to the congregation and introduced her husband and the polite youngsters. She was telling her kids that Win was the brave FBI agent who'd been caught up in all the recent domestic terrorism activity. Win was nodding and smiling and trying to act humble, but his eyes had settled near the rear of the sanctuary on an older gentleman who was following the choir members down the main aisle. The gray-haired man wore a navy dress coat and carried a straw cowboy hat in his hand. He shuffled to the other side of the aisle and sat near the back, beside a large woman wearing a bright-red shawl. Win felt a tinge of unease. Something about the man seemed oddly familiar. The piano began the stirring strains of "To God Be the Glory," and Win saw the older man glance his way, then immediately turn and pat a latecomer on the arm and wave to a woman who had walked in with the choir. *Get a grip, Win—you're paranoid! The man obviously knows people here. Lighten up!*

When the service concluded, Win glanced back as the older man stepped out of the pew, turned toward the large wooden cross over the altar, bowed slightly, and crossed himself from right to left. Must be a Catholic or Episcopalian, Win surmised. Nothing unusual about that—this out-of-the-way sanctuary probably drew members of all denominations. But his internal warning system had been nagging at him throughout the service. He was moving to intercept the man just as Trey grabbed his arm.

"Don't forget the game today at three. The team we're playing is pretty good." Trey noticed Win's distracted look. "You with me, Win?"

"Yeah. Yeah, sure." The older man had already exited the sanctuary into the foyer; no catching him now. Win turned back to the ranger. "I'm looking forward to it, but you know we're gonna look like fools in those yellow jerseys."

"Jazmine put the team together, so she gets to pick the mascot and the colors. It could be worse," Trey replied.

"Can't imagine how. The fightin' Pine Martens? Yellow jerseys with a weasel on the front. Seriously?"

"As I recall, you were once a big-time player with a pig on your helmet."

"It's a Razorback, not just a pig." Win felt his hackles rising at the insult.

The ranger grinned. "I see I've hit a nerve." He slapped Win on the shoulder. "See you at three." Trey turned to talk with one of the choir members and Win walked into the foyer. He took in the intricate stained-glass windows that highlighted the park's wildlife and features: geysers, bison, bears, and mountains. But the beautiful 1913 workmanship was lost on him this morning. He still felt the sense of unease.

He dodged traffic to cross the highway to the small parking lot. It occurred to him as he opened the old Explorer's door and started to get inside. *Catholics don't cross themselves from right to left. They make the sign of the cross—a request for God's blessing—from their left shoulder to their right.* He pulled out his Bureau phone and googled "who crosses themselves from right to left." The answer that popped up on the screen caused his stomach to drop: Russian Orthodox Church. *Uh-oh.*

He frantically scanned the small parking lot. There was no sign of the old man. Light drizzle was beginning to fall and the wind was picking up. Most of the congregation were either quickly walking up the sidewalk toward the historic two-story houses along Officer's Row or were climbing into nearby cars and SUVs. Trey and his family had just pulled out of the lot. A few clusters of parishioners lingered near the church entrance. He closed the truck's door, crossed back over the road, and approached the pastor.

It didn't surprise Win that the minister had no idea who the older man was. He said he'd greeted him after the service near the exit doors; he remembered his firm handshake, but little else. Win thanked him, then flagged down the lady with the red shawl. She'd just opened her car door. The crowd of churchgoers was getting thin.

"Ma'am, excuse me . . . I'm Win Tyler. I'm new here. This is kinda embarrassing, but I can't seem to remember the name of the man you were sitting beside in the service . . . I'm sure I know him . . . the older gentleman?"

"Oh, goodness! No need to be embarrassed not remembering names. Wait till you hit sixty—then the memory really goes downhill! I'm Sally Greene." She smiled a broad smile that squinted her eyes nearly shut. "Ah, he must have been a tourist. Never seen him before, and I've been coming to the Yellowstone Chapel for over three years."

"He didn't introduce himself or say where he was from?" Win asked hopefully.

"No, no, but I invited him to come again, and he said he'd try . . . he seemed nice enough . . . maybe late sixties? Hard to tell his age. I got the impression he enjoyed the service. He was very attentive, and he seemed quite devout."

"Well, thanks for your time, Ms. Greene." Win turned to walk two cars down to his SUV.

The woman pulled the vibrant shawl higher on her shoulders to ward off the damp, then called to him as he neared his vehicle. "Oh, this might help you remember. My husband is from Austin and that older man, he has to be from Texas—classic Texas accent."

Oh, boy.

Win drove up and down all the nearby streets. No sign of the old man from church. The office was his next stop. He called the Seattle Counterintelligence Squad, who put him through to Humphrey, who listened for only moments before patching him through to Brent Sutton. While he waited for the supervisor to come on the phone, Win stared out his office window at the American flag whipping in the wind. A herd of tourists were grabbing for their caps and hats and scurrying toward the Visitor Center. The gray clouds were rolling, but patches of blue now dotted the sky. It was looking like the showers had passed. Sutton finally answered and got right to the point.

"Humphrey tells me you think you saw Sokolov at church this morning?" Skepticism in his voice.

"I'm not a hundred percent sure, sir, but my gut tells me it was him."

"That would be highly unlikely, Win. You've only been back stateside for a week." The supervisor didn't want to dismiss Win's suspicions outright, even if he thought the young agent was imagining bad guys. "What was the tip-off? How close were you to this guy?"

"It was just a feeling, instinct. He was maybe seventy feet away. At the back of the sanctuary. He never made eye contact. Looked to be late sixties, maybe seventy. Physically, he was nothing like Sokolov, but something was off. He crossed himself like they do in the Russian Orthodox Church. The woman who sat next to him said he had a Texas accent."

Sutton paused for several moments before he responded. "Texas has a population greater than eighty percent of the countries in the world. There *could* be a Texan in Yellowstone. A senior SVR officer? Doubtful." His tone eased a little. "Look, Win. You've been through a lot in the last several days. It's normal to be edgy. It would be unheard of for the Russians to move on you this quickly. They could have someone running physical surveillance on you, but not anyone at Sokolov's level. He's probably soaking up the summer sun in Moscow while his underlings scope things out."

"So you're discounting the phone call?" Win asked.

"No, no. The phone call, that's expected. That call could have originated anywhere. Major Sokolov wants you thinking about him—wants you worried, fearful."

Well, that's sure working for him, Win thought to himself.

"You'll know when it's beginning. There will probably be a seemingly chance encounter with someone—in the grocery store, the post office . . . maybe a note on your door. If they want to go bolder, maybe a drop with some cash. If it happens, just be real cool about it. Stash it at your house. Stay calm. Real low-key—that's how they generally play it. That's how we'd play it."

Win stayed on the call and doodled on a notepad while the experienced agent gently gave him the brush-off. When the call ended, Win's eyes went back to the American flag, still flailing wildly in the wind. *He didn't believe me.* He drew a long breath. He tried to reason with himself. Sutton was right. He'd told the supervisor that even he wasn't one hundred percent sure the man in the church was the Russian. He shouldn't have bothered Sutton on a Sunday—on his day off. *The guy probably thinks I'm a coward. I'm sure as hell acting like one.* He rubbed his eyes and leaned back in his chair. Sokolov's phone call on Wednesday had spooked him. Really spooked him. *Lordy, I even pulled a gun on an elk. An elk . . .*

CHAPTER EIGHTEEN

He stroked the fur on the black-and-white cat, and she purred and tipped her head back, her large gold eyes staring into his. He guessed she was thinking how nice this was—same thing he was thinking. The young cat had been a good addition to the family; Ellie had taken her in when one of the families caught up in the Prophet's church collapse could no longer care for her.

A log dropped in the fireplace, sending thousands of twinkling sparks soaring up the stone chimney. The fire had taken the chill from the room; it'd been a wet, windy morning. He stretched his long legs over the coffee table; they were still aching from the last two days of hiking. He was pleased that he'd had no serious physical problems on the outing, just sore muscles from lack of use. Babycat settled on his lap and slowly blinked her eyes as she looked up at him—cat talk for contentment, for security, he reckoned. He closed his eyes back at her, his signal that she was safe, that all was good.

But was everything really good? It was still bothering him, something didn't fit . . . something was off about the men he'd taken to Maxwell Springs. The client, James Donavan, had said everyone was in shape, that they all hit the gym, but the miles and miles of backcountry hiking was rugged and hard. They weren't on one of the park's groomed trails by any means; some of the cliffside paths the men had wanted to explore were just a couple of notches down from technical climbing. They'd bushwhacked through several miles of pure game trails, yet none of the three men had shown a moment of weakness or hesitation.

Then there was their backwoods experience. Donavan had fumbled with his tent setup and one of the men had joked about how to start a campfire, but Luke had the impression that neither of those events was genuine. After they set up camp, he'd explained to the group that the Park Service had taped off a prohibited area where human remains had been found recently. He'd told them to stay clear of the actual thermal areas—to view those fascinating features from the edge of the clearing. It was too dangerous to set foot on the hot crust, not to mention the damage tromping through the area could do to the fragile environment. But when he'd had taken one of Donavan's clients down to the lake for some early-morning fishing, it was obvious that his instructions to stay clear of the thermal areas had been ignored by the other two men—they both had white chert on their boots. He'd started to bring it up, but Donavan surprised him by saying they'd like to hike back out by midafternoon, not stay a second night as they'd planned.

Luke thought back to their arrival at Maxwell Springs. They were the only group there, and the guys had gone on and on about how amazing the site was—they'd said all the right things—but then they'd spent mere hours at the location. It was as if they'd found what they came for, as if they had another agenda. *Or maybe I'm just imagining things, making more outa it than there is.* He took another deep breath. Maybe it's just one of those "been there, done that" things that many folks were into these days—not taking the time to really soak it in, just checking the box on another experience, then on to the next adventure.

His musings were interrupted by Ellie's offer of tea from the kitchen. The comfortable cushions sagged as Ellie eased down beside him on the couch. She took a sip of the sweet tea and handed the glass to him. "I don't like not being in church on Sunday morning," she said. "We need to start visiting, find a new place." She reached out and petted the cat. "You've been quiet since you came home last night . . . was it too hard? Maybe you started back too soon?" She moved closer and adjusted the ice pack higher on his throbbing shoulder.

He drained the glass and set it on the coffee table; the cat stirred again with his movement. "Naw . . . it ain't that . . ." He drew a deep breath that still hurt a little when he exhaled. "Extra padding on the pack straps helped the shoulder. . . . My legs were a little weak and my breath is still a bit short, but it wasn't near as bad as it coulda been. You were right about it bein' good to get back in the woods." He smiled at her, his tone reassuring.

But her soft voice still sounded concerned, "I know you, Luke Bordeaux . . . something's bothering you. . . . Were the clients unhappy with the trip? I wasn't expecting you back till this afternoon . . . y'all got back by dark last night. Was there a problem?"

She could see right through him, and he loved her for that. He moved his hand from the cat to Ellie's long black hair and pulled it behind her neck. She'd been able to read his thoughts since back in eleventh grade, when he'd been shocked to discover that the prettiest, smartest girl in Ferriday, Louisiana, Mary Ellen Miller, liked him . . . loved him. He still found himself humbled by this beautiful, good woman's devotion. He ran his fingers down the back of her neck; he tried to deflect the questions. "Kids takin' a nap?"

"You know better than that," she said with a smile. "The only reason they aren't piled in here on top of us is the *Finding Nemo* video I rented for the weekend. They're lying on our bed, watching it for the third time."

He clicked his tongue and shook his head. "Not the best location fer 'em, given what I had in mind, El . . ."

She took his wandering hand and kissed the back of it. She arched her dark brows and gave him a coy look. "You keep that thought for tonight." Then she looped seamlessly back into her interrogation. "What's bothering you, babe?"

"Maybe nothin' . . . the clients I took out seemed fine on the surface. You saw how much they tipped me above and beyond that ridiculous fee Donavan paid me . . . but somethin' doesn't fit. It was like they were goin' to get a feel for the Maxwell Springs area—the trails in and out, the lake, the thermal area—almost like a recon of some sort. I had the feelin' they weren't there for the sightseein'."

"That's where the rangers found human bones nearly three weeks ago—it was in the newspaper. You suppose they were private investigators of some sort?"

"It's possible. . . . There could still be rewards out there fer the locations of some of Yellowstone's missin' persons. Seems one or two folks get lost in the park every year or so . . . maybe that's what it was."

"You could call Trey. You thought he might have sent those clients your way."

"I called Trey after I got cell service, after those guys split last night. He didn't know anything about it." He shrugged and the cat glanced up and frowned.

Ellie was still trying to be helpful. "I checked them out on social media before y'all left—Donavan and the others—they all looked like regular folks. You know, kids' pictures, dogs, golf, vacations . . . typical stuff." She grinned. "Well, typical if you have lots of money—not exactly like my Instagram page."

Luke smiled and nodded, but he still seemed pensive.

"You could talk to Win . . ." She let that hang there, and she didn't really look at him when she said it. They'd come to words over Win Tyler and the FBI's informant money more than once since he'd come home from the hospital. With the four church militiamen still on the run from the Feds, talking to Win Tyler about his concerns wasn't gonna happen.

He stared into the flickering flames sprouting from the log in the fireplace and his mood dipped a notch lower. The clients weren't the only issue on his mind. There were things that Ellie didn't know. Things it wasn't safe for her to know: the body he'd found at Phantom Lake . . . and his treks to the mountains these last two weeks when she thought he was going to physical therapy in Livingston. He kept his eyes on the flames . . . he told himself for the hundredth time that it was better if she didn't know. He told himself he was bending the truth for her own good . . . that it wasn't really lying. He told himself again that it needed to end.

* * *

Trey threw the ball a good fifty yards down the field, and Win sprinted to make a fingertip catch. He'd left the guy playing safety in the dust ten yards back. Win crossed the goal line and heaved the football back to his quarterback as the guys around him broke into high fives. The volunteer referee blew his whistle to signal the end of the game, and the weighty discussions of who owed who a beer began in earnest.

"Whoo-hoo! The mighty Pine Martens are 1 and 0! Adult beverages at Jazmine's place!" one of his team's two female players hollered for everyone to hear. Win slapped a few more backs and headed off the makeshift football field at Mammoth's abandoned elementary school. The school had been closed for years now, and various parts of the complex were used as a community center of sorts for the park rangers and their families. It was located at the edge of Lower Mammoth, a modern subdivision of sixty-four houses and rental units that adjoined the Historic District of Fort Yellowstone. Park Service budget cuts and changes in the ways rangers educated their kids had shuttered the school; Mammoth's children were now bused to Gardiner for classes.

Win had been hitting the employee gym behind the Mammoth Hot Springs Hotel since his mom had left town, and Trey had talked him into the flag football league a few weeks ago. He'd only managed to make two of their practices, but now that he wore the yellow rodent jersey, he guessed he was in it for the long haul. Playing the game again, even though it wasn't tackle, was a great stress reliever, and he had to admit to himself that he missed football. The social activity outside of work also gave him points with the Headquarters' shrink he was required to video conference with twice a week over the shooting incidents.

The only downside to the practices and games was his constant need for reasonable excuses to avoid Jazmine Jackson after each outing. Trey said the young ranger, who'd transferred in from St. Louis when Win was in the hospital last month, was smitten with him. *Smitten.* Trey had used that word. *Just tell her you're not interested. Be a man!* But Win hated to hurt her feelings, so he avoided her hopeful glances and drifted away with Trey as the team meeting broke up.

Trey tossed the ball to him as they both walked back toward the parking lot. "You headin' over to Jazmine's with the single folks?" Trey cut him a knowing grin.

Win shook his head, but before he could fabricate an excuse to miss the heavy drinkers, Trey lowered his voice and offered him an option.

"I'm cooking steaks on the grill tonight and Cindy made strawberry shortcake. A couple more rangers are joining us. Why don't you grab a shower and come by around 7:30?"

"Strawberry shortcake? For real? That's the best offer I've had in weeks. I'm in."

Win palmed the ball and slapped another departing teammate on the shoulder. Trey had stopped to tease a couple of the losing team's players, and Win handed off his flag belt to the departing referees. He sat in the old Explorer's seat and swapped out his cleats for running shoes. He peeled the sweat-soaked jersey over his head and wiped his face and chest with a towel. The cold breeze hit him, and he marveled that it could be below sixty degrees in mid-June. He reached across to the passenger seat and pulled his warm-up jacket to him. When he lifted the jacket, a bulky manila envelope dropped into his lap. He gasped as he blinked down at dozens of hundred-dollar bills that had fallen free of the package.

It's begun. Good Lord, it's begun.

Brent Sutton had told him to stay cool. Hearing it and doing it were two different things. He figured someone was watching him. *Heck, I'd be watching if I'd just dropped several thousand dollars off in someone's truck.* He fought off the urge to scan the surroundings. He casually scooped up the stray bills and stuffed them back in the big envelope. He casually stuffed the big envelope under the driver's seat. He pulled on the warm-up jacket, waved to a couple more teammates, and made the two-minute drive to his house. He tried real hard to remember to breathe.

*   *   *

The steam was still rolling out of the hot shower as he stepped onto the tile floor and groped for his towel. He decided to pretend nothing had happened. He'd get cleaned up and go to Trey's cookout. If he went to the office, if he made a call, he was afraid he could somehow tip them off. The Bureau folks had told him that after a cash drop there would normally be weeks before he'd be contacted again. He had to wait.

He drew in another deep breath of the warm, moist air and glanced into the foggy mirror. The red streak on the side of his head where the bullet had clipped him was barely visible since his hair had grown back. His fingers felt for the scar on the back of his head—still a little tender, but the dark-brown hair was filling in there as well. Soon the only physical reminders of his near-death experiences would be fading scars. *Wish the mental scars would disappear as quickly.* He forced his mind away from a flashback of last month's firefight that sought to intrude on his thoughts. He sighed. Now there were nightmares of Russia to add to the mix.

He wiped the towel across his face again, turned off the vent fan, and stepped right into a soft chuckle from across the dim bedroom.

"Well, I can say for sure you're not armed." The amused voice had an easy, Texas drawl.

Win pulled the wet towel from his hair and clutched it below his waist. His shocked eyes darted around the room and settled on the man causally leaning back in the leather reading chair in the corner. The man he knew as Jake Stedman continued to talk as he flipped the latest issue of *Razorback Football Preview* down on the side table.

"I don't see the appeal in your American football. . . . It's not much of a sport, really. You stand around in a group, discussing things, half the time. So little action." He shook his head and smiled. "Hockey—now that's a sport for real men! Moscow's Red Army—that's my team. Play any hockey, Win?"

Win didn't move, but his eyes found his Glock in the holster on the dresser where he'd left it after church; his football jersey and shorts were slung across the bed. The Russian's outdoor garb gave him the look of a well-to-do hiker, but the clear latex gloves and the small black pistol cradled in his left hand sure weren't standard attire. Win swallowed down the bitter taste of fear. He tried for a steady voice.

"No. No, never even seen an ice hockey game. Not much opportunity for that growing up down South. You played?"

"Uh-huh." He touched a faint scar above his right eye. "Still got a few souvenirs. Both of us were successful at team sports—just another thing that makes us similar in how we approach our careers. We're team players."

"Yeah, so similar, you and me." Win managed harsh sarcasm in his tone. "You mind if I put some pants on? It's gettin' a little drafty standing here drippin' on the floor."

The Russian laughed softly again. "Naw, no need to get dressed for me. I'm not stayin' for dinner. Just sit down on the bed and we'll talk a little business, then I'll leave and let you enjoy your evening."

Win wrapped the damp towel around his waist and sat on the edge of the bed. Sokolov was only a few feet away. Gruff appeared from under the bed and jumped on the leather ottoman in front of him. The big green-eyed cat leveled a hostile stare at the big green-eyed Russian; Gruff gave the man a low, guttural growl.

Win felt a chill that had nothing to do with the room's temperature. "Don't hurt him."

The man seemed surprised. "I wouldn't harm him . . . he's no threat to me, Agent Tyler." He glanced down at the animal and spoke softly, *"Хороший котенок."* The cat probably didn't speak Russian, but he did seem to get the drift of the "good kitty" message. He appeared to conclude that the stranger wasn't a threat. He flicked his long tail, jumped down, and ambled off toward the kitchen and his food bowl. Win was thinking his roommate wasn't such a great judge of character. Sokolov switched his attention back to Win.

"Where's the gift I sent you?"

Win motioned with his chin toward the walnut bookcases that took up the wall behind the man. "It's spread out in my law school textbooks. Mostly in *Black's Law Dictionary.*" *Thank goodness I listened to Sutton and hid the money.*

"Nobody reads the old law books anymore since you can get everything off the internet. Not a bad spot for a stash—better than your sock drawer." The Russian eased out of the chair and reached toward the antique bookcase. The leather-bound dictionary came down in his free hand, and he lowered the heavy book to the desk. The randomly scattered hundred-dollar bills fell to the side as he thumbed through the book. His eyes never completely left Win and the pistol never wavered.

"Well, now, it's good to see you didn't call or turn this over to your agency."

"I haven't turned it in *yet*. I'm still thinking it through." Win's eyes narrowed and his voice hardened. He had to play his role. "You don't own me."

"Of course not . . . not with this piddlin' amount. It's just $20,000. Chump change. What are you gonna spend this first installment on, Cowboy?"

"Get rid of the pistol . . . I'm not talking to you with you aiming at me." Win willed his voice to remain strong.

The man palmed the black semiautomatic. "This little thing bothering you? It's a Lebedev PLK, new on the market . . . one of my favorites." He gave it an admiring look. "Fine Russian craftsmanship. One of the better compact handguns. Very accurate . . . real deadly for such a small thing." The green eyes gleamed as a shaft of late-afternoon sunlight found a slit in the blinds. He shifted away from the unwelcome light; his lips formed a thin line, and he nodded down toward the open book where thousands of dollars had spilled out. His tone became more serious.

"There's more, much more, where this came from, Win."

Win let his focus drop to the money scattered on the desk. His hand went to his chin, and he bit down on his lower lip. He locked eyes with the spy.

"What do you want from me?" Win quietly asked.

CHAPTER NINETEEN

There was silence on the other end of the line. Complete silence. Then, the Supervisor for Counterintelligence at the Seattle Field Office cleared his throat and repeated what he'd just heard. "The drop was $20,000. Thirty minutes later he was sitting in your bedroom . . . he was holding a weapon . . . he was not wearing a disguise." The man cleared his throat again. Win was thinking his impromptu Sunday-evening report fell squarely into the "very surprised" or maybe even the "shocked" category. After another long pause, Brent Sutton seemed to recover.

"Where are you calling from?"

"I'm at a barbecue, a cookout, at a friend's house . . . using their landline. We've been mostly outside; I don't think I need to be away from the group for very long . . . I'm sure they're watching me."

"Don't let it get to you. The Russians aren't everywhere, Win."

"It sure *feels* as if they're everywhere. And with all due respect, sir, everything y'all told me—on how they behave, when they'll move in, what to expect—it's all been wrong. Somebody on their team is working off a different playbook."

Win heard the supervisor sigh. "I can't argue with that. Give me a quick overview. What did he say . . ." It went on like that for about five minutes, and Sutton told Win to expect a call from Paige later tonight. "Just continue to do what you're doing," he said in closing. "Now that we know Sokolov is in Mammoth, we'll quickly pivot resources your way. You're not alone in this . . ."

Sutton wrapped up the abbreviated pep talk with "You're smart to stay off your phones. No way he has the office landline or your Bureau cell compromised, but I'd bet money he has your house, your personal phone, and maybe your vehicle wired. . . ." Sutton seemed to be thinking it through on the fly. "You're changing your keypad numbers for entry into your office every week . . . so no way he's been in there. Paige is back in San Francisco, but we'll probably send her back to Bozeman. She'll either handle the debrief on today's events . . . or . . . or AD Langford may want to bring in other players." Sutton paused again. "Hang in there, Win. I'll be in touch."

Hang in there. Uh-huh. I'm hearing that waaay too often lately.

Win hung up the receiver and moved into the kitchen to help Trey's wife bring out the homemade ice cream and strawberry short-cake. They all gathered on the small patio at the rear of the modest frame house and toasted the cook. It was one of the few times in Win's life when he had absolutely no appetite.

* * *

When his personal phone rang at eleven, he'd already been back at his house for an hour. He'd gone through every closet, looked under every bed; he'd even gone down in the dingy basement—all with his .40 caliber Glock in hand. Gruff followed him around until he tired of the game, then plopped down on the couch and licked his paws as Win finished his search for bogeymen. Win knew who'd be calling at this hour.

"Babe! We can see each other tomorrow night!" She squealed. She actually squealed. Then, "Can you believe those bozos in Bozeman still can't get all the financials uploaded from the bank fraud cases and sent in correctly? Their loss but our gain, Winnie! They're sending me back there to straighten things out. Tell me you're free!"

Win played along. He had no choice. None at all. Maybe this wouldn't be too bad, he reasoned; the Russian hadn't seemed terribly threatening. Maybe they could set a quick trap, nab him, get this over soon. But deep down he knew better. He knew it wouldn't be that easy. Still, he clung to that hope. Paige ended the brief call with a string of suggestions for their activities tomorrow night that went way beyond dinner. He knew his face was red when he got off the call.

*   *   *

He was mentally running through a dozen tasks when he stepped out his back door at 5:45 the next morning. He'd had a fitful night of nightmares, tossing and turning, of staring into the darkness. His Glock had been lying on his nightstand—he'd only slept with the gun at his side one other time in his life. It wasn't a good feeling. He'd abbreviated his usual routine of running, coffee, Scripture, and prayer down to simply coffee. That wasn't a good feeling either. And it was becoming more of a habit than he cared to admit. Something Prophet Shepherd's daughter said to him the other day drifted through his mind as he locked the back door: *"He wasn't always a bad person—he just got away from God."* Avoiding God seemed to be happening more and more in his life these past few weeks. He knew he wasn't trying real hard to figure out why.

He turned on the top step and took another sip of his coffee. The sunshine that came so early to this northern place suddenly cut through the morning mist and lit up the Lower Terraces of the hot springs. A blinding light seemed to radiate from the glistening white travertine; bold streaks of orange bacteria twisted through the formations as steam rose from every surface. It was so sudden and so beautiful that it nearly took his breath away. A truth he knew from childhood came to his mind: God is ever present. And today's reminder was this spectacular scene just yards from his house. As he stood on the step and took it in, he said a prayer of thanks. Some of the weight lifted from his shoulders, and he reminded himself that he couldn't let fear or uncertainty steal his joy for life. He'd joined the Bureau to be a force for good—that job still remained to be done.

* * *

Tom Strickland could see the front range of the Rockies from his expansive upper-floor office on the outskirts of Denver. The early-morning sun was lighting up the distant mountains. It was a great view. He'd been the Special Agent in Charge here since January, when he'd stepped down as an FBI Assistant Director to take this job back in his home state. He'd been one of the first African Americans to serve as an AD; he was proud of his service at Headquarters. But retirement was coming in two or three years, and he and the wife wanted to be closer to family, closer to home. He'd hoped for smooth sailing here, in a field office that oversaw Bureau activities in Colorado and Wyoming. But it had been anything but smooth sailing these last two months, and Tom Strickland's considerable experience told him things in Yellowstone National Park were headed in the wrong direction again.

Strickland's heavy shoulders were hunched forward as he leaned his stocky frame over his desk. His shaved head dropped as he reviewed the latest classified memo on the Russian case, as he and his second-in-command, Wes Givens, were calling it. He spoke to his ASAC before he even raised his eyes. "Win's in this over his head, Wes. Washington is using him as bait in what could be a lethal game."

Wes Givens dropped his lean frame into a chair across from the desk as his boss waved him down. "Brent Sutton tells me that Win understands the risks . . . but I think you're right. Win has no train-ing in counterintelligence, and if even half the intel I've seen on Sergei Sokolov is accurate, the guy is beyond scary." He paused. "What do you make of Sokolov showing up at Win's place yesterday afternoon?"

Strickland leaned back and drummed his pen on the paperwork. His heavy brows hooded his eyes as he worked through the possibilities. When he finally spoke, the concern hadn't left his voice. "Washington is reading that move as just another logical step for the Russians to reel Win in—in their effort to turn him. Brent's analysts expect them to drop more money, to sweeten the pie a bit more, before they ask him for anything substantial. They may just keep asking for tidbits on those missing persons files . . . using them as a pretext to see how far Win will go in sharing information."

He dropped the pen on his desk and sighed. His small, dark eyes found Givens's face. "That's what Washington thinks."

"You're not convinced that's their play." Givens said it more as a statement than a question.

The SAC nodded slowly. "I worked alongside a Russian army group back twenty-five years ago, when I was with the Army's European Command." He smiled a little. "That was back in my earlier career . . . my much younger days. Back then, we thought we might build something of an alliance with the Russians, but that wasn't their goal. They ended up with our intel and strategic plans on half a dozen former Eastern Bloc countries, some of which they're now in the process of destabilizing. They ended up with valuable intel, and we ended up with the realization that they'd outfoxed us completely.

"Even their junior officers were big into chess and were students of history. The Russians I worked with were calculating people . . . they tended to look further out than we did. They were more willing than we were to lose some assets—whether it be personnel, territory, or status—to gain the greater prize. And they mix their military people in with their intelligence folks. It's not the sharp distinction we have . . . I was never sure if I was dealing with regular army or former KGB. Often it was both. It's no different for them now. Major Sokolov has an impressive military background, but you can bet that's not his primary job."

Wes Givens raised his chin a little and gazed into his boss's eyes. "You're thinking there is more going on here than the SVR trying to recruit a young, up-and-coming FBI agent."

Strickland nodded. "This guy Win is dealing with is way too high up the food chain to be tasked with recruiting low-level assets. Win might be a catch for them, looking at the long game, but why would they risk someone like Sokolov? In a setting like Yellowstone of all places?"

"What's AD Langford thinking?"

"We talked last night. He knows my concerns, but we've got nothing to go on. The background of the Russian geologist who disappeared in the park a few years ago was investigated by Homeland Security when the incident happened—no red flags. Donald says we're looking into her background again, but the folks in Washington still seem to think that the Russians are just using the missing persons angle to get to Win."

Wes straightened his Gucci tie and frowned. "Sutton did tell me they're going to clue Win in a bit more on who he's dealing with—it's way past time for that to happen. And Win should have the option to opt out once he has all the facts. He's gone into this deal blind up to this point. If he elects to stay with the assignment, there's no way he should be dealing with an operative on Sokolov's level without solid backup. Lots of solid backup."

"I'm not happy about how this is going either, but we're sidelined, at least for the time being. Just stay on top of Sutton . . . make sure he remembers Win is our guy."

Givens nodded. "On another matter, is Headquarters really ending the manhunt?"

The SAC's eyes narrowed and he sighed. More rough sailing. "They're letting Angela Holmes make that call . . . but the search in southwestern Montana has been a bust. You've seen all the bad press. The governor out there is raising a stink on all the cable news shows. The Park Service is having a fit that we've still got so much of Yellowstone in a restricted zone and that we've commandeered so much of the park's lodging. Putting a crimp in tourism, I suppose. Haven't gotten the official word, but I expect HRT to fly back to Quantico tonight . . . our SWAT guys will likely convoy back here tomorrow. We should know before noon. They could even shut the Bureau's operation down completely—turn the search in the park, if there is a continuing search, over to the Marshals Service."

* * *

It was just after eight when Win finished reviewing the Bureau's daily bulletins, checking his email, and sorting through phone messages. It had been one week since the Bureau's very efficient rumor mill had run with the story of Win's latest fall from grace. He was thankful that the messages of condolence from his Bureau friends and coworkers were becoming less frequent.

He left Tory a voicemail to let her know he had to work and couldn't meet her for dinner tonight. He was amazed that she'd agreed to the date in the first place, after the fiasco with the gun and the elk at the waterfall last Wednesday. Her artist friend, Lauren, had helped him save face by making him out to be their great protector. They'd ended the evening by all hiking back to the trailhead together, then meeting for ice cream in Roosevelt as darkness fell. The date hadn't gone as he'd planned, but finding himself as the center of attention for intelligent, talented women hadn't done his ego any harm. He'd had fun. He tried to recapture some of that buzz as he thought back over it, but it just wasn't happening this morning.

He was usually good at compartmentalizing issues and emotions. Very good. But he was struggling to finish routine emails—he had to fight to keep his thoughts off the Russian. The man hadn't really given him explicit instructions. Just a few "rules" Win needed to follow, instructions to watch for a text or signal that a meeting was requested, directives to keep working on the missing person files, move things forward, that sort of thing. There had been no hostility, no threats. True to his word, he hadn't stayed long. *Close your eyes and don't move for three minutes . . . I'll be in touch soon.* That's all he'd said as he left the bedroom late yesterday afternoon. Win didn't hear the floor squeak, never even heard a door close; the Russian moved like a ghost. He simply disappeared. And Win Tyler obeyed every command.

Win scowled at the unfinished work on his computer screen, leaned back in his chair and listened. The old building was quiet. Too quiet. The only sounds were the indistinct blend of muted voices and vehicles outside; the tourists had all awakened. But he felt alone—very alone. He even found himself wishing Johnson was back. Win was a team player; he needed a team. He tried to shake the melancholy feeling by heading downstairs to the break room to brew a fresh pot of coffee, but instead he found himself standing in front of the office's metal gun vault. *I'll just check on them,* he told himself as he keyed in the combination on the lock. He opened the lower ammo drawer and pulled out the plastic bag that contained Natasha's ring box and the slender container that housed the bones. A glance told him that the bones were fine; he slid the Coroner's carton back in place. He placed the red velvet ring box on the countertop beside the vault, then set the dark-blue velvet box beside it.

He told himself that he was just making sure everything was safe, everything was as it should be. But that didn't fly. *I wouldn't be pulling a woman's bones, her family's ring . . . my family's ring . . . out of a gun safe if everything was as it should be.* He opened the two ring boxes and stood there appraising their contents. The Russian ring's opulence sparkled under the overhead light. His grandmother's more modest ring—no, it was Shelby's ring—shone just as brightly in his eyes. He blinked back unexpected tears as he gently closed both boxes and picked them up. His heart knew what he held . . . *the rings of the lost.*

* * *

It was nearly six o'clock when he stepped through the door at the Holiday Inn—he was beginning to feel like a regular there. The two men standing in the room introduced themselves as Jeff Ginner and Ramon Santiago; they didn't say who they worked for and they didn't have to. The business cards they handed him set out some innocuous subagency within the State Department. He'd played this game before; he wouldn't get their real names, but he'd be expected to grasp their employer: CIA. They were serious men who looked rumpled from the long plane ride from wherever they came from—they didn't volunteer any information, and they weren't given to small talk.

The smaller guy had thinning brown hair, a ruddy complexion, and wire-frame glasses. His companion, Santiago, had more of an athletic build, tall and muscular—his suit coat was too small for his broad shoulders. He had curly black hair that matched his trimmed beard. His dark eyes had a brooding look.

The Bureau's Russia expert from San Francisco, Ms. Gorski, sat in the corner and seemed content to listen in; Paige and Humphrey had disappeared into the adjoining room moments after Win had arrived. Win couldn't figure why the Bureau folks were letting the CIA guys handle his debrief. They rehashed Win's every movement for the last twenty-four hours. They dissected everything about Sokolov's appearances on Sunday: his gestures, his disguise, his words. For Win, it was exhausting, and it had gone on for almost two hours when they finally began to wrap it up.

"He thinks he's got you on a line . . . he's got you thinking about what he means by 'maybe I can make it worth your while.' He'll want to set the hook, gauge your real interest. He'll ask you for something he doesn't already have . . . to prove you're serious." The smaller CIA officer leaned back in the chair and glanced toward his compatriot. "Anything to add here?"

Santiago leaned toward Win. "We're gonna be real straight with you, Agent Tyler. If what we know about Sergei Sokolov is true, you will be in extreme danger if he gets the slightest inkling you're not falling in line with him. Normally, we'd want you to string him along, see what he's here to target. But with your lack of experience and his reputation, we don't feel comfortable with that tack. Best-case scenario: we're able to bag him and some of his team, even if we have to take them out. Worst case: we lose them. If that happens, we may never know why the Russians were willing to send such a top-tier operative to Yellowstone." He paused for a moment and locked eyes with Win. "If we get burned on this—if he finds out you're working with us—there's always the possibility that he'll kill you to tie up loose ends."

Well, then. Win hoped he'd kept his game face.

Paige moved into the room in a revealing tank top, short skirt, and platform sandals just as the Agency men were standing. Win did a double take when he saw her; he wondered where she kept her gun. Paige looked like a vamp, but she was all business. "We're going to dinner . . . maybe have a beer afterward," she announced to the room.

"We'll be back around eleven and Ms. Gorski will finish the debrief."
She barely glanced at Win. "Tyler, we've been in here nearly two hours
since we met in the lobby . . . you need to leave this room lookin' real
happy. When we're out, you should look and act like a guy anxious to
get back to the room for dessert. You get my drift?"

"Got it."

* * *

Win was still reeling from the Twilight Zone feel of his dinner date
with Paige when he stepped back into the crowded hotel room later
that night. Paige slipped past the Agency officers, who'd both donned
their jackets, and followed Ms. Gorski into the adjoining room. The
air-conditioning unit was rattling, Win supposed that was to thwart
any efforts at audible surveillance, but it made the room cold enough to
hang meat. Humphrey had changed into sweats and was leaning on the
bed, eating nachos. They watched the smaller of the CIA guys, Ginner,
pull a stack of photos from his briefcase.

"Your bosses wanted you to know who you're dealing with, Win,"
Ginner said as he stacked several glossy crime-scene photos neatly on
the small desk. The tall, dark Agency man ran his hand across them
and spread them out like playing cards for Win and Humphrey to see.
The predominant color was red. Humphrey stood up; he and Win both
moved closer for a better view. Win took in the horror in one quick
sweep and looked away. Humphrey made the mistake of holding his
gaze on the depicted carnage a second too long. He pushed past Win
to the bathroom and lost his dinner. While Humphrey reentered the
room and tried to regain his composure, Win tried to force himself to
breathe. His mind didn't want to comprehend this level of depravity—
this level of inhumanity.

"A good operative . . . a good case officer . . . can lull you into
thinking—into believing—that they're on your side, you're in this
together, they're just like you." The tall man pointed to the photos.
"Well, listen up! He's not like you, Tyler . . . he's not like us. Based on
what we know, he's a damn good case officer. He'll have you eating out

of his hand. But don't forget for a second that he's also a cold-blooded killer. Forget that and you'll end up like these poor souls."

Ginner glanced down at the sickening photos. His tone was indifferent. He'd seen this sort of thing before. "This little massacre happened last year outside of Aleppo, Syria. We got the photos from British MI6. The Brits had an informant, who was apparently a double agent, named Ahmad Al Numan. He was feeding intel to them and to the Russians and Assad's boys. Your man, Sokolov, was supposedly his handler for the six or seven months leading up to this. There was a leak, and the Russians realized Al Numan was playing both sides. The Brits sent in a special ops unit to pull him and his family out, but Sokolov and his team beat them to it. Look at the photos, Win. They aren't pretty. Tortured to death. The man, his wife, two little kids. He'll be wanted by Interpol for war crimes once civilization returns to Syria. If it ever does."

Win forced himself to see the photos again. He pictured Sokolov's deep-green eyes.

"Do you want me to take him out?" he asked softly. "Is that the point of this?"

The smaller man shrugged. "Not my call."

Santiago stepped closer to Win and flipped a file down beside the photos. "Part of Sokolov's file that we've cleared you to see . . . look it over." He locked eyes with Win. "Your background is in white-collar cases—bank and securities fraud, public corruption—that sort of thing. This is a whole different ball game, Tyler . . . just watch yourself. We want you to know who you're dealing with . . . if you decide to stay in this operation." He gathered the photos and moved to the side of the room.

Ms. Gorski walked in, sat in the desk chair, and took over the little meeting. Win eased down on a corner of the bed. "Win, you haven't been given a read-in on Major Sokolov's file until now. . . . You have the right to opt out—that word comes all the way down from the top. No dishonor in quitting this assignment. The Bureau doesn't want to put you in an untenable position."

They're covering their butts in case he kills me.

When Win didn't respond, she continued to talk. "That said, we're hoping you can keep Sokolov occupied long enough for us to get an arrest team in place. Since Washington has apparently decided to shut down the fugitive hunt in Yellowstone, we won't be able to utilize any of those resources in dealing with Sokolov." She looked down her nose at Win; she had a habit of doing that. "Brent Sutton has six hand-picked HRT operators flying in; they'll be in Gardiner or Mammoth within twenty-four hours. They'll be under deep cover—you shouldn't worry, Win. It's all being handled . . . just trust the process."

Didn't Jake Stedman—Sergei Sokolov—tell me the same thing?

Win knew his eyes had narrowed. He sat there and studied the three Bureau folks. Ms. Gorski's efforts at reassurance felt as cold as the icy air in the room. Humphrey still hadn't regained his color, and Paige seemed subdued. He knew they were all watching him, wondering if he would quit.

Not a chance. "I'm ready to finish this up . . . I need to get back to Mammoth early tomorrow. Sokolov said he'd be in touch soon."

CHAPTER TWENTY

Paige was hanging all over him as he stepped into the bright hallway at 6:30 a.m. and turned to pull the door shut. She was playing her role, that was for darn sure. Before he straightened to take a step, she stretched on tiptoes and kissed him hard on the lips. She giggled as he forced a grin and nuzzled down her neck. A businessman dodged them in the hall and sent Win a knowing smirk over her head. Win turned with her attached to his hip right into the path of three other guests who were moving down the hall from the lobby.

"Win?" The wavering voice stopped him in his tracks. The sounds from the lobby, doors closing down the hall—everything just faded away.

Tory, her friend Lauren, and another young woman stood blocking the hall. The shock on Tory's face was evident, and he watched in horror as she bit down on her lip, raised her chin, and tried to control her emotions. The awkward silence began to drag out.

"Winnie, baby, you didn't tell me you had friends here," Paige cooed from under his arm. She couldn't get any closer without getting inside his shirt. She turned just enough in her proprietary stance to address the other women. "Hi, ladies . . . I'm Paige Lange, I don't think we've met."

Win wasn't sure what happened next. There were introductions that he heard in the background. Lauren said something about them having had an early breakfast, the other girl said something about a concert last night. But Tory didn't say a word. She just stared up into his face, and the hurt and distrust in those velvety-brown eyes was breaking his heart.

It must have gone silent again, as Paige suddenly turned her attention back to the door. "Oh, crap! Forgot my phone, babe. Let me back in, help me find it . . . I'm gonna be late for work." Win fumbled with the plastic key card and the other three women continued down the hall. Paige kept up the act until the door firmly clicked shut behind them. She slid from under his arm and retreated from his side. The CIA guys were fooling with the room's tiny coffee maker—both looked startled when the couple reappeared. Paige gave them an okay sign and drew a deep breath.

"Ah, Win, I'm really sorry . . . what crappie luck, to run into—I'm guessing here—your main squeeze?" Paige dropped her eyes and seemed to be waiting for him to say something. He shrugged off her apology and raised a hand to silence her.

Humphrey looked up from his computer on the far side of the room; he'd obviously watched the exchange in the hallway on his laptop, from a hidden camera. He locked eyes with Win. "You know you can't tell anyone else why you're here." He shook his head. "Bad luck is all . . . it happens."

Win's shock turned to anger. "You don't have to tell me my business."

Humphrey gave a shrug and changed focus. He held up two fingers. "We spotted two watchers last night for sure, and our folks have already tagged one this morning. The opposition has two cameras in the hall and a 'maybe' in the lobby." He frowned as he glanced down at the laptop. "They're upping their game."

The tall Agency officer finally brewed his cup of coffee. He gave Win his parting advice as Paige reached for the doorknob. "Don't screw this up, Tyler. String Sokolov along until the Bureau gets those HRT guys in place. . . . The Russians aren't invincible. They won't be any more comfortable in a park crawling with tourists than we will."

As Win turned toward the door, the guy's voice followed him. "And forget the girl . . . there'll always be another girl."

* * *

He turned off the highway in front of a minivan—way too close. Then the Expedition bounced over the wooden bridge much too fast, hit the gravel road, and fishtailed. He got it back between the ditches. Win wasn't normally a reckless driver, but he was less than three miles north of Mammoth and still numb from whatever it was he was feeling. He'd been driving south from Bozeman for nearly two hours, and he'd made no attempt to sort it out. He felt as if he were walking in quicksand—he was real damn tired of getting nowhere on nothing.

Maybe it was anger boiling up in him, maybe frustration at not feeling in control of his life, maybe anguish at having caused pain to someone he cared for, maybe all those emotions mixed with the fear of what awaited him. Whatever it was, it came to a head when he saw Bordeaux's green pickup turn off Highway 89 onto the narrow gravel road that led through gently rolling flats toward a tree-covered plateau and Luke's house.

Win flashed his headlights as a signal as he pulled behind the pickup on the dusty road. Bordeaux slowed to a stop and let the dust from both vehicles roll over his truck. No need to pull off to the side— wouldn't be anyone else coming this way. Luke stepped out of the pickup in his bushwhacker garb and leaned back on the dirty tailgate. He didn't look happy and Win didn't care. Win walked to within ten feet of him.

"Trey said your bosses weren't lettin' you talk to me," Luke began.

"That's right."

Luke raised his eyebrows in question.

"We aren't talking."

"Alright, what is it we ain't talkin' about?"

"I'll do my best for those men if you send them my way." Luke might as well know Win was on to him.

Luke's reply was flippant. "What men?"

"You know right well who and what I'm talking about. We never really got to finish our conversation at Phantom Lake . . . and here it's gone on another two weeks."

"Uh-huh, we had a little interruption that afternoon, as I recall. You get that mess figured out?"

"Not my problem. You know as well as I do the body in the snow-drift was the guy who went missing from Prophet Shepherd's bunch back in April. He was murdered—no secret there. But back to Eriksson and those boys. I figure you've been giving them intel, rations, who knows what all, ever since you got back on your feet."

Luke's chin went up a little and he glanced away for a moment. When he looked back, his dark eyes were evasive. "Well now . . . how'd you figure that?"

Win moved closer to the man; his hard look didn't waver. "You know it needs to end. If the Bureau were to pull back and the bounty hunters move in, someone will very likely end up dead. They're trigger-happy. *We know that.*" He emphasized the words.

"Yeah. That we do. Y'all pullin' out?"

"I never said that."

"Didn't have to say it. Feds started takin' radio equipment down, removing the temporary chopper pad—doin' the teardown, as we'd say in the service. Been goin' on since last night. I figure the FBI is outa here before sundown."

He's got that right. Win stared him down. "It needs to end."

Luke made a slight nod; if Win hadn't been really dialed in, he'd have missed it.

"Nice herd of antelope will be crossin' back over the road fore you get back to the highway. Be right pretty to see in the early light. Good fer a man's soul to see beauty every mornin'." Luke turned away, got in his truck, and drove toward home.

The twenty or so pronghorn antelope really were a beautiful sight. Luke was right; sitting in the truck, watching them pass, began to calm him. They were only a few yards in front of him, highlighted by the sun that was gaining height in a crystal-clear blue sky. They were strung out in a line, with the tiny babies running circles around their mothers. The little ones were miniature copies of the adults: long, spindly legs; bright-white heads, chests, and rumps; with tawny bodies. Stumpy white tails flicked constantly. The three bucks swung their short black horns and for no obvious reason raced ahead, then back to the group. Win knew they favored the sagebrush flats and open ridges; he'd read that they were the second-fastest animal in the world. It wasn't quite nine o'clock, but he figured they were headed for some cool spot to spend the heat of the day. As the last of the herd cleared the empty road, he put the truck in gear, and realized he was smiling.

*   *   *

As Win drove past the Justice Center in Mammoth, he met three large utility trucks headed in the opposite direction—back toward Gardiner and out of the park. It was obvious that the remnants of the Bureau's manhunt were on the move. The Bureau had been down to the bare minimum since the bulk of HRT and the SWAT folks had shifted to extreme southwestern Montana on June 2nd, but now, on June 17th, everyone seemed to be folding their tent. Win thought about stopping at the Justice Center to touch base with anyone from Denver who was still working on the False Prophet case, but he decided he'd violated enough direct orders for one day by stopping to chat with Bordeaux.

Gruff met him at the back door with a head bump on his leg and an accusatory glance at the empty food bowl. "Geez, Gruff. I've only been gone since yesterday afternoon, just a few hours." Win reached for the cat food and sighed. *It sure seems like more than a few hours.*

Tory hadn't returned the call he'd made to her as he'd driven down from Bozeman. *No big surprise there.* It might be for the best, he told himself. With a murderous Russian trailing him, it might be wise to distance himself from her until the threat was over. But his barely contained heartache was unexpected; they'd had only two real dates— he'd never even managed to kiss her. Was he doing the rebound thing? Latching on to her for affection because Shelby had broken his heart? He kept reliving the pain and shock in Tory's soft eyes that he'd seen this morning. He kept remembering the words he'd spoken to her only days ago: *You can trust me, Tory Madison. I promise you that—you can trust me.* In her view, he'd broken that trust completely. He had to figure out a way to get it back.

For the rest of the morning, he went about doing the stuff normal people do during their time away from work: laundry, paying bills, calling his folks back home. He set out a grocery list and money for Tia, his once-a-week housekeeper. She was a lifesaver. The kind middle-aged woman cleaned his house, ironed his shirts, and made a weekly hour-long drive to the grocery store and dry cleaner in Livingston for him and several other single residents of Mammoth. He felt guilty about leaving Gruff alone so often lately, so he spent the better part of thirty minutes playing with the cat. He thought about a run, but the trails were so crowded with hikers it would be a hassle this time of day. He settled for several sets of push-ups and crunches on the bedroom floor.

He'd taken to locking his bathroom door and keeping his Bureau phone and his handgun on the sink counter when he took a shower. A little extreme, maybe, but having a Russian killer show up in his bedroom had made him a bit paranoid. *Better safe than sorry,* he told himself while he shaved. It felt weird being at home midmorning on a Tuesday, but he didn't have anything on his calendar until his two o'clock meeting with Chris Warren, and he figured he'd more than put in his time for the Bureau in the last twenty-four hours. He was debating whether to fight the crowd at the Mammoth Hot Springs Hotel restaurant or scrounge up something at home for an early lunch when Jason knocked on his back door. The kid was wearing his Park Service uniform and a smile a mile wide.

"What's up?" Win asked as he opened the door.

"Saw your rig here and thought I'd catch you home." The slender boy headed inside as soon as the door opened, not waiting for an invitation. Win could hear the excitement in his voice. "I got in!" He waved his phone. "Got two emails this morning—I got in!"

"You gonna keep me guessing?" Win was grinning; Jason's exuberance was contagious.

Jason pulled up the emails and scrolled though them with his thumb. "Montana State and, look . . . see the next one, it's the University of Wyoming!"

Win took the phone and read the letters of acceptance out loud. Two months ago, the kid hadn't even studied for his SATs; now he was well on his way to college. "This calls for a big-time party! But grab a coke, how 'bout we celebrate with ham-and-cheese omelets till we can do this right." As Win opened the cabinet beside the stove, he thanked God for the little things that became the big things that made life special.

*   *   *

An hour later, after Jason pulled out of the driveway, Win walked around the house to check on his mother's flowers. He'd told himself he'd check them every day, water them, send her pictures. But he hadn't. He was shocked to see that the shrub the elk had trimmed had grown by at least two feet, colorful buds were forming, and the wildflowers were taking off too. Not the most attractive flower bed, covered in chicken wire as it was, but even with that ugly web of protection, the flowers were blooming. He thought to himself that there must be a life lesson in there somewhere if he'd just take the time to look. Instead he took a few photos and texted them to his mother.

He noticed a large group gathered on the boardwalks; some sort of educational talk was going on across from his house. When he realized it was the geyser guy, Dr. Ratliff, he decided to listen in; he had a few minutes before he had to get back to the office. Simon Dravec was standing on the boardwalk several yards from the group, materials in hand. Win headed that way.

He walked up to Dr. Dravec and stopped beside him. "Dr. Ratliff certainly can draw a crowd," Win commented.

The pale man barely glanced at Win. "Yes. He is brilliant . . . just brilliant. He'll be published again in *The Journal of Geothermal Research* this fall."

"I thought y'all were planning to be at Maxwell Springs checking on that earthquake damage this week." Win wondered how much the little guy would tell him.

It was as if Dravec had forgotten the confrontational vibe of their last encounter. He was borderline friendly. "We've already established our base there—moved our gear in with a helicopter Sunday. We come and go . . . there are lectures like today's event, and meetings with prospective donors. It's just a robust hike in and out of camp. Part of the profession."

"Y'all camp out there alone?" Win asked. Dravec was intent on Ratliff, as if waiting for the man to summon him. He reminded Win of a golden retriever—hanging on his master's every word, every movement. Win was surprised when the guy kept talking.

"Dr. Warren will be joining us for part of the research at the springs. We're shorthanded this summer, no interns," he said softly.

Wonder if that's 'cause they keep disappearing, Win thought to himself. The charismatic volcanologist was gesturing to his onlookers and pointing to something on the white calcite terraces with a green laser pointer. Win glanced at his watch. *Gotta go.*

"Well, y'all have a good day," Win said as he turned to leave.

"Don't move!" Dravec ordered. Win froze.

A tiny gray, lizard-like thing scurried over Win's boot and hid under the wooden plank of the boardwalk. Its piercing reptilian eyes blinked up at him.

"A sagebrush lizard," the small man said. "You almost stepped on him." Dravec's eyes met Win's; Win couldn't help thinking they looked just like the lizard's.

* * *

The tune floated in the darkness, then faded. He knew he heard it . . . was sure he heard it. The water was gurgling in the small stream just a few feet away. Still, he was sure he'd heard a soft harmony, and for a moment it seemed to calm him. But the CIA had told him the Russian would try to get in his head, mess with his subconscious, draw him in with comforting memories from his past. *Can't let that happen!* He stopped as his throat tightened and he tried to swallow down a sudden jolt of fear. It wasn't working for him, so he just stood there on the trail and waited.

He'd been shocked to see the text on his personal phone less than fifteen minutes earlier: **Cowboy, 1/4 mile up Beaver Ponds Trail now.**

He knew Sutton and his folks would see it too; he also knew there was not time for Sutton's crew to react. He had to go alone into the forest behind his house. He had to go meet a killer. His mind formed the words as the faint whistle caught his ear again . . . *Let Thy Goodness, like a fetter, Bind my wandering Heart to Thee* . . . Closer this time, but the direction was unclear. *Has to be up ahead or—*

He whirled when the man behind him spoke. "Whoa there, Cowboy. Keep your hands where I can see them . . . atta boy." The Russian was a silhouette behind him. He was still talking. "Beautiful hymn . . . old-time Baptist favorite. Thought you might know it, since you grew up around your grandmother. I learned it during my stint in Texas . . . thought you might remember it."

Win barely trusted himself to speak. "You some sorta choirboy? You playin' with my faith?"

"Well, I guess you'd call me a choirboy. In the Russian Orthodox Church, we're called chanters, and I still serve as one in my church. And no, I'm not demeaning your faith. You've sure got that American superiority complex! You don't believe anyone besides you knows our Lord. My church thrived for hundreds of years before your country ever raised its flag." Sokolov stepped closer.

Win wasn't sure what to say to that. Something inside told him that the guy had a point. "Why am I here . . . so soon?" he managed to ask.

"Ah, well then, no more small talk." He was close enough now that Win could make out his features in the faint moonlight. "No phone? You're not carryin', are you? You did remember our rules?" The voice was cordial, conversational.

Win held his hands up higher, palms out. "I remembered, I deleted the text, but I'm making some new rules from here on out. I can't go around with no phone, not in Mammoth. Not even for a hike in the dark. If my boss tried to reach me—if I was out of touch—with the trouble *you've* already gotten me in, I'd be looking at the door with the Bureau in a heartbeat. And the gun? I can't hike around unarmed. There could be four domestic terrorists roaming these woods—they almost got me last month. They could still be aiming to kill me."

"Well, there is that."

Silence for a few moments. Win heard an owl calling in the distance, the frogs were singing in the small stream; he was becoming more aware of the night sounds of the forest.

"All right, turn around and lock your fingers behind your head. If you can't follow my rules, we'll have to improvise." The Russian cuffed Win's hands behind his back, frisked him, and laid Win's Glock to the side. He ran a small scanner down him, front and back, and he powered down both of Win's phones. He kept up the conversational tone as he efficiently accomplished those tasks. "If I take the battery or SIM card out of the phone, your compatriots could tell that you'd been off the grid—playin' with it. Not good. The cell phones don't work out here half the time anyway, so I wouldn't concern myself with that if I was you. The gun, well, I'll have to give that some thought. Would hate for you to get killed off by American outlaws after I've invested good money in you. Be a shame."

"Why the cuffs?" Win asked as he tried unsuccessfully to tamp down his fear. Having his back to the guy brought the horrifying photos from Syria to his mind. He closed his eyes tight to force the images away.

"The cuffs are to build a little trust . . . we need to get to know each other, and since you're not real good at following instructions, we'll just have to work this another way. Not to worry, I always keep a spare handcuff key on me . . . or did I forget that key?" Win tensed even more. The Russian patted Win on the shoulder and moved to face him. A hint of the half-moon cut through the tree canopy, and the man's eyes gleamed in the dark. "Just kidding." His teeth shone white as he smiled. "On those missing persons cases you were working on: What are you thinking?"

Win was caught off guard by the question. He tried for a vague response.

"I've got nothing new. I've got several missing women and a missing man still on the table . . . goes all the way back six years. Several of them tied, in one way or another, to thermal research groups, and most of those are tied to one specific group. Nothing concrete. Nothing."

"Dr. Warren didn't show for your meeting today. Is he your main suspect?"

Whoa! How does he know about that? Win tried not to sound surprised. "Warren is a class A jerk, but I don't know that he's a suspect. It's not smart to blow off the FBI on an investigative interview; he'll find that out once I track him down. And the disappearances . . . they could still turn out to be accidents—"

"You don't believe that."

Win shook his head. "I'm trying not to get ahead of myself here. I'm trying to follow the evidence, do a thorough investigation."

"Since there's a Russian national who's missing, let's concentrate on solving something there. Based on what Dr. Orsky told us, we know Warren was involved with her, as was this other researcher, this Dr. Ratliff. We've found some notes, a letter that might shed some light on that woman's case . . . ah, Yahontova, is that her name?" He tucked a folded envelope into Win's front jacket pocket. "Your goal is to get back into your agency's good standing, right? Then let's solve a case or two right quick, get some positive attention coming your way."

"Yeah, right. Positive attention from the Bureau." Win hoped he sounded sulky. It wasn't his normal tone of voice. "Is that it? You order me out here at eleven o'clock just to prod me on cases no one else gives a flip about?"

The Russian took that in and seemed to be studying Win in the darkness. He spoke softly. "Someone cares. You told me that yourself during our time in Kamchatka. Someone cares a great deal . . . and I think you care much more than you're letting on, Agent Tyler."

"Yeah, maybe." Win hoped he still sounded sulky.

"Oh, nearly slipped my mind," the Russian quipped. He slipped a second, bulkier envelope into Win's other pocket. "Turn around, I'll get the cuffs off." Win felt his adrenaline rise as he turned his back to the man again. "I'm gonna want something solid to show my superiors on this real soon, so how 'bout you ease up on the hookups with blondie in Bozeman. Settle down and do the work."

Win whirled to face the guy. "Who I spend my free time with is none of your damn business! Stay out of my private life!"

The Russian tapped Win's chest with one finger. "You don't have *your* life now, Cowboy. You're *mine* . . . and I want to see the bones you found, anything on that Russian national. Keep that local, don't ship any of that evidence off."

Win bit back another angry response; he glanced to the side before he answered. "No danger of that—my bosses couldn't care less what I do or don't do on the missing persons files. Those bones aren't going anywhere. But they're case evidence. You're not getting the bones."

"One step at a time, Cowboy. I just need to see them and anything else you found. You can make that happen." He stepped back behind Win again and fooled with the cuffs.

This could be a chance to trap the guy. Ease up, Win, his mind counseled. "Maybe so," he answered softly, as if he were thinking it over. "May need a little more incentive to—"

The Russian's grip on Win's arm tightened. The voice behind him turned icy. "Don't talk to me about incentives, Agent Tyler. Do the work and you'll get your reward." Win felt the cuffs come off and sensed the man moving way. "Stay where you are for a count of sixty."

Win did the slow countdown to sixty and said a prayer of thanks that he was still alive. He retrieved the Glock and the phones from the rock where the guy had laid them and moved down the trail toward his house. He felt eyes watching him as he flipped on his small flashlight and tried not to stumble on the rocky pathway. He willed his heart rate to slow and his adrenaline levels to drop. The probing light bobbed a bit in the blackness under the big trees, and Win realized his hand was shaking. The Russian's words kept going over and over in his head: *you'll get your reward.* It didn't sound like a good thing; it sounded like a thing to fear.

CHAPTER TWENTY-ONE

There was $5,000 in crisp one-hundred-dollar bills in the thick envelope in Win's front pocket; Win pulled on gloves and flipped the money down on the table. His focus was more intent on the second envelope, which held two pages of photocopies. He threw his jacket over the back of one of the dining room chairs, sat down, and smoothed the pages out on the table. The short letter was in English, sorta formal English; it was addressed to someone named Christopher.

> *Dearest Christopher,*
>
> *I am sorry I have not answered your calls. You do not deserve to be treated this way—you have been very good to me. More than I deserve. I know we will often be together when the expedition begins next month and yes, I remember our plans for that time. But life for me has changed. Truth is, I have met someone here who shares my passion for this work, and yes, it has become more than that. Do not be angry. There is no need for anger. You know I will always hold you in my heart. Yet what can I say? I have moved on and I hope you can as well.*
>
> *Tasha*

There was no date on the letter, but the photocopy of the envelope was on the same page. The postmark was Yellowstone National Park, Wyoming, and it was stamped five years ago on March 15. That was the spring before Natasha disappeared. The envelope was addressed to Dr. Christopher Warren, Geological Sciences Department, Stanford University. Win leaned back. *Well, there you go.*

Two black-and-white photos of Chris Warren and a dark-haired woman were on the second page. The couple was dressed for an event, formal clothes; he noticed a name tag on Warren's jacket. Maybe they were at a conference, or a banquet? The woman had her hand on Warren's shoulder and a ring was visible. Win got up and dug a magnifying glass out of the kitchen junk drawer, then looked at the photos again. It looked like the ring he'd found on the bones—he'd bet money it was the same ring. The second picture showed a front view of the couple; the woman was wearing an elegant necklace. She was smiling; Chris Warren looked smug. Win had seen that look. He sat down at the dining room table and thought about it. They were good photos, clear and crisp, not posed, likely shot from a distance. They looked like the surveillance photos he'd grown accustomed to seeing these last few months. *Surveillance photos? Odd. Why would Natasha and Warren be under surveillance? Why would the Russians have these?*

He picked up the first page again and scanned the envelope. It hadn't been sent to a home address. He thought that unusual for such a personal message—a Dear John letter for sure. Win read it again, this time with a less clinical approach, this time with his heart. His chest tightened, he clenched his jaw, and he tried to force down the sadness that descended on him as he read: *Yet what can I say? I have moved on . . .*

* * *

"Hey Winnie," she purred. "I'm missin' you, babe." It had been nearly an hour since he'd gotten back to the house, since he'd read the letter, since he'd moved Chris Warren higher up his suspect list in Natasha Yahontova's disappearance. He'd hid the $5,000 in books, taken a shower, and played with the cat for a few minutes before he picked up his personal phone and called her. It was midnight.

He tried to sound conflicted. "Got a pretty big day coming up, not sure I can drive into Bozeman tomorrow night. Those drives—it's a four-hour round trip. And well, you're wearing me out, Paige. Not sure I can get up there—"

Paige was quick, she cut him off.

"I've got, like, nothing going tomorrow. The audit with that banker fell through." Then her pouty voice switched to upbeat. "So I'm thinking I might take some annual leave, come down and see Yellowstone. Come down and see you, babe."

Lordy, she is good at this.

"Okay. Okay, that would be good." He tried to ratchet his enthusiasm up a notch. "Be nice to have you down here. Can show you around."

"I *know* what *I* want to see." She was purring again, and he felt his ears go red.

*   *   *

It had been two hours since the rendezvous in the forest, and the man was sitting motionless in the car, watching the rear of the old stone FBI building. The entire area was dark and quiet. The tourists seemed to turn in early here; not having television or Wi-Fi probably had a lot to do with that, he supposed.

He and his mates were communicating with cheap walkie-talkies they'd bought at a sporting goods store in Bozeman. Many of the tourists used them, and if they spoke in code, the Americans shouldn't be clued in that foreign intelligence officers were in their midst. Not exactly high-tech, but sometimes it was better to be old-school—often the simple things worked best. He'd just gotten the hourly report from his team: Agent Tyler hadn't left his house, and he'd made only one brief phone call to the woman named Paige. *Maybe he gave her the brush-off, as I instructed,* the Major thought. *No loss . . . she's not his type anyway.* He'd listen to the recording of the call later; it wasn't important right now. He settled back in the seat. He'd wait just a few minutes more.

Major Sergei Nikolaevich Sokolov did not like being tagged—it just never happened. But Agent Tyler had recognized him in the church ... not so much by seeing through the "old man" disguise, but by instinct. The lad was intelligent and intuitive, and what he lacked in training, he made up for in courage. He'd seen more of that on display tonight. After Agent Tyler's experience in Kamchatka, it had to have been terrifying for him to turn his back to the enemy, to allow himself to be cuffed, to be helpless. It had taken courage. The Major admired that trait; it was a necessary part of his work. He'd have to use great care in handling Win Tyler.

Then the man sighed. *Well, perhaps I'm giving the lad too much credit. Maybe I'm slipping a little.* Becoming careless in the world of espionage could mean an early death. The American had gotten the drop on him in the tunnel twelve days ago. If Winston Tyler had been a CIA assassin, his darling Krestya would likely be attending his wake today instead of preparing for their son's birthday party. *Could I be losing my edge?* He'd seen it happen to other operatives, often because of too much time in the field, losing touch with the people and values they were fighting for. *"Burned out."* Wasn't that what the Americans called it? *Maybe it's happening to me.* He sighed again and his breath formed vapor in the cold air. It was mid-June and the temperature had dipped to near freezing again tonight. The cold was good; it reminded him of home.

Every male in his immediate family had been a military man— every one of them patriots, defenders of the Motherland. His mother's uncles had all died fighting in the siege of Stalingrad. His father's father had been the commander of the 150th Idritsa Rifle Division during the Great Patriotic War—he'd been a Hero of the Soviet Union and had retired as a Senior General in the Russian Federation shortly after the dissolution of the USSR.

Sergei's father had made the lofty ascension to General of the Army for the Southern Military District; he'd died in a helicopter crash in the rugged mountains of Afghanistan one month before the Soviet withdrawal from that country. Another Hero of the USSR. Sergei was barely seven years old when word came of his father's death; he remembered the formal military funeral, the coldness of the cavernous cathedral in Moscow. He remembered his mother's pale face, his grandfather's sunken eyes, and his grandmother's tears on that bitterly cold January day.

His mind drifted to the little photo of Victor that he carried in his wallet when he was home. It was his son's first school picture, and he hated to leave it behind. The blue military jacket of the Visclosky Military Grade School was the same as the one he and his father had worn. The prestigious Moscow institution had its beginnings in 1754. He hoped Victor would follow in his footsteps by enrolling in the Suvorov Military School for the upper grades, then the Military University of the Ministry of Defense. He hoped his son would embrace the proud family tradition of protecting Mother Russia.

Victor was six today. There would be a birthday dinner tonight that he would miss. There would be the gifts that he wouldn't see his son open. He couldn't even risk a phone call to him. He still remembered his own childhood yearnings for his father, for more time together, for words of encouragement and approval. He'd been in the clandestine service now for several years, and before that he'd often been deployed with the Spetsnaz in war zones. He'd recently been asked to consider an indefinite assignment in America, but that would take him away from his family for up to two years. Two more years for Victor to grow up without him, and now there was another factor to consider.

He'd been at their flat in Moscow for only twenty-four hours before he'd flown to Petropavlovsk. He'd spent the previous several months splitting his time between Hungary and the Ukrainian region, with only short breaks at home. He smiled in awe as he reflected on Krestya's words as he was packing to leave for Kamchatka—leaving so much sooner than they'd hoped.

"The Sokolov men do their duty to Russia well, but Sergei, there's another duty due to your family," she'd said.

"It gets harder and harder for me to leave you both. I wonder if we're becoming soft . . . thinking we can have it all. A home life and a lifetime of service."

"Perhaps we can. . . . You've served, mostly out of country, for years now. When is enough? Maybe enough for a time? Maybe something different now? What is our homeland if its families aren't strong? There are other ways to serve, at least until the children become older. They need these formative years with their father." She brushed his sandy hair back off his forehead. She smiled into his green eyes.

For a moment he didn't catch it. He studied her glowing face. Then, "Children?"

Her eyes were gleaming as she pulled him closer to her. He raised his chin in question.

"Da, da . . ." She saw the sentiment in his eyes turn to concern, and she looked into his face to reassure him. "It's been over twelve weeks now—the doctor says everything is fine . . . it's good. I've hardly been sick this time. God has heard our prayers, Sergei. Don't be afraid."

Twelve weeks—three months—and he hadn't known. She'd held on to her own hopes and fears alone, while he fought secret battles for Russia on the vast plains of eastern Ukraine and the narrow streets of Budapest.

"Why didn't you tell me?" His mind went back to those assignments . . . they'd talked by phone many times.

"And worry you? The Lord has seen fit to take two souls from us . . . two babies we'll only know in Heaven. This time it feels so different . . . I wanted to see joy in your eyes, not fear. I didn't want our hearts to break again."

He found himself blinking back tears as the emotion of that memory overtook him. Yes, when this mission was complete, he'd talk with the Colonel. He would do it for Krestya, for Victor, for their new child—and, yes, for himself. But first, there were things to accomplish here in this remote corner of America. He glanced once more at the dark stone building and scanned the area for signs of movement; there were none at 1:00 a.m. on this cold, still night. He crossed himself, touched the GSh-18 9mm on his side, and quietly slid out of the car. The time for thinking was past, the time for action had come.

* * *

The big ginger cat was staring back at her through the open blinds. It was perched inside the window, watching the flow of tourists trekking down the path or clamoring over the hot springs' boardwalks. It was just after nine, and already the place was crawling with people. She saw the cat's green eyes dart to follow a bird that had lit on a bush at the side of the house. Lowering her binoculars so as not to seem too conspicuous, she smiled at a young couple who moved past her along the boardwalk. The cat was still in the window when she looked back.

She sighed. Someday she'd have a cat. Someday she'd be stable enough in her work, in her life, to share it with someone. Even if it was only a cat. She'd never had pets, and she'd always envied those whose hearts were deep and wide enough to invite someone else in. A cat would suit her fine, not too demanding and a bit reserved. Willing to give love, but on its own terms. A bit like her, she thought.

A group of teens moved by her on the wooden walkway, and she shifted to let them pass, annoyed by their noise but aware that fading into the crowd of sightseers was a good thing. Then, refocusing on the house, she tried to clear her mind. *I'm just tired,* she told herself. *It was a short night.* Tired or not, she hated it when she allowed herself to become introspective, to want things she couldn't yet have. She hated that she found herself envious of a man with a cat.

His house was built like a fortress: thick sandstone walls cut from local quarries. It had been the first stone house built at Fort Yellowstone, in 1894. She'd read that in some park brochure. It was used as the fort's original judge's office, residence, and jail, back in the day of horse patrols. She made a sweep of the covered front porch, with its swing and Adirondack chairs, and the two towering evergreens that afforded the porch some privacy.

As she moved along the boardwalk to a better vantage point to see the rear of the house, she scanned the tourists moving up and down the wooden walkways. It was second nature; she'd studied thousands of crowds. Always aware that the enemy could be lurking—watching her as she watched for them. She was dressed to blend in, although her chinos, flannel shirt, and hiking boots had come from high-end shops, not from some provincial big-box store. She trained her field glasses on the home's back door, then swung her gaze over to the shed, the only structure behind the dwelling. The home's back windows were high and small, likely remnants of the jail cells that had once occupied that part of the building. There was a doorway on the side, but the flowering shrub growing below it told her it wasn't used. Someone had covered the shrub with wire, covered the flowers blooming there.

A glance at her watch told her she needed to get back to her car, finish her drive-around, then get to his office. This reconnaissance didn't seem necessary, but that wasn't her decision to make. They wanted to get a better feel for the place, get more comfortable with its layout. They were like her: creatures more comfortable in cities than in this foreign place where cell phone coverage was terrible, internet was almost nonexistent, and access was difficult. She'd been stuck on a two-lane highway for twenty minutes this morning on the drive into the park. A bison jam, the ranger had called it. As she sat in her car, waiting for herds of the big ugly things to lumber off the pavement, she'd forced herself to take phone pictures, to point, to mirror the excitement the masses were showing. She doubted she'd find any place in this tourist trap to get a cappuccino.

She hated this part of the job. Actually, she'd been thinking that fairly often these days—that she hated the job. They hadn't really asked her to do too much. Nothing particularly dramatic or unexpected. Mostly routine assignments, really. And the money was good—very good. A definite upside. But it had been years now, and it was getting old. She was ready to move on, to take on other tasks. They'd promised to relocate her, but the timetable just kept dragging out. She was ready to go; it couldn't happen soon enough. A change of pace, a little adventure—that's what she needed.

She scanned the southwest side of the house a final time and again caught sight of the big orange cat. It was sitting in the window, casually licking its paw. It looked contented, at peace with its world. She sighed again. Yes, she'd get a cat when they moved her to Moscow.

* * *

He watched Paige's little silver rental car pull into an empty spot in front of the Albright Visitor Center. He flipped the shades back down in the conference room and sucked in a breath. She'd called him on her way down from Bozeman. She'd been bubbly and flirty and filled him in on the fun she'd planned for their afternoon—which she assured him included a good bit of "visiting" in the cute little cabin she'd rented at the Mammoth Hot Springs Hotel.

"Gotta go out front and meet someone," Win said absently to Hechtner. The ranger raised his head from the files they'd been reviewing for the last hour on Natasha Yahontova's and Chris Warren's overlapping time in the park. "I've got a meeting in a few minutes, and then I'm gonna be out a good deal of the afternoon . . . feel free to stay and go over this stuff." He sounded uncharacteristically distracted.

Trey sat back and scowled when he realized Win was walking out. "You're leaving? And us right in the middle of this?"

"I'll try to get back on it midafternoon," Win said. "Can you get Warren in here? I'm losing my patience with him." He looked back at Trey. "I'm sorry, something came up."

"Something or *someone*? You've been checkin' that parking lot every five minutes," Trey said. Win just glared at him. Trey paused, then conceded. "All right, all right. I'll go after Warren."

The security pad's intercom came on and Win moved out of the room, into the small foyer, and out through the inner doors. The ranger pushed back from the desk and followed Win out. Trey rested his shoulder against the doorframe as Win opened the wooden front door. Paige leaned into Win and caught him with a solid kiss before he could close the door, then pulled him out onto the broad porch and landed another kiss. She spotted the ranger as she pulled her lips away.

She smiled at Trey. "Oh, now I've gone and embarrassed Win. I can't believe I did that!" She didn't sound one bit remorseful.

Trey stepped to the doorway and nodded. "Trey Hechtner, miss. And you are . . . ?" Win glanced over her head and noticed an older woman on the sidewalk, smiling up toward the lovebirds. Others near the Visitor Center were taking in the show too. Paige was making a scene. He tried to stay close to her, tried to play his role. He was having a hard time pulling it off.

"Oh, surely Win's mentioned me." She snuggled into Win suggestively with her shoulder and hip. He fought the urge to pull back. "I'm Paige Lange . . . Win and I are going for a little road trip down to see some bison, elks, and deers, or is that deer?" She giggled and batted her eyes at the ranger. Somehow she snuggled even closer to Win. She was purring again. "Anyway, first we have to check into my cabin and freshen up a bit." Her bright smile settled on Win's face. "Isn't that right, babe?"

"Uh, yeah . . ." Win gripped her shoulders and peeled her off. "Uh, Paige, I've got to meet with some folks on a case I'm working . . . won't be long. Why don't you go see if you can check into the cabin early." He spotted Ms. Gorski getting out of her car and walking toward the office. "I won't be long."

"Well, okay," Paige said with a pout. "It might be a little early to get the cabin—I'll head down to the hotel and find a café." She gave a fluttering wave to Trey. "Nice to meet you. *Love* the uniform. . . . Don't keep Winnie long!"

Paige gave Win a sultry smile, then practically skipped down the granite steps. She passed Ms. Gorski on the sidewalk and neither woman acknowledged the other. *I could never do this counterintelligence thing,* Win thought to himself. No one watching the exchange would have guessed that Paige Lange had worked on Gloria Gorski's San Francisco Counterintelligence Squad for six years.

CHAPTER TWENTY-TWO

An hour later, Win used a metal key to open the door of the stand-alone cabin. Paige edged past him and methodically pulled every blind in the room, then hit the bathroom as he carried her overnight bag inside and stared at the floor. He had no idea how Paige was gonna play this, but he knew he wanted her out of it. The Russian had mentioned her; she was in danger now.

She came out of the tiny bathroom, then washed her hands in the sink that stood across from the beds. "Cute little bear soaps . . . I'm taking these back to my friend's daughter. She'll love them." Paige held up two bear-shaped soaps. She was trying to loosen him up. Win just stood there looking at her. "Hey, Win. This room is clean. I picked it at random just a few minutes ago at the front desk. Relax. We're good." She bunched the pillows up on one of the beds and sat back against them.

He leaned against the door and reported word for word what the Russian had said about "losing blondie" and cutting out the hookups. He told her about his new orders to show Sokolov the bones they'd discovered at Maxwell Springs. He told her about the money. He didn't sit down.

She was thinking about it. "Sit down. Got to make this look real, so we'll need to stay put for a while."

Win sat on the edge of the other bed; there wasn't anywhere else to sit. She bounced back up and dug in her overnight bag. He was still wondering how this would go.

"Want a drink?" She held up a bottle of red wine.

"Seriously? It's not even noon."

She shrugged with one shoulder and turned back to unwrap one of the glasses that sat on the basin. "Suit yourself . . . it's after five somewhere." She'd pulled a corkscrew from her purse and was working on the cork. "Gotta kill at least forty-five minutes." She glanced back over her shoulder. "Or maybe your flings don't last that long . . . wanta give it a shot and see? Or are the stories I hear about you being a puritan for real?"

He let it pass. She was making fun of his morals—of his values. It wouldn't be the first time he'd run into that from coworkers. It wouldn't be the last. He watched her sniff the cork, hold the half-full glass up to the light. "At least they have real glasses in this place, most of these touristy places have plastic." She swirled the drink in her hand and watched him over the top of the glass. He'd never liked wine.

He moved his hands to his knees and leaned forward. He felt rising anger with the woman in front of him. She was playing with him. Baiting him, trying to get a reaction. And she was succeeding. She eased down on the corner of the other bed; their knees were nearly touching. She sipped the wine and kept watching him over the glass's rim. She kept up the seductive vibe.

"Come on, Win. Loosen up, let's have a little fun. What's it gonna hurt?"

He'd heard that line more times than he could count, often from far more convincing temptresses than Paige. He tried to tamp his anger down a bit. He tried to feel empathy—maybe she was just lonely. But empathy wasn't working for him right then.

"Ain't gonna happen, Paige. So why don't you get down to business? I've got a Russian agent breathing down my neck and you're just angling for a romp in the sack!" Tamping down his anger wasn't working for him either.

She turned off the coy act as if she'd hit a light switch. "Your loss." Her face took on a hard look he'd never seen. She pulled a small silver recorder from her pocket, held it up, and pressed a button.

It was Brent Sutton's voice. "Hi, Win. I know this is stressful . . ."
You think?

"We've run into an issue with the HRT arrest team—I know you thought they'd be in place by now. They're on standby at Quantico." There was a pause before the supervisor continued. "Honestly, it's bureaucratic politics, a turf war. The CIA wants to be involved, and the Justice Department is fighting that. Well, bottom line, you need to try to string things out with Sokolov—give him something he wants, stall for some time. Paige and Humphrey will be in Gardiner, within five miles of you. They're your backup for the moment. I've arranged for Agent Spence Johnson's medical leave to be pulled so he'll be back soon. And Tom Strickland tells me we still have two or three Denver agents working out of the Justice Center on the False Prophet case. He tells me you've been ordered to stay clear of them because of the shooting inquiries, but Tom and I agree that you need to reach out to them, let them know you're around—just in case things start to go sideways with Sokolov. We . . . we know he has a team in place, and we don't want you to think you're totally alone out there."

Win stared at the floor while the recording played on. "I'm assuming you met with Gloria earlier today. She will be coordinating with Paige and Humphrey. I assume Gloria told you that her cover is going to be an investigation of two Chinese nationals who are working with a concessioner there in Yellowstone. That, by the way, is not a fabrication, we do have an investigation ongoing out of the San Francisco Field Office. I also assume that Gloria told you she'd be working out of the Justice Center for at least the rest of the week while we try to get the arrest team in place—she will probably pull Paige into that effort. We're still sorting it out. Paige will remain your main contact. . . . We're putting much of this together on the fly. It will come together."

Sutton went on like that for a couple more minutes, going over what they did and didn't know about Sokolov's sudden incursion into the USA. They didn't know much. The recording was basically another pep talk. A "hang in there and try not to get yourself killed while we figure this out."

One thing was clear: the brass didn't want to bring the hammer down on Sokolov until they had some feel for how he'd gotten there, how large his network was, what his objective was. Win spent the next six minutes recording his report on last night's meeting in the woods with Sokolov. Paige prompted him a few times on details, but otherwise she just sipped her wine and watched him. He finished the report with the time and the date and handed the recorder back. Recounting his observations, his interaction with the Russian—reliving the fear he'd felt—left him drained.

For a moment, Paige seemed to relate to him as another human being. "He's scary, isn't he? You're afraid of him."

Win moved his eyes to the large photo of a geyser that hung above one of the beds. He swallowed hard and nodded. "You've seen the briefings. The reports from Ukraine and the UK, the photos from Syria . . . yeah, he's scary." Win looked back at her; he needed someone to understand. "And . . . and maybe it goes back to Kamchatka . . . when I was drugged . . . when I lost those hours."

"He kinda got in your head. I can see that," she responded.

"He seems to be able to pop up anywhere . . . out of the blue. Seems to know everything I've said or been told."

"They want you to think they're everywhere—all seeing, all knowing. It's part of the way they pull you in. But he hasn't laid a hand on you, probably won't as long as he thinks he can use you. He'd leave that to his team members. His goons."

"We still don't have a handle on who he could have here? How many?"

Paige shrugged, shook her head. "No. Maybe four . . . maybe six. *We* don't have enough assets on the ground to make a firm assessment. And if we decide to play full court, we risk spooking him. This case is checking all the atypical boxes. Why in the world would an operative of Sokolov's stature be personally making a move on someone as insignificant as you?"

Insignificant? Me?

She kept her line of thought going—she never even seemed to notice the insult. "We'd expect him to show up around our embassies, maybe in Washington, maybe go after senior-level diplomats, Fortune 500 executives, or some of our military brass—troll for weak links in those sectors." She studied her wine glass. "Not spend time here in the middle of nowhere courting a low-level nobody."

Well, then.

Paige rose and poured herself another glass of wine; she held up the bottle to Win. He shook his head. She tapped her finger against the glass. "So he tells you to 'lose blondie and get back to work,' something to that effect? Well, we're going to have a bit of a lover's spat after our late-morning tryst." She turned and took in the rustic furniture with distain. "In about ten minutes, you're gonna go storming back to the office in a huff, and I'm going to stay thirty minutes longer, cry my eyes out, and go check out of the hotel." She unwrapped a second glass, poured it half full, and sat it on the sink. "So here's how we're gonna play this. Get in the shower, make a mess in there . . . I'm gonna scatter a few things around—"

"You think they'll check the room? Really?"

"You wanna take a chance on not staging it after our little romp? We're not dealing with penny-ante criminals here, Win. Keep reminding yourself of that. The Russians are not amateurs."

Yeah, but I am. That thought crossed his mind as he watched her throw a comforter in the corner and pull at the sheets.

*   *   *

He stormed out the door, crossed the small porch in two steps, and stomped across the wide lawn between the cabins and the rear of the Mammoth Hot Springs Hotel. He had to work at looking angry, even though that was exactly how he felt. He'd spent a good deal of his life trying hard to conceal his feelings, to always appear calm and in control, and now his life might depend on his emotions riding raw on his face and in his actions. He must have pulled it off.

"Whoa! I'm guessing that didn't go well." Trey was lounging against one of the lawn's big cottonwood trees.

"It's none of your business!" Win snapped.

The ranger's eyes narrowed. He straightened and stood his ground. "You care to tell me what the hell is going on? Are you all right? This isn't like you."

"Are you out here spying on me?" As he said it, Win wondered where the real spies were lurking.

"No. No, I was trying to decide whether to knock on the door and interrupt you . . . you weren't answering your phone. Something's come up with Dr. Warren and you're not gonna like it."

Win stopped under the shade. He glanced back at the cabin behind him and shook his head. He raised his hand in a dismissive motion. He hoped anyone watching from a distance would get the idea that he'd cut things off with blondie. He pulled his phones from his pockets and turned them back on as he stepped closer to Trey. "What's going on?" he asked the ranger.

"Chris Warren has hired an attorney. Chief Randall got a call from his lawyer in Palo Alto . . . said Warren was considering a harassment charge against us, said he would be contacting the federal employees' union rep—seems even though he's a volunteer ranger, he still counts as an employee. The attorney says Warren has no intention of meeting with you, me, or anyone else unless we've got a warrant."

"Where's Warren now?"

"He was scheduled for an educational program at Mud Volcano this morning, then he's leading a group of graduate students on an overnight trip to Tindell Ridge. It's a small, remote geyser field southwest of Roosevelt." Trey glanced down at his watch. "It's 12:30; they should be leaving soon. Supposed to be back tomorrow afternoon, then his schedule says he's at Maxwell Springs doing research for a week."

Win was walking toward the office now. Trey fell in beside him. Win covered his mouth with his hand, as if he was just rubbing his chin. He spoke barely above a whisper. "Can't tell you what's going on with Paige. Can't talk about it."

"You want me to watch your back?"

He glanced sideways at the calm, easygoing ranger. His mind flashed back to Sokolov's icy-green eyes, to the blood-red photos. *I can't put Trey in danger.* "No . . . I'm good."

Win stopped when he reached the office's gravel side lot. "I'm gonna try to intercept Warren before he heads off on that overnight trip."

"Grab a heavy coat before you leave, we've got weather coming in late this afternoon."

Win looked up at the azure sky, not a cloud to be seen. It had to be nearly eighty degrees.

The ranger saw Win's questioning look. "Cold front is supposed to slam us—sorta unexpected, we get those sometimes. With the warm weather we've had the last two weeks, it will be a mess in the backcountry if we get snow."

Now he had Win's attention. "Snow? On the 18th of June? Snow?"

"Yup, snow or sleet at the higher elevations . . . not unusual to lose one or two hikers to hypothermia in early summer. I've gotta go get rangers out to the primitive campsites, put out more alerts. Let me know if you need me." Trey paused before he crossed the street. "Win, I mean that."

*   *   *

The petite girl flicked her wavy brown hair back over her shoulder and followed that with a hostile glare. She was sketching something from her perch on a low boulder set back in the trees near the cabin she shared with Tory.

Win cleared his throat and weighed the risks of approaching her. The girl cut off his dawdling.

"She doesn't want to see you," she said, looking back down at her sketch pad.

"Why not?" he asked as he stepped a little closer.

Her eyes turned to him with an *Are you that dense?* expression.

"I need to explain to her . . . it wasn't how it looked."

"And how *did* it look?" She studied her drawing as she spoke.

"Not good . . . it didn't look good. But it was work—I told Tory I had to work the night before . . . I was working the morning I saw y'all. It was work."

"It *sure* didn't *look* like work." Lauren pivoted on the big rock and draped her tanned legs over its side. A detailed charcoal drawing of a bird stared back at him from the bold white paper as she shifted the sketch pad. Her hands were as small and delicate as her facial features. Her hazel eyes transitioned to sadness, then back to anger.

"You led her on . . . that was low. She doesn't want to see you," she repeated. She could have dropped it there, but she was angry, and seeing him standing there, hat in hand, just made her madder. "She actually trusted you. If you want to explain, fine! But she's gone till tomorrow afternoon. And you're blocking my light."

He retreated to his SUV and sat in the Roosevelt parking lot, trying to decide what to do. The ranger at Roosevelt said he'd missed Chris Warren by less than twenty minutes. The guy said Dr. Warren was leading a group of seven up the Lost Creek and Prospect Trails to Tindell Ridge; it was a strenuous eight-mile hike to the primitive camping area. They'd be out of cell phone range most of the way. Dr. Warren had a satellite phone, but that was only for emergencies. Win decided not to push it. Might be for the best, he concluded. Driving down here to confront the guy had been more of a knee-jerk reaction than a well-thought-out plan. After all, Warren had lawyered up. Win had nothing on the guy that rose to an actionable level—he couldn't file charges on a hunch.

And he'd missed his chance to make things right with Tory. Although he had to admit to himself that he had no idea how to make things right with her. He couldn't talk about an ongoing case with anyone outside of law enforcement unless it became public knowledge. And even then, there were restrictions. It was a challenging part of his job, but a necessary one. *Maybe having Tory out of my life is the safest route right now.* The Russian was still out there somewhere, and he didn't need to put her in harm's way.

He drew a deep breath and tried to regroup. It was nearly 1:30. He stared out the windshield at the tourists milling around in the parking lot, at several excited teenagers starting out single file on horseback. Three yellow chuckwagons with canvas covers were crossing the highway, returning from the advertised cowboy cookout; regular folks who were cowpokes for a day waved to their families and friends. Everyone seemed to be happy and relaxed, soaking in the beauty of this magical place.

Everyone but me. A feeling too close to despair washed over him. He felt totally alone. Shelby, the woman he thought he'd spend his life with, had dumped him four months ago, and he'd moved backward rather than forward in his lame attempts at romance with Tory. *I tried to love again too soon,* his rational self counseled. And his career wasn't going any smoother than his love life. No one in the Bureau would even give him the time of day, and he was having a hard time seeing that little vixen, Paige, as a teammate. All the while, somewhere out there a dangerous man was pushing him to wrap up a case that might have no ending. Some cases couldn't be solved. He knew that. *The lost aren't always found.* That sad truth settled on him heavy and hard.

* * *

He had too much time on his hands here. Droves of tourists, painfully congested roads, terrible cell service. It might be perfect if he were here on holiday, he supposed, but trying to work here was nearly impossible. Everything moved at a crawl . . . all the better to view the wildlife and the geysers, but far from ideal for accomplishing his tasks. Espionage was for patient people, and he wasn't a patient man.

His superiors wanted this ranger, Christopher Warren, followed, wanted Sergei's opinion of the man's culpability in the case. Agent Tyler seemed to be zeroing in on that other researcher, the arrogant professor from back East. But Dr. Warren was checking all of Sergei's boxes. Warren had been in the park when the disappearances occurred. He'd interacted with some, if not all, of the missing women. He intimately knew the thermal areas. And then there was the letter of rejection to Warren from Natasha Pavlovna Yahontova. Dr. Warren was a man Natasha Pavlovna had spurned and then toyed with—Dr. Orsky had told them that, had told them Natasha Pavlovna spent time with Dr. Warren just to make the other researcher jealous. Natasha Pavlovna hadn't been especially smart. Men whose pride was damaged could do foolish things . . . and those things could include murder.

Dr. Warren was also a playboy, a hustler; women seemed to be drawn to him. He was a privileged man who seemed to view his geology research and his park ranger roles as hobbies. And it was clear Agent Tyler couldn't stand the man—Sergei could tell that from his comments the other night. But instead of seeing Dr. Warren as a suspect, Agent Tyler could simply be viewing him as a rival. After all, the tall young lady who'd gotten out of Dr. Warren's high-end SUV before the hike began was the same one Agent Tyler seemed bent on pursuing. It was the woman he'd been with at the waterfall last week, it was the woman he and the blond girl had spoken to in the hotel hallway yesterday. He grimaced as he thought back on that video footage: potential girlfriend face-to-face with current fling. *The lad can't seem to catch a break.*

He'd learned that the dark-haired girl's name was Victoria Madison and she was in the park writing reports on grizzly bears as a part of her internship with a research group. He knew that she had the rustic cabin in Roosevelt rented until next week, and that a tiny girl who painted birds was currently staying with her. His watchers had told him these things. What he'd learned from his own observations was that she was a pretty girl, intelligent, with kind eyes. She reminded him more than a little of his Krestya.

While he was trained to see every hazard, every problem, he knew he should also focus on the positives. Better for his own morale. Surveillance was running smoothly, communications had improved, and his bug placements in the agent's office were operational. He was finally getting better intel from the Office, but he was still frustrated not to know the source of it. The Office wouldn't reveal who they had on the ground here. He scowled as he thought about it. That secret made everything much more difficult. He could accidentally burn his own source; that would really make a mess of things.

He took off his backpack, drank from a water bottle, and leaned back against a large tree near the trail. The other hikers in Dr. Warren's group had stopped just ahead, to stare down at a waterfall. He could hear the melody of the falling water from where he sat. He was just another hiker tagging along near the end of the group, probably hoping that afforded some protection from the resident bears. He suspected that was what the others thought when they looked his way. No one gave him any real notice.

The Russian was dressed like most of the overnight hikers: hiking boots, cargo pants, a tan shirt over a green tee. Always an open shirt or jacket to better conceal his weapon. The worn backpack and sun-bleached hat made him appear to be a backcountry regular. The floppy hat covered his dark-brown wig; the longish synthetic hair was uncomfortable in the heat. The unkempt style, grizzled beard, and heavy-framed glasses gave him a vagrant look. He thought the disguise had enough of a grunge factor to make him nearly unapproachable. When forced to interact with tourists or rangers, he'd done so in a clipped British accent. He'd signed the required forms for a permit to camp at Tindell Ridge and left his fifteen dollars on the ranger's desk. There hadn't been much interaction.

He watched the interchange between Dr. Warren and the Madison girl. They were standing near the trail fewer than twenty paces away. Warren was explaining something about the stream running far below them; Sergei guessed that by watching the geologist's hands as he talked. He was standing very close to the girl, smiling, charming. His ranger uniform gave him authority, and he was using it to play the seducer. The girl moved away from Warren a step, shook her head at something he said. She fanned herself with her wide-brimmed hat and moved another step away. *Maybe she is instinctively sensing a wolf,* Sergei thought. *She should be.*

CHAPTER TWENTY-THREE

Instead of driving back to Mammoth after he left Roosevelt, Win drove south. *I'm missing something.* He drove the Grand Loop Road twenty-nine miles through some of the most beautiful country in the world; the forty-five-mile-per-hour speed limit wasn't hard to maintain—rubbernecking tourists had reduced the pace to a crawl. But he couldn't blame them. Grizzly bears were the main attraction on the slopes of towering Mount Washburn, and he found himself watching the bison that grazed the open hillsides, catching glimpses of eagles swooping down, slowing even more as elk, antelope, or bighorn sheep crossed the road. He lost count of the bison—there were hundreds; it seemed he'd stepped back in time. It was obvious why the eastern part of Yellowstone is called America's Serengeti.

As he pulled off the highway at the Mud Volcano parking lot, he didn't even have to get out of his vehicle to see the dangers. Orange hazard cones on the lot's pavement surrounded two gaping holes that were belching steam. *Not a spot to let your kids or your dog run wild.* And Maxwell Springs was much more dangerous—no raised boardwalks or rail fences to provide protection there. No emergency phones to call for help. Maybe he was overthinking this; maybe Natasha's disappearance was simply an accident.

This was his second trip to the Mud Volcano area, and this time he visited every feature along the three-quarter-mile boardwalk. Trey had told him that the ground below the area was in constant flux, heaving, cracking, and spewing new hot springs and mudpots even as older ones fell silent. The namesake for the area, the Mud Volcano, had gone dormant in the 1870s, but prior to that, it had been a thirty-foot-tall cone of mud that shot grayish-brown sludge sixty feet into the air every few hours. Win cast a wary glance at its seething, chocolate-colored surface as he passed it and walked toward a puff of steam rising from a hole in the hillside. *Dragon's Mouth Spring,* the faded wooden sign proclaimed. Dr. Orsky said it was one of the features that had fascinated Natasha. It was the type of steam vent or spring that could contain subterranean rooms and tunnels. Win stood in front of the six-foot-tall opening and took in its deep rumbling, puffs of hot steam, and cloudy surges of scalding water. *Yep, I can picture a dragon sleeping in there.*

The smell in the area was akin to rotten eggs: hydrogen sulfide—a poisonous, flammable, acidic gas. *An entrance to Hell.* That's how Luke Bordeaux had described it after translating Natasha's handwritten notes. He couldn't imagine a researcher wading into that opening. Win was reminded of Dr. Orsky's warnings: ". . . *The danger, the extreme danger. Those features are live steam vents, wildly fluctuating heat from 170 to 320 degrees Fahrenheit. They sometimes contain hot springs— often toxic—which rise and fall in depth. Very unpredictable.*" Could Natasha have gone into the spring? Could she have died there?

Then how would her remains have ended up at Maxwell Springs? The map showed it to be twenty-six miles northeast of the Mud Volcano area. But getting there was the problem. It was at least a ninety-minute drive and then a difficult four-to-five-hour hike into Maxwell Springs. Dr. Orsky seemed convinced that Natasha was meeting someone at Mud Volcano the morning she disappeared. Who was she meeting and why? He thought back to the interview with Dr. Ratliff. They hadn't used horses to carry in their equipment in five years . . . then what did they use? A helicopter? Dr. Dravec had said they'd ferried in their gear with a helicopter on Sunday. Who had one when Natasha went missing? This was going to take some old-fashioned cold-calling. He'd never used the satellite phone in the Bureau SUV, and he decided it was time for the taxpayers to get their money's worth. He used the hands-free device to pull up numbers and make his calls as he slowly drove the mountainous road back to Mammoth.

He started with what he considered to be the longest shot. He called Headquarters and asked for an intelligence analyst he'd known at the Academy, Judy Wade. She seemed thrilled to hear from him and intrigued when he posed several questions: Could Facebook pull up public photos that had been taken from specific coordinates in northwestern Wyoming or southwestern Montana on August 26th or 27th five years ago? On Instagram too? Can we see those without a warrant? Win wasn't a tech guy—he had no clue—but Judy was a techie, and she was big into social media. He remembered that about her. He also remembered she'd been a little sweet on him and might be willing to do him a favor.

The Russian volcanologist had said there were tourists in the parking lot taking photos of bison the morning Natasha went missing. There wouldn't have been reliable cell service in Yellowstone then, but if tourists uploaded photos to social media from their hotels in West Yellowstone, Gardiner, or Cody, or anywhere they had access to Wi-Fi, he might get lucky. Among the tourists' bison photos there could be one that offered clues into Natasha's disappearance. Judy seemed pleased that he called, said she'd work him in. She asked him to send the coordinates and said she'd give it a try.

He struck out with his first three independent aviation companies. On his fourth call he hit pay dirt. "Yeah, we've been ferrying all sorts of researchers around the park for the last ten years out of West Yellowstone," the gruff voice replied. "But you ain't on my good side right now . . . you FBI boys have had us shut down in half the park for over a month. Do you have any idea how much it's costing me to keep two choppers on the ground?"

Uh-oh, the aviation restrictions because of the fugitive manhunt are still in place. Win switched gears quickly and appealed to the guy's sense of compassion. "I'm real sorry about that—I'm just working on finding a missing woman, someone you might have ferried five summers ago . . ." He kept talking and the man finally gave in.

"Oh, all right . . . I'll look through the logbooks. Not like I have much else to do since you've got us basically grounded," he groused. "I'll get back with you tomorrow."

Win was on a roll. Next on his list was Rock Man.

The guy finally answered after seven rings. Win hurried through the pleasantries, then asked, "Has anyone brought in a necklace that matches the ring I showed you? Might have been several years ago?"

"No, I haven't seen it and I wouldn't forget jewelry of that quality. But I've only had the shop a couple of years." Win's spirits sank. Then Rock Man added something unexpected. "Did your folks get what they needed on the ring?"

"What?"

"My sketch of the ring . . . you know, I posted it on Instagram . . . you know, those two agents were going to contact you about it."

"When?" Win's internal alarm bells were ringing.

"Oh, it was the same day I got a big shipment in . . . it was . . ." Win could tell he was thumbing through some paperwork. "Ah, yes, it was late afternoon of June 3rd, the day after you showed me the ring."

Win was puzzled. "When did you post the sketch of the ring?"

Rock Man seemed contrite. "Well, it was the same evening you were here. I was so inspired by it, I had to paint it. I know you asked me to keep it to myself, but, well . . . I hope I didn't do something wrong. The other agents seemed interested in who had the ring. I gave them your card."

Whoa. That was before I found out I'd be going to Russia. That's when the paperwork for that trip suddenly got rubber-stamped. Win found out very little more from Rock Man, but he did get him to text a screenshot of his Instagram post with the "sketch" of the ring. It was a beautiful painting—the guy was a true artist; it was a near-perfect likeness of the ring—and he'd added a short description of the ruby and the green Russian garnets in his comments. Someone had been trolling the internet, waiting for the ring to surface. But trolling for *five years*? Win stared out the windshield at the slowly changing scenery. *Who was Natasha Yahontova?*

* * *

She knew this wasn't smart. Knew this wasn't a good idea. But still . . . she was mad. Really mad. She'd been a fool. She kept moving down the trail quickly, hoping that her soft singing would warn bears of her approach. The bears took the easiest routes up and down these mountains too; the bears used the trails. Hopefully they'd move away—they most often did. But hiking down by herself was stupid. She'd tell anyone else it was unwise, bear spray or not, it was just plain old stupid. She launched into another song—a hymn this time. Honestly, she wasn't much of a singer, but the words gave her comfort. She'd expected to see more hikers coming toward Tindell Ridge, but she hadn't met anyone in over two miles.

The last couple she'd met warned her about a black bear and two small cubs, about a half mile farther down, they'd said. But what really got her attention was the man's weather report. "It's gonna come a squall, I think they said." He'd noticed her summer clothing. "Weather is gonna take a bad turn," he added. The woman was more direct. "You'd better come with us, we have a tent." She gave Tory's shorts, T-shirt, and light day pack a once-over. "You don't look prepared for a snowstorm."

She thanked them as she turned to go—it was June 18th, for good-ness' sake. *A snowstorm?* The woman called after her, "They're saying it'll come through early this evening. It's already six o'clock, you'd bet-ter come with us."

Tory waved her thanks again, but she continued down the steep slope, through the clearing, and into the deep forest. She couldn't face walking back into the primitive campground and seeing Chris.

An hour later she was breathing heavily, sweat stinging her eyes, as she continued her solo trek over two unnamed mountains in the Washburn Range toward the trailhead at Roosevelt. Building clouds had blocked the sun about thirty minutes ago. Since then the tempera-ture had dropped at least twenty degrees. The wind was blowing the tops of the lodgepole pines; pine needles and small limbs had begun to fall, littering the trail before her. She usually found the sounds of the forest to be calming and peaceful, but with the wind shredding the tops of the trees as the storm approached, all she felt was a building sense of alarm.

She'd been delayed for nearly fifteen minutes when she'd had to stop and wait patiently for a bear and her two tiny cubs to move into the woods. Black bears weren't normally aggressive, but any sow with cubs shouldn't be trifled with. The cubs were probably only three months old, less than ten pounds each, but full of playful energy. They finally bounded off across a fallen tree to follow their mom deeper into the forest. The trail was open again for her retreat.

A gust of wind chilled her, and she could smell moisture in the air. She pulled off the day pack and her stomach knotted when she realized her packable down jacket and change of clothes was in Chris's larger overnight pack, not in hers. She checked her phone. She wasn't expecting cell service, and she got none. But the phone was also her only flashlight. The battery showed only twenty-five percent. The mobile battery charger was in her jacket pocket. *Dang it!* She drew a deep breath and swallowed down an emotion that was almost foreign to her: fear. At least she knew how to handle that unwelcome feeling. She stopped for a moment and prayed for safety.

She kept hiking, every step bringing her closer to the trailhead. Closer to the corrals and the lodge. Closer to her cozy cabin in the woods. After she saw the sign for the Lost Creek Trail, she knew she was less than three miles from safety. But it wasn't a cakewalk. Those last miles were strenuous, up and down steep slopes—the side ridges and ravines of Brock Mountain.

She remembered a roaring creek paralleling the last part of the trail. Chris had stopped the group about two miles in earlier this afternoon to take pictures of the waterfall. That's where she'd found herself wondering for the first time if this overnight trip with Chris was really a good idea. But it wasn't until they'd reached Tindell Ridge and everyone had begun to set up camp that she realized he'd been carrying only one tent in his backcountry pack, not two. He'd told her she'd have her own tent. Told her the trip would be a great chance to get to know each other much, much better . . . she remembered his sly look when he'd said that. She wasn't thirteen, she should have known that look. She'd been so angry at Win Tyler that she'd missed it, she'd heard what she wanted to hear, not what this older man was telling her. It wasn't really Chris's fault, she reasoned; he probably related to every woman that way—expected them all to fall in bed with him. *Nope, I'm the one who was an idiot,* she told herself again.

She paused at the bottom of a sharp incline. She knew exhaustion was setting in, but she could finally hear the rushing of the stream in the distance, and it gave her some assurance that she was getting closer to her goal. The sky was much darker now, and the wind in the trees was nearly blocking out the sound of the water far below her. She gave herself five minutes to rest on a mossy rock before she began the steep climb up the mountainside. Her legs were still shaking from the stress of coming down the last switchback a bit too quickly. She emptied her water bottle, ate her last granola bar, and wiped sweat off her face with her bandanna. The sudden chill in the air caused her to shiver as the first cold raindrops began to strike her.

She needed to climb at least four hundred feet to the crest of the next ridge, to the spot where they'd viewed the falls. If she remembered right, the trail was more moderate after that . . . but maybe it had only seemed that way because of her early enthusiasm for the trip. The sky was quickly becoming darker; it was only a little after eight o'clock, but the gray clouds had turned black. The thunder that had been a steady background noise for the last fifteen minutes now grew intense. She knew lightning strikes in the Rockies were an extreme danger, but she reasoned that walking within the deep forest offered some protection. She kept moving upward until she was within fifty feet of the ridge crest. A bolt of lightning split the sky and shattered a tree just across the ravine. The close concussion of thunder nearly caused her to fall.

The cow moose suddenly loomed over the trail twenty feet in front of her. It had stepped from behind a boulder the size of a house and now stood blocking the path, its head held high in fright. A tiny calf quivered at the cow's side, spindly legs spread wide. With barely a snort of warning, the cow dropped its head and charged. Tory dodged in shock as the huge beast lunged toward her, its nostrils flaring, sharp hoofs extended, eyes frenzied. The combination of the storm and an intruder had sent the cow into a rage. Tory thought she'd screamed, but she wasn't sure. She stumbled off the trail, grasped for a sapling, but fell. She felt herself tumbling as rocks were sliding, dirt was flying—then an abrupt, jarring stop as her boot caught on a root and held her.

She was dangling nearly upside down, staring up at the rolling clouds, the swaying trees, and the blackish-brown movement on the trail forty feet above her. The moose was still there. The rush of water in the ravine two hundred feet below her cancelled out all other sounds. She was stunned. She lay still as stones continued to slide past her, she reached for a low limb on her left, but her fingers couldn't quite touch it. The pain in her foot from being lodged below the root began to overwhelm her. *Please, God, help me.* She talked to herself to try to regain calm, to ease the pain. *Focus! Focus!* She blew out a breath and realized she could see condensation in the air. Pellets of sleet stung her face. *I have to get free!*

* * *

"Sheeees! Don't do that!" Win exclaimed in surprise and anger. "You scared five years off my life by sneaking up on me like that!" His hand was on his chest as he tried to slow his heart's pounding. He couldn't see a thing in the dark shed, but Bordeaux's Louisiana dialect was unmistakable.

"Wouldn't be givin' you such a fright iffen you'd pay more attention to your surroundings." Luke quietly replied. The man's voice didn't sound friendly, and Win had no real idea what was coming. Luke shifted in the darkness, and Win's hand found the Glock's grip.

"I do not like being spied on, dammit! What are you doing outside my house?"

"Waitin' in the shed fer you to get home . . . and I's 'bout to give up on that. Interestin' choice of words you got there—bein' spied on. I come by cause Trey thinks you have a problem—he asked me to check on you, and to make sure you'd be around . . . say tomorrow and the day after."

Win's pulse was finally moving back toward normal; he eased his hand away from the gun and stepped closer to Luke in the deep darkness within the old garage. He still couldn't make out much of the man, then he realized Luke was wearing a black ski mask and black overalls—his ninja garb, Win had once called it. He was invisible in the night. Luke had lured him into the old garage by leaving the door open and making cat sounds. He'd unscrewed the single light bulb. As soon as Win had stepped out of his truck and heard the "cat," he'd entered the shed—he'd fallen for the trick hook, line, and sinker. Bordeaux had a knack for making him feel like a fool.

Luke dropped the country-boy accent and switched to his precise military tone. "You were followed from your office to Roosevelt, then to Mud Volcano, back to your office, to the Terrace Grill and probably on to the house this evening. They're tailing you with at least four—all men, far as I could tell. Right now there's a spotter up on the second level of the terraces to the southwest. He can't see us from there, even if he's got night vision—which I'm betting he does—but he'll be wondering why you haven't gone in the house in a minute or so. Looks like a blanket surveillance." He lost the military timbre. "Whata ya gotten yourself into?"

Win just stood there breathing in the dust from the old garage and tried to make sure his mouth hadn't dropped open in shock. Luke kept talking. "I followed you around all afternoon and evening and got here in the middle of that last thunderstorm. Didn't see anyone. Changed in here and did some recon after it got dark from that last cloud . . . weather is fixin' to turn."

Win tried to dodge the real questions. "Weather is already awful . . . it's completely dark at nine o'clock, temperature's droppin' like a rock, and those two electrical storms that came through earlier coulda put most Southern storms to shame."

Luke was still on point. "Well, it's gonna get worse, but that might suit what's comin'. You gonna be here fer the next two days?"

"Far as I know." *Maybe Luke's gonna set up a meeting for me with the fugitives.*

"Alright then, why are you bein' tailed by foreigners?"

"How . . . how do you know they're foreigners? Can you describe them?"

"Yeah, but we don't have time for that—spotter will know you're on to him if you don't get in the house. Here . . . here, carry this shovel back. He'll think you were just in the shed, rootin' around fer it."

Win realized that Luke was pushing a garden shovel toward him. He groped for it in the dark. "Okay. Okay, I'm gonna go in the house and get a flashlight and come back out here like I'm looking for something. You can give me the details then." Thunder rumbled, drowning out the sound of the wind. "I don't wanna make myself a target."

"You've been a target fer at least a day with these guys on you . . . I don't think it's that. I've met with two of them."

"What?"

"Get on in the house or you'll blow this."

It was real hard to walk the fifty-some-odd feet from the garage to his back door in the dark. He mentally pictured a bull's-eye stuck to his back as he faced away from the threat Luke had seen on the cascade boardwalks. He grabbed his hat from the rising wind, leaned the shovel against the house, and flipped on the lights as he opened the back door. He realized he was still holding his breath when he entered the mudroom. His palms were sticky with sweat and there was a low ringing in his ears. He put on a heavier coat and got a flashlight from under the sink. Cloud-to-cloud lightning snaked across the black sky as he walked back outside to a garage that was now empty.

CHAPTER TWENTY-FOUR

Trey knew it was gonna be a tough go of it. He ducked his head as another freezing gust blew the stinging sleet into his face. He put his back into the wind and tried to adjust the hood tighter over his ball cap; the LED light on his headlamp was the only thing getting him up this mountain. He'd called dispatch and asked for anyone they could spare to report to the corrals at Roosevelt. He was trying to quit fuming—anger wasn't going to help him solve this crisis. Chris Warren hadn't reported that Tory had left the Tindell Ridge Campground until dispatch had called him to check on the primitive campground's status at 8:30—nearly an hour ago. Warren told dispatch that Tory had begun the hike out at 5:00—she should have made it to Roosevelt by 8:30 or 9:00 at the latest. Trey had no authority over the interpretative ranger, but he was still furious. Warren knew not to let someone hike out of there alone with a summer squall on the way. He knew better. Here it was nearly 9:30, Tory hadn't signed out on the backcountry trailhead's logbook, and her roommate hadn't seen her. It had gone nearly dark before 9:00 because of the intense storms, and that ass, Warren, hadn't had the good sense or the decency to even call and ask anyone to check on her. Trey really wanted a few minutes alone with the guy. Why someone had allowed Warren to wear the proud uniform of a park ranger was beyond him.

Ease up, he told himself. *Ease up or you'll miss something.* And missing something would be real easy in these conditions.

The storms were much worse than predicted. Chief Randall had rangers and volunteers calling or hiking in to check on each of the primitive campgrounds in the northern half of the park. It was a monumental task, since most of the backcountry campers didn't have satellite phones and only a few of the primitive campgrounds had cell service. And then there were situations like this, where a hiker or small group of hikers hadn't signed out when they returned to the trailhead. Most had safely made it out, but each case had to be verified. They'd already found one older man incoherent on the far side of Bunsen Peak; thankfully, they'd located him before his hypothermia passed the moderate stage. Too many hikers were unprepared for the dramatic shift in the weather.

So here he was, by himself in the darkness a mile up the trail from Roosevelt. His folks were spread thin. Real thin. Just hours ago, it had been seventy-five degrees and sunny—now it was thirty-four degrees with a howling wind, freezing rain, and sleet. Often these early-summer storms impacted a small area and lasted for only a few minutes; this one was lashing the entire northeast quadrant of the park and had been coming in waves for hours.

He blew out a deep breath, pulled the rain poncho's hood closer to his face, and continued trudging up the icy trail. *Never let your guard down with mountain weather,* he remembered his father's warnings from his childhood. They were ranchers, and they'd lost dozens of calves and lambs to these squalls in Idaho's Salmon River Mountains. He was no stranger to the dangers. Seemed every year these sudden cold fronts would sweep in and the park would lose someone to hypothermia—just a fancy word for freezing to death.

* * *

She had long since lost all feeling in her foot, but spasms caused by her body's uncontrolled shivering sent stabbing pain down her leg every few minutes. The intense waves of pain may have been the only thing keeping her conscious; she knew unconsciousness was one step closer to death as her core temperature continued to drop.

She could see her luminated watch; it had been nearly two hours since she'd tumbled off the trail and lodged here, her left foot caught under a root, her head lying near the lip of the cliff. For at least the first half hour, she had kept her wits about her, she'd tried to use her body strength to raise herself toward the root that entangled her; that hadn't happened, but she had worked the day pack off her back, managed to get it under her neck, and used it to raise her head to a level where all her blood wouldn't pool there. She'd succeeded at that one task, which kept her from blacking out.

Her cell phone was nowhere to be found; she'd checked her pockets. It had likely gone off the cliff when she fell. She'd shouted for help every few minutes, but she didn't know if anyone on the trail—if there was anyone—could hear. The waterfall was roaring two hundred feet below her, thunder was rolling through the mountains, and the wind was tearing at the trees. At least two thunderstorms had passed, then the sleet and freezing rain had begun in earnest. She was completely exposed to the icy wind and soaked to the skin. She was smart enough to know that was a lethal combination.

The uncontrollable shivering had begun over an hour ago, and at first, she'd moved her arms back and forth to try to warm herself. Once the convulsions became near constant, she'd pulled her arms into her to conserve warmth and put a nylon pack strap between her teeth to ease their chattering. She began to slip in and out of consciousness. Lucid thoughts were becoming few and far between. Somewhere she'd read an article that said freezing to death was painless—an easy way to die. She was coherent enough to reflect that the author was a fool.

At least she had stopped blaming herself. She'd prayed and asked God to comfort those she'd leave behind. Her prayers became jumbled as her circulatory system concentrated her blood in her core for warmth; the lack of blood in her extremities began to starve her brain. She asked the Holy Spirit to pray for her since she could no longer do it herself. Tory found great comfort in the assurance that He would pray—that He was with her. She saw the faces of those she loved drift by; she was a bit surprised to find Win Tyler's gentle smile floating through her mind among the others.

Tory managed to raise her wrist one last time . . . but the numbers on the watch's face were meaningless at first—she forced herself to process them. Every time she'd looked at her watch, she'd thought of her mother. The sports watch had been a gift to celebrate her acceptance into the Interagency Grizzly Bear Research Project this spring. Her mother had reminded her that her cell phone wouldn't be a constant companion in the wilds of Yellowstone; she'd have to go with an old-fashioned wristwatch to tell the time. Earlier she'd cried each time she looked at it, but then the cold had stolen her tears. She knew if she stopped shivering, she'd have entered an even more deadly phase of hypothermia. Her watch told her that phase had passed ten minutes ago. Now the only thing keeping her awake—and alive—was the pain.

* * *

He saw the large hoofprints first. He stopped and took in the shadowy surroundings for just a moment. Wandering into a cow moose with a calf could be just as disastrous as surprising a grizzly bear. The cows could weigh over 1,100 pounds, had notoriously short tempers, and used their sharp hoofs as weapons. Fortunately, they also had terrible eyesight, and if he remained still, he could go unnoticed. He didn't move as his eyes scanned the forest and jumbled boulders near the crest of the ridge. Years of training had enhanced his night vision far beyond most people's, but still he used caution. The blackish-brown beasts could blend into the forest with ease. He'd had one run-in with a moose in the Ural Mountains, he didn't want another. But no eyes stared back at him. Nothing caused him alarm. He thought about pulling his night-vision optics from his pack, but those might attract unwanted attention if he did meet another hiker. The white on the ground had brightened the surroundings. He could still see well enough.

And what he saw were tracks that were fresh; the steady sleet that had been falling for the last half hour hadn't completely covered them. He crouched down with his Maglite to confirm that, yes, there were smaller hoofprints among the giant ones . . . a cow with a young calf.

Probably moving from the grasslands around Roosevelt up toward mountain lakes. He stood and took one step toward the large boulder that stood at the trail's crest when he saw it: a wide-brimmed hat lodged just off the trail to his left, nearly covered in white and just out of reach. The edge of the trail fell off into the ravine there—he could hear a stream rushing below. He shifted his pack and leaned into a skinny pine to try to see down into the ravine. The ice was making the footing treacherous near the trail's edge. He wouldn't risk a fall for someone's wayward hat. He dismissed it and took another step up the trail toward the huge boulder, but something was pulling at him, and he glanced down again. He saw her.

* * *

It was a bright white light, and within the fog of her mind it brought her comfort. In the last few moments, she had begun to feel warmth and now the light, now the light was here to take her home. But something was wrong... she tried to move her eyes away from the light's intensity. Her arm was covering part of her face, shielding it from the stinging sleet. She tried to blink and saw a dark form coming down from the sky, coming toward her. Something in her barely conscious mind registered fear; she tried to strike out, but her arms weren't obeying her feeble commands.

"Don't move. Be still." A man's deep voice ordered. She blinked again as the dark form loomed over her. *How is he standing in the air?* She felt a hand at the back of her neck. She saw a large knife inches above her face. Before she could close her eyes, everything went black.

* * *

He cursed. Shook the freezing rain off his floppy hat and cursed again. It had taken him only seconds to set up the ultralight pop-up tent; it was hard against a large boulder and partly beneath a massive fallen tree. Those obstacles would protect it from the worst of the winds. He'd chosen a spot about twenty yards off the trail. He could see the path, but the tent would be impossible for a passing hiker to spot. Only the front side was approachable. A fine defensive position. But the reason for needing a defensive position in the middle of the night in this foreign place was what had brought on the curses. This wasn't his problem. *I should have kept walking.*

But he hadn't. Instead he'd gone into action: he'd strung his rappel ropes, eased down the near-vertical incline from the trail, and examined the woman. At first he'd thought he was too late. Vacant eyes stared at him through the sleet; she wasn't moving—no shivering, no convulsions. He made the sign of the cross over her from habit. But when he shined the Maglite into her eyes, she blinked. Then she tried to move her arm from her chin . . . then groaned. At that point she had him. He knew it and he cursed.

A few seconds of calculations told him that he wasn't urgently needed anywhere else on this night of terrible weather. He'd been thinking of stopping along the trail and camping—he'd wait the storm out and get back to Mammoth tomorrow. The call on his satellite phone that had caused him to leave the Tindell Ridge Campground hadn't been that urgent. Some worrisome intel the Office had communicated and an unexpected visitor at the agent's house. But nothing that couldn't wait a few hours. He had a few hours, but he knew the young woman did not.

It wasn't his first experience with the dangers of hypothermia, far from it. A fellow recruit at the training academy had died after passing out while walking back to the barracks after a night of cards and vodka. He'd lost another comrade to the cold during a Zaslon Spetsnaz mission near the Finnish border. Russian winters were no more forgiving than Russian bears. He suspected that this park, with its high mountains and fickle weather, was much the same.

Sergei dug out what he needed and hung his pack on a rope in a nearby tree. No need to invite the local bears to the tent. He made a quick call to keep rescuers at bay, then powered down the sat phone. He'd removed the girl's wet clothes with slow, gentle movements; he'd hung them to dry from the straps inside the high-tech two-person tent. He'd eased her into his goose-down sleeping bag and checked her pulse often. It was still far too faint. Her left foot was likely injured, but that was a secondary concern. He'd feared that carrying her up the slope and to the tent could have caused the cold blood in her limbs to flood her heart. That was a common cause of sudden death in those suffering hypothermic shock. He'd seen no signs of that complication yet, but she hadn't regained consciousness either.

He knew he had to warm her core gradually. She'd need to regain enough awareness to sip warm liquids; his tiny Coleman stove was set up under the storm flap. It had been less than twenty minutes since he'd first seen her, but every second mattered. He knelt inside the entrance of the tent and pulled off his clothes down to his shorts. He slid beside her in the sleeping bag, wrapped her icy body close in his arms, and touched the gold cross that hung around his neck. He whispered another prayer that he'd found her in time.

*　*　*

Trey huddled at the side of the trail with his back to the blowing sleet. He repeated what he thought the dispatcher had said. "This is NPY5 . . . you're saying campers reported that Tory Madison is safe with them on Prospect Trail?" The reply on the sat phone came back clearer this time.

"Roger that. A couple made camp approximately two miles east of the Tindell Ridge Primitive Campground." Trey felt immediate relief, then doubt. If Tory left Tindell Ridge when Chris Warren told them she did, she should have been much closer to Roosevelt than was being reported. Warren had also told the dispatcher earlier this evening that he'd checked in with everyone who was permitted to camp at the site and everyone was there, except for one man—not a couple. "NPY5 to base . . . who verified that report? Copy?"

"Copy that . . . uh, says a man called in the report . . . will check further . . . we have lots of extra folks here tonight."

"Roger that." Trey started to punch off the heavy phone when the dispatcher's voice returned.

"Base to NPY5, dispatch requesting you assist at Tower Fall Campground. A tree blown down with injuries. Copy that?"

His feelings of relief dissipated. He was nearly to the waterfall lookoff . . . nearly two miles up the trail. He sighed. "NPY5 here . . . I have a sixty-minute hike out on Lost Creek Trail to Roosevelt. Will call in my ETA when I reach the Roosevelt staging area. Copy?"

Trey's instincts were telling him something was off. He knew from experience when the weather got this wild—when hundreds of visitors were impacted, and dozens of rangers were responding—things often went haywire. But someone had apparently used Tory's full name in the communication—that was reassuring. Maybe Tory had doubled back toward Tindell Ridge when the weather worsened and found refuge with someone who had a sat phone. Someone who hadn't filed for a permit to camp in that area. Campers skirting the permit process happened all too often. It sounded like that was the case. He'd almost called Win to come help in the search. Now he was glad that he hadn't. Something told him Win Tyler had enough irons in the fire, no need to compound that stress with a false alarm about Tory.

He shifted his heavy backpack and turned down the mountain the way he had come. It was going to be a long, long night.

* * *

She blinked her eyes open in the dim light and caught her breath as pain shot through her foot. "Ow . . . that hurts."

The big rough-looking guy with the gentle hands looked into her face and she self-consciously pulled the sleeping bag up higher under her chin. "Much more alert now . . . well, that's a good sign, lass." He turned his attention back to her foot; her left leg was extending from under the cover. He propped the small flashlight against the tent wall as he probed her ankle with his fingers again. His British accent was crisp. "Pays to buy good hiking boots, bloody right it does! Probably saved you from having a broken ankle or worse." He was applying some sort of ointment and taping her foot as she watched. He was quick and precise. He talked softly as he worked. "Lots of abrasions on the lower leg . . . I'm taping your ankle . . . it may be sprained, but it hasn't swollen much . . . nothing too bad."

She still had her watch on—she was aware it was all she had on. She was surprised to see that it read 5:14 a.m. Her clothes were hanging from various spots in the cold tent. He caught her eyes as she looked at them. "Your shorts are dry enough, I think. I had a clean T-shirt in my pack. I wouldn't think you'd fit in any of my other kit. You can get dressed when I finish here." He eased up from his knees and sat back on his heels. He had cargo pants on, but no shirt. His wild hair brushed the top of the green tent. A small gold cross stood out against his tan skin. She looked away from his chest.

"Don't be embarrassed, lass. It was survival, it wasn't sexual. Skin on skin was the best way to slowly warm your core. I started giving you warm sports drinks about two this morning . . . had to take you out a few times . . ." Her mind flashed back to at least two hazy bouts of vomiting; swallowing warm, sweet liquid; of relieving herself outside in the sleet. The muscular man was still talking. "Embarrassed? Aye, that's rubbish. Pretend I'm a doctor." He grinned. "You're a tough one . . . you pulled through." He was putting on a khaki shirt; his rain jacket and hat were now in one hand.

"Thank you. . . . Have . . . have I even told you thank you?" she asked in a shaky voice.

"Aye, several times in the night." He smiled again as he turned to crawl out of the tent.

"I need to get back . . . they'll be looking for me . . . ," she began as she tried to sit. Suddenly she felt very dizzy and very tired.

He was moving out of the entrance when he spoke. "Ahh, the weather's still dodgy, ice melting on the warm ground has turned to fog—thick as pea soup. Not likely anyone comin' or goin' for a bit, but someone will show up after a time, I expect."

He stuck his head back inside for some final instructions. "Move slowly getting dressed, you'll be weak and light-headed. There's more Gatorade and some protein bars here." He pointed to the bars and a water bottle near the entrance. "You'll need the calories and electrolytes to get some strength back." He spoke again just before he dropped the tent flap; she could see his eyes shining in the dim light. "Aye, Saint Michael petitioned God for your life—you're a blessed one, lass."

Tory leaned her head back on the pad, flexed her foot and winced. It hurt. The small flashlight was still on; it provided a little illumination. She reached for the clean T-shirt the man had laid across the bag. Her day pack was sitting near the tent's entrance with her boots. The bear spray was lying near the water bottle. There was no sound outside the tent, and she knew he was gone. Then she heard distant thunder. *I didn't even ask his name.*

CHAPTER TWENTY-FIVE

He was still breathing heavy from the five-mile run as he pushed open the wooden back door into the mudroom at 5:30. The black storm clouds had transformed the early-morning light back into night; he groped in the dark for the light switch. A roll of thunder rattled the windows and he instinctively dodged as another flash of lightning brightened the darkness outside the door. He'd made it back to the house just as the storm was hitting. It had been another restless night with his Glock on the nightstand, but he'd somehow managed several hours of sleep. The thunder and lightning had kept it up for hours, but it gave him some consolation that the Russian watching him from the terraces likely had an even worse evening.

He shook the rain off like a dog—heavy drops splattered the floor from his Gore-Tex running suit. He pulled the jacket off and draped it over the washer to dry, pulled off the wet running shoes, and padded into the dark dining room in his damp sock feet. He froze as a pistol muzzle lodged hard against his right ear. His heart skipped as his breath caught in his throat.

"Hold it . . . don't move." Win recognized the deep, low voice immediately. It was Jon Eriksson, the militia sergeant. The huge man was standing just inside the dining room, off the hall that led to the stairs. Win felt the gun move away as the man spoke again. "Real slow now . . . bring those hands up behind your head . . . lock those fingers. Slowly . . ."

"Still all clear." Another voice called softly from the darkness in the den.

Another man patted Win down, checking his legs for an ankle holster, then found the pancake holster in the small of his back. He pulled the small Glock 43 free. Win's mouth had gone completely dry. He tried to speak and choked a little on the first words. "I'm . . . uh . . . only carrying the one on my back." Thunder rumbled through the house again and rain pelted hard against the room's tall windows.

"Then you don't mind us checkin' real good," the low voice growled. "Harold, get the rest of those blinds and curtains pulled."

Win's eyes were adjusting to the dark room. He could see all six feet ten of Eriksson out of the corner of his eye. The black form of another man materialized from near the kitchen counter. Win couldn't see them very well in the gloom, but he sure could smell them. It was the earthy, musty smell of men who'd lived in the woods without bathing for far too long. It was a familiar, deer-camp smell from Win's youth. He didn't know why he hadn't noticed it when he came through the back door. Apparently his sense of smell hadn't made a full recovery.

One of the men hit the lights in the kitchen. Eriksson motioned with the gun for Win to move toward the oak dining table. "Sit down right here. We're gonna have a little powwow. Ain't no need for anyone to get hurt."

Win was finally beginning to get his wits about him as Eriksson pushed him down into one of the antique dining chairs. His mind flew to yesterday afternoon's bulletin from Denver on the manhunt. Four individuals matching the fugitives' descriptions had reportedly been observed by an anonymous caller at a gas station—which conveniently had no surveillance cameras—outside of Sheridan, Wyoming. Win knew that the five Deputy U.S. Marshals who'd been in Mammoth to continue the search had been pulled away and were on the hunt three hundred miles to the east. The fugitives obviously had outside help— the good guys had been played again.

Be cool . . . be cool. Maybe they want to surrender. Win thought that to himself as he tried to get his breathing back on track. Eriksson slumped into a chair at the end of the dining table. The .45 caliber

Colt 1911 semiautomatic looked like a toy in his massive hand. No one said a word for a minute as a sharp clap of thunder caused the stone house to shudder. Win sized them up while they waited for the rumbling to subside. The three men looked beyond ragged: dirty, scruffy beards; matted hair under their camo field caps; filthy, torn camo uniforms; and scuffed combat boots. There was a beaten-down, fatigued look about them. But they hadn't forgotten that they were soldiers; all three had clean AR-15s, there were knives in scabbards and pistols in holsters. Their hard eyes and faces didn't show defeat, not yet anyway.

Win knew their names by heart, knew their jobs, their relatives, their histories—all that information was neatly stacked in working files on his desk at the office. Jon Eriksson, the huge third-generation sheep farmer, had a small ranch north of Gardiner. Harold Peck, a thirty-year-old heavy equipment mechanic, had been employed by Park County. Ronnie Olson, the oldest at forty-six, raised a few cows and did private snow-removal work during the winters. All three were family men with wives and children. All three had served with distinction in the Army in Iraq or Afghanistan. These men were capable soldiers, honorable patriots, they'd call themselves, but they'd been terribly deceived. They'd fallen for lies and followed a madman. And they'd been on the run since May 12th, over five long weeks. There was a fourth man . . . Cabe McDonald; he was the guy who'd been wounded in the firefight. *Where's McDonald?*

"Can I lower my arms?" Win found his voice and asked.

The big man nodded, but he glanced down at the handgun. Win got the point as he slowly brought his hands to the top of the polished oak table. The adrenaline spike was starting to drop.

"Where's Cabe McDonald?" Win looked directly into Eriksson's bloodshot eyes.

"We laid him down in the hall. He needs a doctor, bad. That's why we come in."

"That's the only reason you came in?"

For the first time, the man looked away. Win watched him chew a little on his lower lip. He was struggling for something to say. The other men were quiet. The thunder carried on in the distance. The rain was letting up. "We were told you'd be fair with us. We were told it'd be best to come to you direct. Those other Feds were gunnin' for us." The guy paused a long moment. He was staring down at his handgun.

Not exactly what I had in mind when I tried to get Luke to set up a meeting, Win thought.

"We have families . . . we have kids . . . and . . . hell, Cabe is gettin' worse by the day," one of the other men added.

"We ain't going to jail." Harold Peck said in a raspy voice. "I ain't going to jail!" Win saw Peck's hand settle on his pistol's grip. *Easy, Win,* he told himself, *this could go off the rails real fast.*

The timer on Win's coffee maker dinged and everyone flinched. He always programmed it to brew right after his run, while he showered.

Win drew a breath and nodded to the big guy. "Alright, then. Let's get some coffee and see what we can work out. I don't need that .45 pointing at me."

"Harold, go check on Cabe," Eriksson ordered softly. He kept the gun where it was, with his big hand just touching it.

Just as Peck turned to leave the kitchen, the injured man stumbled into the room and collapsed against the doorjamb. His dirty face was a picture of pain as he slowly slid to the floor before Peck could catch him.

"Hell, this ain't good," Win heard Olson say under his breath. "Damn."

Eriksson got to his feet as Win moved to McDonald's side. The gaunt man was hot to the touch. His greasy brown hair was plastered to his scalp, and sweat was beaded on his brow. Win knew Cabe McDonald was only thirty-five, but the hardships of being on the run had etched lines through his face that made him look years older. Win crouched beside him, balanced on the balls of his feet. One of the other men eased the olive poncho back to reveal the dirty gauze bandages covering McDonald's upper arm. Win had adjusted to the stench of their body odor, but the putrid smell of rotting flesh hit Win's nostrils and he fought the urge to gag. He was no medic, but he knew that smell wasn't a good sign. The man shivered against the chill of fever.

"Mr. McDonald . . . ," Win started slowly. The hazy eyes rose to meet his. "We'll get you some help . . . take care of that arm."

The dazed eyes climbed above Win to the huge man leaning over his shoulder. "Brother Jon . . . you boys . . . leave me here." McDonald drew a labored breath. "You boys get outa here. You stay, they'll send you to prison." The voice was thick with emotion and pain.

"Be still, Cabe, it'll be all right. Got to get you some help." The low, deep voice was directly above Win.

The house shook again as thunder rolled through. Win was aware of rain hitting the line of small windows high on the back wall of the stone house. Win stood and Olson dropped down to take his place, putting a wet dishrag against the wounded man's forehead. Harold Peck was standing watch near the mudroom door, fingering his AR-15. Win took a step back. He looked up at Eriksson and cleared his throat.

"This man needs medical attention immediately." Win knew the smell of gangrene from his upbringing on the farm. Shock, then death were its close companions. He nodded toward McDonald with his chin. "We both know that. Every minute we wait makes it worse for him . . . and for you. Right now there are federal agents hunting you. If any one of them were to be injured or die, even in an accident, their injury, their death, would be on you. *On every one of you.*" He emphasized the words as the huge man blinked down at him. "Turn yourselves in to me now. I call off the hunt—that takes one risk off the table. Then we can get McDonald to the hospital where he belongs."

The big man looked down at his suffering companion. "He was gettin' better . . . gettin' better. Then he fell and ripped the wound open again. After that it got worse pretty quick." He was still hesitating. "We've all got families . . . got people we love . . ."

"That's even more reason to give this up now. You've done some things wrong, but you've also done some things right, Eriksson. You men saved some folks' lives in that firefight, you fought alongside our people. I can attest to that. You turn yourselves in peacefully, put an end to this manhunt . . . that'll count for something too."

The man kneeling beside McDonald had a shell-shocked look. He seemed to be blinking back tears. "I haven't seen my kids in so long, Jon

... but I can't let my sons see me on TV being led off in handcuffs. I'm not a criminal."

The younger man leaning against the doorframe with the rifle looked like he might bolt. He didn't move, but his frantic eyes reminded Win of a cornered animal. Ready to lash out if prodded once more. All of them had suffered through the weeks-long pursuit—each one of them was near the breaking point. It could go either way. Win knew he needed to give them something they wanted, something they needed.

"How 'bout we do it this way. You agree to surrender to the FBI. We'll get McDonald to the hospital, and I'll call a stand-down on the manhunt. We'll ask the U.S. Attorney to release you today, after a preliminary hearing. You'll have four days of confinement to your homes. Then a formal arraignment on Monday afternoon at the Justice Center. That will give you the weekend at home with your families and allow you time to secure lawyers. No handcuffs. No orange jumpsuits. None of that today or Monday."

Eriksson nodded and motioned for Win to sit back down at the table. He handed Win a phone. Eriksson wasn't dumb. It was a burner phone. It would take time to track it, to get a firm location. If Win had called on his Bureau phone, the cavalry could have been here in minutes. He punched in the number for his supervisor's cell phone, laid the phone down, and put it on speaker mode.

"Jim, this is Win."

"What's up?" Win's supervisor was puzzled, but in typical FBI fashion, he answered on the second ring and seemed completely alert at 5:45 in the morning.

"Boss, I need a conference call with you and the ASAC on the False Prophet case now."

"At this time of the morning? C'mon, Win. You want me to call him now? You're not exactly winning any popularity contests down in Denver these days."

Win had momentarily forgotten he was deep in the Bureau doghouse. He drew a breath and regrouped. He started to call them fugitives, then thought better of it. Harold Peck, the guy with the edgy look, leaned in closer to him, the black muzzle of his AR-15 rotating Win's way.

"I'm, uh, with some gentlemen who may want to turn themselves in today, and I need your help getting through channels to firm up a deal."

There was silence. Then concern. "Are you all right?"

"For the time being. Wanna make that call, Boss?"

Silence again, then, "Hold on, I'll patch the ASAC through on a three-way."

Win sat there and tried to remain calm. He stared down at the cheap throwaway phone while they waited. In less than thirty seconds, Wes Givens's cultured voice came over the speaker.

"Win, where are you and what's going on?"

"I'm not at liberty to give my location, sir. I'm trying to facilitate a resolution to the ongoing manhunt related to the False Prophet case." He hoped the formal language would clue the ASAC into the situation.

"Are you a hostage?"

Depends on how you define hostage. Win eyed the .45 caliber handgun resting on the oak table in front of the giant Eriksson. He cleared his throat. "This doesn't have to get categorized that way . . . this doesn't have to go sideways on us, sir."

"Okay . . . okay." The ASAC was tentative. "Do you have something in mind?"

"First, we need to call a stand-down on the manhunt and get their man, Cabe McDonald, to a hospital. I can get a paramedic to him quickly, but we'll need a med flight to get him to the trauma center in Idaho Falls." *That should tell him I'm in Yellowstone.* "The three other men are willing to appear before the Magistrate today on the condition that they be bonded out till, say, Monday afternoon. That gives them enough time to get with their families, retain lawyers, take care of personal business before a formal arraignment with the U.S. Attorney. No handcuffs . . . no extraordinary police presence or press at the initial appearance today."

There was a long pause on the phone. Win was afraid they'd lost the connection. Mr. Givens finally responded. "This is one of the biggest manhunts since Eric Rudolph. Win, those men are domestic terror-ists." The militiamen were hearing every word, and all three stiffened. Eriksson's huge hand flexed on the pistol.

"Sir, all four men were solid citizens of this area before the inci-dents with Daniel Shepherd. They're willing to come in peacefully . . . they want their say against the charges, but they are holding some cards right now. The Marshals and our teams are looking for them in the wrong places." *Not to mention they've got me at gunpoint.*

The ASAC only paused for a second. "I'll reach out to Tom, and I'm sure he'll need to touch base with DOJ. It could take a few minutes . . . make sure the gentlemen are comfortable with that."

Win's eyes met Eriksson and he nodded. "You've got fifteen minutes to decide. Agent Tyler will call you back." He said it into the speaker on the phone and hit the END button.

Win glanced down at McDonald. "Let me call Trey Hechtner, he's a paramedic with the Park Service. I'll put him on standby to help Cabe. I won't give anything away," Win said, as the man groaned softly in the background.

Eriksson nodded. He pushed the burner phone back across the table to Win.

The ranger answered his cell on the first ring. "Hechtner here."

"Hey, it's Win."

"Problem?" Trey could hear the strain in Win's voice; he noticed the unknown number.

"Uh-huh. Just wanting to give you a heads-up that I may need an EMT or the doctor from the clinic on standby here at Mammoth." Another clue to tell them where he was.

"Okay." Trey answered, hesitation in his tone. "Talk to me."

"Not free to say too much. Can you sit tight and put the chopper on standby?"

"The helo left here before that last storm with two campers injured by a fallen tree. It won't be back for at least an hour. The doctor went out with the ship to keep the patients stable. I just rolled in to my house from that callout." Trey paused again, puzzled. "Look, Win, if someone needs medical help now, I can be there."

Win's eyes rose to Eriksson again. He glanced at the handgun. No way he was putting Trey or anyone else in danger until these guys were disarmed. McDonald groaned again from the hallway. The guy was suffering.

"Maybe you could give me some advice on what I should do for shock, gangrene?"

"Yeah, right. Where are you? You at home?"

"Trey . . . I'm going through channels here to resolve this. I can't let you get into a situation. Can't have any law enforcement in this . . . right now."

Trey didn't even pause. "Look, Win. I'm trained to save lives. If you've got a potential gangrene situation, every second counts. Are you at your house? I can just drop in for a cup of coffee in my personal truck. Nothing official. My medical bag will be with me."

Win rushed his response. "I can't put you in—"

Trey cut him off. "I'll see you in a minute. I won't make a call to anyone else, and I won't be armed. You . . . and whoever you're with. You have my word on it."

CHAPTER TWENTY-SIX

Things were picking up a little too quickly to suit her. Her sources were indicating that the Bureau had lost its interagency battle to deploy HRT as the arrest team in Yellowstone—inserting the CIA into the mix had raised the stakes considerably. She stared into the steamy mirror and ran a hand through her damp hair. A quick peek out the door told her that he was still asleep. She'd gotten next to no direction from her handlers in the last several hours; they seemed to have been caught off guard by the speed at which the situation was developing. Allowing the team to be faced with a potential confrontation with HRT or, Heaven forbid, the CIA, seemed to have sobered everyone up a bit. The original plan to allow Tyler to methodically plod along and hopefully solve some case before everyone moved in was now completely out the window.

She pulled out her makeup bag and began with the firming lotion; the bags under her eyes were a bitch this morning. When this was over, she planned to take a week's leave and sleep for days at a time. She dug in the bag for her foundation, then paused at the sound of snoring from the adjoining room. A glance at her watch on the counter told her it was 7:34, she needed to get moving. *Get moving . . .* She paused again. This might just be the break she was waiting for. She hadn't gotten much useful intel during last night's drinking, schmoozing, more drinking, and, well, a lackluster main event. She rolled her eyes at herself in the mirror—too much drinking. Ah, well. But why not turn this into an opportunity to insert herself deeper into the operation . . . the Major was one of the Office's stars. Impress him and her career could skyrocket. Her role had already been elevated, why not take that even further? What was that old saying her mother used to tell her in junior high school? *Nothing ventured, nothing gained.*

* * *

The waiting had been agonizing. More so for the three armed militiamen who were still standing in his house, Win supposed. Harold Peck had paced back and forth from the kitchen to the den dozens of times; he was completely on edge. Ronnie Olson seemed resigned to his fate; he'd helped Trey with McDonald, hardly saying a handful of words. Eriksson had just stood around holding the pistol and looking distressed. He was obviously too tired and preoccupied for small talk. Win had offered them all the protein bars he had in the pantry; he'd made a second pot of coffee and fed the cat. When the final call came in from Wes Givens ten minutes ago, the tension had finally begun to ease. Win glanced at his watch: only 8:36. Time was crawling.

The ASAC had been on speakerphone when he assured them that Judge Walters, the Federal Magistrate for Yellowstone, would go along with the deal they'd worked out with DOJ. He told them that they'd be free to call their families as soon as the impromptu hearing concluded. Trey had been at work on Cabe McDonald for the last two hours; the morphine that he'd administered early on had taken effect, and the man's eyes now had a foggy, unfocused look instead of the tortured fixation on pain. The opioids were doing their work; he finally had some peace. Win had watched Trey work with the wounded man and marveled at the ranger's calm concentration. Eriksson kept bending over them, wanting to know what the outcome would be. No telling on that, Win knew. He'd seen Trey's face go a shade paler after he cut away the wet, dirty bandages and first saw the wound. Trey's eyes had found Win's just for a moment before he began his work, and the look said a lot: *This ain't good.*

It would have been helpful if they'd had real backup, but they didn't. That was part of the deal. Win knew there would only be the ambulance crew and Johnson to transport the fugitives to the clinic, then just a short walk across the street to the Justice Center's courtroom for Eriksson, Olson, and Peck. No lights. No sirens. Two of the Denver agents who were still in Mammoth would be guarding the courtroom. The goal was to attract as little attention to the arrests as possible. Win knew the national press would be ticked, but he couldn't care less. For him, one more phase of a nightmare was over—for the four militiamen, another phase of the nightmare would soon begin.

Harold moved to the den and peered through a crack in the blinds. "There's an ambulance coming into the parking lot . . . it's turning onto the gravel." That would be the gravel drive that ran between his house and the cascading Lower Terraces. Win drew a deep breath. *Finally!*

"Y'all need to place all of your weapons—knives, everything—here on the counter," Win told the men. Ronnie Olson, who was holding the bag of liquid saline attached to the IV Trey had inserted into McDonald's arm, eased the assault rifle off his shoulder with one hand and gave it to Win. He followed that with a Smith & Wesson .40 caliber from its holster. Eriksson had been holding the Colt 1911 ever since Win's first call to Jim West nearly three hours earlier. The big guy cleared his throat and placed the black handgun on the granite countertop; his AR-15 was propped in the corner, and he moved across the room to retrieve it just as Harold walked back in the room and laid his rifle on top of the growing pile. Harold laid his commando knife down and fidgeted with his holster flap. Win heard the low growl of the ambulance's diesel engine; he heard a vehicle door slam in the backyard. *Time to go.*

Trey was holding the back door open for two Park Service EMTs who were totally focused on the prone form of McDonald. The three militiamen began filing out the door; they'd agreed they would all crowd into the back of the ambulance for the less-than-half-mile ride down the street to the clinic. Better to keep prying eyes off them, better to secret them to the hearing and the reunion with their families. Win moved away from the counter to make more room for the medics.

He did a mental check of the weapons . . . *Crap! One short . . . oh no!* He pocketed his Glock 43, which Eriksson had laid on the counter, pushed the screen door open, and stared down at the group gathered in his backyard. *Eriksson . . . Olson . . . Where's Peck? Dammit!* Harold Peck was running up the Beaver Ponds Trail. Harold hadn't turned in his gun.

Spence Johnson was standing by the Park Service ambulance, looking like he just got out of bed. He glanced around the ambulance's open door and called to Win. "Got a runner!"

Win took both steps down at once. "You can catch him!" he shouted to Johnson.

Johnson never even looked toward the trail. "Bad knee."

Win moved past the back of the ambulance, past Johnson and the other two militia guys, and stared after the escapee. He saw Harold push two hikers out of the way as he sprinted across the short wooden bridge a hundred yards above the garage. Win called out to Trey. "I've got this . . . can you help Johnson get these guys to the Justice Center?"

Trey didn't break his focus on the patient litter that he and two other EMTs were easing out of the house. "Got it!" was his quick reply.

Eriksson grabbed Win's arm as he turned for the trail. "Harold . . . Harold might shoot himself—he's been real tore up over this." The grip tightened. "And he might try to take you with him."

Win didn't even answer, he just nodded and began his run. The guy was fast, but not as fast as Win Tyler. He'd been an All-SEC receiver, he still had the speed. Win paused for a second at the bridge as one of the hikers, a heavyset, balding guy, was pulling himself off the ground, slapping the mud off his cap. He looked angry; his female companion just looked scared. She looked even more scared when Win pulled the compact Glock from his pants pocket. "I'm FBI, y'all get back and keep any hikers from coming up this trail. Can you do that?"

The man had frozen at the sight of the weapon. He stood quickly and nodded. "Sure, sure thing." Win knew that people generally liked to be helpful. And Win needed all the help he could get. The two hikers trotted back across the bridge toward the trailhead at the side of his house.

Win turned and resumed his race for another couple hundred yards up the gentle slope. He slowed to a jog as he neared the tree line above the house. *Don't need to run into an ambush. No telling how many hikers are up here,* he thought.

The storms had apparently moved on, the sky was crystal clear, the sun was trying to clear the clouds to the east, and the well-worn path he'd jogged up before dawn had begun to dry. He neared the second wooden bridge over Clematis Creek and paused. The trail paralleled the small stream for a good ways, winding deeper into the spruce and lodgepole pine forest, then got a bit steeper and climbed for over a mile until it leveled off at a scenic overlook. Harold Peck was from this area, he'd likely know the spot high up on the ridge where the view went on forever. Maybe he'd been there with his wife, with his kids. It was a spectacular place in the early morning. Win figured that's where the desperate man might go to end things. Win cut off the main trail and took a much steeper game trail, a shortcut he'd found, that led to the overlook. He'd try to flank the guy, or at least cut him off. He ran up the slope like his life depended on it. He was thinking someone's did.

*   *   *

He'd gotten back to Mammoth before eight; his mates thought things were going badly for the agent and they were certainly right. He'd seen night vision–enhanced images of heavily armed bandits entering Tyler's house during one of the predawn storms. Then more images of Agent Tyler walking right into them after his run. Then the negotiations, the back-and-forth of trying to work out a surrender for the hooligans. He'd listened to bits of the recording. And now this. One of the men hadn't bought into the surrender, he'd bolted. That man was now sitting on a boulder on this high ridge, holding a Colt 1911 in front of his face. That man was crying.

Apparently this one had eluded the authorities for weeks now and he couldn't face defeat—he couldn't bring dishonor on his family or his comrades. Sergei could understand those desperate thoughts, he'd faced them himself on the rocky shores of Crimea and in the Caucasus highlands. Death before dishonor. It was a theme never too far beyond his consciousness.

He'd made the climb from the Lower Terraces above Tyler's house to the high overlook a few yards behind the fleeing man. He hadn't known where the bandit was going, but he knew he couldn't run any distance. The man's initial burst of adrenaline had carried him away from the house quickly, but the hardships of the last weeks were evident. He was spent—he wouldn't go far.

And the only reason to stalk the fleeing man was to protect their investment. Agent Tyler was as predictable as the rise and fall of the sun every day. He'd concluded that based on the new intel the Office had sent him this morning—his early impressions of the lad had been correct. Sergei knew the agent would follow the man, would try to reason with him, would try to apprehend him. Agent Tyler could very easily get himself killed doing that; reasoning with a man who has decided that dying is better than living is a horribly risky thing. So that's why he and his mate hunkered down in the rocks, stilled their breathing, watched, and waited. Losing Agent Tyler at this stage of the game would be disastrous for the mission. And the mission was everything.

*   *   *

"Harold? Harold . . . no need to do something drastic. C'mon, Harold, drop the gun, come down off that rock, and let's go on back." Win kept his tone gentle, tried to sound reassuring.

The answer was a choked sob. Then, "I can't do it . . . I can't face them . . . I can't . . . whata my kids gonna think? I can't—"

"Look, Harold, think about those kids . . . you love those kids . . . you've got plenty to live for. . . . Put down the gun. C'mon, man, trust me." Win stepped out from the tree cover and moved into the small clearing a few feet closer to the boulder that seemed to overlook the world. The sun was clearing the last of the black storm clouds that stood miles in the distance, the purple and blue mountains south and east of Mammoth rose to touch the emerging sun. The cold rain had cleansed the air and the view from the overlook was breathtaking. But

Win wasn't here for the scenery. He took another step closer; he kept his Glock pointed down. Harold Peck's thin shoulders were heaving from his sobs, but his pistol wasn't budging.

Harold sobbed again, the muzzle of the .45 caliber handgun tight against the side of his head. "I . . . I don't know what to do . . ." Then as if a plan had suddenly materialized, the anguish in his face disappeared, he blinked to clear his eyes and slid off the rock to face Win, bringing the Colt down in a shooter's stance.

Win realized a second too late that he needed better cover. *Uh-oh . . . death by cop—death by me! He's gonna try the martyr route!* Win dropped to one knee as he brought his weapon to bear. "C'mon, Harold, you don't wanna do this!"

Harold's hands were shaking when he took the first shot and he missed Win cleanly at forty feet. Win rolled to his left into a patch of sagebrush as everything in his world morphed into slow motion. *I can't kill again!* his mind screamed as he sighted in on Harold Peck's chest. The man rose out of the two-handed stance, aimed the gun wildly in Win's general direction, and took a step closer. He fired again—two loud shots that kicked up the damp ground less than five feet from Win's head. Win rolled again as two more rounds found the spot where he'd been lying a heartbeat before. There were no options now; firing to wound was a made-for-TV ploy. There was only firing to kill. His eye found its mark, his finger eased back on the trigger. *Please God,* he whispered, *I don't want—*

The shot sent parts of Harold's fingers flying away with the Colt. He screamed as he grabbed for the wound with his free hand. Blood drained from his face as he stumbled back several steps and fell against the huge boulder. Win had no idea where the friendly fire came from, and he didn't care. He sprinted toward the injured gunman and threw him facedown to the ground. Win had him pinned with a knee in his back, but the fight had already gone out of the poor guy, who just lay there whimpering in pain. Win blinked to clear his mind and realized he had no cuffs, nothing to tend to the wound, not even his phone.

Then Luke Bordeaux stepped from behind the huge rock, dropped into a crouch, and grabbed Harold's bleeding hand. Blood was everywhere.

Win glanced at Luke and noticed he was breathing heavily. "You got here right in time . . . thank you."

Bordeaux started cutting a piece of Harold's jacket sleeve off to make a tourniquet. "Harold . . . lay still, lay still," he commanded. His dark eyes flicked to Win. "I got here a little late, seems to me . . . we got company, but they ain't showin' themselves."

Win stared at Luke in disbelief. "You didn't shoot him?"

Luke raised his eyebrows and barely shook his head. "Nope. Damn good shot, whoever he is. What *have* you got yourself into?"

CHAPTER TWENTY-SEVEN

It was messy, wasn't any other way to see it. In Bureau-speak, it was just plain messy. No one was satisfied with the process or the outcome. Judge Walters had been stupefied that after millions in federal dollars and countless hours of manpower poured into one of the largest manhunts in recent times, two of the fugitives were being quietly released on their own recognizance and two others were to have family and attorney visits within hospital settings. Jon Eriksson and Ronnie Olson, who reeked to high heaven from weeks in the woods, stood in his courtroom and loudly proclaimed that they were patriots—innocent of all wrongdoing—even though the judge told them they couldn't make formal statements without their attorneys present. The Assistant U.S. Attorney was ticked because she'd had to throw documents together with no notice and wasn't even getting any press time on the biggest case she'd ever worked. The cable news companies were really going to go ballistic when word broke of the surrender. All of their reporters and satellite vans were still off chasing a false lead halfway across Wyoming. And the special agent orchestrating this circus was bloody, unshaven, and dressed for a jog. The judge liked order, decorum, formalities. This was messy.

Cabe McDonald, who was technically released, was now on a med flight on the way to the Eastern Idaho Regional Medical Center with a very good chance of losing his arm, if not his life. And then there was Harold Peck. Harold had forfeited his chance at four days of freedom by trying to commit suicide by cop and nearly killing a federal agent in the process. Harold was across the street in the park's modest medical clinic, being stabilized before his ambulance trip to a Bozeman hospital. In Judge Walters's view, Harold needed medical treatment, a suicide watch, and a good dose of jail time, but DOJ was wringing their hands over how to handle the two wounded militiamen without violating their surrender agreement and incurring the wrath of every ultraconservative cable news network. The judge ordered an FBI guard for Peck for the ambulance ride, told the two Denver agents to remain with Eriksson and Olson until their families arrived, and stepped down from the bench. He stormed out of the smelly courtroom, thrilled that the matter was now out of his hands.

Win was still in his running pants. His bloody T-shirt clung to his chest as he pushed through the heavy glass-and-metal doors of the Justice Center. The preliminary hearing had concluded, but Win still had his hands full. He thought back over it as he trotted down the steps and dodged the tourist traffic to cross the street to the low-slung, stone-clad building that housed the park's medical clinic. *It didn't go smoothly, but it sure coulda gone worse.*

Trey had gotten two armed rangers up Beaver Ponds Trail within ten minutes of Luke's phone call for help from the overlook; they'd left one ranger on the ridge to secure the crime scene. Win had asked the second ranger to make sure no one entered his house. He and Luke had gotten Harold down off the ridge and to the clinic in time for Win to appear before the judge and give a statement alongside Eriksson and Olson. Two of the Denver agents who'd been working the False Prophet case stood at the back of the courtroom in bulletproof vests, armed to the teeth. Win wasn't sure what they'd been told by the ASAC, but they both followed Win's directions to stay clear of the militiamen. It was obvious that Special Agent Winston Tyler was running the show.

A glance at his watch told Win it was just after 10:30 as he pushed open the door into the clinic's small waiting room. The agents they'd requested from the Bozeman RA to accompany Harold Peck in the ambulance should be here soon. The receptionist pointed him in the right direction, and he pushed through another door to find Harold lying on his back on an exam table. The tiny room was barely large enough for the table and the two rangers who were standing guard. Win noticed that Harold's uninjured hand was cuffed to the table's side rail. The thick bandages padding his right hand were already spotting bright red. A nurse walked in just ahead of Win to check Harold's IV, and Win saw him open his eyes. No one said a word. Win paused at the door for a moment. He'd walked over here to wait for the Bureau's transfer team, yet he felt as if he needed to say some word to Harold Peck. Harold beat him to it.

"I'm real sorry . . . I'm real damn sorry." He said it just a little louder than a whisper, and the others in the cramped room turned to look at Win. "I don't know what come over me. . . ."

Win took a step into the room and looked down at the man. "Mr. Peck, you know you're under arrest, it's best for you if you don't say anything until you've talked to your lawyer. I'm sure they've got you on pain meds . . . best you not say anything."

The man's face crumpled and tears began leaking down his gaunt cheeks. Win's mind flashed back to Harold holding the gun to his head as the sun cleared the eastern mountains less than two hours ago. *Dang it.* Win took another step into the room and spoke quietly to the guy. "Judge Walters is going to allow your family to visit you in the hospital . . . I understand they'll be taking you to Bozeman . . . they're calling in a hand surgeon."

The man blinked the tears away and stared up at Win. "I'll get to see my kids?"

Win nodded.

"Will you . . . will you forgive me? It wasn't about you."

Win was suddenly aware that all the eyes in the room were on him again. *Well, hell.* "Sure, Harold." He drew a deep breath. "Yes, I forgive you. Remember what I said, you've got a lot to live for . . . make your life count."

He couldn't handle any more sentiment, especially in front of others, so he turned abruptly into the hall and ran smack-dab into a short nurse in bright-purple scrubs.

"Look out!" she exclaimed as she dodged back.

"Whoa! I'm so sorry . . . Cindy? I didn't know you worked here." It was Trey's vibrant wife wearing the purple scrubs.

"Oh, I fill in sometimes. They sure needed help last night and this morning. It's been wild! Are you here to see Tory?"

"What?" Win's pulse jumped a few notches.

She looked puzzled. "I just assumed . . . well . . ."

"Tory's here? Is she okay?" His chest was suddenly tight; his mouth was suddenly dry.

"Ah, HIPAA rules . . . I can't *officially* say, but if you walk down the hall to room 3, you can see for yourself." She gave him a quick smile and held up a chart. "I've got to get this to the doctor."

He made it down the short hall in four strides. He tentatively knocked at room 3 and cracked open the door.

She was lying on an exam table with a cotton blanket draped over her. He took in the IV with two bags of liquid dangling over her head. He took in the monitor—the vital signs looked pretty good. She shifted and he could see her face. She was very pale, and there was a cut near her chin that had been taped. He could see a purple bruise above her left eye. She raised her head just a little and smiled at him. "Hey, Win."

"Hey, you okay? What happened?"

Her voice was weak. "Uh-huh . . . I'm okay."

You don't look okay. You don't sound okay.

She kept talking softly. He had to step into the room to hear her. "I think they'll let me out . . . ah, when the drips finish." She motioned up toward the IV bags with her eyes. "How'd you know? Did Lauren call you?"

"No. No, I'm here 'cause a guy got injured. What happened?" he asked again.

"Oh, I did . . . I did something incredibly stupid." She closed her eyes for just a moment. When she opened them, it was clear she didn't want to go there yet. "Lauren went to find me a coke. I need some caffeine and they don't believe in giving patients coffee."

Cindy came in and stood beside Win. She smiled down at Tory and set a cup on the counter. "Brought you some apple juice, Tory. We should have the labs done in an hour or so . . . your vitals are staying constant. If you haven't developed a headache and are continuing to improve, Dr. Phelps will probably spring you late this afternoon. You're one tough cookie!" Cindy glanced back out the door, where someone was calling for her. "Push the button if you need me. I'll bring you another warm blanket in a sec," she said as she hurried from the room.

Tory nodded and managed a feeble smile; she shifted on the uncomfortable-looking exam table and tried to get her head higher up on the stack of pillows.

"About the other morning in Bozeman," Win began.

She raised her hand and limply waved his efforts at an explanation away. "Lauren said you came by . . . she said you told her it was work. . . . We can talk about it later."

"It *was* work, but I'm sorry, so sorry that I hurt you. We need to talk soon, okay?"

She nodded and gave him another weak smile. "Okay . . . I think they put . . . something . . . in the IV a few minutes ago . . . I'm feeling a little loopy." She drew a deep breath. "The doctor said I came close to dying . . . hypothermia. I thought about you . . . then I . . . I got rescued by an angel. He had . . . ah, such intense eyes. . . . Saint Michael, I think." Her words were coming more slowly.

A guy in a white coat, who didn't look to be over twenty, stuck his head in the door, glanced at Win, and scowled. "Ms. Madison should be resting. Are you a relative, sir?"

Win didn't budge. "Yeah, I'm her brother. How's she doing?"

The young doctor's eyes narrowed. He motioned Win outside the room with his head. Win squeezed Tory's hand. "Don't go anywhere," he grinned down at her. "I'll be back." Her eyes were closing.

In the hallway outside of Tory's room, the doctor took in Win's bloody T-shirt as he identified himself. Win thought being an FBI agent might carry some weight with the doctor, but it didn't. "I only want relatives in with patients," he said. "I can't tell you anything about her condition." He immediately turned and walked into another exam room.

Cindy appeared in the hall and huddled with a frowning Win Tyler. "That was Dr. Phelps." She rolled her eyes. "He's a newly minted physician and totally full of himself. He's also a stickler for the rules. Many patients we see in the park have no family out here. We have to rely on friends for information." She sighed. "Here's the deal: Tory's got a mild concussion and a sprained ankle—neither one is a big issue. But she had moderate to severe hypothermia last night. A few minutes ago we gave her a sedative to help her sleep for a few more hours—her muscles are exhausted from the uncontrolled shivering and convulsions that the drop in body temperature causes. Based on what she told us, she was unconscious before the angel found her . . . and likely unconscious off and on throughout last night. It's really a miracle anyone found her. She'd fallen off a trail west of Roosevelt. Jimmy Martinez did the rescue—you know Jimmy. He could give you the details."

"An angel?"

The short nurse shrugged. "Tory was sorta delirious when the ambulance brought her in about an hour ago . . . she said an angel saved her." Cindy leaned back against the pale-green wall. "Bottom line: we think she'll be fine. She does need to stay quiet and rest for a few more hours. I know she had another friend in here earlier. That girl, Lauren, told the doctor she was her sister." She smiled. "Well, sister in Christ, just like you're a brother in Christ. Come back in a few hours if you can; she should be awake and more alert by then. Give me your number and I'll text you when she wakes up."

As they traded numbers on their phones, Win noticed some commotion up the hall at room 1, where Harold Peck was residing. Three FBI types were congregated outside the door. The folks from Bozeman had arrived.

* * *

Win really wasn't expecting anyone to be in the office, but he heard voices down the hall as soon as he cleared the small foyer and pushed open the ornate wood-and-glass doors leading into the lobby. Sounded like a woman's laughter.

He walked through the narrow lobby past the conference room, the oak staircase, and two small offices. The break room at the rear of the building was empty as well, but as he turned toward the locker rooms, he heard laughter again. He made the corner and sitting on the counter next to the gun safe was a jovial Paige Lange. She was gesturing with a drink in her right hand, but it was her left hand that attracted Win's stare: it was firmly attached to Johnson's arm.

"Win! Spence is showing me the office—you didn't tell me you had such a *darling* partner," she cooed. "Now that you and I aren't a thing . . . well, I've got some time on my hands." Johnson was closing the heavy metal door to the big gun safe. He abruptly straightened and his ruddy complexion became even redder. Paige was still latched onto his arm.

Win didn't know what to say. Johnson had the expression of a kid who'd been caught with his hand in the cookie jar. "Ah, just showing her the art . . . uh . . . the paintings you put up . . . just looking over the office renovations," he stammered.

"In the gun safe?" They could both tell Win wasn't pleased.

"Ah, Winnie, I never get to see the guns . . . you know how it is as an FBI support staffer. Just work, work, work—none of the really cool Bureau stuff!"

Paige slid off the counter, dropped her grip on Johnson, and swirled the drink in her hand. "Spence, I'll bet you have a little more booze in your desk, let's go back upstairs and get some for Win." She dropped her chin and gave Win a sour look. "Or are you too much of a stiff shirt to indulge on your lunch break?"

Win held up his hand and stared her down. "No thanks, I'm good." He shifted his eyes and gave Johnson a hard look. "Why didn't you stay with the fugitives in the courtroom? We've got agents from Bozeman with Peck now. Where have you been?"

Johnson had regained his composure. He gave Win an indifferent shrug. "The Denver guys showed up at the courthouse, and we're waiting for an Evidence Response Team to show up and process your house and that overlook on the trail. I think they're coming out of Lander or . . . maybe Billings . . ." He stared over Win's head and shrugged with one shoulder. "Doesn't matter . . . no telling when they'll roll in. I just got yanked back off my leave, so I've been monitoring it all from the

communications room. I figured someone needed to be in the office."
He scowled at Win. "You'll get all the credit for the collar, dammit. I
figure you've got everything under control."

Win was fuming, but he didn't want to launch into the older agent
in front of Paige. She brushed past him as she walked back down the
hall. Her tone was biting. "Not that it's any of your business, Win, but
I've been pulled into some case that's being worked out of the San
Francisco office—I'm gonna be doing the digital filing for some dudes
over at the Justice Center for a few days. So I may see you around."
She kept walking down the hall as Win and Johnson drifted along
behind her.

She raised her cup. "Thanks for the tour and the refreshments,
Spence! Gotta go change and meet some geek for lunch. I'd better let
you get back to work before Win has a hissy fit." And with that she
moved through the foyer's door, out the entrance, and into the sunlight. Win and Johnson just stood there in the small lobby, glaring at
each other.

"What?" Johnson said. "You think you still have a claim to her? She
doesn't seem to see it that way."

Win shook his head. He hadn't even thought about the Russians
for several hours. Paige's unexpected appearance changed that. *This
is probably part of Paige's new cover . . . ease up.* He was still scowling
at Johnson, but he held up both hands in mock surrender. "Whatever.
I've got no claim on her." He turned away from the other man. "I'm
gonna go get cleaned up and check on my house." He was already walking toward the exit. "Call me if anything comes up." He knew Johnson
wouldn't be calling today.

* * *

Win had just parked beside a Park Service Tahoe at the rear of his house
when his Bureau phone buzzed. He stepped out of the Expedition on
the off chance that the truck was bugged and answered the call.

"Are you where you can talk?" It was Brent Sutton from Seattle.

"Yes, sir. I just got out of my vehicle."

"Oh, we were able to sweep your SUV—it's clean. And I hear we got the fugitives. Wes Givens tells me you brought them in."

"Yes, sir. More or less. Thanks for the backup. I needed it."

There was a long pause. "We don't have anyone in place yet. What backup?"

It was over seventy degrees in the midday sun, yet Win felt himself go cold. "Someone took a shot at one of the militiamen who was in the process of trying to kill me this morning. Disarmed the guy with a shot to the hand. I . . . uh . . . I assumed it was one of HRT's arrest team."

"HRT is still in Quantico. Paige and Gloria got to the Yellowstone Justice Center around 9:30 this morning. Humphrey is driving down there from Bozeman now. Wasn't any of our folks."

Now it was Win's turn to pause on the call. Luke had denied taking the shot. Luke had said, *"We have company."* The number of possibilities for the shooter's identity immediately dropped to one. *Well I'll be damned.*

CHAPTER TWENTY-EIGHT

L uke had disappeared as soon as they'd gotten Harold Peck to the clinic this morning. That was probably for the best. There would be mounds of paperwork and reports to complete once the dust cleared on the fugitives' surrender, but for the moment that crisis was winding down, and Win had bigger fish to fry. Brent Sutton's call a few minutes ago was a game changer.

"We're afraid the Russians have someone on the inside—on the immediate inside." That's what the man had said. Win had stood in his backyard and finished up the call, raising two fingers in salute to the park ranger sitting on the back steps of his house, guarding its entrance. Win was trying to figure out what to do next. He thought back to Sutton's words.

"It looks like the CIA is going to send in a paramilitary unit and go after Sergei Sokolov. We're losing the turf war on this one from the top. Major Sokolov is considered too great a national security threat to just let him continue to wander around Yellowstone for no obvious reason."

"Why not HRT?"

"Well . . . honestly, the powers that be are leaning toward a policy of neutralizing the threat immediately . . . lessening the possibility of an escape—"

"Shoot first and ask questions later?" Win interjected.

Sutton paused, then added, "No one in the Bureau wants to go that route. That's not the way we do things."

"And the Agency does?"

Win heard him blow out a breath. "The CIA's paramilitary units are accustomed to operating out of country, where the rules of engagement aren't as restrictive as we have here."

"But we are *here* . . . in America. You're saying they'll just kill the guy if they get the chance?"

Sutton didn't answer the question. Win took that as a *yes.*

"This is all coming down in the next forty-eight hours. The CIA wants you to lure the guy out, stage it. I know the fugitives have been a distraction, but you need to start setting something up. Start pulling him in. I'm leaving Gloria and Paige in Mammoth on the pretense that they're working that Chinese espionage case. Humphrey will move between Gardiner and Mammoth as he's needed. Humphrey and Paige will rotate on and off . . . they'll be your primary backup."

"What makes you so sure someone's on the inside?" Win asked.

Sutton paused again. Win figured the supervisor was trying to decide how much he could tell him—how much he needed to know. "We've gotten some intel from overseas, intercepts by NSA. We're learning there's been way too much information on this case getting back to Moscow. It's coming from someplace other than the bugs we know about, someplace other than the sources we know are compromised. It's possible that your office is bugged, but if we run a sweep, we risk tipping Sokolov off. But there's more than just that. . . . Headquarters is . . . ah . . . thinking it's personnel."

Win's mind flew back to the meeting with AD Langford in the rainforest outside of Seattle—what had he said? *"The Russians, among others, I'm afraid, have eyes and ears in our government. We must use great care, even in the Bureau."*

"We're just now thinking we've got a leak?" Win asked. He wondered if Sutton would tell him the truth. He heard the supervisor take a deep breath.

"No. We've suspected something for nearly a year—other cases, other situations. We think we're closing in on it. The situation you're in could blow it open for us . . . I can't say any more at this point, Win. What you just heard stays between me and you."

Brent Sutton had wrapped up the call with a warning: "Watch what you say in your office, and watch your back. Get the meeting set up with Sokolov and keep your head down. This will all be over soon."

*　*　*

Win could have stood in the hot shower for hours, but it was nearly noon, and his mind was overrun with issues. *One thing at a time,* he counseled himself. He'd found no sign that the fugitive militiamen had been upstairs, so he coaxed Gruff into an upstairs bedroom with cat food and apologized for imprisoning him until the Evidence Response Team cleared the rest of the house later today. He'd made sure the site of the shoot-out up on the ridge was still being guarded by the Park Service. He'd gotten a call that Harold Peck was in an ambulance on his way to Bozeman with two FBI agents on board. One of the Denver agents had texted him that Eriksson's and Olson's families had shown up, and that the men would be escorted back to their homes to serve out their four days of house arrest before the formal arraignment on Monday afternoon.

By some miracle, the press still hadn't gotten wind of it, but that reprieve would likely be short-lived. The Denver Field Office had a charter flight coming into Bozeman with the ASAC, the office's press agent, another Evidence Response Team, and some additional folks from the Violent Crime Squad to help wrap up the fugitive surrender. Jim West and two agents were driving up from the Jackson Hole RA; they were due to be here any minute. Win had been told to keep the lid on things until they all arrived. Now he at least looked like an FBI agent, as he straightened his tie and pulled a western-style sports coat on over his starched white shirt. He was back in his khakis and cowboy boots; his Glock was in its holster and his creds were in his pocket. His world was falling back into some semblance of order. He sure as heck needed that right now.

Win walked out of the house with two packages of cheese crackers and a coke just as Ranger Jimmy Martinez pulled up in a Tahoe and got out. He waved to Win before turning to intercept a troop of Girl Scouts setting off on the Beaver Ponds Trail; they'd already passed one *Trail Closed* sign. "Sorry, girls, this trail is closed." The slender ranger pulled on his Smokey-the-Bear hat and motioned the group back. The girls ignored him until he stepped directly into their path. "A *'Trail Closed'* sign means the trail is *closed*." The girls were grousing at him, and he was trying to pin down who was in charge. Win needed to talk to the guy; he stood next to his SUV and checked his texts again. The pack of young ladies finally retreated, and Ranger Jimmy walked his way.

"I just saw Tory at the clinic—she's improving. Cindy Hechtner said you'd rescued her," Win said.

The ranger smiled at him. "We didn't do any rescuing. Someone very capable had already handled that task. We just brought her down Lost Creek Trail."

Win thought about that for a few seconds. "She said an angel saved her."

Jimmy raised his eyebrows. "I'm sure not gonna argue with that. I checked the spot where she fell off the trail—found her phone at the edge of a cliff, saw where she'd been hung up. I saw where someone had to cut through roots to get her free, had lifted her back to the trail, all while dangling on a rope two hundred feet above a ravine. That would have been a gnarly rescue attempt even under good conditions, but in darkness, in an ice storm, with her unconscious and suffering hypo-thermia?" He nodded. "An angel sounds about right."

"No idea who it was?"

"Nope, very strange that he didn't stick around. Tory hobbled out to the trail after daylight . . . it was awfully foggy up there. A couple hiking down found her. They said they didn't see another soul. If it was an angel, he must have a darn good credit line, 'cause he left a really sweet tent, a sleeping bag, and a camp stove with her. The *angel* also knew exactly what he was doing to slowly warm her, to bring her back. She may have been near death when he found her, Win."

Win felt his stomach drop when he heard those words. He swallowed hard and drew in a breath as the ranger continued talking.

"There was professional taping on her sprained ankle. And I found where he'd cut a bit of the rappel rope to tie down a flap . . . here . . . I kept it, it's a little unusual." The ranger dug in his cargo pants pocket and came up with twelve inches of black nylon rope. He handed it to Win.

"Why is this unusual?" Win asked as he fingered the 9.9 mm cord.

"It's black. Who uses black rope? You want to be able to see your rappel lines. No one uses black rope."

HRT does. Special ops do. Anyone who doesn't want to be seen. Win just nodded.

Win reached for the Expedition's door handle, then he turned back. "One more thing . . . maybe you could check the backcountry log y'all keep . . . maybe this guy's first name is Michael. Tory was a little out of it at the clinic, but she said the angel might be Saint Michael."

The ranger straightened and smiled. "Ah, Saint Michael the Archangel." Jimmy crossed himself and bowed his head slightly. Win stood there looking puzzled.

"What? I'm Baptist, don't know much about saints."

"I'm Catholic. Saint Michael is the patron saint of soldiers." He grinned. "Still, that angel or *somebody* will likely turn up looking for that high-dollar camping gear. It's at the Tower Ranger Station, by the way. Tory gets it if no one claims it." He turned toward his SUV and waved. "I'll check the trail log and the backcountry permits for that area. I'll bet he'll show up."

Win had a sinking feeling in his stomach as he opened his truck's door. *Yeah, I'm afraid that he will.*

* * *

Sergei Sokolov was dressed in upscale hiker clothes, complete with a tan ball cap sporting a Masters golf tournament logo. He was casually leaning against a big half-dead evergreen that was clinging to the side of a steaming stream. One arm was outstretched, braced against the gray bark, and his other hand was resting behind his back. His relaxed stance didn't fool Win. The alertness in those green eyes told him worlds more than the man's posture. Win stopped on the little-used trail less than six feet from the Russian.

"This some kinda initiation? Some kinda test?" Win asked. He hadn't expected the summons from the Russian in the middle of the day, not with what seemed like half of Denver's FBI contingent swirling around him, competing for his attention. It hadn't been easy to get away at 2:30 in the afternoon. And the location was scary, families with kids within ten yards. Sokolov was using the tourists as a shield of sorts, to make an armed takedown impossible without civilian casualties. The guy might be ruthless, but he was also smart, real smart.

"I suppose you could look at it that way. As a test." Sokolov smiled a thin smile that didn't make it to his eyes. "So, Cowboy, are you gonna pass that test today? What do you have for me?"

Instead of answering, Win pulled in a long breath and glanced back down the empty path leading from Upper Terrace Drive, a one-way paved road that looped around a thermal feature called Orange Spring Mound. A steady stream of vehicles pulled slowly by, folks searching for a rare parking spot or taking photos out the windows. The sound of voices seemed close—yet somehow far away. All the activity was just a few yards from this small clearing in a stand of heat-stunted pine. Win's anxious eyes combed the dense evergreens directly behind the Russian; he knew Sokolov wasn't alone. He could feel it. He wondered how many of the "tourists" he'd passed on the brief walk from the Upper Terrace parking lot were working for the bad guys. He was less than a five-minute drive from his office, yet he might as well have been in the wilds of Eastern Russia. The sound of water trickling over the lichen-covered rocks beside him began to cancel out the noise from the tourists. Win's world shrank into the six feet of parched ground between him and the Russian.

"Keep your hands where I can see them." Sokolov cocked his head. "Nervous?" he asked.

Win dropped his eyes to the trail. He had to keep playing his role. No one from Brent Sutton's team had contacted him; he knew the CIA team couldn't be in place this quickly. *Play your role.* "This isn't . . . uh . . . this isn't a place I thought I'd find myself." He shifted from one foot to the other and kept his hands clenched at his sides. "I'm not gonna betray my country . . . I'm not a traitor." He made his voice sound desperate as his eyes found the man's face again. *Is he buying this?*

Sokolov's chin came up and he straightened a little against the big tree. Win still couldn't see that left hand clearly. "I'm not asking you to betray anything, or anyone. I'm interested in the same thing you are: justice. That's what we're working for, you and me. No damage done . . . no one's gonna get hurt. We're just moving you back on track here. Back into the mainstream of the FBI—where you belong."

Sokolov paused, then nodded. "You've apparently scored some points on the arrests of those bandits today. Isn't that so? I want to help you achieve a bit more." He glanced at a couple of old-timers who were slowly walking beside the road, several yards away. His eyes quickly moved back to Win. "Did you get the bones I wanted to see?"

"I've been a little busy since we talked . . . hasn't even been forty-eight hours. Real busy, with real work. I expect you know that."

The big man nodded. "Yes, I know that . . . and I know that you nearly got yourself killed by a hooligan this morning." Then his tone softened a bit. "You hesitated too long, Agent Tyler. You can't hesitate to pull the trigger when someone is firing at you."

Win shrugged. "Yeah, that has occurred to me."

"You didn't want to kill the poor man, even though he was intent on taking your life. He nearly succeeded. You can't waver and effectively do your job. You're still traumatized by last month's firefight. You're still tormented because you were forced to kill."

Win swallowed hard and tried to think of a comeback. He couldn't.

"I learned that when we had you under the drugs in Kamchatka . . . I learned that you're struggling with unworthiness before God. You don't trust God to absolve you of the killings."

The guy sure nailed that on the head. "I guess I'll just have to take that up with my shrink."

"Either that or with your priest. . . . You can't be a warrior if you can't use your weapon."

They said he'd be conciliatory—gentle, even. They said he'd have me trusting him. Win stiffened. *No way!* Win spread his hands out in front of him. "Yeah, well . . . we're not here to deal with my mental health issues, are we?"

"That's true, so where are the bones I asked to see? You're being paid very well, and it appears you aren't delivering." The man took a step toward Win and Win felt the intensity of those green eyes. *"His eyes were so intense."* Wasn't that what Tory said?

"Look, I didn't have time to get the bones, and there are too many agents wandering around the building today for me to get them. Too many folks there who could ask questions. Tomorrow it oughta calm down. Give me till tomorrow afternoon and I'll have something for you." *I hope he's buying this—the CIA can surely get set up by then.* "How 'bout we meet somewhere late tomorrow afternoon." Win cut his eyes to a group of hikers coming down the main trail that paralleled the Upper Terrace Drive. "Somewhere away from the tourists."

"Perhaps that would work." Sokolov's gaze swept the trails before coming back to Win. "Do you have your thumb on your suspects? Have you forgotten you're supposed to be solving missing persons cases?"

"What are you now? My supervisor?" Win tried to sound indignant. "Yeah, I know where they are . . . or at least where they're supposed to be. Like I said, I've been a little busy."

The guy studied him for a minute. For at least a full minute. Win had learned long ago that the one who did most of the talking was often the one who knew the least. He waited the guy out—he didn't say anything more.

"All right. There's no hurry. We're just trying to move you back up the ranks, give you another score." He nodded toward the road with his chin. "Go back down the trail. I'll be in touch."

As Win turned to go, he met the man's eyes and caught something there that he hadn't expected. For just a fleeting second, Win was aware that the Russian was playing him. And this play had nothing to do with turning Special Agent Win Tyler into a Russian spy. They weren't trying to develop an asset—they were after something else. He was a means to an end, a tool to be used and then discarded. Like a match starting a fire—once the kindling ignites, the match is tossed into the flames and consumed. Every fiber in him flashed a warning, yet he forced himself to turn his back to the man and casually walk down the path.

* * *

His Bureau phone buzzed seconds after he stepped into the Expedition. He took off his jacket and wiped a sleeve across his damp face before he answered. "Win Tyler." He was still trying to tamp down his nerves from the meeting with Sokolov. His eyes were scanning the trees on the far side of the small parking lot for the Russians.

It was Judy Wade from Headquarters, and she sounded excited. "Win, I'm sorry I didn't get back with you sooner, but it took a while to go through the hoops with Facebook on the photo search. They wouldn't let me see anything archived without a warrant."

Another closed door. He felt a letdown. "That's okay, Judy. It was a long shot anyway. I really appreciate you taking the time—"

"No, I didn't mean I didn't find anything. I just didn't get anything from their archives on Facebook or Instagram. So instead I launched a current search, just on my own social media." She paused, and he could tell she was fooling with her computer. "I just sent you something from the coordinates you gave me . . . you said to look for something weird. Well, this is weird."

His phone dinged and he swiped over to his email. He put her on speakerphone and pulled up the image. "Whoa. Geez!"

"Is that what you were looking for?"

"Yeah . . . yeah. I didn't think they were releasing anything from five years ago—"

"This wasn't five years ago, Win. This was yesterday. Last night, just after ten."

Win was staring down at two still shots and a fifteen-second clip from a camera phone. Someone in a very shiny suit was at the entrance to the Dragon's Mouth Spring. He enlarged the image of the sign with his fingers; he enlarged the date stamp. Yep, someone had gone in that hellish opening last night.

Judy gave him a few moments to take it in. "I've enhanced the images some; they were greenish. Odd color. I've also sent you the Instagram page of the guy who posted the shots and what appears to be his cell number. He posted the images from Mammoth, Wyoming, this morning. I can message him and ask him to call you if you want, or you could try the number."

"Yeah, send the message and let's see if he'll call me. Since this is on public social media platforms, I don't think we're crossing any privacy lines. Wow, Judy, thanks. You're amazing!"

"Happy to help, Win." She paused. "Hey, I heard about you getting sent to Yellowstone this spring and ... ah ... your issues overseas. I just want you to know that anyone who knows you thinks you're getting a bum rap. You're one of the most decent guys I've ever met. I remember you telling me you joined the Bureau to do good. There is no doubt in my mind that's just what you're doing."

"Thanks, Judy. I appreciate that." Win tried to sound upbeat. "I owe you a lunch when I get back to DC."

"I'll hold you to it. Take care."

He sat in the Expedition with dozens of tourists milling about the tiny parking lot. Finally he started the engine to turn on the air-conditioning and stared at the house-size mound of orangish-white calcite—the Orange Spring Mound—sitting directly in front of him. Steaming streams of water were coursing down the mound's side and pooling at the bottom near remnants of long-dead trees. Someday he wanted to visit these magical places and really take in their wonder. He sighed and sat back in the seat. Wasn't happening today.

He reviewed the images on his phone again and tried to make sense of it. Someone had gone into that steam vent at ten last night. The cold front was coming through with a vengeance about that time. Couldn't have been many people around. There was only one figure in the photos, and the images weren't clear enough to give him much information. But one thing was for certain: someone had gone into that steaming gaping hole. *Why on earth had they done that?*

His phone buzzed while he was still staring at the images.

"This is Brad Packer . . . uh. I got an Instagram message to call you." The youngish voice sounded tentative, suspicious.

"Mr. Packer, this is Win Tyler with the FBI. I really appreciate you reaching out to me. We're investigating an intrusion into one of the thermal features at Yellowstone National Park. We understand that you witnessed and photographed that intrusion."

"Uh . . . yeah. You mean the posts I put up this morning?"

"Yes sir. Can you tell me about them?"

"I normally post to Instagram several times a day." The guy still sounded timid. Then he switched gears. "Do you know that the Albright Visitor Center is one of the only places in the whole park that has Wi-Fi? Do you know how lame that is? We haven't had an internet connection for three whole days!"

Listening to the guy, Win was thrilled with his decision not to be on social media. "I think that's part of the point of being here, Mr. Packer. You know, back to nature, getting off the grid. Can you tell me about the photos?"

Win heard a woman's voice in the background. "Brad, just talk to the man and hold on to Emma's hand!"

The guy turned his attention back to Win. Win strained to hear; a mechanical-sounding voice was announcing something in the background. "Not much to tell really. The weather was horrible last night. We were driving from that lake area back to our lodge at Canyon. Can you believe what they charge a night for that lodge? And no TV, no Wi-Fi, terrible cell service! It's outrageous!"

Win ignored the rant and the guy finally continued. "Well, our little girl needed a potty break, so we pulled into the Mud Volcano parking lot. They have bathrooms there. Well, it was sleeting and blowing, and we just sat there and gave her a snack after everyone got back in the car. I pulled up away from the toilets toward the front of the lot. And then I see this dude on the boardwalk and Emma starts screaming 'It's a spaceman!' and I thought it was unusual, so I took some shots. We were there ten minutes max."

"Could you tell if the person in the suit was a man or a woman? Was anyone else with them? Did you see his or her vehicle?" Win's pulse was ticking up again.

"No clue on the gender, 'cause of the suit. It was like one of those suits the firemen wear at airplane fires—shiny silver. I was guessing it was a guy, but the helmet thing was pulled back at first, it was dark, and he was walking away from us. Didn't see another soul out of their car, but there were only maybe two, three other vehicles in the lot. By the time I got my phone out and had calmed Emma down, he had the helmet thing down and he was going in that steaming opening." Win strained to hear over the boarding announcement for a flight. The guy was calling him from an airport.

Packer began talking again. "We'd seen the spring yesterday morning. Emma was hyped on the dragon thing. I couldn't believe someone would just walk in there—it was wild." Packer paused, as if he still couldn't believe it. "He stayed in there five minutes . . . almost exactly five minutes. I timed it 'cause I didn't have anything else to do. He had like a pouch in his hand when he went in, I didn't see the pouch when he came out. We left before he walked down the boardwalk to the lot. It was getting late and we had to drive to Canyon to get our daughter in bed."

"You were seeing this pretty clearly . . . over ninety yards down the boardwalk? In the storm?"

"Well . . . well, I was using the night-vision scope my brother-in-law loaned me—he's a big hunter. The scope helped us spot the animals in the dark, had it rigged to my phone camera. Probably shouldn't have been spying on the guy like that, but, you know, I was bored."

That explains all the details and the green color, Win thought.

Win got the guy's contact information and learned that the family was sitting in the Bozeman airport, waiting to fly home to Portland. He asked Packer to send him a copy of the photos and video and to not modify them in any way. He figured having them provided by the photographer was more by the books than Judy's pilfering them off social media. He thanked the man and wished them a safe flight.

He backed the Expedition out of the parking space and tried to sort through way too many things on the five-minute drive back to the office. Whoever went in that steam vent picked a time when next to nobody was likely to see them: well after dark and right in the middle of a sleet storm. But why? And then there were the Russians. He was sure they were still watching him, wondering why he hadn't made the slow drive down the mountain to his office where all sorts of problems awaited. He still had at least a million loose ends to tie up on the fugitive arrests. The Evidence Response Teams were due to be hitting town about now, along with reinforcements to plow through all the required paperwork on Eriksson and those boys. Win still wasn't sure how much or how little of Bordeaux's involvement to include in the mix. And who shot Harold Peck? At least Win's gun hadn't fired—no one could pin that on him. Then there were Brent Sutton's folks to deal with—was he supposed to be in contact with Ms. Gorski or not? Where were Paige and Humphrey in this? Why weren't they shadowing him? And a band of CIA assassins was coming to town—*really?*

CHAPTER TWENTY-NINE

Win's supervisor, Jim West, called him before he made it down the mountain into Mammoth, telling him to come to the Justice Center to give his FD-302s on the fugitives' surrender and the near shoot-'em-up with Harold Peck. They had interview rooms set up in the Justice Center, and the ASAC had called an operations briefing for four o'clock. Win rushed into his office long enough to type a brief overview of his meeting with Sokolov on the Upper Terraces; he sent it to Ms. Gorski's secure email and jogged down the street to the Justice Center.

From Win's perspective, there was an odd dynamic going on when he hit the second-floor conference room in the modern building. Agents he barely knew were slapping him on the back, offering high fives, wanting to chat. Word was definitely out that he, Win Tyler, who'd been the office outcast for the last ten days, was suddenly back in the fold. He wasn't sure how to take it. He moved toward the coffee pot in the back of the crowded conference room and poured a cup, then leaned back against the counter and waited for the parade to begin. He had a nagging feeling he needed to be doing other things.

The Denver Field Office's National Security ASAC, Wes Givens, came through the open door with Jim West on his heels. He wasted no time. "Before we start assignments for today and tomorrow, I want to thank everyone for making this unexpected trip back to the wonders of Yellowstone." He scanned the crowded room and smiled. "It feels good to be wrapping this chapter up . . . and it feels especially good since all of the fugitives were brought in alive *and* they were brought in by one of our own." He nodded toward Win. "Win Tyler did an outstanding job of handling a very dicey situation that could have turned deadly. I want everyone in the office to know his work is an example of how we want things done in the Denver office."

Wes went on with the attaboys for the Denver folks who were still working False Prophet and for the agents who'd been dragged in from Bozeman to help. The good guys had scored a big win, the ASAC told them. There would be time to celebrate soon, but now there was work to do. He gave everyone a brief overview of where things stood, then turned it over to Jim, who began handing out assignments.

There were interviews to hold, papers to file, calls to answer—all before the formal arraignments on Monday afternoon. The Evidence Response Teams were working up on the ridge and at Win's house. Things were hopping, but at least the mood was upbeat. The meeting broke up and everyone began to scatter. Win was moving for the door to head to his interviews when Wes motioned him over.

The ASAC took a few steps away from the others lingering in the room . . . he looked Win in the eyes. "Good job. Really good job. Are you okay?"

Finally someone is asking that question. Win nodded. "Thank you, sir. Yes sir, I'm fine."

Givens kept the eye contact. "Your shooting inquiries came in this morning. The Shooting Incident Review Group voted that all of your shots were justified. You're cleared for full duty."

Win nodded again and took that in. *Sure feels like I've never been off full duty.* Wes glanced out the tall window toward the clinic; he seemed to be processing something. Wes Givens was nearly as tall as Win, but with a slender build—probably did rowing or one of those other Ivy League sports, Win figured.

Wes lowered his voice and met Win's eyes again. "Brent Sutton tells me it's going down tomorrow. Some folks have arrived in Gardiner."

"Not our guys, not HRT?" Win wanted to hear about the CIA from his boss, not just rely on Sutton.

Wes shook his head just slightly. "No, not our folks. We're not happy about it." He blew out a breath that sounded almost like a sigh. "We don't know how many the other team is playing with, what their capabilities are . . . in my opinion, we don't know nearly enough." He stared out the window again. "Sutton tells me you're going to be setting it up."

"Yes, sir. As soon as the man tells me where to meet late tomorrow afternoon—I'm guessing it will be down in the park, away from everything, but I don't know. . . . The guy is sharp."

"He's sharp *and* he's dangerous. Sutton says they've got some folks covering you. Are you good with that?"

Win shrugged. "I'm sure they know what they're doing." *Sure as hell hope so.*

"Win, this should be easier for us—this is our home turf—but the remoteness of this place, the lack of communications capability, of infrastructure . . . it levels the playing field." The ASAC patted Win on the shoulder as he turned away. "You can handle this, Win. Just stay on your toes and don't get caught in the middle."

*   *   *

As soon as Win finished the lengthy interviews, he walked down the hall to the little office that Gloria Gorski and Paige were using as their base. The two women were supposed to be his main contacts on the counterintelligence case, but he'd heard next to nothing from them since they'd set up shop in Mammoth. He certainly didn't count Paige's dance through the office with Johnson this morning as helpful.

He knocked on the door, entered, and got a tepid greeting from Ms. Gorski. The small, windowless room was claustrophobic; two metal desks had been pushed together near the middle of the room and four chairs lined the walls. He was guessing this had been spare storage space before the counterintelligence folks hit town.

"You've been distracted by the fugitive hunt apparently." She was looking down her long nose at him; even sitting back in the chair, with him towering above her, she was managing quite well to be condescending. Her red hair was tied up tight on her head again; he guessed she must always wear it that way. She didn't ask him to sit, didn't offer any pleasantries. Her dark eyes darted back and forth between her computer screen, her phone, and his eyes with unnerving frequency.

She looked at the watch on her wrist. "It's nearly 5:30."

"Yes, ma'am, I've been a little busy with the fugitive incident since early this morning. Then I met with Sokolov at 2:30 this afternoon. You've seen my preliminary report, my email, on that meeting?"

"Yes, I saw your email. Not much of substance there. Did you get a sense that Sokolov's demeanor had changed? Any sign that he might know we're moving on him?"

"No. No indication that he was anxious. None," Win replied.

"You know you'll need to be available for your contact with Sokolov by late afternoon tomorrow." She frowned up at him. "Do you think you can be free of these other distractions, be on task, by then?"

"Yes, ma'am." His voice had an edge. *I know my job. I know how to focus.* He was being a little chippy . . . not his usual manner. He forced himself to take a few shallow breaths.

"The Russian will be in touch with you tomorrow. We're certain of that based on his last few contacts. He's trying to establish a level of trust with you—it's how they operate when they really want something." She glanced at her computer screen again before she looked back up. "But he certainly can't safely make contact while you sit in this building, surrounded by a dozen agents."

"I've finished my 302s on the incidents that happened this morning. I'm heading out. Do we have any idea where Sokolov might call the next meeting?"

She looked back at her phone for a moment, then raised her eyes again. "We're getting something on and off on satellite phones; it's in code. Could be the Russians or could just be kids fooling around—this place is nearly impossible to work. Seems as if every other hiker and camper has some form of satellite device. The chatter we're focused on is coming from an area about twelve miles southwest of here." She pointed to a Yellowstone map that was spread out on her cluttered desk. "Sheepeater Cliff . . . Indian Creek Campground. Do you know that area?"

"No, ma'am, I've passed those points on the highway; both are on the road toward the Norris Geyser Basin. But any campground would be crawling with tourists. I told him to pick a place with no tourists."

"Well, what you requested and what he'll do are likely to be two completely different things. Just keep working on those missing persons cases tomorrow . . . I'm sure he'll have someone watching you. You've got to show him you're toeing his line."

"Yes, ma'am." Win turned toward the door.

"Oh, and Agent Tyler, he is a Russian; he will have thought things out several moves ahead. If you value your life, you'd better do the same."

Win left the room, closed the metal door behind him, and leaned back against it. He took a deep breath. *Gee, that was fun.* He nodded to a couple of Denver agents who passed him in the hall as he checked his phone. Sure enough, Cindy Hechtner had texted him fifteen minutes ago that Tory would be leaving the clinic soon. He drew another deep breath and headed for the stairs. His mood brightened at simply seeing Tory's name in the text. That spoke volumes.

*   *   *

They were coming out of the clinic's entrance as he came down the sidewalk. Lauren spotted him and went into a protective stance that would have made any mama grizzly bear proud. She wasn't going to let Win anywhere near Tory.

"Doctor said to get her back to the cabin and to bed for twenty-four hours." The tiny girl held Tory's arm and glared up at him.

Tory took her focus off her footing for just a moment and smiled when she saw him. "Hey, Win . . . I'm outa here."

Win looked for a way to circumvent Tory's determined bodyguard. "I can at least help you get to the car. You don't need to be hobbling on that ankle." He switched back to Lauren with narrowed eyes. "I'll help her." He scooped Tory up in one swift movement before either girl could protest. Lauren pointed to a silver Camry parked a few yards down the street. Win weaved through a group of Boy Scouts and got her into the passenger seat. He stood at the open door and looked down at her, worried that she still looked pale and weak, and now maybe a little embarrassed.

"Are you okay?" he asked.

She smiled again and worked to get the seat belt on. "Yeah, yeah. I think so . . . but whenever I fall asleep . . . I'm having nightmares." She looked up at him and tried to smile again, a hint of red touched her cheeks. "I caused a lot of people a lot of trouble because of my pride and stupidity." She saw his questioning look. "I know better than to hike alone anywhere, much less out here."

"Chris Warren is a park ranger; no way he should have let you hike out alone from that campground," Win responded. "This isn't on you."

"It isn't really Chris's fault. He is who he is. I was the one who was foolish."

Yeah, foolish to go with that scumbag, Win was thinking, but he didn't say it. "Did Warren do something to you? Something to scare you?"

"Lord no. Chris is a charmer, and I . . . ah, wasn't in the mood to be charmed. I just decided to hike back out instead of spending the night up there. That's all. Really, it is."

"It doesn't matter now." Lauren interjected. She shut her door and put the key in the ignition. "What matters is that you're safe, that you're going to be fine."

Win straightened and looked down at Tory. He still wasn't ready to let her go. He was blocking Lauren's escape by holding the car door open. "All of that high-end camping equipment will be yours if your angel doesn't claim it." He was grinning to try to lessen her unease.

"I hope he's already gotten it. Cindy told me I'd been telling everyone my rescuer was an angel." Her blush got a little deeper. Win was thinking that made her even more attractive. Then it occurred to him that he needed some facts, some actual information.

"Remember anything more about him?" Win tried to be cool, tried to make the question sound casual.

"He was big, strong, and gentle. Wild hair and beard." She drew a deep breath and Win noticed again how pale she looked, saw the bruise on her face more clearly. "He spoke with a British accent, kept calling me *lass*. It was dark most of the time, his flashlight was on very little. He wore a small gold cross around his neck. . . . He's a believer . . . I could feel it."

"I'd like to find him . . . I'd like to thank him. Anything else? Hair color?" Win asked. Lauren cleared her throat and scowled at him. He ignored her. Some impulse was pushing him on with the questions.

"It was so dark . . . but when the flashlight was on in the tent . . . ah . . . his hair wasn't light . . . maybe medium or dark brown." She stared up at Win as she thought back over it. "His eyes were intense. Green . . . his eyes were green."

Win nearly lost his grip on the car door. He knew what his instincts had been hinting at, had been telling him. He forced himself to compartmentalize that frightening bit of intel; he forced himself to refocus on Tory.

Lauren cleared her throat again. "Hummm, I'm supposed to be getting our patient back to bed soon." She gave Win a look that could kill. "How about you come visit in a day or two. I'm extending my stay in Roosevelt until she's one hundred percent. Tory can call you when she's up for visitors."

Win nodded and dropped down beside Tory. He took her hand. "Take it easy and I'll see you soon. Let me know if you need anything." He didn't want to let go of her hand, and the look in her soft-brown eyes told him she was feeling the same way. For a moment, just for a moment, Win forgot about the danger, chaos, and loss that surrounded him. For a moment he was holding something he wanted—something he needed. He squeezed her hand, nodded, and moved away. He tried to smile but wasn't sure he'd made it.

He didn't know how the relationship would develop with Tory, but one thing he now knew for sure: Tory Madison was alive because a Russian SVR officer had saved her. And he might have to kill that man sometime in the next twenty-four hours—if the Russian didn't kill him first.

* * *

"You are kidding, right?" Trey asked.

"No."

There was a long, long pause as Trey studied him. They were standing in the shade of a massive cottonwood tree near the Visitor Center, the late-afternoon sunlight highlighting every kelly green leaf. Several yearling elk sauntered across the road to the old parade ground, seemingly oblivious to the excited tourists angling for the perfect Yellowstone photo. Trey had been doing his ranger thing, pointing out two fluffy great horned owl chicks in a large nest of sticks about thirty feet up in the cottonwood. The crowd of visitors was still milling around the tree, taking pictures and pointing, when Win pulled the ranger aside and laid out his plan.

"You really think someone went into the Dragon's Mouth—and came back out again?" Trey said in disbelief after Win had shown him the photos on his phone and made his request.

"Uh-huh. Do you have the gear or not?" Win was impatient.

"Well, yeah, but it's for emergency fire rescue or recovery, hazardous chemical situations. That sort of thing."

"Well, what I'm thinkin' of doin' sure falls into the hazardous chemical category. Might fall into the recovery category."

Trey wasn't impressed with Win's logic. "It certainly falls into the stupid category. You're just trying to justify a foolhardy stunt. You're talking about something that probably has low odds of survival, even if the gear works as designed."

Win wasn't deterred. "Will it fit me?"

"Don't know. We've got six suits, probably different sizes. They're called proximity suits—proximity to fire, I suppose. Feds gave them to us as part of some block grant program three or four years ago. The packages have never been opened. I'm guessing they're military surplus." Trey still couldn't believe they were having this conversation.

"Let's go check 'em out."

Less than an hour later, Win was standing in front of a full-length mirror in the lockers at the Park Service Fire Response Building,

staring back at himself. He looked like a spaceman. He felt like a frog-
man. Trey was adjusting the air cylinder on the back harness; the gear
was heavy, hot, and cumbersome. He'd need to practice just to walk
around or bend over.

Win finally freed a hand from the long-sleeve, metallic glove, then
pulled the shiny hood off, slipped the buckles of the face mask free, and
took in a deep breath of real air. "Would it work? You've had some time
to think about it . . . would it work?" he asked Trey.

Trey moved to face Win as he set the silver hood to one side. "You
said that even the volcanologists don't go into the springs or the steam
vents—you told me they thought it was too dangerous."

"You saw the photos, the video. Someone went in there and came
back out." Win fumbled with the air canister's straps and glanced back
at Trey. "And according to the time stamp on the photos, he or she
was in there for five minutes . . . and whoever it was left something in
there."

Trey shook his head. "No point in me looking for a permit—no way
anyone gets a permit to do that sort of thing. Not even a legit research
team. Whoever it was, it's a rogue deal." He helped Win remove the air
tank and the breathing apparatus. Trey was still pensive.

"I can see it in your eyes. You're gonna try it," Trey said.

"It worked for someone last night. We can make it work. But I can't
do it alone. Gotta have someone hold a safety line. Gotta have someone help me gear up." Win tried to sound confident. He glanced at the
ranger; he was hoping Trey would come around.

"Safety line may not work in that heat, in that acid. Win . . . I don't
know."

Win began removing the rest of the sixty-pound fire suit. He was
afraid Trey would talk him out of the risky excursion.

"Let's sleep on it!" he called as he loaded the fire suit into the Bureau
SUV. He pulled away before Trey could say *no*.

*   *   *

He went back to the office for a couple more hours, then headed to his house, dreading the chore that awaited him: wading through the aftermath of the fugitives' and the ERT's visits. He paused on the steps outside his back door, held up his phone light, and read the note that was attached to the screen.

> Win. Everything is clean, finished at 6, but I will need to work some more to get all the blood stains out of the hall rug. Will get a different cleaner and try tomorrow. Groceries in the fridge and dry cleaning in your closet. Tia

Thank you, Lord, for small favors!
He struggled to get the back door open with the bulky fire suit in his arms. He finally managed to get the key in, open the screen and wooden doors, and push his way into the mudroom. He piled the suit on the washer, sat down on the bench, and pulled his boots off. The house smelled of pine-oil soap; the kind Tia favored always reminded him of his grandmother's house. One glance into the dining room told him all was in order. The awful smells, the stack of guns, the dirty blankets on the floor, even the crime-scene tape had been removed. But while the physical evidence of Eriksson's ambush was gone, all he had to do was close his eyes and he could see it again, smell it again, feel it again. He drew a breath, hit the lights, and walked into the dining room. *Wonder where Gruff is?*

That question got answered as he walked into his dark den to turn on the TV. His cat was sitting on the couch, getting his head scratched by one of the men Win had met at the Bozeman Holiday Inn. Win stopped just inside the French doors and stared at the guy. He felt another presence behind him and cursed himself for walking into yet another ambush. *Hope they know the house is bugged.*

The Agency man, Ramon Santiago, held up a small electronic device in his free hand. "In layman's terms it's an audio countermeasure—a jammer," he said. "The Russians won't be able to hear a thing while this is on . . . they'll just figure their equipment has a glitch. And for some reason, the watchers who've been tailing you for days disappeared this afternoon. No one has seen us come or go. We're clean."

Win just stood there. He didn't say a thing.

"Cat got your tongue?" Santiago chuckled and scooted Gruff off the couch. "What are you thinking, Tyler?"

"That I need to change the locks on the doors," Win replied. The second man stepped around and planted himself at Win's side, hands clasped in front of him. He was burley and stout. Even in hiking clothes, he looked like someone to avoid. "Mind if I turn on some lights? Or do you people only work in the dark?"

Santiago reached over and turned on the lamp on the side table. "You've got a bit of an attitude. We're on the same side here."

"I guess I'm just getting tired of being the bait and not getting the full story of what's going on. I feel like I'm swinging in the wind here, Santiago."

The guy shrugged. "Goes with the territory sometimes. In this case it can't be helped. Based on the pattern Sokolov has set up with you, I take it you're expecting a text from him late tomorrow afternoon—on your personal phone?"

"That's what he'd done before, but . . . if I was him, I'd go off pattern. Make the contact in a different way, not be predicable."

Santiago nodded. "Yeah, be ready for anything. You'll need to take those remains to your rendezvous with him—just the bones, not the ring. We don't want to give him everything he's after in case we have to abort the takedown tomorrow and set up something later. We need to still be holding a few cards."

"Okay. Who's in place?" Win asked.

Given the terrain they had to cover, it wasn't much. The CIA had a team of twelve working loosely out of Gardiner, as well as two fast-response helicopters and their crews. The helicopters were at the small Gardiner airport—a modest asphalt strip with a few older hangars, on the northwest side of town. The team had come in at night and concealed the choppers in a rusty hangar; the arrest team and the air crews were all bunking there. Not the best of accommodations, Win thought, but in the shadowy world these guys operated in, he figured they'd seen much worse.

"Our advance folks rented the hangar under the guise of needing a temporary home for a couple of choppers doing aerial electrical-grid inspections," Santiago said. "We're laying low, trying not to attract any attention from the locals."

Good luck with that. As a small-town boy, Win knew keeping secrets from the locals in a rural community was next to impossible.

Santiago told Win his guys would come in hot when the trap was set on the Russians. "Keep your head down," he said, "nothing to worry about."

Their sensors had been picking up chatter on sat phones from an area southwest of Mammoth for two days; that confirmed what Ms. Gorski had said earlier that afternoon. Win's job was to notify his FBI contacts—that would be Paige, Humphrey, or Ms. Gorski—of the location of the meeting with Sokolov and then get out of the way when the raid went down. Santiago told Win that if he felt contacting the FBI folks was too risky, he should just go to the meeting with Sokolov.

"Not to worry," Santiago said, "we'll be tracking you all the way." They affixed a tiny metal dot to the back of his watch, and another to the back of his ear. "We use an advanced form of GNSS, uh, the global navigation satellite system, to track you; it's classified above your level. Nearly foolproof . . . nothing to worry about."

After the third assurance of "not to worry," Win was really beginning to question this plan, or lack of one. He was worried.

Santiago wrapped it up by telling Win they'd decided against having him swallow a transponder—that was apparently one of their preferred methods of surveillance. Win hoped he'd kept a straight face while Santiago discussed the disadvantages of that method.

"The Russians have really good countermeasures, Win. We'd normally go with having you carry around a twenty-four-hour tracker in your gut—they're no bigger than a vitamin pill. But there are GPS scanners out there that can pick up the signals off those internal devices just as easily as if you were carrying it around in your shirt pocket. And there's a big downside. The Russkies would have to kill you to silence the tracker. So not a great option."

No kidding, Win was thinking. It wasn't gonna be a restful night.

CHAPTER THIRTY

Win made the forty-three-mile drive from Mammoth to the Mud Volcano parking lot in the dark. It was slow going even before five in the morning. There were the early risers who were out waiting for the 5:35 a.m. dawn, with its prime wildlife watching, and the animals themselves, which seemed to be everywhere as the new day arrived. He drank strong coffee, watched the road, and replayed Natasha Yahontova's handwritten instructions on entering the steam vent over and over in his head. *Directions to the entrance to Hell.*

Hechtner was leaning against his big white-and-green SUV in the parking lot, sipping coffee from a thermos, when Win pulled up. "You're set on doing this?" Trey asked.

"Yeah. What do you think?"

"That you're crazy. But you're also bullheaded, so let's get to it before we attract a crowd."

It didn't take Win long to suit up; he'd practiced at home for over an hour last night after his unexpected guests had departed. Walking around in the metallic suit, he'd probably scared Gruff half to death. Now he and Trey stood below the boardwalk's viewing platform next to the Dragon's Mouth Spring, laying out the rest of their gear around a camp lantern. Trey had blocked the raised boardwalk with a *Trail Closed* sign well before dawn, but there were already half a dozen folks watching them from the parking lot.

Trey checked the water's temperature and finished tying the safety rope around Win's waist. Trey was wearing a proximity suit identical to Win's; he was struggling to get the high fireman's boots pulled on as Win reached for his gloves. Win was surprised. "Why are you suiting up? I'm the fool goin' in there."

Trey managed to get the second boot on. "Well, I'm the fool who's holding your safety line, and if anything goes wrong in there—and what could go wrong—I'll be able to help. Yeah, what *could* go wrong? Water's at 180 degrees, not much shy of boiling, steam is nearly that hot, we have no idea how deep the standing water is in there . . . no idea how toxic the vapor is within the cavern . . . if there even is a cavern . . . we have no way to communicate. . . . Want me to go on?"

Win held up a gloved hand. "I get it. I know. But you saw the photos . . . someone else did this—*yesterday.*"

The ranger glared back at him in the dim predawn light. He wasn't finished. "Yeah, maybe someone who knew what they were doing." He shook his head and held out his hand for Win's phone. "I'll only use one glove . . . I'll be filming this on your phone—great for evidence if you live long enough to get prosecuted for trespassing on a national park thermal feature." Now Trey was scowling.

Win knew he needed to get going before the ranger talked him out of it. He sucked in a deep breath of real air before he pulled on the full-face scuba mask over his Nomex hood, pulled down the silver fire helmet, and squinted to see through the face shield. Trey checked the air valve for a final time—it registered twenty-six minutes of air—and covered the tank with fire-resistant material. He handed Win the fire-man's flashlight and a hiking pole and attached their straps to Win's gloved wrists. Trey stepped back just a bit and gave Win a thumbs-up. Win nodded and returned the signal.

"You don't have to go through with this." Win saw the ranger mouth the words, but he heard nothing except the soft hissing of the air flow. It reminded him of a snake. He closed his eyes tight for a moment and whispered a prayer for protection. *Let's do this!*

Signaling for Trey to begin the video, Win grabbed the bottom of the platform above his head and stepped off into the tidal pool that lay in front of the ridge's gaping hole. He expected his boots to sink into the goo, but he was standing on solid rock. He used the hiking pole to probe the area in front of him; it was firm. He inched forward toward the opening. A cloud of steam and a deep roar met him, and the wash from the push of steam sent the chocolate-colored water higher on his boots. A glance down told him it was about mid-calf. Even through the protective boots, he could feel the heat. *Here we go,* he thought to himself, *walking into the entrance to Hell.*

The opening in the rock was about six feet tall; Win had to stoop to enter. He waited for the dense steam cloud to dissipate, then ducked his head and moved inside the opening. Everything went completely dark. The beam from the light in his hand didn't carry more than a foot, and as he shuffled forward another few inches, it didn't carry that far.

He tapped at the tunnel ceiling and found it to be the same height as the entrance. He probed the floor and realized it was a gentle downward slope. The sloping floor allowed him to stand upright, and he began probing the area with the pole. The near-boiling water was deeper here, maybe thirteen inches, not far below the top of his boots. He'd gone maybe six feet from the entrance when he realized that the light's beam was carrying further, that he wasn't touching the walls when he extended the hiking pole to each side. He was within a cavern—a room of sorts.

He moved to the right side and gingerly ran his gloved hand over the rough surface of the wall . . . there were shallow ledges and crevices in the rock. He was so engrossed in exploring the wall that the sudden blast of steam caught him off guard. He'd forgotten to count down the seconds before the next steam burst—the first thing Natasha had written in her notes—so he was completely unprepared for the violent rush of superheated air.

It was a good thing they'd attached the hiking pole and flashlight to his suit with straps, because he dropped them both as his gloved hands grasped at the shallow stone ledges, as he fought to stay upright. He tried to find a handhold within the crevices, tried to hug the rock wall. He could hear the roaring from the throat of the cavern, could see nothing but blackness, feel nothing but the deadly steam lashing his suit; heat was rising on his boots as the toxic water rose. Had he closed his eyes? He wasn't sure. His left hand found a deeper hole in the wall. He thrust his hand inside and was shocked to feel it touch something soft.

He knew the gush of steam and water from the vent would last less than a minute. He and Trey had stood outside and counted it—the cycle was consistent at forty to fifty seconds. But in his panic it seemed like an eternity. Then as suddenly as it began, it ended. Except for the hissing of the tank's air flow, everything went quiet.

Win groped for the dangling flashlight, but he kept his left hand in the crevice, gripping something that he instinctively knew shouldn't be there. It was lodged deep in the rock wall; he had to yank it free. He stuffed the bundle into the pouch at his waist and realized that he had no idea which way to turn to exit the vent. He fought down a moment of terror as he fumbled for the safety rope. He yanked it twice. The rope pulled tight—Trey was leading him out. *Thank you, God!*

Win staggered out of the opening and pitched the hiking pole and flashlight onto the bank of the tidal pool. He glimpsed Trey's worried face staring at him, holding the safety rope in a death grip. As he stumbled toward the bank, another wave swept into the pool, nearly causing him to fall. The ranger grabbed his arm and pulled him out of the scalding water, and he collapsed on the bank. For a long minute, Win just lay there on the ground, facedown in the fire suit, listening to the snake sound of the compressed air and praying his thanks to God. He drew a final breath from the sweat-soaked mask as Trey worked to remove his helmet and gloves.

Win was glad the raised viewing platform and boardwalk blocked the tourists in the parking lot from seeing what was going on. He figured he was probably trembling, but he was too drained to know. He scooted farther away from the swirl of steam and foul-smelling vapor and coughed to clear his throat. Then he opened the pouch at his side as Trey disconnected the air canister. The ranger paused above him. "What is it?"

"It was on a ledge, sorta wedged in . . . I nearly fell trying to get it loose. It's wrapped in this same fire-resistant stuff . . . it's metal . . . a box?" Win touched it with his fingers and immediately jerked them back. "Geez, it's hot!"

Trey was holding the air tank and breathing apparatus, staring down at Win's find. "Let's get out of these suits before we roast. More importantly, let's get out of here before we get caught trespassing on a thermal feature."

"Ease up a little, we're here on an official investigation. That will fly."

Trey's eyes looked doubtful and Win had to concede the guy had a point. They both scrambled to get out of the aluminized suits and heavy boots. By the time they'd shed the cumbersome equipment and had finished lacing up their hiking boots, the metal container was cool enough to touch. Win realized at the last minute that he needed evidence gloves. He fumbled with his cargo pants pocket and produced a pair. He repositioned the camp lantern and handed Trey his Bureau phone. "Okay, I'm gonna open it. Film this."

The box looked to be about a foot long and eight inches wide, maybe six inches deep. It was a dull gray color with a sliding latch. Trey knelt beside Win with the flashlight and the phone as he slid the latch back and opened the sealed lid. The interior was padded with a material that had to be heat resistant, because the soft fabric pouches inside were cool to the touch.

There were several gray pouches in the box, none of them large. Win chose the one that looked the heaviest. It fell open when he picked it up. The same ornate necklace that he had seen in the Russian's surveillance photograph dropped into his hand, its blood-red ruby and green garnets appeared dull in the faint light.

"Oh, man," Trey whispered.

Win dug in the pouch with his thumb, and an international driver's license and a thick lock of brown hair appeared. The face on the photo was a much better likeness than her passport shot. Natasha P. Yahontova stared up at him. *Lordy.* He swallowed hard and laid the items down on a clean towel. The steam from the Dragon's Mouth washed over them again, emitting a low roar.

The second pouch he chose was lighter. A lock of blond hair, a driver's license, and a small gold cross was deposited on the towel. He knew without even looking at the license—Missy Sims had been found.

"How many more?" Trey asked. Win glanced up at the ranger and saw how pale he'd become. He figured he must look the same way.

"Several," Win answered.

"Proof of life," he'd heard this called on kidnapping cases he'd studied at the Academy. In this situation, the items appeared to be proof of death. Trophies kept by a serial killer. He remembered that course of study at the Academy—it had caused him nightmares. He'd been taught that no one truly understands the psyche of a monster who methodically preys on other humans. Or why over ninety percent of serial killers keep some token from their victims. He knew that some mass murderers even collected such trophies as they stalked their victims, well before the kill. He was grateful that he didn't understand the heart and mind of such evil. His gloved fingers lifted another gray pouch from the box.

The third pouch was no surprise to him: Janet Goff's license, hair lock, and wristwatch. The fourth was not as expected. The trophy item for Conner Chen was a small silver multitool with *Yellowstone Adventure Tours* stamped on it—a merchandizing trinket from one of the park's concessioners. *Why Conner?* he wondered as he laid the little tool down beside Conner's license and hair lock. There were two other pouches on the bottom. Both held hair locks and personal items; one contained the University of Arizona ID of a middle-aged man from the school's geology department, and the other contained a young woman's California driver's license. Win did the math in his head; the killing spree had been going on for at least eight years.

The last of the lot was the lightest. He wasn't even sure anything was inside when he picked up the pouch. It seemed to contain only a card or ID that had stuck to the cloth on the inside. He shook the pouch twice and a driver's license fell onto the towel. He drew a sharp breath when he saw it—Paige Lange's face staring back at him, a sultry smile on her lips. Nothing else was in the pouch.

Trey was still looking over Win's shoulder. They both flinched when the steam vent let loose with another roar and belch of vapor. They waited until the steam cleared to talk. Win was already placing the items back in their pouches. Win was in a hurry now.

Trey recited the required evidentiary information and turned off the cell phone recording. Then he moved away and climbed onto the boardwalk. Win could tell he'd had enough. The ranger was standing on the boardwalk's platform, silhouetted against a spectacular orange-red sunrise. *Storms comin'. That's a bad sign,* Win thought as he climbed the railing to the platform.

Some guy yelled at them to ask when they'd open the trail. Trey ignored the tourist and turned to Win. "What does it mean?" he asked, and then answered his own question. "I'm thinking it means your friend Paige is in real danger. I'm thinking that's what it means."

Win was thinking exactly the same thing.

*   *   *

The sun was nosing over the mountains far to the east, and the few high clouds that draped the sky had turned a vibrant orange. The cold night had retreated, and he could now see the brush-covered landscape in front of him clearly. He took a sip of tea from his thermos and wished it were hot. The hood of the rented SUV was sparkling with frost, but the heavy parka he'd pulled over him had kept him warm in the night. They'd slept in the vehicle in a small parking lot only a few miles south of Mammoth. Too many federal agents wandering around Mammoth; too great a possibility their satellite transmissions could be intercepted. Better to sleep leaning back in the vehicle than risk exposure. The man sleeping in the back seat made a snoring sound and shifted. His mate in the passenger seat still had his eyes closed, head leaning against the window. Soldiers—like him, they'd been soldiers. They could grab sleep in any position whenever the opportunity came. On these types of missions, it never came often enough. He glanced at his watch. It read 5:38. He'd wake them in a few minutes.

Two huge bison bulls plodded up the grassy slope to the near-empty parking lot, slowly moving away from the winding highway, which was surprisingly busy with traffic. The bulls stopped in front of the vehicle. They were nearly as tall as the car—two meters at the shoulder, he was guessing. They must have weighed over a ton each—all muscle, vigor, and strength. They lifted their huge black heads, their ebony horns glistened, and the whites of their eyes shone bright for just a moment. Sergei surmised that was a bison's expression when startled or perhaps just plain annoyed. The bulls were probably wondering what a car was doing here, blocking the easiest path to the turquoise lake that lay on the other side of the hill. The larger bull shook its head once and snorted, condensation rising from its nostrils. The frost had settled on their broad backs, and every hair shimmered as the first rays of sunshine found them. Then the bulls seemed to conclude that the car was no danger, and they slowly walked past the vehicle. If he'd had the window down, he could have reached out and touched them. *Amazing.*

He took another sip of tea. The word from the Office last night had been unsettling. He'd known at noon yesterday that a team from the CIA was likely en route to Yellowstone. He'd known that the Americans were fighting an internal turf war over who would do what and when. Sadly, that wasn't uncommon among his comrades either. There was constant infighting between the GRU, the military intelligence service; the FSB, the internal investigative branch; and his agency, the SVR. All three agencies were formed after the KGB was dismantled following the fall of the Soviet Union in 1991, and all three agencies had some claim on intelligence gathering and protecting the Motherland from external threats. He supposed it was no different in America—agency budgets and prestige depended on results.

Originally he'd understood that the FBI planned to send in an arrest team; now the hazards seemed to be ratcheting up. He'd been told that the CIA operators cared little about actual arrests. He had a team to protect, and more importantly, he had a mission to accomplish. It looked as if the timetable on that mission had shifted, but at least he now knew the identity of their people on the inside. The Office had finally concluded it was just too risky for their spies to remain unknown to the team on the ground. He'd run enough of these missions to know that wasn't a particularly good sign. Moscow was risking internal assets, spies who'd been in place and moles who'd been cultivated for years. Moscow was thinking the same thing Sergei was thinking: the opposition was closing in, they had to move quickly if the mission was to be accomplished. With the CIA paramilitary team's arrival, the stakes had gotten considerably higher.

He'd already moved his extraction options out of Canada. He had one jet helicopter sitting on an airstrip outside of West Yellowstone under the pretext of filming aerial scenes for a Hollywood western and a second bird on standby at an even more remote landing strip just east of Cooke City. He had options on opposite sides of the big park. The Cooke City bird was closest to their current location; he'd probably call for it to go on red status this morning. He knew the aircrew would be thrilled with that development; they'd sat for days in the absolute middle of nowhere waiting for something to happen.

He watched a small car enter the lot—its lights were still on. It pulled into a parking space several yards away. The interior light in the car went on for a second, then off, then on again, then off. Their contact was here. They'd all sit tight for two minutes, then make the exchange. The tradecraft of spies didn't really seem necessary in this deserted wild spot, but protocols had to be followed. He spoke softly to wake up his mates.

The dawn had transitioned to a brilliant crimson hue. It was beautiful, inspiring, yet he knew what it heralded: storms approaching. *Red sky in morning, shepherds' warning . . .* He subconsciously touched the gun he wore under his jacket. *Bring it on.*

CHAPTER THIRTY-ONE

Trey had walked over to visit with a Park Service crew who'd pulled in to clean up the restrooms. It was looking as if they'd lucked out and their excursion into the steam vent hadn't been spotted by anyone official. Win sat in the Expedition and tried to get in touch with someone—anyone—who could give him Paige's whereabouts. She hadn't answered her cell phone and neither had Ms. Gorski. And that was odd. FBI agents always answered their phones. *Well, not always.* He glanced at his watch—only 6:25. *Calm down,* he told himself, *it's early, maybe they're both in the shower.* He hated to do it, but he finally called Johnson on the sat phone. He obviously woke the guy up.

"Whata ya want?" Johnson growled.

Win had to bite his lip to make a civil response. "I need to know if you saw Paige after she left the office yesterday. It's important."

The guy cleared his throat. Sounded like he was yawning. "You trying to move back in on her? I don't think she's interested."

Win was growing impatient. "This has nothing to do with that—nothing. It's case related. Did you see her or not?" Win could tell Johnson was weighing it.

"Saw her having lunch in the Terrace Grill . . . not long after she left the office. She was with one of those geyser guys who gives talks here once in a while."

"Which one?"

"How should I know? I'm not into that stuff. Maybe middle-aged ... brown hair ... coulda been grayish hair ... not sure."

"Come on, Johnson! Give me more than that on the man." *Geez, this guy is an FBI agent, and he can't even give me a suspect description!*

"For your damn information, I was lookin' more at her than I was lookin' at him. And I didn't want her to think I was following her around. Wasn't even in there half a minute, didn't even order . . . I turned around and left."

"You didn't see her or hear from her again yesterday or last night?"

Now Johnson was getting a little hot. "No. Where are you and what's this about?"

"I'm down in the park. Mud Volcano area. I'm working on the missing persons . . . I think Paige could be in danger. If I can't locate her in the next hour or so, can you check and see if the restaurant has surveillance cameras? I may need a better description of the guy she was with."

Johnson was thinking about it. "Yeah. They have cameras . . . I've had to use them before. Have you checked the Justice Center? Paige told me she was working with some lady supervisor over there. Oh, by the way, the place is crawling with the press. Jim told me before I left last night that they were setting up a press conference for the ASAC at noon today. You better get your butt up here before that kicks off."

"We'll see. The missing persons files are turning into way more than just that. I'll fill you in on this later. If anyone needs me have them call the sat phone."

"Yeah, right."

* * *

He tried calling Paige and Humphrey again and got nowhere. His Bureau phone buzzed just as he was getting ready to call Ms. Gorski. It was the guy from the helicopter rental service in West Yellowstone. "Found the records from the date you gave me five years ago," he immediately said. "We chartered for Yellowstone Geothermal Expedition from a makeshift chopper pad we use just south of Mud Volcano—the flight was to Maxwell Springs. The ledger says it was at six in the morning, two passengers, a man and a woman. No cargo. One-way trip."

"Nothing on the passengers? No names? Descriptions?"

"Nope." The guy sounded like he was in a hurry.

"Can I talk to the pilot, maybe he would remember—"

The guy cut him off. "Well, wish you could, but that would be Bill Dunklin and he died of cancer two years ago. Best pilot I ever had. Good man."

Win needed to keep the guy talking while he thought through the new intel. "Do you fly into Maxwell Springs often?"

"No, but we did fly this same group in last Sunday afternoon, June 15th . . . three trips of gear, lumber, two passengers—both men, Dr. Ratliff and his assistant, Simon. I flew one of the runs and it was a windy, bumpy ride. The man who booked the trips, uh . . . that would be Simon, told me they were setting up a base camp for their research. We're loosely scheduled to fly everything back out in another couple of weeks when they finish up."

Win started to ask him about a helicopter rental for that day, but the guy answered Win's question before he even asked. "I gotta go. I've got two ships and they're both down today. Choppers are a pain to keep in the air."

When the call ended, Win stepped out of the Expedition and called Trey over; he told the ranger he needed to get to Maxwell Springs pronto and then get back to Mammoth by late afternoon. Trey didn't see the urgency, but Trey didn't know about the Russians. They stood beside Win's SUV and talked about it.

"Our chopper is in Livingston for its two-day quarterly mainte-nance," Trey said. "We won't have it back until late tomorrow after-noon. We can get an emergency ship up here from Grand Teton if they aren't using theirs. Takes them at least two, three hours for everyone to get organized and then fly up here from Jackson. It would have to be an emergency . . . have to be approved way up the ladder."

"Seriously? You don't have a helicopter available all the time?"

"You know as well as I do how short we are on funds. The Park Service isn't the FBI, Win. We're not rolling in cash and resources."

Win shrugged to concede Trey's point, but he knew that the Bureau's vast resources weren't available at the drop of a hat either. "Warren and Ratliff are probably both at Maxwell Springs. You told me they'd been permitted to camp there for two more weeks. How can I get to Maxwell Springs this morning? It's off the beaten path."

"That's an understatement," Trey said. "I've never even hiked all the way in. There's a primitive campground about four miles in—that's as far as I've gone. I don't think the trail is well maintained after that point. You'd need someone who's familiar with it." He thought for a few seconds. "What about Luke?"

"What about Luke?" Win asked.

"Luke and Ellie had dinner with us last night. Luke said he was meeting a carload of folks from, ah, Maryland or somewhere back East for a crack-of-dawn wildlife safari in the Lamar Valley. They should be wrapping it up well before midmorning. Luke could get you to Maxwell Springs on foot. I'll see if I can get ahold of him. He could meet you, maybe save you some time."

Win nodded. "Can you get the evidence back to Mammoth if I go with Luke?"

"Yup. Want me to take it to Johnson?"

Win opened the SUV's door and picked up the metal box from the front seat. "Yeah, sure. I'll call my supervisor and Johnson and tell them to be expecting it." He looked down at the metal box again, wrapped it back in the fireproof pouch, and drew a deep breath. "It's . . . uh . . ." The emotions hit him as he handed the parcel to Trey. He tried again. "It's—"

"I know," Trey replied softly. "It may be all that the families will ever have of these folks. . . . It could provide some closure." Trey placed the box in his Tahoe, made the call to Bordeaux from the Tahoe's sat phone, and gave Win a thumbs-up.

"I'll wait for Luke at the Roosevelt junction," Win said. "I'll call you when I get back." He hesitated before getting into his truck. "Thanks, Trey. Thanks for helping with this."

"Helping people is what I do, partner."

*　*　*

He listened to the radio chatter as he drove. It was nearly eight now, and traffic was crawling along on the north side of Dunraven Pass. He'd already flipped on his blue lights twice to move creeping vehicles out of the way. The pace was slow, but he never tired of watching the wildlife, or watching the visitors delight in the wildlife. It was one of the favorite parts of his job. The hours were long, the housing wasn't great, and the lack of manpower and resources was frustrating, but still, it was the best damn job in the world.

He glanced at the precious cargo he was carrying on the passenger-side floorboard. He'd tried to keep his mind off the sad fact that the small box likely contained all that was left on this earth of several lives. Win Tyler's hunch had been right: they had a serial killer in the park, and if they didn't act fast, he could kill again. It had to be one of the geologists—no one else would dare enter that hellhole.

Except Win Tyler . . . and he wondered about that. Trey knew this morning's high-risk exploit wasn't about proving his bravery; after the events of the last month, no one would question Win's bravery. But he wasn't sure it was really about pursuing justice either. They had evidence someone had entered the Dragon's Mouth . . . they could have waited. Win didn't have to be the one to go in the spring; they could have called in national experts, let more experienced hands solve the mystery. It was almost as if Win had a death wish, a recklessness he'd never seen before. It wasn't like he'd known the guy for that long, but Win's obsession with going into that spring was unnerving. *A death wish.* That thought crossed his mind again. Win hadn't seemed the same since he'd come back from Russia. And maybe it went deeper than that. Trey knew the guy was dealing with some weighty stuff: he hadn't just survived the firefight last month; Win Tyler had killed.

But there was another side to consider. If they'd gone the prudent, reasonable route, the trophy box might not have been found and they wouldn't have known Paige was in danger. *All true.* Trey drew a deep breath and tapped his finger on the steering wheel as he waited for the two cars in front of him to turn off at the Roosevelt junction. Still, he needed to call Win in a day or so and ask him to go grab a beer—see if he needed to talk things out, see if that would help.

Trey powered down his window, and as he drove on toward Mammoth, he waved back to Win, whose big gray SUV was pulling off at the Roosevelt gas station. He knew Luke would be meeting Win there in the next few minutes. If anyone could get Win through the wilds of the northeast part of the park in record time, it would be Luke.

Trey was making better time now. The wildlife watching was a bit less frenzied as he left the steeper, wooded mountains and fertile valleys behind and drove toward the more barren ridges and plateaus surrounding Mammoth.

He'd just passed Blacktail Deer Creek when a white Toyota suddenly stopped right in front of him. He slammed on the breaks to avoid hitting it. He didn't succeed. He felt a hard thump as the big Tahoe hit the smaller car's bumper. He said a swear word that he never used, flipped on the blue lights, and keyed in his radio. A short woman in shorts and a T-shirt jumped out of the driver's door and walked back to check out the damage. *She's not hurt, thank goodness!* The woman tossed her long red hair and glared at him. She was livid.

He held up a finger to let her know he was aware of her outrage. "NPY5 to base, copy . . ." He got that much out before she whirled toward him and appeared at his open window. Other cars were slowly passing to the side; someone honked. He glanced in his rearview mirror and saw a ranger exiting the passenger side of a car that had stopped directly behind the Tahoe; he was pulling on his flat hat and motioning to the traffic. *Thank goodness, one of the interpretative guys can help me keep the road open.*

"Ma'am . . . ma'am, can you move out of the road?" Trey asked.

The ranger behind him was waving a huge RV around the fender bender. The noise from the big diesel engine drowned out everything. Instead of returning to her car, the woman jumped on the Tahoe's running board, yelling something at Trey that he couldn't understand. Trey tried to turn his attention back to his radio, but somehow the woman managed to open his door. He dropped the radio's mic and grabbed for the door handle just as his passenger door opened and a big man smoothly slid inside.

Time seemed to freeze. As Trey jerked away from the woman to face the intruder, he glimpsed the ranger calmly directing traffic outside the vehicle, he saw a dark thunderhead building on the blue horizon, he heard the voice on his radio—"Base to NPY5 . . . do you copy?"— but most clearly, he saw the black muzzle of a semiautomatic handgun pointed right at him. He heard the man say, "Do it," just before he felt a sharp stab in his neck. His mind flashed to Cindy, to McKenna, then before he could speak, everything went completely black.

* * *

Win finished gassing up the truck, got a coke and a prepackaged turkey sandwich from the filling station, and sat down at a picnic table to eat his breakfast and wait for Bordeaux. It was windy and he could tell clouds were building in the north. He shielded the sandwich from the blowing dust with his hand, finally gave up on the picnic table location, and moved back to the truck. He hadn't even gotten settled when the satellite phone buzzed. He wasn't really expecting Johnson.

The guy was still grouchy. "I didn't wait for orders from you. I walked over to the Justice Center to see if Paige was there. That office she was working out of was shut up tighter than a drum. No one has seen her or that lady supervisor today . . . but it's still early."

"Okay . . . thanks—"

"Then I went ahead and checked the video from yesterday noon at the Terrace Grill. I'm sending you a screenshot of the guy Paige met. With any luck, you can get it on your phone as a text. May take a minute to come through . . . damn phones are slow today."

"What did you see on the video?" Win asked.

"The guy was already seated when Paige came in. They weren't strangers. She seemed *real* friendly toward him, if you know what I mean."

Win knew exactly what he meant.

Johnson kept talking. "She sat at the table and played with her phone and the guy got up and ordered for them, they both ate a sandwich and then left arm in arm at 12:41." Johnson paused. "The cameras outside the building aren't great, but we lucked out and he was parked right in front. He got into a dark-green Range Rover, but there was no view of the passenger side . . . I can't be sure if she left with him. I can text you the plates."

Win's Bureau phone dinged a message alert and he swiped it open to find a very good photo of Dr. Preston Ratliff standing in the crowded café with Paige. The man was dressed in hiking garb, no surprise there. But Paige had on cargo pants and hiking boots and she was carrying a sun hat—that was a surprise. He'd never seen her in that getup before. They looked like they were going on an excursion, and he had a sinking feeling they were going together.

"Got the photo . . . it's Dr. Preston Ratliff, the lead geyser expert around here. Yeah, text me the plates. You still haven't heard from her?"

"No. What's going on, Tyler?" Johnson was dead serious now.

Win's phone dinged with the text of Ratliff's plate numbers. Win was hesitating. Paige Lange was supposed to be his backup. And she seemed to be AWOL. *I have no backup.* That unsetting thought crossed his mind. "It's part of the missing persons files," he said. "It looks like there's a serial killer who's been operating in the park for a few years now. Trey Hechtner is on the way back to Mammoth with a trophy box that the killer had stashed in a steam vent at Mud Volcano . . . Trey should be there before nine. It would help if you could coordinate with Jim and take care of the chain of evidence on the box."

He paused, wondering how much he should tell Johnson. "Evidence is pointing to someone related to one or more of the geological research teams. . . . Part of this case is being worked out of Headquarters. I can't say much more about it. I'm sorry that I can't."

Johnson responded with silence, then three words. "Serial killer? Here?" He snorted. "Hell, if you're trying to create work for yourself, don't you think that's a bit of an overreach?"

Win bit back an angry response. *Stay on point,* he cautioned himself. "Bottom line, I think Paige may be in danger," he said. "Ratliff is supposed to be at a research camp in Maxwell Springs, and I think Dr. Chris Warren may be there too. If there's any evidence that Paige has gone to Maxwell Springs with one of those geologists, I may go over there this morning and check it out."

"Maxwell Springs?" Johnson scoffed. "You'll be one of the missing persons if you trek off by yourself up there."

"Bordeaux may guide me . . . that is, if I go. I've gotta make some calls first, gotta call Jim and give him a report, and—"

The satellite phone made a weird clicking noise and went dead. No sounds, nothing on the screen. Win sat there and stared at it. He pulled out his other phones. No service bars on either. He took a deep breath and reminded himself that he was in Yellowstone National Park—these sorts of things happened. Usually it was just a hassle, but today it could be far more than a minor inconvenience.

CHAPTER THIRTY-TWO

While Win waited on Luke to arrive, he debated whether to risk walking to Roosevelt's rustic cabins and checking on Tory. *Her cabin's right beside the lodge.* He'd left things on good terms with her yesterday. He thought back to Tory's smile when he'd touched her hand. He thought about how he'd felt—*good*—he'd felt good. Then he had a reality check. It was very possible he was under surveillance by the Russians. Ms. Gorski had warned him about it; he knew they'd followed him around in the park two days ago. No need to expose Tory to that danger, wiser to wait. Later today the CIA would get the guy—one way or another it would be over. Better to wait.

Win had already gone back inside the gas station and discovered that their telephone was out. The guy behind the counter didn't seem concerned. "Happens all the time," he'd said with a shrug. "Oh, and don't bother checking with the lodge. If mine is down, they're all down. Probably working on the line . . . it'll likely be back on later this morning."

Luke Bordeaux pulled in and stopped his pickup beside Win's SUV. He waved out the open window to some folks who were exiting their car near the front of the lodge. The family all gave Luke enthusiastic waves and shouts—apparently the early-morning wildlife safari had been a hit.

"Trey says you're needin' a guide this morning," Luke said by way of greeting. He stayed in his truck. His voice was direct and to the point.

"Maybe . . . I'm trying to find out if a woman hiked back into Maxwell Springs yesterday afternoon with one of the geyser researchers. If she did, she could be in danger."

"I don't have any other clients lined up the rest of the day. You gonna be a paying customer?"

"Yes, I can do that." Luke still wasn't being friendly and it bothered Win.

"Alright, let me make a pit stop and grab a sandwich. I need to call Ellie and let her know I'll be late. My sat phone is out."

"Their phones aren't working. . . . My satellite phone isn't working either."

Luke glanced at the billowing gray clouds far over the northern mountains. "Could be the weather comin', I suppose. Still odd that everything just went dark."

*   *   *

A few minutes later, Win was following Luke's pickup on the scenic drive on Highway 212 east from Roosevelt toward the Lamar Valley. They crossed the Yellowstone River and flowed along with tour buses, RVs, and a multitude of cars and SUVs. It seemed to Win that a good portion of the four million tourists who'd visit Yellowstone this year were driving the road in front of him. And he couldn't blame them a bit. Large herds of buffalo, as he'd grown up calling them, covered the green rolling hills. Smaller groups of pronghorn antelope ignored the traffic and lounged by the side of the road. He'd seen at least three coyotes— with this much meat on the hoof wandering around, he figured plenty of predators were lurking in the background. He breathed a deep sigh and thought about Paige. It chilled him to think that another sort of predator was also stalking its prey in this special place.

Win couldn't figure out why Paige would have gone with Ratliff. He knew she and Humphrey were rotating on and off duty as his backup on the Russia deal. From what he'd seen of her yesterday, she'd been working—if you could call her flirting with Johnson at the office "working." But Ms. Gorski likely had Paige staying closer to Win than he knew—after all, she was in the business of catching spies. Maybe she saw cozying up to Ratliff as a way to keep Win close by . . . Win had told her Ratliff was one of his suspects in the missing persons cases. They'd talked about it some while they killed time in the cabin at Mammoth the day before yesterday.

But before he found the killer's trophy box this morning, all he had was circumstantial evidence—nothing solid. And Paige didn't know about the danger. She'd seemed flippant and bored when he'd seen her at the office yesterday. Maybe she was trying to stir something up on the cases, maybe even solve the cases herself. Or maybe the charismatic geologist was just a convenient excuse for fun on her day off. After all, she was technically off duty until noon today. She wouldn't have any reason to think she was one of the killer's targets. He frowned at the road as he drove; he tried calling her number again on the sat phone. No connection. Nothing.

They left the pavement and most of the tourist traffic behind. After a winding drive down a gravel road for several miles, Luke pulled into a gravel parking lot that spelled the end of the line. Win got out of his truck and held on to his hat to keep the wind from snatching it. There were only five other vehicles in the lot. Win immediately spotted Ratliff's dark-green Range Rover and the luxury SUV that he knew Chris Warren drove. Luke stood by his truck, waiting for Win to decide what to do. Win stopped near him, wondering the same thing himself.

"There's a big grizzly bear on that far ridge; he's diggin' fer roots or ground squirrels." Luke motioned with his head toward a green expanse probably a quarter mile away. Win took off his sunglasses and squinted to see it.

Win pointed. "There?"

"Nope. That's a big glacial boulder. Glaciers dropped boulders here and there as they melted back in the last ice age thirteen thousand years ago." Win tried harder but he still wasn't sure about the bear; the hillside was dotted with large brown and black dots. "How do you tell the bears apart from the big brown rocks?" Win asked.

"The bears move. The rocks don't."

"Oh."

"Check the trail log," Luke said, motioning toward the trailhead. "I'll ask around." He walked toward a small camping area where several folks were lounging by a camp stove.

Win touched the hood on the Range Rover. Even without checking the plates, he was sure this was Ratliff's ride. The hood was cool and the numbers matched the ones Johnson had texted. One of the compact cars in the lot looked like the little silver Toyota Paige had been driving, but Win hadn't memorized her license plate—he mentally kicked himself for that oversight. A windshield sticker told him it was a rental, but likely two-thirds of the vehicles in the park were rentals.

The covered trail log stood next to the ever-present warning posters about bears. A worn wooden sign read *Slough Creek Trail*. He scanned the waterproof ledger and found that Chris Warren had signed it yesterday at 1:20 p.m. and Preston Ratliff had signed it at 2:30 p.m. There was no woman's signature. No one had signed the log today.

Luke walked back over. "A guy camping here is a wolfie I know."

Win gave him a questioning look and glanced at the grizzled-looking man who was looking their way. "A what?"

"We call 'em wolfies—folks who are wolf groupies. It's a thing . . . like a hobby. They stay in the park most of the summer and document wolf pack sightings, pup numbers, and such. They give me tips on where I can set up to show my clients wolves. Everyone who comes to Yellowstone wants to see a wolf . . . there are fewer than a hundred wolves in the whole park, they're not easy to find."

"I'll go talk to him," Win said, starting to turn toward the man.

"I wouldn't. He's not high on law enforcement types. Told me once he was out on parole for bank fraud. He won't help you."

Win looked toward the wolfie and frowned.

"Anyway, he saw Ratliff gear up and hike up the trail with what he described as a 'real hot number' midafternoon yesterday. The woman followed Ratliff's rig in—less than fifteen minutes behind him—driving the silver Toyota. The guy's seen Ratliff up here on and off this week, but he'd never seen the woman before. Said she had short blond hair, petite, real built. Sound like your girl?"

"Uh-huh," Win said. "How long would it take to hike in there?" He noticed that the wolfie had decided to forgo a conversation with law enforcement by bugging out. The guy got into an old blue-and-white GMC with a battered camper shell and pulled down the gravel road. He never looked back.

"Four, five hours if you take the main trail—and it's not an easy trail. I kin get you there in half that time by goin' cross-country and then down an old patrol trail. That route is not maintained. It ain't a leisure hike."

Win glanced at his watch. It was after nine. He wished he'd told Trey to request a helicopter from Grand Teton—but he hadn't. And now . . . now he had no good options since the phones still weren't working. He really didn't expect the Russian to contact him until late this afternoon—he'd told Sokolov it would take him that long to get the bones—so he had maybe seven, eight hours to work with before he had to be back in Mammoth. He was cutting it close. But he reminded himself that at this point meeting the Russian didn't matter, he could string that out another day. What mattered was getting to Paige and getting her out of danger—what mattered was preventing another killing. He pulled his jacket out of the truck and opened the back compartment. *Time to saddle up.*

"Okay, let's do the short route. I'll follow you," he said.

Luke moved back toward his truck, talking as he went. "Take only a day pack, extra jacket, plenty of water . . . protein bars . . . first aid kit . . . nothing too heavy. This hike ain't for the faint of heart."

* * *

Spence Johnson knew no one in the Denver Field Office was going to accuse him of working too hard. Or working at all, he supposed with a resigned sigh. He'd been with the Bureau for twenty-seven years and it hadn't always been this way. He'd had a string of bad luck: incompetent supervisors, lousy postings, and dead-end assignments. He had plenty of excuses for the less-than-stellar performance evaluations that filled his personnel file. By the time the Bureau stuck him away in the Yellowstone satellite office, he'd long since given up on trying to improve his lot. He'd told himself that he'd just wait until he could pull in full retirement benefits at age fifty, then move on with the next phase in his life. But that hadn't happened. He'd been in Mammoth for over five years, and he was nearly fifty-six—mandatory retirement was just over a year away. What was he waiting for? Why couldn't he pull the trigger and retire? He drummed his pen on an empty legal pad on an empty desk, he pivoted in his chair, and stared out the window at the rain that was hammering down. *Because I have nowhere to go, damn it.*

He'd been divorced for nearly fifteen years now; he didn't even know what state she lived in. . . . No children—he'd always said that was a plus, now he wasn't so sure. His folks were in their late seventies, they were talking about moving to Florida, leaving Pittsburgh's long winters behind. He hadn't liked the thought of that, but then he hadn't kept up with any of his school friends, didn't even follow the Steelers, no longer called that place home. He drew another deep breath. *I have nowhere to go.*

He leaned his considerable bulk back in the chair and loosened his tie. He took another sip of his coffee. *No need to get into a funk.* It was after 10:30 and there were at least half a dozen Denver agents over at the Justice Center getting everything in order for the ASAC's noon press conference. He told himself again that he should go over there and try to be helpful, or at least have a cup of coffee with some of the folks. Couldn't hurt.

But he hadn't liked what he'd seen in the mirror when he'd headed out for the office this morning. He'd put on an actual suit and tie— hadn't done that in ages, but with all the brass in town, he wanted to at least make some effort. And he *was* the senior resident agent in Yellowstone National Park . . . he might get a background spot at the press conference, but that upstart, Tyler, he'd steal the show. Johnson tried for a moment to generate some actual resentment toward Win Tyler, but he couldn't pull it off. Tyler was hard to dislike, as much as he wanted to dislike him. Tyler was serious about the job—the kid was out to save the world from evil, and Johnson had to concede he was pretty damn good at it. *Wonder if I ever felt that way? Surely I did.* But he couldn't remember when.

A sharp clap of thunder shook the Pagoda, the nickname given to the square gray stone structure that housed the FBI's Yellowstone office. Johnson instinctively dodged back from the window as another bolt of lightning crashed down somewhere nearby. He'd wait till the weather let up to walk the two hundred yards down to the Justice Center, that was for sure. Thinking about Tyler got him thinking about what Win had said this morning—that Paige, the little cutie who'd been making a play on him yesterday, might be in danger. He wondered about her ... something didn't fit. He had to admit it had puzzled him that she'd shown up yesterday and turned up the heat around him. Had he been fool enough to think he was gonna attract a babe like her? No ... no, he could see her going for Tyler—every female around tried to catch that kid's eye—but *No, not me. That ship's done sailed.* He subconsciously sucked in his gut and straightened in the chair. *There was a time . . .*

He stared back out the window again. *Didn't Tyler say Hechtner would be bringing me some proof of this supposed serial killer?* He looked at his watch: it was 10:35. The second call with Tyler had been well over two hours ago. Maybe the thunderstorms had balled up the traffic. It took over ninety minutes to get to Mud Volcano during the summer on a good day. No telling what the ranger had run into . . .

But something was bothering him. He walked down the hall, passed Tyler's closed office, went down the stairs, and ended up in front of the gun vault. It had seemed odd that Paige was so keen on seeing the guns, on seeing how the safe worked. He keyed in the access code, turned the handle on the heavy door, pulled it open, and did a quick check of the weapons. Didn't seem to be anything out of place. He opened the lower ammo drawer, where he knew Tyler was keeping the bones and those ring boxes. He stood there and stared down into the empty drawer. *Well, hell.*

* * *

Luke wasn't kidding about the trail being rough. Win couldn't tell there was a trail, but Bordeaux seemed to know where he was going. And much of that going seemed to be straight up the side of a very high mountain. They'd veered off the Slough Creek Trail after four miles and bushwhacked up the side of a fire-scarred ridge that seemed to go on forever. They stopped on a fairly level spot near an impressive cliff and rockslide. Both men shed their packs and reached for their water bottles. Luke sat down on a weathered log out of the wind. It was starting to blow pretty good this high up.

"Where are we?" Win asked after he'd gotten his breath.

"On the northeast side slope of Frederick Peak. The summit is 9,585 feet, but we're not going there. We're going to the top of this saddleback—it drops off the other side directly into Maxwell Springs. Good views of Mount Hornaday and The Thunderer from the saddle-back crest. Both of those mountains are over 10,000 feet." Win couldn't see the taller mountains yet, but he could see dark storm clouds to the northwest, toward Mammoth. He heard the distant rumble of thunder.

"You don't seem to be having any trouble with the climbing—you're moving like a mountain goat," Win remarked, wiping sweat from his face with his sleeve.

Luke shrugged with his good shoulder; his expression was pensive. "It's gettin' better . . . easier . . . but it ain't back to normal. I'm blowin' pretty hard. Gonna take a bit more time, I reckon." He was watching something on the higher ridge. "Speaking of mountain goats, look off to your right at two o'clock."

Win saw the five white goats clearly; they weren't more than sixty yards away. They were standing on what appeared to be a sheer cliff, with nothing but air below them.

All five adult goats were looking back at him—all with identical quizzical expressions on their long faces. All five had glowing-white coats, with trailing white beards and pointed black horns. They looked like creatures from mythology. They seemed to be wondering why these humans had invaded their alpine world, but they quickly lost interest in the trespassers and continued on their jaw-dropping traverse of the near-vertical cliff.

"How in the world?" Win was awestruck by the beasts.

"They've got pads on the bottom of their hoofs. And they're all muscle." Luke was pulling on his pack and looking down the slope they'd just climbed as he continued his tutorial. "Pretty special, gettin' to see 'em up close. They stay in the high mountains. The Park Service says they're not indigenous to Yellowstone. They were introduced to the region back in 1940s and '50s. Some dudes thought they looked really cool and would be great for trophy hunting. But they took hold in this high, remote part of the park. They've bloomed where they were planted. . . . Ellie always said that was what we needed to do since we moved here from Louisiana." Luke smiled as he watched the goats.

Whoa... Win forgot the cramping in his legs for the thirty seconds it took the nimble creatures to bound from one tiny ledge to another and out of view. He found himself smiling too. He stood and stretched and checked his phones again. Still no satellite service, and that was becoming worrisome. It was after 10:30. He figured Trey and Johnson had gotten some of the higher-ups' attention with the killer's trophy box by now. He was hoping someone would reach out to him. He was hoping this little trek over the mountain was all for nothing, that Trey or someone had gotten through to the researchers and discovered that Paige was safe and sound.

He had to get back to some semblance of civilization so that he could be contacted by the Russian . . . or the CIA . . . or both. Santiago had told him they'd be tracking him with a mixture of high-altitude drones, the cell locator, and the tiny GPS-like devices that were attached to his watch and his ear. The man had said that the Agency did this all the time. He'd said not to worry. But Win was worried. Without phone service there was no way for the Russian to contact him—no way to set the trap.

Luke stood up on the big log he'd been sitting on. "I'm worried."

He had Win's attention.

"I'm thinkin' someone may be followin' us."

Now he really had Win's attention. "What?"

"Not fer sure, but twice now I've heard somethin' when we'd stop, when we'd rest." Luke dug in his pack as he spoke. The big pistol came out in his hand. He unbuckled his belt and slipped the holster on.

"That all you're carrying?"

Luke gave him a scowl. "What do you think, boy?" He pulled out a spotting scope; he was watching the switchback down the hill. "If there's someone down there, they're smart enough to stay off the trail in the open spots." He gave Win a hard look. "You told me we were goin' to Maxwell Springs to check on a woman. Is there more to this?"

"It's a case, Luke. I can't talk about an open case, but there could be someone following me . . . if that's so, it should be some of our guys." *Unless, of course, it isn't.* He realized he didn't sound too convincing.

Luke motioned upward. "Well, let's stay ahead of whoever it is . . . maybe it's nothin'."

Win glanced down the mountainside and saw no one. He pulled on his pack and adjusted his holster so that his Glock was within easy reach.

CHAPTER THIRTY-THREE

Wisps of steam that looked like white smoke were all they could see of Maxwell Springs from where they stood on Frederick Peak's high, narrow saddleback. The mountain fell off in front of them toward the valley—the expanse below was dotted with stands of whitebark pine that clung to the steep terrain; rockslides and deep ravines cut the sides of the slope. They'd been climbing the opposite side of this mountain on grades that were often more than sixty degrees. It was tough work to reach the crest, and now they'd have to descend to Maxwell Springs down a landscape that looked even more impenetrable.

Both men huddled behind a huge gray boulder to get out of the wind. Win leaned forward to catch his breath. He'd seen no sign of anyone coming behind them, and Luke hadn't commented on it again.

"Reckon it'll be a sight quicker gettin' down than it was gettin' up here. That is, iffen we don't fall and kill ourselves," Luke observed.

Win collapsed on a rock, took off his hat, and ran his hand through his wet hair as he tried to catch his breath. Then he took in the amazing view. He could see a pear-shaped turquoise lake and dark-green forests nestled between high peaks. Thin trails of steam were rising from an area between the mountainside they sat on and the lake. Maxwell Springs was about 2,500 feet directly below them—getting there in one piece would be the trick. Win saw no sign of a trail.

Luke handed Win a spotting scope from his pack. "This is where the trail splits." He pointed to the north, down the spine of the ridge. "There's an old warming cabin 'bout half a mile down the top of this ridge . . . it ain't hard to get to from here, lots of exposed rock. And there's a fairly decent game trail that leads off this crest to the valley. It's a quick descent. Back seventy years ago there was a patrol trail that snaked down to the valley from the cabin. Hasn't been used in years. The Park Service never restored the old trails up here. Too dangerous, I reckon."

Win was scanning the valley below them with the scope. "I can't tell if anyone's down there . . . the steam is obscuring the thermal areas . . . we're still too far away. I'd have to get down a lot closer to check it out from above."

"Well, watch your footing when you do. Cliffs and shale slides fall off a thousand feet into ravines in a couple of places. The loose shale will slide out from under you."

Luke was also scanning with his scope, but it was pointed down the near-vertical trail they'd just climbed. When he spoke, his voice was hard. "Win Tyler, it's time you come clean with me. There's three men comin' behind us. . . . They ain't having any trouble with the terrain, and two of them are carryin' some kinda sub gun. They ain't out here fer the scenery." Luke lowered the scope and looked at Win. "And worst of all, they're not very far behind us."

Win looked back down the way they'd come; he saw nothing except twisted trees, boulders, and the occasional rockslide. He heard nothing except the wind. *Come clean, he said. . . . You can't put him in danger.* Win drew a breath and locked eyes with Luke. "Well, you were deputized by the FBI once . . . I guess that might technically still be in effect." He had no idea if the deputization of citizens had a time limit. He nodded down the slope. "It's likely a group of CIA paramilitary . . . they're in the park to nab some foreign nationals who seem to have taken an interest in me. I've got locators on me so the Agency guys can track me."

Luke's eyes narrowed even more. "You said 'likely'—who else could it be?"

Win pulled his hat down tighter and stared off into space.

"Who else?"

"The foreign nationals that the CIA team is after—"

"Russians?"

"How'd you know that?"

"Trey had me read that Russian clipping a few weeks ago, then some folks hired me to take them into Maxwell Springs—two of the boys behind us move a lot like those fellas. And Trey said you ain't been yourself since you got back from overseas . . . he said you went to Kamchatka."

Win didn't respond, he didn't meet Luke's eyes.

"It ain't rocket science, Win. Somebody you're scared of is tailing you . . . and you ain't scared of much. You're sensing somethin' ain't right, and you've got good instincts. Let's assume the folks behind us aren't friendlies."

Win nodded and drew a deep breath. *Deal with the fear later—focus on the job.* "I need to get down to the springs and see if Paige is alright . . . I need to get her away from those geologists—Warren and Ratliff. One of them may be a killer. And"—Win nodded down the slope—"I need to lose those guys."

"Alright. You go down to the springs, follow the game trail in front of you. When you hit the lip of the cliff about a quarter mile down, go left on an old trail, you'll see blue diamond markers. Follow those markers down a ravine to the bottom, then the trail splits again—to the left goes directly to the lake, to the right goes more toward the geyser field." Luke leaned back against the big boulder, then stuffed the scope in his pack. He looked back up at Win. "Watch yourself. It's rough goin' the first couple thousand feet. I'll cover your tracks and try to lead 'em off toward the cabin, then I'll try to lose 'em. If it's your guys, I guess they'll be on you. If it's the Russians . . . well . . ." Luke shrugged with his eyebrows as he turned away.

* * *

Johnson wasn't sure what to do. He'd poured himself another cup of coffee and tromped back up the stairs after finding the bones and ring boxes missing. He'd double-checked the security codes on the office; nothing seemed off there. He'd tried Paige's number again and it went straight to voicemail. He called Trey Hechtner's number and got the same result. He called the park's Dispatch Office and was told they hadn't heard from Hechtner. The dispatcher connected Johnson to the secretary in the park's Administration Building. Chief Randall was at the Justice Center helping organize the press conference, but his secretary said they were concerned that Trey hadn't reported in after they'd lost radio contact with him just after eight. They'd sent rangers to drive the Grand Loop Road toward Roosevelt to try to locate him.

The damn thunderstorm that had sat over them for the last several hours was finally beginning to peter out. That was the only positive thing that crossed his mind. Johnson turned away from the window and drummed his fingers on his desk. Somehow he felt as if *something* was his fault, he just wasn't sure what. Maybe if he hadn't taken that bogus leave of absence, he'd have been involved in the case. If in fact there was a case. A serial killer in the park? Been going on for several years, Tyler had said. Well, those would be years when he was the only FBI agent in Yellowstone. *Did I blow something that big? A serial killer? Possible . . . it's possible,* he had to concede. He exhaled a deep breath and picked up the landline. *Well, hell.*

Jim West put him on hold for a minute, then got on the line. "Spence, we're kinda busy over here. Must be every TV network in the country trying to squeeze into the conference room. It's nearly eleven o'clock . . . press conference is at noon. When are you coming over?" Johnson could tell by the tone that Jim's expectations of his contributions to their efforts weren't high.

"Was waiting till the lightning let up, Boss. But we've got an issue." He told the supervisor what little he knew. Jim stopped him after he said the words *serial killer* for the second time.

"Win actually said he thought there was a serial killer—that someone else might be in danger? Said he had evidence? Said the ranger was bringing it in?" Jim sounded incredulous.

"Yeah, he told me that this morning on the sat phone . . . it was, uh, 6:28 when I got the first call from him. I was still at home. We talked again at 8:15 after I did the checking he wanted done, and I sent him the screenshot of Paige Lange with Dr. Ratliff. That's when Win said he'd be going to Maxwell Springs to try to find Paige. She's a Bureau support employee working here on some Chinese espionage deal out of San Francisco. There's a lady supervisor that she's with—they're working out of room 223 over there in the Justice Building. But no one was there when I checked early this morning. Win seemed concerned that Paige could be in danger."

Johnson caught his breath and continued. "And Boss, Hechtner hasn't shown up with the killer's trophy box—dispatch can't locate him. The bones and ring Win found up at Maxwell Springs are missing out of the office gun safe." He could tell Jim West was trying to take it all in. Johnson added one more thing to the mix. "Win said part of this case was being handled out of Headquarters. Do you know anything about that?"

Jim ignored the last question. "Why haven't we heard anything more? You heard from him last at, what, 8:15?"

"Satellite phone call dropped while I was talking to Win. He was gonna reach out to you, but, like I said, the call dropped. I haven't been able to get him back on the office's sat phone or the cells. I talked to Park Service Dispatch and apparently there's been no satellite or cell service in the northeastern part of the park since early morning. They've got the cell tower folks working on it, they've called in the techies for the satellite network, but you know how weather can really screw up communications out here."

* * *

Win kept following the faint trail down between smooth gray rocks that were the size of cars. At times the path was near vertical; he had to lean back into the mountain to remain upright. He balanced with his hands against the boulders and grasped for whatever handhold was available. He focused on just the few feet in front of him; he couldn't afford to lose his balance, to fall. He was rapidly dropping in elevation, that was for sure.

At one point the trail cut back across a rockslide that was at least fifty yards wide. The narrow path through the rock field was worn smooth—likely thousands of elk, pronghorn, and who knows what all had worn the path level with their hoofs over hundreds of years. At least for a short while Win could walk upright, that was the positive. The negative was that he was exposed as he crossed the slide—anyone on the crest above could see him. No other options; there was no other way down. He quickly cleared the rockslide and moved into an area of stunted pine. He was grateful for the cover of the trees.

A few minutes later, he stopped and knelt at the edge of the forest beside a huge fallen log. He pulled the spotting scope from his pack and looked up the mountainside to the exposed area of the rockslide. If anyone was behind him, they'd be in the open for fifty yards. He drank from his water bottle and waited. It wasn't long. His breath caught, his chest tightened, and his pulse accelerated. The man following him moved on the trail just like Luke Bordeaux—easy and fluid like a cat, quiet and quick like a hunter. He was dressed for backcountry hiking, carrying a day pack . . . no sign of a weapon. His floppy Tilley hat shaded his face, but Win didn't need to see that face. Major Sergei Sokolov was less than a quarter mile behind him and closing fast.

That meant that two of the Russians were on Luke—they saw Luke as the greater threat. *They got that right.* Win drew a deep breath and felt a stab of fear. He slid behind the nearest boulder and told himself to breathe. *Get a grip,* he lectured himself. *This guy is human, he's no superman, he's just like me. Get a grip!*

Luke had said there was a clearing below, maybe a spot for an ambush. He told himself to be cool, he pulled his Glock from its holster. The weapon in his hand calmed him. *I'm an FBI agent, for Pete's sake. Just arrest the guy, put him in cuffs, and get down there to Paige.* He told himself it was just that simple. He told himself he could go up against this guy. His mind flew back to the Scripture his brother had quoted to him twelve days ago: *Those who are with you are mightier than those who are with them.* He moved off down the steep trail and whispered a prayer that God's mighty angels would indeed protect him.

* * *

Jim West knew something was very wrong. He barely knocked on the door of the Assistant U.S. Attorney's office before turning the knob. He knew she and Wes Givens were going over the final details for the press conference on the fugitive surrender. But this couldn't wait. Johnson had told him that Win said Headquarters was handling the serial killer case . . . or handling *something*. He was out of the loop, and it was looking more and more like one of his guys was in trouble. Givens stood when the supervisor entered the room. He shifted some paperwork in his hands and didn't look pleased with the intrusion.

"Sorry to interrupt you, sir," Jim began, "but we may have a situation." He ran through what little—what very little—he knew. He wrapped it up with a question. "Is Win in something I don't know about?"

Wes had listened to Jim without a question. Now he had one. "You're telling me that no one has had contact with Win since 8:15 this morning, and that all communications are out for a good part of the park? Even satellite phones?"

Jim nodded. The ASAC asked the attorney if she would excuse herself so they could talk privately. As soon as the door closed, Wes was on the phone to Seattle; in seconds Brent Sutton was on the line. Moments later Jim West was quickly walking down the long hall to room 223—the room where Ms. Gorski and Paige Lange had set up their office. He was trying to make sense of what he'd overheard on the phone call—Wes had put Sutton on speakerphone. *Russians? CIA? Arrest/neutralize operation?* He wasn't liking being left in the dark one little bit.

Sutton had said Supervisor Gloria Gorski was at the Gardiner Airport coordinating an arrest operation with elements of the Agency. While Ms. Gorski dealt with the CIA, Agents Paige Lange and Antwon Humphrey were Win's backups in Mammoth on something Sutton called "the Russia deal." They'd been rotating twenty-four-hour shifts, and while they weren't expected to be in constant contact with Win, they were expected to be in Mammoth and be available if Win needed them. Paige had been on duty through noon yesterday. Sutton knew that Humphrey had been in Mammoth yesterday afternoon and evening. Paige should be relieving Humphrey by noon today. The planned arrest of foreign nationals by the Agency team could take place late this afternoon.

Jim reached the closed metal door—he rapped hard on it and got no answer, then tried the metal knob but it was locked tight. He hit the speed dial on his phone for the building's security office; the officer with the master key was moving up the stairs in seconds. Jim put in calls to Win while he waited. Both his personal and Bureau phones went to voicemail; the sat phone didn't even connect. Jim tried to remind himself that communications in Yellowstone were sometimes unreliable, but this didn't fit. The phones worked fine in Mammoth. It seemed to be just the northeast quadrant of the park that was impacted—the area Win had called from early this morning. Jim's fifteen years of experience in the Bureau told him that his young agent was in trouble. He started punching in Chief Randall's number just as the security guard arrived with the keys.

The guard got the door open and flipped on the lights. Jim nearly dropped his phone. He rushed into the windowless room. Maps and papers were scattered over two desks and over the floor. A metal chair and coffee cup were overturned, and a man Jim didn't recognize lay cuffed on the carpeted floor. He was lying on his stomach and hadn't moved when they'd barged in. Jim couldn't tell if he was breathing. He had a bad feeling he was looking at Win Tyler's backup on the Russia deal.

* * *

The clearing was just the solid rock lip of a cliff; the stunted trees stopped thirty feet from the edge. Win jogged to the edge and looked over; the tops of eighty-foot lodgepole pines looked minuscule below him. *Nowhere to hide here, no cover.* He moved to the left and spotted a faded blue trail marker attached to a tree with a rusty nail. He moved down the path along the bluff, looking for better cover. He could see the steam rising from the spring below; it was much closer now.

And the thermal area wasn't the only thing that was closer. Win had caught a glimpse of Sokolov with the scope moments ago—he'd cut the distance between them in half and was now holding a handgun. Win needed a plan. The trail downward was easier now, but still plenty steep. He'd gone about thirty yards from the cliff's edge when the path cut between an eight-foot-tall weathered stump and a massive boulder. An open area where a shale slide dropped off the mountainside was just beyond the stump. Win pulled off his pack, dug in the bottom of it, and came up with the spool of fishing line that he always carried. He strung the line at boot level across the trail between the stump and the huge rock. He needed to get Sokolov's attention diverted to the potential booby trap for a few seconds—he just needed him to look down. Win knew that once Sokolov saw the trip wire, either he'd be caught off guard or he wouldn't—only one way to know.

Win leaned back into a crevasse in the boulder, said a prayer, and waited. He heard a footfall in less than a minute. It was nearly impossible to traverse the steep grade without sliding. A few seconds later the nearly imperceptible sound of a twig snapping, then another sound of sliding. Sokolov saw the line just in time and sidestepped, slipping a bit as he did. Win spun onto the trail with the Glock in a two-handed grip. He was down on one knee with the pistol pointed right at the Russian's chest.

"Stop . . . lower the gun to the ground! . . . Now!"

The Russian didn't even seem startled. His expression never changed. "Stupid of me to underestimate you, Agent Tyler." The big man bent and slowly lowered the semiautomatic to the trail.

"Unbuckle the pack . . . use one hand . . . drop the pack . . . then hands behind your head, lock your fingers." Win methodically moved through the commands, got the guy on the ground on his chest and cuffed his hands behind his back. Win wasn't sure he had taken a breath since the confrontation began. He inhaled deeply, whispered a prayer of thanks, and began the process of searching him.

He turned Sokolov over and started through his pockets, looking for another weapon. He'd already tossed the Russian's semiautomatic to the side; he figured the guy had another small semiautomatic stashed somewhere. He found it in a pancake holster on his back. A folding knife was in a pocket. Win stared down into the hard face. The Russian hadn't said a word. Win unzipped the breast pocket of his jacket and a small black corded rope interspersed with beads fell out. Win held it up and the sunlight caught the varied shades of the beads: bright green and ebony. The breeze moved the black wool tassel. Win's mind flashed back to something Tory said yesterday: *"He's a believer, I could feel it."* Rosary beads?

Sokolov answered Win's unspoken question. "It's a prayer rope . . . a chotki." The man tried to shift on the ground, he kept talking. "It was my father's. The green beads are malachite and the black ones are onyx. It is very special to me." For just a second Win thought about the tiny Bible he carried in his own pocket. He had it with him now, just as this man—his enemy—carried a tangible symbol of his faith. Win nodded. He put it back in the guy's pocket and zipped it shut.

"Can I sit up? It's a little uncomfortable down here . . . I'm lying on a dozen rocks." The Russian was calm. His tone was conversational. Win was kneeling beside the prone man, methodically going through the remaining pockets. "Tyler, come on . . . let me sit up. You've got me, dude." Win glanced up the trail, he strained to listen for sounds of any approach. He heard nothing.

He found a small black phone of some type in a pocket. Cyrillic letters scrolled across the screen . . . it was operating, but Win had no idea how it functioned. "How'd you get your phone to work? We've had no satellite service for hours." Win didn't expect an answer, he was just talking to hear his own voice, to calm himself. He was surprised when Sokolov replied. "Well, for all practical purposes, much of Yellowstone has no satellite coverage, no cell towers, no repeaters. . . . Russians are the world's best hackers, Win. In the realm of cyberspace, we simply made those physical assets of yours temporarily disappear.

My satellite"—he glanced at the sky as if he could see it—"my satellite works just fine."

Win fished his sat phone out of his pocket—still dead as a doorknob. He looked down at the Russian's smug expression. *Could they have actually done that? Hacked the systems? And if they did, what about the locational trackers on me?*

The Russian seemed to be reading his mind. "You're not in counterintelligence, Win, so I'll give you a little lesson." His voice was unhurried. "I figure you've got one, two . . . maybe even three transponders on you somewhere. That would be standard tradecraft. Those tiny little suckers can be tracked by satellite or drone—they'll show your location within half a meter. Your people could be taking pictures or video from drones positioned miles away. Or if the stakes were high enough, they could reposition a satellite and follow your every move from a hundred and fifty miles above. Have they told you that's how it works? That you don't have a thing to worry about? That Uncle Sam will be there just over your shoulder, ready to pounce on the bad guys if they sense a hint of danger for you. Is that what you were told?"

Uh . . . yeah. Win was sweating this now.

"Your people *think* they're tracking you. The locator beacons are showing you in a forest just south of Sheepeater Cliff near Indian Creek Campground. You've been in that area since midmorning, as far as they can tell. They're analyzing their high-altitude drone feeds—which we've also hacked—and they *think* they're seeing you hiking through the backcountry . . . with me traipsing along behind. But your boys aren't seeing today's footage, they're seeing edited footage of all that meandering we've done out in the woods the last few days, plus a bit of deep-fake imagery. The images look just like you, look just like me. We have folks who can weave footage together so that even you wouldn't know it wasn't you. Remember the bar fight scenes from Kamchatka we sent your agency? Same process, just a bit more high-tech today. Without someone on the ground, they'll take it all at face value and begin searching for you in those areas—nearly thirty miles southwest of here. Whata ya think, Cowboy?" He was grinning.

Win hoped the shock he felt wasn't plastered on his face. He didn't respond at first. What could he say? He had a sinking feeling that everything the Russian said was true. He cleared his throat and nodded. "Well, Major, you've already underestimated me. I wouldn't get too cocky if I was you . . . you're the one in cuffs. And I wouldn't bet against the Americans on this deal just yet. Folks who've done that have regretted it throughout history."

Win focused back in on his search. He needed to go through the guy's backpack next. Win was still kneeling as he holstered his Glock and reached across the guy for the pack.

"May I sit up? My arms are cramping."

"Okay, sit up."

The Russian struggled to a sitting position as Win lifted the backpack and unfastened its top. A small gray cloth pouch fell from a zippered compartment, the elaborate ruby-and-garnet necklace dropped into the pine needles in front of Win's knees. The Russian had gone still. Win blinked down at the necklace and went cold as ice. He'd held the pouch and necklace in his hand just hours ago. He'd seen Trey walk away with it . . . *Dear God, no!* Win grabbed the front of the Russian's jacket and yanked him closer. The man's face was as hard as stone; the green eyes were evasive.

"Whoa, Cowboy, easy," he softly said.

Win shook the guy—hard. His rage was barely contained. "Where is Trey Hechtner? . . . The ranger who had this . . . what did you do to him?"

Two quick shots faintly echoed from somewhere far above them. Win eased his grip on the Russian for just a second and glanced up the mountain. *Luke?* The next thing Win knew, two strong fists had clubbed each of his ears. He was stunned for a moment, then suddenly fighting for his life.

CHAPTER THIRTY-FOUR

He'd dodged down behind the fallen log when the two rounds slammed into the tree trunk three feet above him seconds ago. He knew it was a warning—a *stop now or the next bullets will be on target.* He knew it because that's how he would have handled it. They'd caught up to him much quicker than he'd envisioned; he was still yards away from the heavy forest surrounding the cabin. He was gasping for air and moving much slower than normal; his reflexes were sluggish. The lung shot he'd taken last month was impacting him at this altitude much more than he'd expected. And now, because of the lack of cover on the crest of the saddleback, he was pinned down.

He slumped lower behind the deadfall and hoped he hadn't been outflanked. He didn't have solid cover, and he knew if either of the gunmen let loose a volley with their automatic weapons, they'd likely get him. His pride had gotten him in this fix—he wasn't yet physically healed to the point where he could climb for three thousand feet, then fend off a combat assault. He'd told himself he was healed, that he was capable, that he was ready. *I was wrong, dammit!* He'd spent years teaching solders not to overestimate their own ability, not to get themselves into indefensible positions, and here he'd done it himself.

The plan had been to get all three of the men who were following them up the mountain to break off pursuing Win and come after him. That would free Win to get down to Maxwell Springs. But their pursuers had split up . . . one was still on Win Tyler. Two were on him, and he had to admit he was kinda glad there were only two. Two was enough. And these two were good.

He'd spent his military years in Army Special Forces; he would normally have no problem with two against one. But as he'd watched his two adversaries move through the maze of rocks and scrub trees behind him, he had a sinking feeling these guys had done the same— they were clearly operators. Tyler had said they were probably CIA paramilitary . . . that would mean they were officers from the CIA's Special Operations Group. He knew the Agency usually recruited their operators from Delta Force and the Navy SEAL teams. He knew they were pros. What he didn't know was why they were here in the high country of Yellowstone, tracking him down. It didn't make sense. Why not come in with a chopper? Why spend two hours climbing one of the toughest trails in the park? Unless, of course, they weren't CIA. Unless they were the Russians.

Russian soldiers were known to be tough—were known to be brutal. Maybe that went with living in a country where the temperature hovered near or below zero for a good part of the year. Or maybe it was because of their country's history of ruthlessly killing off millions of their own countrymen every few decades. But if they were Russians, why the warning shots? He had a bad feeling he was fixing to find out.

* * *

The dark bird's wings formed a sharp V as it dove down the front of the yellow limestone cliff on the opposite side of the ravine. A second gray flash careened down the face of the wall, the sunlight glancing off its wings. Win had been watching them swoop and dive for the last couple of minutes as he lay on his back amid the jumble of small, loose rocks. Any movement caused him to slip farther. And there wasn't much farther to go. He'd come to rest on a shale slide fifty feet below the trail and just above the lip of the abyss—an eight-hundred-foot cliff that stood above the valley. If he slid much more, his boots would extend into open space.

They were much too small for ospreys or eagles; he knew those predators often made their nests on ledges along the canyon walls. They were too fast and agile for hawks or harriers. *Maybe kestrels?* His mind was eliminating bird species instead of focusing on the obvious problem: he had mere minutes to live. The only thing keeping him from flying into the canyon with the birds was a rather tenuous, two-handed grip on a scroungy-looking shrub of some sort. Both hands were above his head in a death grip on a thin, spindly limb. He'd done a quick inventory when the terrifying slide stopped minutes ago—he seemed to be unhurt—not that it made any difference with hundreds of feet of sheer cliff just below him and no way to climb to the top.

The hand-to-hand fight with a Russian who'd spent years as a special forces operator hadn't been a fair match. Win thought he'd gotten in a few good licks, but Sokolov didn't even bother to go for his weapons—he'd yanked Win's Glock free and gone at him with one hand still in the cuffs. And the cuffs? Win's mind had immediately gone to the Russian's comment Tuesday night: "I always keep a spare handcuff key on me." *Should have remembered that earlier.* Win had tried to reach for the smaller gun in his pancake holster, but Sokolov had pinned him in a neck hold, pulled that gun, and thrown it over the bluff. The battle had been short and intense. The only surprise in the outcome was that he remembered Sokolov reaching for his outstretched arm just before he tumbled down the shale slide. He'd missed.

He didn't know what Sokolov was doing up on the trail. . . . He'd heard him speaking Russian—probably calling someone to report that their prospective turncoat had fallen off a cliff. Now the man was softly whistling that old hymn. This time, Win remembered more of the words: *Prone to Wander, Lord, I feel it; Prone to Leave the God I love; Here's my heart, O take and seal it; Seal it for Thy courts above.* This time, with his life hanging in the balance, the meaning hit home. He'd given God his heart long ago, now he had to continue to trust that God had indeed sealed it. He hadn't lived a perfect life, but his sins, even the deaths he'd caused, couldn't break that seal. He was God's child, sealed by Christ's sacrifice on the cross. He thankfully accepted the grace he'd been avoiding these last few weeks and watched the birds soar through the air.

"That a pair of peregrine falcons?" The Russian's voice floated down from above. He'd lapsed back into the Texas drawl.

Win tried to blink the stinging sweat out of his eyes as he forced a reply. "Looks like it . . . I've read that . . . that we have them out here."

The birds seemed to know they were being admired; they dove in unison toward the bottom of the cliff and out of Win's view.

"You people used to have them on your protected species list . . . saw that in a brochure. We have them in Russia. Beautiful birds. . . . Look at them fly straight up!" The whoosh of the wind whipped through the space below. Then quiet for a moment. "Do you know what my last name means in my language?"

"Why don't you tell me—" The roots on the little bush gave a little to Win's 205 pounds, and he slipped a few inches farther down the sharply-angled slope.

The Russian either didn't notice or didn't care. "Sokolov means 'falcon.' Bet you didn't know that most Russians didn't have surnames until the late 1800s, then lots of families adopted the names of common things: rivers, animals, or birds. So I'm a falcon, watching rare American falcons. . . . It has to be an omen, a good sign."

Win's effort to dig in his heels caused more of the loose shale to scatter off the cliff. It was too far down to hear the stones hit bottom. Sweat was trickling down his face, and his grip on the shrub was slipping. Time was suspended. He'd seen a steady stream of faces he loved—they all came to him slowly and gently, yet he knew from experience that they actually passed in less than a second. A final, kind gift from this world. He whispered another prayer before he tried to speak.

"I'd love . . . to hear more . . . more about your family history, but I'm a little preoccupied here. You gonna just wait it out?"

"You were going to kill me."

"Arrest you . . . not kill you . . . I coulda shot you when you were exposed on the slide or when . . . when you came down the trail." He struggled to pull in a breath. "I'm . . . I'm not like you . . . not a killer."

"There is no 'arrest' for me, Win." He said "Win" with the Russian accent; it came out "Ven." "If you take me back to your people, I disappear into a black hole. I don't exist here . . . there is no 'due process.' It won't go good for me—I know that. You know that."

Win thought of the CIA team that was supposed to be handling this task. He blinked away the very real possibility that the man was telling him the truth. But that didn't change things—this guy was the enemy.

"Arrest me. Kill me. Same difference. You don't understand the rules of the game we're playing, Agent Tyler."

"Why don't you . . . get me off this cliff, then . . . then you can explain it to me." Win heard the strain in every word. His arms were beginning to cramp; he knew it was just a matter of seconds now.

"Just waitin' for you to ask." A length of black nylon rope landed near his side. Win stared at it in disbelief for a millisecond, then dropped one hand from the bush and looped the rope around his wrist.

"I've got you. Pull the rope under you with your other hand. You're not gonna have much strength in your arms for a few minutes." Win hesitated. He drew what he feared might be his last breath. The voice from above was steady. "You'll just have to trust me. Eventually each of us has to trust someone, Win."

He caught a glimpse of the falcons diving for the canyon bottom just as he let go of the slender branch. He held his breath as he dropped another two feet toward the edge before the rope pulled taunt.

"I've got you," the voice said again.

* * *

Ramon Santiago was pacing back and forth the length of the hangar's dirty, greasy concrete floor. The wind and rain were finally beginning to let up. Finally. One of his operators, who was from this part of the country, said they occasionally got these big summer storms that blew up, sat over one spot, caused a flood, then dissipated. Good thing it was winding down; there'd been no chance of getting the choppers up during that torrent.

He walked over to the consoles they'd set up to monitor the satellite and drone feeds. The storm had caused significant disruptions, but they were still hitting on both of Tyler's transponders. Tyler was near a place called Indian Creek Campground and fortunately the weather hadn't moved that far south. On the downside, they had visuals that Sokolov was already in that area too. Tyler and the Russian were both on a little-used trail, just out for a hike from all appearances. The Russian was staying more than a hundred yards back from the agent. Looked like it was going to be a rendezvous deep in the woods, or maybe Sokolov just wanted to drag things out a bit and make sure Tyler wasn't setting him up. *Troop around for a couple of hours, then loop back to the parking lot for the actual exchange of the bones. Could be.* He wondered about that. It felt odd, and the timing felt off. Sokolov had told Tyler yesterday that they'd do the switch-off with the bones late in the afternoon. He glanced at his watch again. It was just past noon.

His eyes swept the hangar: everyone was ready, everyone was waiting for the word to go. They wouldn't roll the choppers out the door until he had the word from his bosses; they were also monitoring the satellite and drone feeds from Langley—the last indication he'd heard was a likely rollout in thirty minutes. He ran his hand across his forehead; he was getting a headache thinking about everything that could go wrong.

And way too much could go wrong. He didn't approve of this ops plan . . . too damn many things were left wide open. Generally a recipe for disaster, based on his considerable experience. And he didn't like operating in-country, and neither did his boys. It wasn't what they'd signed on for—taking out a guy, and it might turn out to be several guys—within the boundaries of the United States was not in the rule book. Obviously, someone way up the chain of command thought Major Sokolov and his crew were too dangerous to leave the takedown to law enforcement—even the FBI. He knew everyone in the Bureau was ticked, and he didn't blame them.

Most of his boys were rechecking their weapons and gear. He would have four on each helicopter. He already had four plainclothes folks at the Indian Creek Campground and along the banks of the Gardner River, pretending to fish. Everyone there was dressed as tourists. They'd reported that the campground was absolutely crawling with people: tent camping, an RV parking area, picnic tables, two popular trails, and old service roads that meandered along the river.

They were planning to set down one of the choppers at a Park Service maintenance lot just north of the river, but he had other sites as backups; there was quite a bit of open area along the streams. The second bird would lower its team by rappel into the main contact area, which he hoped like hell would be well away from the tourists. There wasn't anything simple about this operation, and he had no idea how the Agency and the Bureau had gotten the go-ahead to do an armed tactical operation square in the middle of a national park teeming with civilians. He was definitely starting to get a headache.

And speaking of headaches, Ms. Gorski was coming his way again. He stopped in the middle of the hangar and waited for her. He drew a deep breath and tried to force a smile. He didn't like this interagency crap, didn't like it at all.

"Any word from Tyler?" he asked her.

"No . . . no, but I'm really not expecting anything at this point." She was wearing a rain jacket that was dripping on the floor. She pushed back the hood and wiped strands of damp red hair back from her face. Santiago thought she looked tired and stressed—they all probably looked that way. He wondered why she'd been out in the storm, maybe getting something from her car? It was miserable outside and not much better in the leaky metal building. He focused back on what she was saying.

"Based on your monitors, it appears that Sokolov managed to contact Win and get him to that part of the park. We haven't picked up any communications between them—so the contact wasn't by phone. Win's tracker beacons are showing he's 14.3 miles south of our position. He was in the Mud Volcano area early this morning . . . we have an 8:15 a.m. satellite call with him from his office as our last contact. I don't know why he's gone dark, but he may simply be trying not to spook Sokolov. Obviously, the Major called the meeting much earlier than Win expected."

She stepped closer to the front of one of the MH-6M Little Bird helicopters. She gave it an admiring look and nodded to the pilot, who was checking the sensor guards. "I flew Apache AH-64s during two tours in Afghanistan," she said. Apaches were the U.S. military attack workhorse. They were a beast to fly; the pilot was impressed with the Bureau supervisor. "I understand the Bureau's HRT is using Little Birds for insertions . . . I'll bet these babies can really move out," she said to him.

"Yeah, HRT is now flying UH-60s, plus a couple of these bad boys. The MH-6 was reconfigured a few years ago; these are quite an upgrade. Over ninety knots loaded . . . can land on a roof, turn on a dime, quiet as a church mouse," the young pilot said, smiling at her. Ms. Gorski touched the night-vison optics on the helicopter's glass shield. The pilot started explaining its function; he climbed on the railing, opened the door, and invited her up.

Santiago drifted away and left them rummaging through the choppers and discussing aeronautics. They were all looking for diversions to kill the time. And speaking of killing, his tendency to see the worst-case scenario reared its head again. If everything went perfectly, they would swoop in and surround Sokolov by surprise. He'd have no avenue for escape, he'd drop his weapon and surrender. His team would sense defeat and melt into the tourists and the landscape. The Agency would score big if they managed to get two or three of them. But Sokolov's crew wasn't the target, the target was the Major himself, and Santiago knew he wouldn't go down that easily. Major Sergei Sokolov was Zaslon Spetsnaz, badass SVR special forces. He'd want to take a few folks with him . . . and he very well could.

And then there was poor Win Tyler. If the good guys fouled up and he was left hanging out to dry, there was little doubt Sokolov would kill him. Tyler was a loose end for the Russian. Tyler had spent time with Sokolov, and the agent was intuitive; he'd tagged Sokolov in the Yellowstone Chapel early on . . . he'd developed an instinct for spotting the guy. Some people had that ability, and in this case it was a serious liability for the agent. If Major Sokolov managed to escape them today, he could only remain an effective covert operative if Win Tyler was dead.

* * *

The rope went slack, his legs buckled, and he collapsed on all fours as soon as he topped the rim of the slide. His breath was still coming in gasps, and the pain in his arms from the lactic acid coursing through his veins brought tears to his eyes. He fought the urge to drop and hug the solid ground.

"That was a waste of fifteen minutes." The Russian had tied the rope off on a tree and was leaning back against it, his semiautomatic resting against his thigh. "We don't have time to squander. We need to get down to the geyser basin."

Win forced himself to push up to his knees. His breathing was still ragged, but his mind was forcing the pain away. "Why . . . why save me?"

"We've got an investment in you, Cowboy." Sokolov rubbed his fingers together to indicate the money. "Not to mention we've got a case to finish. There's no going back till I see justice for my countrywoman . . . ah, what was her name?" He pushed off from the tree trunk and closed to within ten feet of Win at a hobble. He was favoring his right leg. Win's focus shot there. The man was barely putting any weight on his boot. He'd finally caught a break—he'd done a little damage after all.

Sokolov settled himself on a boulder near their gear and pitched Win a water bottle from his pack. Win drained it and wiped the sweat from his face with his sleeve. He still wasn't sure he could stand. He had to ask the question, but he was afraid he didn't want to hear the answer.

"How'd you get the necklace? . . . The ranger?"

The Russian shrugged. "It belonged to my countrywoman. It's all I took from him." He locked eyes with Win and Win nearly flinched at their intensity. "The ranger was drugged. He is fine . . . out for six to eight hours or so. But no harm." Sokolov could read the disbelief in Win's face. "You have my word as a Russian officer, he was not harmed."

He glanced at his watch. "I scouted this route when we did our little campout with Bordeaux last week. No idea that excursion would be this helpful. Oh, by the way, your friend Bordeaux, he's still trying to evade my lads up on the mountain . . . they'll keep him occupied so that you and I can get on with our work." He sighed. "Ah, and apparently another of your colleagues, Blondie? She has perhaps decided to solve the case of the missing women by herself—she has gone with Ratliff to the springs below us. Why are you so concerned for her?"

He tapped into the Bureau satellite phone this morning. Geez, he knows everything. "Her driver's license was in one of the gray pouches in the fireproof box. I'd thought you would have seen it."

The Russian straightened a bit on the boulder. "I took only what was Natasha Pavlovna's—I didn't look into the other pouches." He seemed puzzled. "Her driver's license?"

"Sometimes serial killers do that . . . steal items from their next intended victim, days, even weeks, in advance. She's at Maxwell Springs with Ratliff and Warren—she has no idea she's in danger. I need to get down there."

The Russian turned his head, and Win caught a look of concern in his eyes before the practiced look of indifference returned. He seemed to be considering the options.

"Why'd you save Tory Madison?" Win asked.

Sokolov seemed surprised at the question. "What would you have done? God put me there to help, I suppose."

Win's mind flashed up an image of the bloodied bodies in Syria. "How in hell can you claim to be a Christian and massacre a family! You're nothin' but a butcher . . . less than an animal!"

The hard eyes were on his. The Russian cocked his head in question. "What are you talking about?"

"I saw the pictures from Aleppo. Your asset, Al Numan . . . the man . . . all of them. I saw the damn pictures. You slaughtered a family—no, you did worse than slaughter them!" Win's voice was shaking and he didn't care.

There was a long silence between them, then the Russian rocked back on the boulder. He shook his head. "That wasn't me. That wasn't our team. The Brits must have gotten photos . . . they were close behind us." He drew in a fractured breath as if he could still smell the death. His voice became softer. "The bodies were still warm when we got there . . . the blood was still running. We were after Al Numan, that much is true, but his family . . . the woman, those children . . . no. No." He shook his head as if that would clear the horrifying images from his mind. "It was the Syrians who got to them, Al Numan's old gang . . . five of them."

"Sure it was. And you know that how?"

"Because we took them out two days later. The savages who massacred that family died in a firefight, which was better than they deserved. Al Numan was our problem to deal with, but his family was innocent. I've seen some terrible things, but that night in Aleppo was one of the worst. It still haunts me."

They both flinched at the sound of distant gunshots. The four steady pops sounded like firecrackers. This time the reports came from below. Sokolov was on his feet before the echo of the last shot died. Win saw him wince as he stood. "Something is happening at the springs," Sokolov said. He was staring into space, trying to make sense of it. He pulled the small black phone from his pocket.

"I need to get down there," Win said. "You're hurt—I can move faster. Give me my gun." He paused. "I give you my word I won't go after you until Paige is safe, until we get Natasha's killer."

The big man seemed to be considering it. Win slowly stood. "We could lose the guy. C'mon, I swear. You have my word." Win knew the Russian was worried; he pressed him. "And call off your dogs on Bordeaux. He isn't a threat to you . . . I shouldn't have drug him into this."

The guy might have been hurt, but he still moved with the quickness of a cat. He pitched Win his backpack and pulled on his own pack. "Go. I will follow." He touched Win's shoulder as he handed Win the

Glock. "Don't even think about going back on your word. You and I, we'll deal with each other once the dust settles."

Win nodded and holstered the weapon. He started off down the steep trail at a jog.

CHAPTER THIRTY-FIVE

It didn't take long to hit the relatively level ground of the valley. Win had gone full tilt down the steep slope, grabbing at trees every few yards to slow his momentum, finally pausing at a small stream that trickled through the path below the mountain. His hands were on his knees, his legs were shaking from the rapid descent. He wasn't real sure where he was or where the thermal field was—he couldn't see any sign of the geysers from this spot in the deep forest.

Wherever it was, he needed to find it fast; he heard two quick shots from somewhere far to his right—short pops—small caliber. He cautiously moved down the trail through a mature stand of lodgepole pines, some probably ninety feet tall; they were swaying in the slight breeze. He could smell the sulfur from the springs now. The thermal area had to be somewhere directly in front of him. The cloud bank that had hovered over the northwestern horizon all morning was moving in. Clouds covered the sun, dropping a curtain of deep shade over the forest. Win felt a chill that likely had more to do with stress than the dropping temperature. He moved forward with the Glock in his hand and soon spotted a faded blue trail marker on a decaying post where the trail split. He remembered Luke's comments about the trail to the left going directly to the lake, while the other path led toward the geyser field. He veered to the right.

He stopped when he heard what sounded like a man's voice through the trees. He was shouting something, and then there was a shot—a single *pop*—from something small caliber. Win plunged off the trail and dropped to a knee. Several answering shots, higher caliber. A rifle of some sort; it was close. A man's voice yelling something again.

He caught a glimpse of someone in blue staggering through the woods, moving from tree to tree, but not with purpose, not with intent. The small figure he was watching was obviously injured . . . and obviously armed. The sun made another stab at holding off the storm clouds; its rays gleamed silver from a small gun in the individual's hand.

"FBI! Put down your weapon! FBI!" Win called out as he moved toward the one person he could see.

The figure in blue collapsed on the trail about twenty yards in front of him. Using the big trees as cover, he cautiously moved toward the still form. He could see short blond hair and narrow shoulders under the jacket. He could see her better now. He'd found Paige Lange.

He picked up his pace, then slid to a stop like a baseball player sliding into base—one leg extended, his Glock sweeping right and left above the motionless woman lying in front of him.

She was on her side, facing away from him; a small silver semiautomatic lay in the trail where she'd dropped it. He kneeled at her back and whispered a prayer that he wasn't too late. He realized he was holding his breath as his trembling fingers found a weak pulse at her neck. He bent low over her face and felt her warm, shallow breath. She was alive, but just barely. He paused to listen to the woods around him. *Where has the other shooter gone?*

He quickly pulled off his pack and dug out the modest first aid kit. He'd spent all of two hours at Quantico learning first aid, but he saw no blood or obvious wounds. He didn't know what to do. What he did know was that seconds were ticking away, and somewhere in those deep woods there was a gunman with a rifle. They were too exposed. He whirled on his knees when he heard footfalls behind them. How the Russian had made it down the slope so quickly on a bum leg was beyond him. But the guy was nearly to them, his weapon moving with his eyes as he swept the woods around them, his free hand holding that small black phone to his ear.

"She is alive, yes?" He'd lost the Texas accent. He pocketed the sat phone and dropped down on a knee beside Win, near the woman's head.

"Yeah, but her breathing is shallow," Win said. "No blood that I can see, I was just fixing to get her to better cover."

The clouds moved away again, and the sunlight filtering through the canopy of trees outlined Sokolov's hard face inches from his own. "Don't move her yet . . . we'll check her injuries." Sokolov reached for the small handgun that lay in the dust. He pocketed it.

"Hey," Win hissed. "This is a crime scene. You can't do that—"

"You've got bigger problems right now than securing a crime scene!"

Point taken.

They eased her flat on her back. Sokolov told Win to roll his jacket and use it to support her head, to stabilize her neck. Win stripped off the jacket and did as he was told. Paige seemed to be fighting for consciousness. Win's stomach clutched as she groaned with every touch.

Sokolov ran his hand through the woman's hair. "Look . . . here." A patch of blond hair was gone, cut clear to the scalp.

"He took a hair lock . . . he took a trophy," Win whispered. He forced his eyes away to scan the forest again while he fought down a wave of revulsion. This woman was an agent—his teammate, his partner—and she'd become the target of a serial killer. *Why is she even here?* he asked himself, gently brushing the blond hair away from her battered face. *Why on earth did she go with Ratliff?*

The Russian was digging in Win's first aid kit for something. He broke open a foul-smelling capsule and waved it under Paige's nose. "I think she's been drugged," he said, "but she must have put up a fight . . . maybe the scum didn't get the dosage right, maybe she fought him off . . . before a lethal dose . . . maybe." She stirred just a bit and Win heard her gasp. She was coming to.

Thank you, God. Win drew a long breath and flinched when the woman unexpectedly tried to jerk her arm away, tried to roll to her side. Now he could see Paige's face clearly; one eye was nearly swollen shut and was beginning to blacken, blood was oozing from scratches on her ghostly pale face. There were blotchy purple bruises and swelling around her throat. She was clutching a canvas messenger bag to her chest. Her blue tank top and jacket were covered in dirt and dried sweat. She moaned and tried to pull away again. Regaining consciousness wasn't such a good thing.

"Ease her off the trail, I'll hold her neck," Sokolov said. "He strangled her to knock her out. She could have damage to her spine." The Russian put down his weapon and held Paige's head in his hands. "Go slow . . . slowly." He removed the messenger bag, then probed her neck with his fingers. "I'm not feeling a knot or a break . . . that's good." He seemed to be talking to himself as he worked.

Win was holding his Glock to his side with his right hand while he cradled Paige's shoulder with his left. The Russian was intent on Paige, and for the moment he was unarmed. When Win's finger moved toward the trigger, Sokolov didn't even glance up from his task.

"Uh-uh . . . don't touch it. Don't dare forget your pledge to me. . . . We're not finished here yet."

Win had only a second to consider the threat; Paige groaned again and tried to cough. "Who did this to you?" Win asked softly.

She was blinking rapidly, trying to move.

"Who—"

She came fully awake with a start and blinked again. "What? What?" She managed to swallow. "I . . . I don't know . . . early morning . . . they'd gone to the geysers . . . they'd all gone." She stared into Win's eyes, her pupils wildly dilated. "Someone came . . . behind me . . . I ran to the camp . . . then to the woods . . . I ran. He . . . he chased me . . ." The words fell away at the end and she fainted back against the Russian's leg. Sokolov eased her head down on Win's jacket.

Win's eyes went to Sokolov's. "Ratliff, his assistant, Dravec, and Warren are all here. There could even be others, but those were the names on the research permit."

"You move on up. Find the one who did this," the Russian ordered.

Win glanced back down at Paige. Sokolov was propping her on her side so she wouldn't choke if she threw up. "Not to worry about her.

You have my word we won't harm her." The intense green eyes found his again. "Go! My lads are coming off the mountain, they'll help her."

"Bordeaux?" Win asked.

"They'll leave him at the cabin, unharmed." Sokolov met Win's doubtful gaze. "Why should I lie?" He shrugged with a shoulder. "There is no reason to kill him. He can't recognize me or disrupt our mission."

But I can. I'm the one you can't leave alive. That sobering thought flashed through Win's mind.

Sokolov motioned toward Paige with his chin. "I want this thug, this killer, to pay—I want justice, a confession, same as you do. . . . He knows you're on him now. Go do your job."

* * *

Win made good time moving through the trees at a low crouch. The big timber began to thin, and he crossed the small stream again as he neared the campsite. The sulfur smell of the steam vents and mudpots was much more distinct now. He remembered that the primitive campsite was about a hundred yards from the area of superheated ground where he'd retrieved Natasha's bones nearly a month ago. He was coming full circle; he was coming back to the place of the lost.

He ducked behind a wide spruce that sat just back from the camp and waited a moment, watching. The four nylon tents in orange, red, yellow, and blue reminded him of brightly colored balloons at a child's party. A thin wisp of smoke drifted up from a central fire ring. He started moving forward but stopped when he saw movement near one of the tents. He wished he had his binoculars, but those were in his pack back on the trail. His mind went to Paige as he zigzagged to a low boulder to get closer to the tents. He dropped beside the big rock and whispered a prayer of protection for her and for everyone else caught up in this tangled mess.

He forced down lingering doubts about his plan, then pointed out to himself that he didn't actually have a plan; he was simply taking orders from a Russian SVR officer, who was reported to be a cold-blooded killer. He was trusting that man's word that he wasn't a murdering assassin, that Trey and Luke were unharmed, and he'd just left an injured FBI special agent in the man's care. *Geez, Win! Are you nuts?* his rational self cried out. But some other force within him, something much more powerful, called on him to trust—to listen to his heart. Proverbs 3:5 kept floating through his mind: *'Trust in the Lord with all your heart, and lean not on your own understanding.'* He told himself he was choosing to trust.

He was thinking of moving forward again when he saw a stooped figure emerge from the largest of the tents. A man pushed back the bright-orange flap and straightened. His back was to Win, and Win couldn't see much, but he could see a scoped hunting rifle in the guy's right hand.

Win was within accurate pistol range for his Glock: about eighty yards. It was a long shot with a handgun, but Win knew he was deadly accurate at that range. His name was on top of the marksmanship plaque at the FBI Academy. "FBI! Drop it! FBI! Drop the gun!" he yelled as he braced the Glock against the boulder and took aim. He had the monster now.

The guy with the rifle didn't have time to turn. Instead he crumpled to the ground like a puppet whose strings had been cut. Win stared in shock as the sound of the gunshot reached him less than half a second later. He instinctively ducked and tried to make sense of what had just happened. He'd given away his location, so he had to advance. He skirted the camp, using the larger trees for cover. He could see no movement on the trail leading to the thermal area. The prone figure by the tents hadn't moved. Win wouldn't have any cover at the campsite, but he had to risk it. Whoever was lying there with a high-caliber bullet wound could bleed out if he didn't hurry—if he wasn't already dead.

Win dodged around the yellow tent, crept to the front of the orange one, and was surprised to see Chris Warren lying on his back, still clinging to part of a rifle. He wasn't expecting Warren. Win went down low to make himself less of a target, kept his Glock aimed at Warren's chest, and pulled the fragments of the rifle stock away from the man. Warren's mouth and eyes were wide open in shock. The round had hit the stock of someone's very expensive hunting rifle. It had shattered the stock, probably broken a few ribs, but Win saw no entry wounds on the man's shirt, no blood; even the shreds of the wooden stock had missed him. Warren was stunned from the bullet's impact.

"Why'd . . . why'd you shoot me?" Warren stammered as his breath began to return.

"Shut up, Warren. I didn't shoot you." Win picked up the detached barrel and chamber from the rifle. It was cold to the touch. He fumbled to open the breach with one hand and finally did: no smell of discharge. The rifle hadn't been fired recently. *Who's shooting?*

"What's going on?" Win asked as doubts began to creep into his mind.

"I . . . I heard shots . . . I was up at the thermal area, checking the seismometers . . . I was afraid that woman Preston brought in yesterday . . . was afraid she'd seen a bear, got Preston's rifle, and freaked." Warren tried to sit, and Win pushed him down hard with a hand to the shoulder.

"Whose gun is this?" Win motioned to the rifle pieces scattered about. He glanced back toward the woods and still saw nothing.

"It's Preston's . . . ah, he always keeps a gun or two in camp. I heard more shots on the way back down here . . . I didn't see the woman." He winced as he tried to take a deeper breath. "I . . . ah . . . I don't do firearms. But I got the gun out of his tent when I got back . . . something's off."

That's for damn sure. "Who else is out here?"

"Just me, that Paige woman, Preston, and Simon. The sat phone isn't working, I tried to call Preston when I heard the shots . . . called the park dispatch. No connection. Preston hiked toward Mount Hornaday this morning to see if there was any sign of heaving or fracture from the localized seismic activity last month . . . Simon's working near the lake, with all the sampling . . . documenting any aberration in heat radiation—" Win could tell the guy was morphing into geyser-talk. He got right to the point to snap him out of it.

"You're under arrest." Win hit the RECORD button on his phone and flew through a recital of the Miranda rights, his Glock still in Warren's face.

The geologist had a moment of clarity. "Under arrest for what?"

I'll figure that out later. Win stared at him in disgust.

"I want a lawyer!" The guy tried to squirm away. Win held him down.

"Fine! Look around and tell me if you see one! I'll leave you here to sort it out with whoever took that shot at you." Win started to stand.

"You wouldn't leave me."

"I can't think of anything I'd rather do," Win replied.

"Hold on . . . who's shooting? Who's out there?"

"That's what I'd like to know. Are you freely talking to me now?"

Warren bit his lip, but he nodded. "Yes . . . I waive my right to counsel. What's happening?"

"Well, someone just tried to kill you and they tried to kill Paige too. I'm thinking someone is tying up loose ends. Now why in hell would you be considered a loose end, Dr. Warren?" He glared down at the man. "It's about Missy Sims, isn't it? She was pregnant, wasn't she? With your child? What happened to Missy Sims, Dr. Warren?"

The geologist's handsome face paled even more and his eyes went even wider. "I didn't hurt Missy . . . she was a good girl . . . it was just a summer fling. I would never hurt anyone."

"Then what?" Win struggled to keep calm. He had never lowered the Glock. It occurred to him that he should lower it, but he didn't. "Then what?" he nearly shouted.

"Preston and I had a partnership back then . . . it didn't last, but . . . but our research was taking off . . . we were in line for a major research grant, and Missy's issue—well, it could have damaged my reputation, could have damaged the reputation of the expedition. It was a glitch."

Missy's issue? A glitch? Win fought again to compartmentalize his anger.

"I . . . I gave Preston some money for her . . . actually a lot of money. He said he'd take care of her, that he had some friends in Missoula . . . that she'd be fine, and I'd never have to hear from her again. I went back to Stanford, and I never did hear from her again."

"You knew she was missing!" Win hurled the words at him. "You knew there was a search. You were interviewed!"

"No one ever asked many questions," the prone man sputtered. "The authorities never asked—"

"And you damn well didn't volunteer any help. Six years you put a family through hell, six more years of killing, because your research couldn't be interrupted!"

Warren's expression changed as it dawned on him. He closed his eyes and shook his head. "Natasha? Janet? Oh no," he whispered.

Win's mind flashed back to the two-sentence statement Warren had made to the agent after Missy's disappearance so many years ago: *She was good with the horses, a competent wrangler, but I didn't know her. No idea where she'd go.*

"You're under arrest for lying to the FBI—among other things."

* * *

They'd found Hechtner's locked Tahoe in a stand of trees, down a seldom-used service road just south of the Blacktail Deer Creek parking lot. It had been staged to look like the ranger was sleeping; his bucket seat was reclined, and he was lying on his side, thank goodness, so the vomit hadn't choked him.

Johnson stood nearby while the EMTs eased him out of the big SUV and onto the gurney. Johnson used his handcuff key to remove the restraints from his wrists. He glanced in the vehicle, where the ranger's weapons—the Sig Sauer handgun, the shotgun, the Colt M4LE—were all visible inside. The EMTs had said his heart rate and breathing were slow; they hadn't been able to get him fully conscious. The symptoms of whatever this was were identical to what he'd just seen with that agent from Seattle they'd discovered in the Justice Center less than an hour ago. The paramedic was communicating with dispatch on his radio; the phones still weren't working. They were told to get an IV in, get oxygen on him—get him to the clinic. Maybe by that time someone would have figured out what drug they were dealing with. Johnson knew they were trying to get quickie toxicological results from blood they'd pulled from the Seattle agent. It was tricky; giving the wrong antidote might make the symptoms worse. Johnson stepped farther back to let the EMT check Trey's vitals again.

When the call had come in about Hechtner, right after noon, he'd been standing in that tiny office in the Justice Building, watching some doctor who looked to be about sixteen puzzle over the unconscious agent from Seattle. Jim had ordered him to Blacktail Deer Creek ASAP, telling him he could take some of the Denver folks with him if he wanted. Those agents were all on the other side of the building, watching the ASAC tell the press that the FBI had had a good day—a national crisis had been averted—unaware that another crisis was unfolding. Johnson had decided to walk up the street, get in his vehicle, and deal with Hechtner's situation alone.

It had only taken a few minutes to get here, but he'd nearly forgotten how to engage the concealed lights and siren on the Suburban; he hadn't used them in a couple of years. The small gravel lot was less than eight miles south of Mammoth, and with the vehicle's siren and lights going, the tourists moved out of the way. He'd pulled into the small parking lot and taken charge. He'd told two young law enforcement rangers to call for more backup and secure the area as a crime scene. He'd pulled on a pair of nitrile gloves as he ordered the rangers to not let anyone touch or move anything near Hechtner's Tahoe once the EMTs got him into the ambulance. Interview anyone who was parked nearby, who might have seen something—get statements, get contact information. Don't let any potential witnesses leave, but get rid of the gawkers who were slowing on the highway at the sight of flashing lights. It felt good to be in charge.

He wasn't contributing anything to the effort to help Hechtner, so he walked around the vehicle to the passenger-side door and opened it slowly with his gloved hand. Tyler had told him Hechtner was bringing a box—a serial killer's trophy box—back to Mammoth. There it sat, on top of what looked like a fire-retardant pouch in the middle of the passenger seat. Johnson reached to open it, then he realized he needed to be taking photographs. He still couldn't believe there was a serial killer in the park; he still couldn't believe Tyler hadn't been blowing smoke. But there it sat.

He pocketed his phone after taking a few photos and reciting some evidentiary facts. Then he reached over and opened the box and stared down at several gray pouches—*several pouches*. He opened one and saw a lock of brown hair, Janet Goff's driver's license, and a silver wristwatch. He vaguely remembered the search for her a couple of years ago. He closed the pouch, closed the lid on the box, and slid the latch shut. He picked it up and carried it toward his black SUV.

As Johnson watched the EMTs load Hechtner into the ambulance, he thought the guy seemed to be moving some—that was positive. Johnson set the metal box on his passenger seat, pulled off the purple nitrile gloves, and threw them on the back floorboard. For some reason he looked in the rearview mirror and adjusted his tie. He picked up the mic on the radio to call the park's Dispatch Office—they could convey his message to Jim West. He started to key the mic, but he looked down at the box again and felt a wave of sadness and regret pass over him. He'd been the resident agent in the park for five years . . . five years. *How in hell did I miss this? How in hell?*

CHAPTER THIRTY-SIX

W̲in left Dr. Christopher Warren sniveling in fear after hog-tying him and telling the scumbag he'd better pray that the FBI, not Ratliff, came out on top in the next few minutes. He glanced at his watch as he moved into the trees beside the trail and began covering the short distance to the thermal features. He'd been gone from Paige's side for nearly twenty minutes. He had no idea where Sokolov or his crew was, and that wasn't his only disadvantage. Ratliff had worked in this area off and on for several years; he'd know it like the back of his hand.

And then there was Simon. Could Ratliff have pulled off years of killing without his assistant knowing? It was possible, maybe even likely. He remembered his lessons from Quantico. His instructors taught that serial killers almost never worked in pairs, and that those closest to them—wives, children, coworkers—were more often than not totally clueless about their murderous madness. He needed to get Simon to safety before he went after Ratliff.

Ratliff had a rifle, so making himself less of a target was a no-brainer. Win stayed off the main trail and crept slowly through the thick stand of lodgepole pines that separated the camp from the thermal area. He caught sight of steam rising above the treetops and began to hear the gurgling and spewing of the geysers and steam vents. He could feel the heat under his boots as he inched closer. The trees were more scattered now, some already dead and gray from the heated ground, others dying.

He reached the edge of the thermal field; there wasn't really much cover within the five acres of chalky-white ground that lay between him and the tall pines on the far side. But there were low berms and rises, patches of decaying trees, and a few areas of jumbled rocks where the hot earth had pushed up. Plenty of places for a gunman to hide.

Steam and spurts of water were spiraling straight up—there was little wind here, and the sun was out again. He wished he had his sunglasses and his binoculars—it was hard to see what was out there in the bright light. He spotted a tall, white open-sided tent that had been set up by the researchers on a slight rise near that roaring hole in the ground, just yards from a wide sinkhole filled with churning gray goo. That was close to the spot where Natasha's remains had been found. He guessed the tent, with its wooden platform, provided the researchers some shade while they worked or took breaks. There were several areas where wooden boards had been extended and linked together into rough boardwalks, giving the researchers better access to other points within the field.

He moved in the fringe of the trees, keeping low, as he edged closer to the open tent. He dropped to one knee and scanned the sparse trees around him. *Careful . . . someone's out here with a rifle,* he reminded himself again and again.

Then he saw the man. Less than a quarter mile away. The guy was skirting the thermal area, walking along the edge of the pines, carrying a backpack, a scoped rifle slung over his shoulder. *Ratliff? He's playing me,* Win thought. *He wants me to think he just walked in on this, totally innocent.*

* * *

The rain was suddenly coming down in buckets again, pounding on the prefabricated metal roof of the fifty-year-old hangar. The interior lit up white as lightning struck nearby; the clap of thunder caused the building to shudder. It was so loud in the building that he couldn't think. And thinking through this situation was real damn important right now.

Santiago was standing next to one of his analysts, staring down at the big monitor's live drone feed—staring down in disbelief. He'd just gotten off the sat phone with his team leader at the Indian Creek Campground; she had reported that a storm had popped up and it was raining cats and dogs, her team was dodging lightning. Yet he was watching a clear video feed of Win Tyler hiking through a sunlit meadow near a stream, both transponders showing a location within two hundred yards of the campground. He put in a call to Langley as he watched the screen. The analyst switched the camera to Sokolov—still trailing Tyler by about a hundred yards, no evidence of wind or rain. He had another guy pull up the satellite weather radar; the new thunderstorm over Gardiner showed up clearly, as did a bigger storm over the exact coordinates he was staring at from the drone feed. A sick feeling hit his stomach as he realized what he was seeing. What he was seeing was the good guys getting seriously outplayed.

*　*　*

He could hear thunder in the distance again. Thought the thunderheads to the north were all gonna die out, but if he'd been standing up and looking off toward Mammoth, he would have seen the black clouds building again. Did that ever so often this time of year.

He was thinking about the weather to take his mind off the inevitable—the man who had flanked him could take him out anytime he wanted. The man on the other side of him was likely within a few yards now, behind that last timber slash. The fallen log he was beneath gave him little to no protection from rifle rounds. He knew that. They knew that. The standoff had lasted over fifteen minutes. *What are they waiting for?*

The flanker finally called out over the whistle of the wind. "We're getting tired of this. It's over. No need to die, Bordeaux. Pitch that gun out and hold your hands up!"

Luke recognized the voice—it was one of the men he'd taken to Maxwell Springs last week. He remembered that the man was fit and capable during that outing; he'd worn a gray ball cap and dark-framed glasses almost the entire time. Luke now realized it was a part of his disguise. He'd caught a glimpse of the guy ten minutes ago, dodging through the rocks. On this trip the guy was sporting a dark balaclava and sunglasses and pointing an SR-3 Vikhr at him. No doubt they were Russians; that compact assault rifle was one of the weapons of choice for their elite forces, one of the few that could easily be concealed. He wondered how they'd gotten those guns into the States.

Luke had been taught that Russian soldiers rarely strayed far from the chain of command; they weren't trained to operate as independently as Americans. He figured they were waiting on some word from their boss before they killed him. He'd seen the gunman on his phone, so somehow their communications were working, while his still was not. He'd checked his sat phone a dozen times—nothing. Luke had never seen Russians fight in Afghanistan or Syria, but he'd talked with folks who had. Their special forces were good, some would say as good as ours. He doubted that, but then he sure didn't have braggin' rights in this deal today.

He drew a deep breath and whispered another prayer. He tried to shut down a string of regrets that darted through his mind, but the thoughts kept coming. . . . He'd promised Ethan a puppy this summer, he still had to build the kids a treehouse, Ellie wanted him to make peace with Win Tyler—his pride was holdin' that up. And Ellie . . . He swallowed hard. *Hell, I don't wanna die up here. If they haven't killed me yet, maybe there's a reason.*

"Alright! I'm standing down!" Luke called out. He pitched the big pistol into a patch of purple flowering lupine growing five feet away; his bear spray landed beside it. He slowly scooted out from under the log with his hands up. He was holding his breath, hoping he was making the right move, knowing he had few options.

The second man came around a boulder from behind him. "Hands behind your head!" that man shouted. Luke had barely gotten them there when he felt the guy pull his Beretta from the holster on the back of his belt. *There goes that option.* The second man was also wearing a mask; that gave him a little comfort.

The flanker was on his sat phone now, letting his buddy cover their captive. He was standing only a few feet away, and even with the wind, Luke could overhear parts of the phone exchange. They were speaking Russian, and they didn't have a clue he was fluent. "We don't need civilian casualties if they can be prevented," he heard the man on the other end of the line say. Luke didn't catch all the rest of it, just "Come down . . . then . . . and take the trail to the lake . . ." Luke heard those words before the wind snatched the rest of the conversation away. The man finished the call, and Luke wondered about Win Tyler. Win was FBI— the Russians wouldn't consider him a civilian. Luke drew another deep breath and hoped like hell that Win was faring better than he was.

The flanker turned to him as he pocketed the sat phone. "Let me tell you how this is going to go, Bordeaux. Remember that cabin you told us about when we were scouting out the springs a few days ago? Well, it's just down the way. . . . We have orders to leave you there, tied up but unharmed. You'll be inside so the bears won't eat you. We'll even leave your satellite phone so you can be found when the networks come back up. Cooperate, and you'll just look back on this as a day you'd rather forget."

* * *

They'd made record time on the five-mile drive from Mammoth to Gardiner until they hit what seemed like a wall of water less than a half mile south of town. The traffic on the two-lane road had come to a near standstill. Everyone's hazard lights were flashing, several vehicles had pulled off to the shoulder to wait it out, and others were blocking the road. He slowed the Suburban and leaned into the steering wheel, trying to see though the deluge. He was from central Virginia; he'd never gotten used to the Rockies' violent, unpredictable weather.

"Whoa! Sheees!" The agent in the passenger seat glanced up from adjusting his body armor and realized they were coming to a sliding stop. Jim West kept looking in his rearview mirror, hoping the agent behind them didn't plow into them. He finally saw the flashing blue lights and the big headlights. The second Suburban had slowed, thank goodness.

"Who exactly are we after and why?" It was a female agent from Denver asking the question. Jim had met her in passing this morning before the press conference; he couldn't remember her name.

Jim sucked in a breath, squinted through the windshield, and tried to formulate an answer. "We're going to, uh, potentially head off a situation at the Gardiner Airport . . . there are some CIA folks there. One of our supervisors out of San Francisco is there, her name is Gloria Gorski. There are some Russian nationals involved somehow—"

"What?" both Denver agents in the back seat asked in unison.

"We'll know more when we get there." *Sure hope that's true!* "We'll pull up at the end of the runway and wait to hear back from the ASAC. He's running this show. Get yourself ready, the airport is tiny. This could be confrontational—or not."

"Gorski? Isn't that a Russian name?" It was the female agent again.

"No, it's Polish," one of the guys in the back answered.

Jim tuned them out and tried to see around a large RV that was directly in front of them. They were within a hundred feet of the Yellowstone entrance booths. They'd have to drive all the way through the small town and across the Yellowstone River bridge, then a couple more miles up the highway until they reached the gravel road to the airport. And there wasn't much there. Just a handful of metal hangars, a couple of fuel tanks, and a modest office. He wasn't sure if the asphalt strip even had working landing lights. Jim couldn't believe a CIA team with two Little Bird helicopters was sitting at the little airstrip at the park's back door.

Wes Givens had jumped on the phone with Seattle as soon as he made a few remarks and turned the press conference over to the Assistant U.S. Attorney. Jim knew they'd been trying to get this supervisor, Ms. Gorski, on the phone for at least the last hour. No one on the ground with the Bureau had any contact numbers for the Agency folks except her, and she wasn't answering her phone. Since Agent Humphrey had been attacked, Brent Sutton was afraid Gorski could be in danger. And where was Agent Paige Lange? She was supposed to be on duty at the Justice Center by now.

He knew the Denver office was trying to get some answers out of Langley, but he'd heard the Agency folks were scrambling too. Was someone in the CIA camp working with the Russians? And why were the Russians in Yellowstone in the first place? No one had even tried to explain that to him. He squinted back at the rain and tried to force the questions from his mind. His job was to remain cool and calm and get to that airport.

He managed to steer around the stalled RV, the second Suburban followed. He couldn't see ten feet in front of the hood in this torrent. He asked the guy beside him to check the weather radar on his phone.

"It's not a big cell—we're in the worst of it," the guy said. "It's sinking south, it's already cleared the airport and the area north of town."

Jim wasn't sure if that was a good thing or a bad thing.

*　*　*

Win hunkered down behind one of the big dead pines on the fringe of the thermal site and watched the man with the rifle approach. He was still a good distance off, much too far for an accurate shot with his Glock. Ratliff had an aristocratic, landed-gentry look—he'd probably grown up trap and skeet shooting. And he was probably a pretty good shot with that rifle. Win knew he needed to sit tight, stay concealed, and wait. Waiting was hard.

He was guessing Ratliff was going to try to lull him into believing he'd just walked in on everything. That he had no idea there was an FBI agent in the woods, an injured woman on the trail, or a lucky-to-be-alive geologist tied up by the tents. Just walk in, gain the FBI agent's trust, then shoot the trusting FBI agent in the back—that's what Win figured he had in mind. Ratliff was just the type of arrogant psychopath to think that might work. *Not gonna happen.* Win tightened his grip on the Glock.

He fiddled with his phone, and although he had no service bars, he tapped in an email with his left hand, attached the recording of Dr.

Warren's interview, such as it was, and sent it to Jim West. He figured it might get to Jim once the phone was carried to some spot with cell service, but honestly he didn't know. He wished he had a better grasp of technology; it wasn't his strong suit.

As the man got closer, the waiting didn't get any easier. *No need to jump the gun here,* he warned himself. Ratliff was still just piddling along, stopping every so often to look at some sputtering, churning feature on the fringe of the white plain. Win's watch told him it was almost one. He tried to keep focus, but his mind was going in too many directions. He knew his spiked adrenaline was fueling his chaotic thoughts, but he couldn't seem to rein them in. It shocked him that he hadn't seen Shelby's face during what he'd thought were his final few moments hanging on that cliffside an hour ago. She'd been the center of his world for so many years. *Why wasn't she there? Have I let her go? Have I moved on?*

He wondered about Luke, about Trey, about Paige. He'd prayed— he'd turned their lives over to God. He needed to get better at trusting, at accepting that those souls mattered more to God than they did to him. And God was ultimately in control; he was not. He was a slow learner—Luke had said that about him once. And where were the Russians? It was as if Sokolov had stepped back to let this chapter play out. What had he said? *"I want justice, a confession, same as you do. . . . Go do your job."* Could this whole drama be as simple as that? Someone in Russia wanting justice for Natasha Yahontova?

He checked his weapon again, more out of nervousness than necessity. He continued scanning the thermal area and the woods around him—still no sign of Simon. Warren had said Simon was working near the lake this morning; Warren seemed to be expecting both men back at camp soon. Win didn't need an innocent bystander walking in on a gun fight. But if Ratliff was tying up loose ends, what if he'd already disposed of Simon? *Naw.* He couldn't picture that. The little wormy guy seemed to worship Dr. Ratliff, and they were both so research focused, Simon might even overlook a little killing. *That's a cynical way to view the man,* his better nature rebuked him.

One of the field's geysers erupted and water spewed fifty feet into the air. A couple of the smaller ones also began spouting off. The sky had cleared, and the plumes of scalding water were striking against the deep-blue sky. The gaping hole near the researcher's tent started belching steam and roaring, and a bunch of the smaller fumaroles began to spew water and vapor. It was like the whole place was suddenly coming to life. "An event cycle," Dr. Warren had called it. Whatever it was, it was noisy and smelly and highly distracting.

As Win scanned the field again, he saw him: a second man, standing less than fifty yards away. He was small and wearing dirty white overalls and a sun hat. The white outfit probably reflected the sun, keeping him cooler in the heat, but it also made him nearly impossible to see against the chalky landscape. The man was waving at Ratliff and walking across the boards toward the open-sided tent.

Ratliff had picked up his pace. He was now cutting across the ashen ground, easily moving from board to board across the dangerous terrain to meet his assistant at the tent. He was holding the rifle in one hand, using it to help him balance as he traversed the hellish landscape. They'd meet in minutes—with Simon there it could turn into a hostage situation. *This ain't good.*

*   *   *

They'd rolled the Little Birds out a couple of minutes ago, as soon as the heavy rain let up. The small helicopters' skids were set on rollers so that they could be quickly moved. The choppers weighed only 1,575 pounds empty; all it took was four guys to push each bird to the concrete pads near the runway. The sky was black as pitch just to the south and west of them, but the radar showed plenty of open sky inside the park. Now if he just knew where inside the park he needed to be.

His boss at Langley was having a fit. They'd lost Sokolov and an FBI agent. Darn shame about the agent, but Sokolov was their target—their mission. Losing him was big. He buckled the chin strap on his dark-green Kevlar helmet, slipped on the clear Oakley glasses, and glanced at the team. It was go time, and they needed a place to go.

The pilots and copilots had unlashed the rotors and locked down the external personnel pods—just the fancy term for the metal fold-down benches that the operators were strapped onto during the ride. No room in the little ships for more than one internal passenger—the operators rode outside the chopper. It wasn't a ride for cowards. He watched the crews continue manual checks, although everything had already been checked a dozen times. The pilots started the warm-up on the rotors.

He'd told Ms. Gorski that they'd keep the team in the hangar until the very last minute; he didn't want them out on the landing pads for more than a few seconds. A busy highway was just on the other side of the runway, and he didn't want the tourist traffic seeing a bunch of heavily armed commandos standing around the ships. He hated working in-country; he hated this interagency deal. Ms. Gorski had told him she'd ride in the #2 chopper; he'd agreed since he knew his bosses wanted him to accommodate the Bureau. If anyone had asked him, which they hadn't, she wouldn't be riding along at all.

Waving to him, she walked across to the #2 bird, then held up her phone and smiled. Minutes earlier she'd told him that the Bureau's Seattle Counterintelligence Supervisor was going to call her with coordinates for a location on Agent Tyler at any time. Find Agent Tyler and they'd find Sokolov: that was the plan for the moment. It seemed to be the only plan they had. Santiago wasn't so sure Tyler wasn't already dead, and he wasn't so sure they'd ever get that Russian. Sokolov had outfoxed them every step of the way so far.

He held up his hand to put the team on ready, then noticed the copilot of the #2 bird jogging back to pick up Ms. Gorski's duty bag . . . she'd left it over near the cars. He inwardly cringed in exasperation—this was feeling way too much like the Keystone Cops. The rotors were beginning to spin now; at least they didn't have dust to contend with, the rain had carried that away. He saw the copilot hustling back with the bag and he'd started to bring his hand down when he realized that the #2 bird was five feet off the ground. He saw Kelly, the pilot, tumble out the door, bounce off the personnel pod, and hit the pavement. He heard the Rolls Royce turboshaft engine engage with a deafening roar as the small craft pivoted and quickly pulled away. Loud popping noises and black smoke were coming from the #1 ship's engine as that pilot tried to stop its rotors. Everyone else was just staring at the scene in shock.

The small helicopter skimmed down the 3,200-foot runway straight toward the town of Gardiner. It passed over the top of two black Suburbans that had just turned off the highway onto the gravel access road leading to the hangars. Gloria Ivanovna Gorsky—that was her real name—eased back on the throttle, trimmed the main rotors, and turned the chopper south across the Yellowstone River. She would skirt the thunderstorm, then plug in the GPS coordinates for Maxwell Springs; a glance at her watch told her it wasn't yet one o'clock. She looked down and watched the earth rush past her; she passed over the stone arch entrance to Yellowstone at an altitude below one hundred feet. Gloria allowed herself a thin smile. She felt a sense of freedom she hadn't felt in so many years—she was going home.

CHAPTER THIRTY-SEVEN

He hit the RECORD button on his phone and moved out of the tree line quickly with his Glock pointed down. It was now less than sixty feet to the open tent, but much of that was across the chalky, unstable crust or above pools of scalding water, hazards that had to be traversed on makeshift wooden walkways. He had to watch his step. He shouted for Ratliff to drop the rifle, he shouted for Dravec to move away from the other man, he remembered to call out that he was FBI, but they knew that already. Both men stared back at him in surprise; they both froze in place. He thought he had everyone where he wanted them, then suddenly he didn't.

The small chopper would have been hard to hear as it dove toward them, even if every thermal thing on the site hadn't been making some sort of hissing, spewing sounds. MH-6Ms were designed to be stealthy by helicopter standards, and this one snuck up on Win. Its rotor wash took down the tent, Ratliff dropped the rifle into the bubbling water and grabbed for his head, Win instinctively ducked low, lost his hat, and covered his face. Simon just disappeared. When Win raised his eyes, he saw the little black chopper skimming over the geysers toward the lake. His mind registered that the CIA had arrived; it also registered that there were no operators on board.

Sokolov was coming parallel to him on the boards. He'd used the distraction of the chopper to reach them from the cover of the trees. Win had seen no sign of the man in the forest, but there he was, Paige's

messenger bag slung over his shoulder, armed with a handgun, hobbling up one of the makeshift boardwalks. The Russian nabbed Simon
on the boards—the little guy had tried to escape, and despite his injury,
Sokolov was still amazingly quick. The Russian held Simon up by his
collar like you'd hold a cat by the scruff of its neck. The poor guy's
boots were barely touching the boards and his pale face was a mask of
fright as Sokolov half carried, half shoved him back toward the wreck-
age of the tent. Win made it there and was holding Ratliff at gunpoint.
The geologist's rifle had landed in an iridescent blue pool of boiling
water—it was clearly out of play.

Win swallowed down what tasted like fear; now, in addition to
dealing with the killer and his assistant, he had the Russian to contend
with as well. He tried to project a degree of calm, a confident manner.
He kept the gun aimed at Ratliff. He shouted over the commotion in
the geyser field. "Get your hands up now! You're under arrest—"

"What's this about! What's going on here!" Ratliff shouted back
at Win. He'd lost his hat when the chopper came in, and his gray hair
was speckled with sweat. His face was red and his eyes were narrowed.
His hands were at his side; he hadn't raised them. He hadn't folded yet,
no sir.

"Hands up now!" Win repeated. He kept the Glock aimed square at
Ratliff's chest. He glanced to the side and saw Sokolov grimace in pain
as he threw Dravec down on the boards in front of them. They were
all within talking distance now, even with the thermal features still
billowing. Then as if on cue, the noise stopped: the waterspouts died
back, the hissing subsided to a constant gurgling. It was as if this place
wanted to hear the explanation as well.

"You're under arrest for the murder of Janet Goff, Natasha
Yahontova—"

"No!" Simon howled. The little guy had managed to stand. "Preston
wouldn't harm anyone!"

Win realized his Glock was shaking. *Geez, Win! Hold steady!* His
first thought was that his hand was trembling. Then he felt it under his
feet, the boards began to move ever so slightly—then the movement

was more pronounced. Win glanced down at the churning milky-blue water on either side of him. It was sloshing.

"Earthquake!" Sokolov announced as he struggled to balance on the boards.

"It's just a tremor," Dr. Ratliff corrected in a completely calm tone of voice. He crouched a little to keep upright, but he still hadn't put his hands up.

Win looked around for more stable footing; the shaking was getting worse. He took two steps back to the plywood platform that had held the tent—then he saw it. The stock of another rifle, lying beneath a pile of jumbled equipment on the platform. *Another shooter . . . Simon?* He went down on one knee to keep from falling off the platform as the ground gave one final long lurch.

The Russian's bad ankle wasn't helping him any. He tried to drop down to the boards, but he staggered. One boot went into the water and he groaned in pain. He lost his handgun to the boiling springs and grabbed for the timbers to keep from following it in.

Ratliff had gone down on his knees as well and was finally raising his hands. Win's eyes went to Simon—whose eyes were on the stock of the previously hidden rifle. Simon swung those creepy eyes back to Win just as he pulled a small handgun from the front pocket of his overalls. Sokolov said something Win would've bet was a cussword in Russian. Simon scooted back off the boards onto two sheets of plywood that had been laid end to end near the steaming entrance to the Devil's Breath Spring. He obviously wasn't a marksman—he held the revolver straight out in front of his face, his arm extended awkwardly.

"You didn't search him!" Win growled at the Russian.

"I normally shoot them first, then take their weapons," the Russian growled back. Win figured that might just be true.

"Simon . . . put down the gun. Do it now!" Win ordered as he stood. But Simon didn't obey the commands. He was trapped and he knew it. Win and the Russian were blocking the two boardwalks leading to the woods. The puffing mouth of the Devil's Breath was behind him. He stood there ten feet in front of the gaping hole, looking more and more sinister as the white vapor swirled around him.

"Preston wouldn't hurt anyone! He didn't know!" the small man yelled.

"Simon . . . put down the gun . . . let's walk out of here and talk about this." Win tried for the calm, cool approach. That was not what he was feeling. What he was feeling was confusion, revulsion, and humiliation. He'd jumped to conclusions; he'd let his prejudices create tunnel vision. He'd missed the real culprit.

Ratliff was still on his knees; he was staring at his assistant in horror. "What are you saying? Simon, what?"

"None of them suffered!" Simon shouted it at Win. "None of them suffered! They would have destroyed Preston's work . . . my work. I couldn't let that happen! We're making progress in charting the innermost workings of the earth . . . surely you can see that! I used Napotizine, we have it for mineral analysis . . . it's painless."

"Paige was beaten—strangled!" Win railed at him.

"She was trying to tie Preston to some crime." The compact revolver was still pointed in Win's direction, but Simon looked down at the kneeling geologist. "I know you couldn't see it, but she was deceiving you. I searched her things, she had Natasha's bones . . . I used a much lower dose, I didn't want it to be detectible—the dose was too low, she woke up, she fought. I didn't intend to hurt her. I just wanted her . . . needed them all . . . to go away." He looked back at Win. "Preston couldn't know . . . it could have upset our research. . . . Preston couldn't know."

Ratliff had covered his face with his hands. He began scooting back toward the platform, farther away from the Russian.

"The bodies?" Win wasn't projecting calm. He yelled it.

Simon motioned across the plain with his free hand, an almost wistful expression on his ghostly pale face. Win noticed that the guy wasn't even sweating. "Oh, into the acidic springs . . . here . . . Natasha." He pointed to the spring. "She loved it here. At Mud Volcano—the sulfur springs are especially well suited—Janet Goff; that young girl, Missy; and that nosey boy who had no business approaching me about Natasha. The Sulfur Caldron is just below the highway. It's a lovely spot, really it is . . . back to the earth, dust to dust . . . you understand."

"You killed Tasha? I thought she left me. . . . Simon, you killed Tasha!" Ratliff cried, pure anguish in his voice. He'd gotten behind Win on the platform, but Win had a gunman directly in front of him; he couldn't cover everyone. It did occur to Win that having the guy flank him was a bad situation, but it didn't occur to him how bad until the rifle blast—then another, and then the solid click of the trigger on an empty gun.

Win dropped to his knees at the sound of the blasts and saw Simon stumble backward—all in slow motion, yet all in seconds. Win saw the revolver fall to the boards, saw the man's thin arm continue up . . . then begin to drop. Simon's gaunt face was framed by the steam. . . . Win saw hollow eyes, the thin line of his lips, parted as if to scream. Then Simon Dravec fell backward into the Devil's Breath—into the entrance to Hell.

Win got to his feet and pulled the empty rifle away from Ratliff, who sat back on the crumpled tent and covered his face with his arms. He never looked up. Win saw Sokolov hobbling down the boardwalk toward the trees; he was nearly to solid ground. The Russian was getting away, but he was unarmed. *I have to find Paige . . . go after Sokolov.* This was Win's chance to get him.

He grabbed a length of rope from the jumbled mess of the tent, roughly pushed Ratliff down on the platform, tied the man's hands behind him, then tied his feet. He was working fast, listening to the man's barely contained sobs. Ratliff was whispering over and over: "How . . . how did he do it? . . . How could I not know?"

Win didn't have an answer.

*   *   *

He ran. He ran the way he'd been trained, with the Glock pointed downward in a one-handed grip, his gun arm bent at the elbow and close to his body. The most direct route to the lake was across the lower half of the thermal field. Win slowed slightly at each low rise in the steaming landscape of white ground to look for the Russian, to watch where he stepped. He tried to land each step on wooden boards or the darker earth; he dodged the colorful pools, milky water, and long-dead trees. He was quickly catching up with him.

The man trying to run away on the injured ankle wasn't armed, but Win still had the overwhelming sense that he was the one at a disadvantage, not the Russian. He was close enough to fire now, to hit the man in the back if he chose to. And as if he could sense that, Sokolov suddenly stopped and turned. He'd lost his hat somewhere, his tan jacket was covered with grime, his hands were raised above his head. He was holding the messenger bag in his left hand, but his right hand was free and closed in a fist. Win could see the sweat coursing down his face. His balance went to his left leg, away from the injured ankle; if the scalding water had done more damage, it hadn't slowed him much.

Win brought both hands to the grip of the pistol as he stopped his charge. They were within ten feet of each other, and Win was staring into the man's face. That face could have been cut from granite.

"Drop the bag, now!" *Did Dravec say Paige had the bones? Could Natasha's bones be in that bag?* Win fought to slow his heavy breathing. "You're . . . you're under arrest, Sokolov. Drop it now! Where's Paige? Where is she?" Win tried to see beyond the barren landscape; they weren't that far from the lake. He refocused on Sokolov. "Keep your hands over your head."

The Russian drew a deep breath and squared his shoulders to Win. They were standing within thirty feet of a gurgling steam vent—the hot steam swept behind the man and formed a wispy cloud between him and the lake.

"Drop the bag, do it now!"

"I don't think so, Win. Look down at your chest."

The guy couldn't jump him from ten feet, but Win really didn't want to take his eyes off him for a second. The calm assurance in the man's green eyes was unsettling. Win hazarded a glance down at his sweat-stained shirt. Two bright red dots were bouncing around on his chest.

Lordy! A sniper . . . I've been sighted in.

He must have said part of his stunned thoughts out loud. The Russian spoke calmly. "Not one sniper, Win—there are two. The copilot, and one of the other lads seems to have you targeted as well. If I unclench my fist they will fire."

Win was suddenly running low on options. *Distract the guy!* He held the Glock steady. "Where's Paige? The girl? Where is she?"

"That answer I can give you." Sokolov nodded with his head to the right. From behind a smooth boulder forty paces away stepped Paige Lange, battered and bruised. She took several unsteady steps off the lake trail toward them, bracing herself against a stout Russian with one hand. The small silver semiautomatic pistol was in her other hand.

"Agent Tyler is worried about you," Sokolov called to her.

"Let me kill him for you, comrade," she called back as she sighted in on Win with the gun.

Paige? . . . She robbed the gun safe—she lifted the bones. Paige was the mole Brent Sutton was after. That's why she was here . . . she must have known Sutton was closing in.

Sokolov called something back to her in Russian. Paige lowered the gun, gave Win a final glare, and moved back toward the lake trail with the help of her muscular wingman. Sokolov's expression was one of annoyance. He looked back at Win and shook his head. "We hardly ever call each other *comrade* anymore—and she didn't seem especially grateful. You saved her life a little over an hour ago." He shrugged with his eyebrows. "Women are sometimes hard to understand."

Sokolov gave the retreating couple one more glance, then drew a deep breath. "We're ready to go . . . don't make me give the signal to fire, Win. Don't force my hand."

"If they fire and hit me, you know damn well pure reflexes will cause me to pull the trigger. Dead or not, the chances of me pulling the trigger and taking you out are real, real good at this range." Win's pulse hadn't slowed much from the run; now it was really ramping up. He was having trouble swallowing, and his hands felt damp on the pistol grip.

"Hasn't there been enough death in this place? Think about it." Sokolov took a limping step forward. The bag and the closed fist were still raised high above his head.

"Stop right there. You're under arrest—give me the bones, the ring. That's evidence."

The man's green eyes were intense, but they weren't hostile. "Yes, it's evidence, but you have plenty of other evidence to prove that little weasel killed those others—many others. Several families will now know, they'll know what happened . . . perhaps they'll find some peace in knowing. You've done a good thing here, don't negate that by getting yourself killed at the last minute.

"This evidence"—he shook the bag above his head—"this bag contains the last remains of a daughter of the Motherland, who never came home. And the jewelry? Those objects that were most precious to her? If they stay with you as evidence—if they remain locked away in a vault—where is the closure for her family? Where is the justice for them? Her bones and her things go back to Russia with me."

It hit Win as the man was talking. Suddenly it all made sense. "She was one of yours, wasn't she? Her name wasn't Natasha Yahontova. She was SVR—she was a spy. Your agency thought she'd defected or just quit." The man's expression didn't change. Nothing in his face gave him away, but his eyes did. Just for a moment Win saw those green eyes acknowledge the truth. "So it's one of those 'leave no man behind' things . . . you can't leave her here among the enemy. This had nothing to do with turning me."

"That's a little melodramatic, Win."

"Melodramatic, maybe, but true."

The Russian shrugged. "You would have figured it out sooner or later. These things will bring great comfort to her parents, to her daughter. It will make life easier for them in ways you can't imagine. Her family is . . . is very well positioned in Russia. They wanted to see American justice for her. After the ring surfaced, after you asked to interview Dr. Orsky, we thought that was finally possible. You gave us a chance to find the lost."

Sokolov glanced toward the lake, then back to Win. "You have your recording of that demon's confession; I have one also, and my mates filmed the entire thing from a drone." Sergei raised one finger from his raised fist and moved it in a whirling motion. Almost immediately, the unmistakable high-pitched sound of a jet helicopter engine engaging came from behind the stand of tall lodgepole pines near the edge of the lake. Then a second engine engaged—they had two choppers. *Two! Lordy!*

The Russian was still talking. "Give me the gun. I need to be leaving. Your buddies will figure this out and be here any time. And I'm getting tired of holding my hands over my head. I didn't have to give you any explanation, Agent Tyler. I didn't have to stop . . . I could have just let you run into the ambush—it would have saved me some time." He limped forward another pace, but he kept his arms raised.

Win stayed in his shooting stance, but the gravity of his situation settled on him. He could fire to wound the man, to disable him, but then two high-powered rifle rounds would cut him down. He could fire to kill the Russian before the snipers fired. But he couldn't imagine himself killing an unarmed man, and even if he could force himself to pull the trigger, the snipers would fire as well—there would be two dead. Or he could give the man his gun, in which case the Russian would probably kill him with it. In all three scenarios he died here among Maxwell Springs' fascinating thermal features, on the edge of what everyone said was a magical lake. Win just couldn't see the logic in there being two more deaths here. One more was enough.

Major Sergei Sokolov seemed to know Win was coming to that conclusion. He spoke softly. "You'll just have to trust me, Win."

"Heard that from you in Russia . . . it didn't go so well for me then."

"Ah, that was unfortunate. Don't make this that much more so."

"What about the money you gave me?" Win asked.

"Just the cost of doing business."

Win slowly dropped his left hand away from the two-handed grip and eased the barrel of the pistol upward while slowly moving it to the side. His trigger finger moved alongside the guard. He expected the snipers to shoot, but they didn't. Instead one of them rose from behind his cover near the trees and started jogging in their direction, rifle at the ready.

Win stole a glance down at his chest—one red dot still there. Sokolov took the Glock from Win's hand as Win forced himself to keep eye contact with him, to face whatever was coming. The masked man in a dark-blue flight suit stopped a few feet away; the muzzle of the lethal-looking sniper rifle reacquired its target. He reported something quickly to his boss in Russian.

The whine of the helicopters was increasing, and dust was rising from the lakeside and whirling above the lodgepole pines.

Sokolov never broke eye contact with Win. He nodded to acknowledge the message from the gunman as he leveled Win's pistol at him. As he slowly backed away, he continued to talk quietly. "Your work on this case has allowed us to take a hero home. . . . She has done her duty for the Motherland. I thank you for that." He cleared the chambered round, ejected the magazine from the grip, then pocketed the magazine and extra round and dropped the empty Glock to the ground. "Government bureaucrats hate it when an officer loses a gun. I'll just take these bullets along with me."

Win blinked in surprise. He allowed himself to draw in a breath. He silently thanked God.

The man reached into his jacket pocket and pulled out a small blue velvet box. "This was in the bag. It doesn't belong to us." He opened it with the fingers of one hand. The sunlight danced across Shelby's ring—no, his grandmother's ring. The small diamond's fire was brilliant. The man snapped the box closed and held it up. "Find a worthy home for this, Cowboy. It doesn't need to be locked in a vault any more than Natasha Pavlovna's ring does. They're both now free to find their intended homes." He lightly dropped it near the gun.

The Russian took the copilot's arm for support and started to leave, then caught himself and turned back to face Win. The Texas drawl was now in full play. "You know, in that interrogation . . . in Kamchatka? Do you remember your final words to me when the drugs were kickin' in?"

Win swallowed hard and nodded. "Yeah, I remember . . . I told you I wouldn't disgrace my country."

"Well, Cowboy, that night and every day since, I'd say you've done your country proud."

EPILOGUE

The tiny white fly floated over the pool below an overhanging willow sprout. . . . The tippet and leader settled gently onto the sparkling surface of the stream. He'd been casting in this spot, where the narrow Madison River exited the tree line, for the last thirty minutes—not even a nibble. He was a seasoned fly fisherman; he'd done it his entire life. He'd grown up just a stone's throw from Arkansas's Little Red River, one of the best trout streams in the country. But this beautiful morning he hadn't had a bite, and his frustration was taking away the joy he usually found beside a stream. Trey was mending his line less than twenty yards downstream—he'd seen the ranger catch and release several good-size trout already.

He glanced at the small herd of bison grazing across the water; he didn't want to get caught unaware and let them get too close. His eyes did a practiced scan of his surroundings, best not to get surprised by a grizzly bear. His fingers found the bear spray at his belt, and he tried to force his focus back onto the calming flow of the river, but it wasn't happening. His mind was still running through the aftermath of the last few days, still trying to put pieces of the puzzle into convenient spots. He was still trying to understand how he could have missed the obvious—that Simon had been the monster, that Ratliff had been the tagalong. He could see it in hindsight, not so much in real time.

He'd been given the task of calling the next of kin—an honor really, for closing the case. In reality, it was a gut-wrenching process of anguish and tears. He'd called everyone on the list, after other agents had arrived at their doors to deliver the news that the lost had been found . . . though not in a way that family and friends had hoped or prayed for. But at least there was something tangible to touch, to hold onto. At least there was that.

Win had driven to Missy Sims's house, since she was local. He'd sat down with Mrs. Sims in the living room and gently told her what he hoped was actually true—the killer's words—that her precious daughter hadn't suffered. He'd handed her the hair lock and the delicate gold-cross necklace, since the judge had waived them as evidence. He figured Major Sergei Sokolov had sat on a formal sofa in a living room somewhere in Russia and carried out the same solemn and sacred duty with another grieving family. Picturing that in his mind gave Win some comfort.

Win's debriefs and interviews on Simon Dravec's killing spree had gone on for hours, and he knew there would be hours more to come. He was coordinating the investigation of Simon's earlier murders with agents in Arizona and California. Everything was pointing toward Dr. Ratliff being clueless about the serial killings, and Win was sure Ratliff's high-powered attorneys had already written up an ironclad self-defense position on the shooting of his assistant. Dr. Warren would also likely avoid jail time based on a guilty plea to something minor—he'd wave the trauma of being a near victim and his family connections in the prosecutor's face. They were only four days out from the incident, and Warren's lawyers were moving fast to cut a deal.

Win retrieved his line and made another cast; he saw a big trout's dorsal fin break the surface just above the spot where he dropped the fly. *Nope,* the fish showed no interest. *Geez!* He let his mind wander to Paige Lange. Headquarters was keeping everything on the Russia deal really close to the vest, but the ASAC told him they'd concluded Gloria Gorski had been working for the Russians since before she joined the Bureau. She'd apparently recruited Paige several years ago, shortly after Paige transferred to her squad in San Francisco. It would take months for the Counterintelligence Division to sort it all out, to try to determine how much damage had been done, but everyone knew a great deal of damage had indeed been done.

Paige had come under some suspicion last winter, but there'd been nothing significant enough to remove her from the job. And Ms. Gorski wasn't on anyone's radar. In a major blunder, she was given the task of investigating Paige. That had probably been the tipping point that caused them both to defect last week. And while they were on their way out, they'd managed to grab a little glory by impressing Major Sokolov and embarrassing the Americans. There were lots of red faces in the Counterintelligence Division over the entire disaster.

Red faces didn't begin to describe the outcome for the CIA. They'd lost $4 million in helicopters, had a pilot with a bad concussion, and had been made to look like the junior varsity compared to the Russians. Win didn't expect to do a debrief with them for a while; the Agency folks were all too busy licking their wounds.

"Right pretty cast . . . might move downstream a hair, cutthroat ain't quite as likely to hit the fly in the deep as your Ozark rainbows. . . . Try fer the point in the current below that downed log." A pause, then, "You can't force a strike . . . reckon sometimes it's best to just trust and let it go." The Louisiana drawl came from behind him, from near the tall cottonwood that stood twenty feet away.

Win didn't turn, he just smiled to himself, recast the thirty-foot line and leader, and softly dropped the top-water fly into the spot Luke suggested. The big fish hit the white-feathered fly before it even settled onto the water's surface. As Win pulled back to set the hook, he smiled again and spoke. "We're good?"

"All good."

Yes, Lord, just trust and let it go.

ACKNOWLEDGMENTS

First, I thank God for the generous blessings He has given me that allowed me to have the time and resources to follow my dream of becoming an author. Foremost of God's blessings in this regard was the leading of the Holy Spirit in nudging me forward to write more of Win Tyler's stories.

I also want to thank my husband, Bill Temple, whose thirty-one-year career in the FBI provided practical insight into the workings of the Bureau and its agents. Several of Bill's former colleagues at the FBI, both retired and currently employed, contributed to the realism of the text. They have asked not to be acknowledged by name, and I have respected that request. You know who you are—thank you so much for your help! Several park rangers also made significant contributions and helped me understand, and hopefully convey, the hardships, hazards, and joys of a career in the National Park Service. Special thanks to Park Rangers Kevin and Melissa Moses, and to Dr. Jeff Hungerford, Yellowstone National Park Geologist. Dr. Hungerford provided insight into Yellowstone's fascinating thermal features and geology. Thanks also to Jon Swanson, who read the manuscript and made excellent recommendations on issues related to emergency services, paramedics, and EMTs. Any errors on factual, technical, or procedural issues within the novel are mine alone.

The book could not have been completed without invaluable input from my faithful beta readers. Special mention goes to Barbara Mills, Anna Anthony, Sherry Holcomb, and Annette Maples, all of whom read the manuscript. Thank you to all the associates at Girl Friday Productions, whose professionalism and enthusiasm helped me navigate the intricacies of the publishing process. Heartfelt gratitude also goes to my outstanding editors, Allison Gorman and Brittany Dowdle, who improved the text while kindly allowing some deviation from *The Chicago Manual of Style.*

Lastly, I want to thank you, the reader. I received so much encouragement from the readers of *A Noble Calling* to get the second book in the series out soon! I can't thank you enough for all your kind words. I hope you enjoyed this second foray into Win Tyler's world in Yellowstone National Park. I would encourage you to go there and visit—as Win discovered, it's a magical place. Most of the locations mentioned in the book are real; a few are fictional or were modified to accommodate the story. Of special note are the new and expanding thermal areas within Yellowstone. Since the park's staff frowns upon tourists venturing into these remote, dangerous areas, Tindell Ridge and Maxwell Springs are fictious names and locations. Join me at www.rhonaweaver.com and I'll provide more insight into what is real and what is not in Win Tyler's world. Let's go have a little adventure!

ABOUT THE AUTHOR

Rhona Weaver is a retired swamp and farmland appraiser who had a thirty-five-year career in agricultural real estate and founded a program for at-risk children in Arkansas. She is a graduate of the University of Arkansas, a Sunday school teacher, and an avid gardener. Growing up on a cattle farm in the Ozarks gave her a deep appreciation of the outdoors and wildlife. Her novels draw on her love of the land and her profound admiration for the men and women in our law enforcement community, who truly share a noble calling. Those park rangers, FBI agents, and other first responders are her heroes. Rhona's husband, Bill Temple, is a retired Special Agent in Charge and Deputy Assistant Director of the FBI; he helped immeasurably with researching the books. Rhona and Bill live in Arkansas on a ridge with a view, with three contented rescue cats.

A Noble Calling, Rhona's debut novel and the first in the FBI Yellowstone Adventure series, won numerous publishing awards, including the 2021 Bill Fisher Award for Best First Book from the

Independent Book Publishers Association, Best 2021 Action/Adventure, Best 2021 Christian Fiction, and finalist for Best 2021 Thriller from the Next Generation Indie Book Awards. The book was also a finalist for the 2021 Christy Award for First Novel from the Evangelical Christian Publishers Association, and the Eric Hoffer Award for Commercial Fiction from the Eric Hoffer Foundation. *A Sacred Duty* is the second in the FBI Yellowstone Adventure series. Please visit her website, www.rhonaweaver.com, and follow her on Facebook at https://www .facebook.com/RhonaWeaverAuthor/.

CPSIA information can be obtained
at www.ICGtesting.com
Printed in the USA
LVHW090906240723
753027LV00090B/252/J